SONS of SAMSON

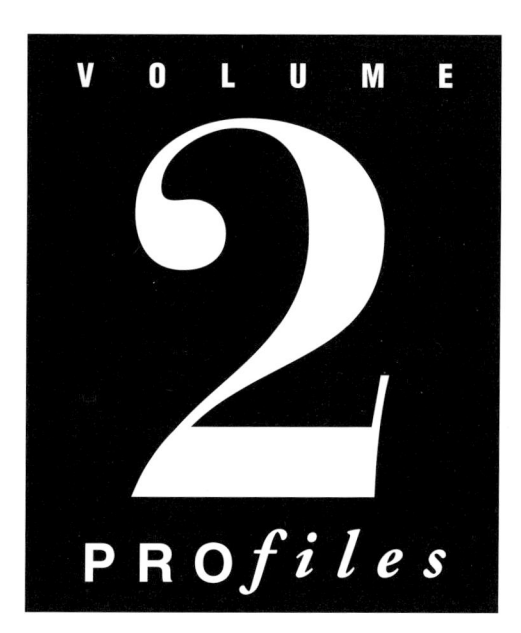

VOLUME 2 PROfiles

DAVID WEBSTER

IronMind Enterprises, Inc.
Nevada City, California

Other IronMind Enterprises, Inc. publications:
- *SUPER SQUATS: How to Gain 30 Pounds of Muscle in 6 Weeks* by Randall J. Strossen, Ph.D.
- *The Complete Keys to Progress* by John McCallum, edited by Randall J. Strossen, Ph.D.
- *IronMind®: Stronger Minds, Stronger Bodies* by Randall J. Strossen, Ph.D.
- *Mastery of Hand Strength* by John Brookfield, foreword by Randall J. Strossen, Ph.D.
- *MILO: A Journal for Serious Strength Athletes*, Randall J. Strossen, Ph.D., Publisher & Editor-in-Chief
- *Powerlifting Basics, Texas-style: The Adventures of Lope Delk* by Paul Kelso
- *Of Stones and Strength* by Steve Jeck and Peter Martin
- *IronMind Training Tablet No. 1* by Randall J. Strossen, Ph.D.
- *IronMind Training Tablet No. 2* by Randall J. Strossen, Ph.D.

To order additional copies of *Sons of Samson, Volume 2 Profiles*, or for a free catalog of IronMind Enterprises, Inc. publications and products, please contact:

IronMind Enterprises, Inc.
P. O. Box 1228
Nevada City, CA 95959
tel: (530) 265-6725
fax: (530) 265-4876

All rights reserved. No part of this book may be reproduced or transmitted in any form or by any means without written permission except in the case of brief quotations embodied in articles and reviews. For further information, contact the publisher.

Sons of Samson, Volume 2 Profiles
Copyright © David Webster

Cataloging in Publication Data
Webster, David—
Sons of samson, volume 2 profiles
1. Weight lifting   I. Title
1997   796.41   97-77883
ISBN 0-926888-06-4

Book and cover design by Tony Agpoon, San Francisco, California
All photos courtesy of David Webster, except where noted.

Published in the United States of America
IronMind Enterprises, Inc., P. O. Box 1228, Nevada City, CA 95959

Printed in the U.S.A. First Edition
10 9 8 7 6 5 4 3 2

CONTENTS

Part 1:
Introduction   2
    My Story: Where It All Began   2
    I Win the Toss   8
Chapter 1—Meeting the Strongmen: The Company I Have Kept   12
    Zass, "the Amazing Samson"   12
    More Wartime Encounters—and Beyond   17
    Mario Maciste   18
    Wilfred Hegginson, "the Amazing Briton"   19
    Al Murray, "the Benefactor"   21
    Mighty Mac Batchelor   24
    Willie Beattie, "the Scottish Apollo"   26
    Stefan Siatowski   28
    Reub Martin, Strength Athlete Supreme   29
    Rusty Sellers   31
    Yorkshire Lads: 31
    Brian Varley, "Britain's Funniest Strongman"   31
    Jim Schofield   32
    Keith Cockcroft, "the Amazing Magnus"   34
    Arthur Robin   34
    Jimmy Evans   34
    Monohar Aich   36
    Peter Lindop   37
    Ronnie Tait—Dicing with Death   38
    Graham Brown, "the Highland Hercules"   40
    Joe Falzon, "the Maltese Falzon"   42
    Charles Saliba, "the Iron Man of Malta"   43
    Manjit Singh   43
    Siegmund Klein   44
Chapter 2—The Association of Oldetime Barbell and Strongmen   46
    Faith Lift   46
    Strong to the End   47
    A Gripping Show   48
    Joe Rollino   48
    Steven Sadicario, "the Mighty Stefan"   49
    Slim "the Hammerman" Farman   49
    Ironfists: Dennis Rogers and John Brookfield   51
    Joe Ponder   53
Part 2:
Chapter 3—A Sport is Born: The Development of
    Modern Strength Athletics   58
    Dr. Douglas Edmunds, Scotland   61
    The World's Strongest Man TV Competitions   64
Chapter 4—The Contestants   66
    The Vikings of Iceland   66
    The Iceman Cometh: Jon Pall Sigmarsson   67
    Hjalti Arnason, the Great "Ursus"   71
    Andreas Gudmundsson   73
    Magnus Ver Magnusson   73

Torvi Olafsson	74
Gerrit Badenhorst	74
Brian Bell	75
Raimonds Bergmanis	75
Tjalling van den Bosch	75
Anton Boucher	75
Derek Boyer	76
Rick "Grizzly" Brown	76
Jean-Pierre Brulois	77
Geoff Capes	78
Forbes Cowan, Scotland's Strongest Man 1992-96	78
Colin Cox	79
Roger Ekstrom	80
Gregg Ernst	80
Laszlo Fekete	81
Lou Ferrigno, "the Incredible Hulk"	81
John Gamble	83
Yngve Gustavsson	83
Allan Hallberg	83
George Hechter	84
Lars Hedlund	84
Manfred Hoeberl	84
Nathan Jones	86
Svend Karlsen	86
Bill Kazmaier	87
Doyle Kenady	90
Ilkka Kinnunen	90
Riku Kiri	91
Rudi Küster	92
Curtis Leffler	92
Pavel Lepik	92
William (Bill) Miles Lyndon	92
Tom Magee	93
Dusko Markovic	93
Phil Martin	94
Stasys Mecius	94
Ilkka Nummisto	94
Pius Ochieng	95
Jorma Ojanaho	95
Chris Okonkwo	95
Heinz Ollesch	96
Joe Onasai	97
Ted van der Parre	97
Ken Patera	98
James Perry	99
Bill Pittuck	100
Evgeny Popov	100
Daniel Poulin	100
Wayne Price	101

Steve Pulcinella	101
Flemming Rasmussen	102
Henrik Ravn	102
Jamie Reeves	103
Don Reinhoudt	104
Bernard "Spinks" Rolle	105
Magnus Samuelsson	105
Adrian Smith	106
Markku Suonenvirta	106
Gary Taylor	106
Henning Thorsen	107
Vladimir Tourtchinski	108
Ron Trottier	108
Aap Uspenski	108
Regin Vagadal	109
Marko Varalahti	109
Berend Veneberg	109
Cees de Vreugd	109
Dave Waddington	110
Bruce Wilhelm	110
O.D. Wilson	111
Ab Wolders	112
Simon Wulfse	113

Part 3:
Chapter 5—The Contests 116

Universal Studios, California, USA 1977	116
Universal Tour Center, California, USA 1978	117
Universal Studios, California, USA 1979	118
Great Gorge, New Jersey, USA 1980	119
Great Gorge, New Jersey, USA 1981	122
Magic Mountain, Southern California, USA 1982	125
Christchurch, New Zealand 1983	126
Mora, Sweden 1984	127
Cascais, Portugal 1985	129
Nice, France 1986	132
Hungary 1988	135
San Sebastian, Spain 1989	138
Joensuu, Finland 1990	141
Tenerife 1991	144
Reykjavik, Iceland 1992	147
Orange, France 1993	151
Sun City, South Africa 1994	153
Paradise Island, Bahamas 1995	160
Mauritius 1996	162

Chapter 6—Beef Encounters 168

The Crunch Bunch	168
It's Tough at the Top	169
The Ultimate Challenge	170
I See a Strongman Die	174

Author David Webster, kneeling front, with strongmen (l. to r.) Evgeny Popov (Bulgaria), Gerrit Badenhorst (South Africa), Forbes Cowan (Scotland), Hjalti Arnason (Iceland), Phil Martin (USA), and Bill Lyndon (Australia).

The Performers

PART 1

Sons of Samson

Introduction

The fascination with physical strength has been in evidence over the centuries and throughout the world. Since earliest times when might was right and only the strong survived, awesome displays of power were seen not just as a means to an end but as an end in themselves. Indications of this have come down to us from primeval caves, Egyptian tombs, Greek vases and other artefacts from ancient civilisations.

Having already published histories of several strength sports, the *Sons of Samson* series focuses attention on the strongmen who have entertained the masses in circuses from Rome to Ringlings', from penniless itinerant showmen to wealthy movie muscle men and the incredible "World's Strongest Man" on television.

This is the second book in the *Sons of Samson* series, and while providing essential information and statistics where necessary, there has been a determined effort to avoid tedious lists of dates and names. There has also been pruning of narratives and incidents which in themselves could fill the allotted space. Some omissions are deliberate (I will gladly defend this policy, confident that my study has been much deeper than most others), and there will be good reason for my cheerful prejudice. Perhaps personal bias is inevitable, but a great deal of care has been taken to avoid this, and it is hoped that only judicious emphasis remains.

My Story: Where It All Began

It has been suggested that it would be appropriate to relate my own background in strength activities, linking my personal experience and the old-timers, before dealing with the most modern strength athletes of television. My long career in physical culture, competitive weightlifting, strandpulling, bodybuilding and sport in general has allowed me to meet a great many all-time greats, and through my firsthand involvement in these activities, I can truly appreciate the enormity of their achievements. I have been told this has also helped performers and competitors relate to me, knowing that I was a long-standing member of the brotherhood of iron, rather than an armchair expert.

Mostly I was a successful international amateur sportsman and coach, but there was a time when I also appeared on stage as an entertainer in Herculean handbalancing and strength acts; however as I climbed the ladder of success with Councils of Physical Recreation, Sports Council and at chief officer level in local government, my extra-curricular activities were not particularly welcomed by my employers. Now that I have retired from these rather political arenas, it is with a sense of pleasure that I can recall and relate some of the interesting and amusing incidents of that extremely happy period of my life when I was an active "Son of Samson."

I still have the Sandow chart of expander exercises my father gave me when I was ten years old. He used the strands in the 1920s, and throughout my life he constantly encouraged me in all my efforts. A boy's paper called *The Adventure* published a serial about Little Toughie Muggins, a mild-mannered school teacher who bought an old expander, which unknown to him had been used in a gimmick with two circus elephants. He practised until he could pull it and became fantastically strong although few people realised just what a mighty man he was. My folks bought me a very strong set of Terry's strands and like my hero, I became a mild-mannered (?) schoolteacher, and eventually I stretched the world's strongest expander. I also hero-worshipped a similar fictional character by the name of Wilson, and no doubt his exploits influenced me in my formative years.

My eleventh birthday was a very special one as my parents bought me a ticket to a gala professional wrestling event at Pittodrie, the Aberdeen football ground. Thousands queued to see the top of the bill match with the sensational Ali the Wicked, making his final appearance in

Scotland before heading for America. His opponent was Jim Anderson, one of the favourite Highland Games athletes of that famous clan. I had previously not been allowed to go to wrestling but followed the sport closely through the newspapers and barbershop gossip, and even waited outside the Music Hall to collect autographs after the bouts. Many years later when I was mixing freely with professional wrestlers, I heard that Ali had been decapitated in a horrendous accident in America.

Even as a lad I did not confine my activities to watching, I had to participate in wrestling, and with my brother and close friends, practised a variety of throws and holds. In the summer of 1940 with my father called up for the army and bombs falling around us in Aberdeen, we packed our bags and gas masks and evacuated to Garlogie, just ten miles from town but far enough to be much safer.

Without cinemas, radio, playgrounds or sports fields, all our activities were of our own making, and naturally wrestling figured high on my agenda. Apart from my fiery-tempered brother Ron, a boy called David Cheyne holidayed in Garlogie, and he gave me many great bouts; but his mother was terrified by our spirited encounters, and eventually he was banned by her from our grassy arena. On reflection, I find that hardly surprising since my bouts were mainly won by vigorously applied full Nelsons' or back-hurting Boston Crabs.

My favourite throws were a simple cross buttock and young George de Relwyskow's classy monkey climb. In the early 1940s I met the de Relwyskows in Yorkshire and again met George when he was advancing in years and recovering from a heart attack, which he suffered while attending his wrestling promotions in Aberdeen. Having to stay in a hospital there, miles from his home in Leeds, he welcomed some Scottish support. George's father, G.F.W. de Relwyskow was 1908 Olympic gold medallist and world champion. Young George won the British and Empire lightweight title from Rashid Anwar of India in the pre-war years.

My father, back from France, was billeted at Mirfield in Yorkshire's West Riding and it was then, in 1942, I began my communion with weights at the age of fourteen when I personally carried a secondhand 60 lb. set of weights from Huddersfield to Mirfield—about six miles in two buses and half a mile on foot. It was a memorable experience. From 1942 until 1945 I appeared in that county's Clubland as a strongboy; it was my first act and nearly my last. I rehearsed enthusiastically for my premier, pulling large expanders and lifting human weights, including supporting in the Tomb of Hercules. I read Syd Harmer's book on how to do strength feats and decided to add one of these feats to my repertoire.

In this stunt, a rope was looped round my neck and two of my pals pulled on each end as I contracted my neck muscles to resist being strangled. I know now that you can bind the rope in a manner which eliminates most of the danger, but I did not know this then, and my very strong mates gave me a very tough time. I found my voice cut off completely and I could not tell them to stop. They took my hand signals as encouragement to increase their efforts, and if it had not been for the changing colour of my face, I would not have been able to write this or any other book. It taught me a lesson on the need for safety, and on the odd occasion when I did forget, there was usually a price to pay. To all would-be strongmen I emphasise that the need for safety precautions is absolutely essential.

For some time I did this little strength act at fêtes, galas, local shows and social occasions. Then, in spring 1945, our Boys' Club was at a late stage of training for the annual physical training shield when our physical training leader, Mr Leask, had to give up, owing to other pressures. Although our team had not previously done very well in these contests, we all desperately wanted to compete as usual; so although I was only seventeen years of age, I was already an army cadet physical training instructor, and my club mates persuaded me to take over to complete the task of training the team. We had learned only half a Swedish exercise routine, which had to be executed in unison to a strict waltz tempo. To this I added a few coordination exercises which looked rather complicated and clever and which we performed to modern music, the change of rhythm and style making a nice finale. We filled the rest of the allocated time with an acrobatic wrestling match between my brother Ron and myself; it was actually well-rehearsed since we were always grappling with each other, but at the show we took a few accidental tumbles so it looked very genuine.

Our team got a tumultuous reception from the young people present, but I was afraid that my departure from the norm, with popular rather than classical music and the violence of our wrestling would probably cost us the shield. I need not have worried. We won comfortably, and Captain Peter McOnie presented us with the big shield. It was my first experience as an instructor and already I was "doing my own thing" and enjoying myself rather than conforming to the accepted pattern.

In Yorkshire I saw many great wrestlers, such as Bert Assirati, George Broadfield, who wrestled under the pseudonym "Farmers Boy," Rough-house Rawlins, Francis St Clair Gregory, Vic Hessle, Douglas Clark, George Clark and the notorious Jack Pye; I also saw some fine strongmen, described a little later in this book.

Soon after finally winning the Clubland shield, I returned to the North East of Scotland but travelled far and wide performing shows and entering strandpulling competitions, and I succeeded in winning the Scottish Championship and breaking some records. While representing Scotland against Ireland in 1947 at the Hercules Club, Dublin, I became the first person ever to pull 300 lb. (136 kg) on steel strands, becoming the founder of the famed 300 lb. club. This of course was done with the very small handles of those days, although I did have a long reach. My first world record won me a solid gold, seventeen-jewelled watch. I won a number of strandpulling titles and my record-breaking activities had been reported in the newspapers, so it was little surprise when I was asked to take part in a fund-raising show at St. Katherine's Club in Aberdeen. As part of the act, I had a man jump off the top of a high-

David Webster, right, with partner Alex Thomson, left, c. 1953.

backed piano on to my unprotected stomach. The fellow volunteering to jump was Alex Thomson, who after this meeting became my partner in training, and in a handbalancing and strength act. We also became firm friends and remain so half a century later.

We were called "the Spartans," although our friends called us "the Mangy Spartans," which may have had something to do with my leopardskin leotard, made as a Christmas present by my mother who gave me every encouragement. For a short period we were billed as Adonis and Arethusa until we discovered that our research had been far too superficial and that Arethusa was a girl's name!

We could offer show organisers two spots on the programme, one a strength act and the other handbalancing, and for ten years we were very active, having tremendous fun and physically doing ourselves a power of good. Alex and I had mastered the art of quietly talking to each other without moving our lips and were able to communicate as necessary during the act. One night at the Music Hall, Aberdeen, Alex said, "Look at your fly." It wasn't open but under my stage trousers I was wearing trunks with a draw cord and about three inches of white cord was hanging out between the buttons. I was mortified and Alex could hardly contain his mirth, his eyes rivetted on the offending cord which dropped down each time I went into a handstand and then fell back as I lowered. I could not very well stop to make adjustments so carried on with a very flushed face.

I got my own back soon afterwards for Alex's belt snapped while he was doing a "get up"—from back lying to a standing position supporting me in a balance throughout. Being a great trouper he decided the show must go on and the stunt was completed with me in a high hand-to-hand overhead as his pants slowly descended to his knees! There was great applause, which I told him puzzled me as I always thought his torso muscles decidedly better than those on his legs, which had accidentally been revealed.

These were good laughs, but an incredibly frightening incident once occurred during our strongman turn. Here I assumed the Tomb of Hercules position and supported a large block of Aberdeen granite on my chest. Alex then proceeded to attack this with a sledgehammer until it broke into pieces.

As a change on the night in question we got a very muscular Mr. Universe contestant to wield the hammer, and granite, being the hardest of stones, is not easy to break. Making little impression on the boulder seemed to frustrate the new assistant, and he began to swing wildly while I watched in terror as the sledgehammer hit the edge of the stone near my face. Heedless of my pleas, he seemed to go berserk, and as the stone began to shift, I had to "crab" along the floor in an effort to prevent it from falling off. At this stage Alex stepped in and took over before any real damage was done to me. To cap it all, Alex set the stone straight and smashed the block of stone with three mighty, but controlled, strikes. That's how it should be done.

On a few occasions we introduced some comedy into our acts, such as when we appeared with Frank Jamieson as "the Noxas Trio," "Noxas" being Saxon spelt backwards. It was not particularly successful as the audiences seemed unsure when to laugh and when to applaud so we soon went back to our standard routines.

In October 1949, although I was studying very hard at college, I decided to organise a show starring Hal Harper of Jamaica, a fellow student, who had been fifth in the heavyweight category at the World Weightlifting Championships that year in The Hague, Holland; I booked the large St. Ninian's Church Hall for the occasion. We got a terrific reception from press and public alike, and this encouraged me to do other shows with Alex Thomson and Willie Cardno's assistance.

In the 1950s, our physical culture shows in the Music Hall, Aberdeen, were extremely successful and highly acclaimed as amongst the best of the genre. The hall was the biggest in town, holding 1,430 people and invariably there were many disappointed enthusiasts turned away when the "house full" notice went up.

The physique and figure competitions to qualify for the Mr. and Miss Britain finals in London were a main attraction, and we ran the first Miss Scotland event well before other organisations became involved with the title. Our shows always included strength items of a high calibre—Vern Barberis of Australia, Olympic bronze weightlifter; Mr. Universe guest stars Reg Park, Monohar Aich, Don Dorans, and Reub Martin; the Amazing Evans; Gordon Mackay; Henry Downs; Tom Cameron; Oscar Heidenstam, World Strandpulling Championships; Poses Plastiques (living statue items) with Syd Baker, Jimmy Wood, and others; handbalancing and acrobatics with the Mackins; Alan Remo; and the Spartans.

The music hall shows were our main events, but most of our appearances as the Spartans were with one-night stands, often in farming districts at agricultural shows and Highland Games, sometimes followed by a dance. It was disappointing to find that yokels who had not matched their strength with us in our challenges would sometimes want to tangle with us at night by trying to pick a fight. We avoided these whenever possible, but we did have a couple of classic punch-ups, quite unavoidable, though to tell the truth we quite enjoyed them.

Left: David Webster supported by Alex Thomson.
Above: David Webster and Alex Thomson before a 7,000-strong crowd in Aberdeen, 1954.

Alex and I had a fair grounding in the arts of self-defence, having been keen wrestlers and, for a time, members of Tommy Begg's boxing club beneath the old Shiprow Tavern in Aberdeen. There we both beat their wrestling champ who, somewhat peeved, invited us to box with him. Alex had the doubtful honour of being first, and it was only after they had started mauling each other, we discovered he was a very much better boxer than he was a wrestler. This local hero got his own back by breaking Alex's jaw and yours truly, threatened with the same fate, insisted it was time I took Alex home. Naturally I never went back! At least I was able to keep eating while poor Thomson had his jaw wired up and was on a liquid diet for many weeks. I am extremely glad he went into the ring before me as I would have undoubtedly suffered the same fate or worse. Incidently, in spite of this incident, all three of us remained friends.

At the music hall we had many open challenges and private events. These were always very popular. Apart from modern challenges, such as my own giant steel strands, which I alone have stretched to extended arms, I also introduced the famous Thomas Inch dumbbell, unlifted for nearly half a century, and "the Stones of Strength." The *clach nearts*, to give the stones their Gaelic name, were historical, almost legendary, objects, for which I had to search long and hard before discovering them in the valley of the Dee. Forgotten for many years, they were neglected and totally overgrown at the time.

We offered a £20 prize to anybody able to carry for 20 yards the lighter of the two Dinnie Stones from Potarch. The cash represented nearly three weeks' wages in the early 1950s, so it attracted some well-known strength personalities. We later featured the larger Dinnie Stone and the *clach neart* from Dinnet. The latter was contested in traditional style, lifting the boulder to a mock wall at waist height. Won by Henry Downs of London, it was the forerunner of the McGlashen Stones competitions, which became world famous.

These competitions were an immediate success, and when TV became more common in Scotland, I was able to arrange some items for the BBC. After winning the World Strandpulling Championships in 1954, against opposition from as far afield as India, I contacted Jim Buchan, head of outside broadcasts of BBC Scotland and, later, programme controller of Grampian TV. He invited me to do some strandpulling before the cameras, and I appeared with Bernie Lewis of India in a show televised in Rutherglen Town Hall. I also arranged the first TV stone lifting and carrying contest in 1955, this time in Edinburgh. The winner was Bill Acraman, a champion weightlifter from London, and these I believe were the very first such televised strength competitions. Other well-known competitors included Oscar Heidenstam and Ewen Cameron, the Highland Games heavy.

Around this time I was doing a good deal of weightlifting, winning area titles at lightweight and middleweight level and even setting a Scottish record. As well as Olympic style lifting, I entered Scotland's and Britain's Best All-rounder contests in order to learn my "trade" thoroughly. In fact I entered every competition open to me and won prizes for repetition press-ups at St Andrews Halls in Glasgow, the Palladium Theatre, London and at the Scala Theatre while representing Scotland in novelty strength competitions, involving pull-ups and repetition presses. These were usually part of Mr. Britain and Mr. Universe shows, at which I was a regular judge. I even judged the Miss Britain and Junior Miss Britain in those days.

Weightlifting took more and more of my time, but I began doing less lifting and more coaching and finally became Scottish national coach. This lasted for many years, in addition to coaching the British team on numerous occasions. I officiated at European and World Championships and Commonwealth and Olympic Games. This allowed me to travel worldwide, including trips to Austria, Australia, Italy, Bulgaria, Romania, Czechoslovakia, Jamaica, New Zealand and a whole lot more. Indeed my sporting involvement has taken me to every country in Europe except Albania. I also received invitations to lecture and coach in other countries such as America, Denmark and on behalf of the EEC in Portugal, where at the Sports School in Lamego I was bestowed with the title of Professor.

At the European Weightlifting Championships in 1965, part of the event was transferred to the National Circus HQ in Sofia where I had the good fortune to meet up with a Herculean handbalancing act of exceptional merit; coincidentally they too were called "the Spartans." As their balances were very similar to the ones I did with Alex, I was able to fit in well with them and it was a proud moment for me when I was invited into the ring to do some balances with them. One was a hand-to-hand in a wrestler's bridge and then a Jap roll, transferring into a very shaky one-hand balance.

When I moved to Glasgow, Alex got a new partner and for a time joined a circus. However we still appeared together occasionally, performing our last handbalancing number in East Berlin in 1966 to entertain weightlifters at the World Championships. We even introduced a new stunt at that time, not very successfully. In the past after performing a high hand-to-hand on Alex, I would return to his shoulders and back somersault from there. Alex had meantime been working with his new partner and suggested that this chap's back rolling dismount was very effective and we should try this. Effective? Maybe not. It was certainly sensational for I landed flat on my face, making deep indentations on the ground with my face and nose. All this was recorded on film, and the cameraman Willie Cardno had great difficulty holding the camera steady, being overcome by laughter at my expense.

My last public appearance as a solo strongman was in Sweden in 1973. A very small party of us had to provide two hours of outdoor entertainment, and as one of our heavies was not able to appear, I found myself having to fill many gaps. I had already wrestled with Tom Barlow, Highland danced with champion Jean Swanston and demonstrated hammer throwing (doing my best ever 93 feet with the 7.3 kg/16 lb. wooden-shafted hammer); all this left me almost exhausted before I started my strongman act. As usual nobody managed to pull my big expander. I did this standing on a roller while they were allowed to do it on terra firma—the more firm, the less terror!

Towards the end of the act, I produced some six-inch nails, or spikes as our American friends say, for a nail breaking contest, offering a 40 oz. bottle of Whyte and Mackay's whisky for the best. Out of the crowd came a huge, beautifully tanned Swede whose physique proclaimed him what he was, a champion weightlifter. It resolved into a contest just between the two of us and no sooner had I began bending my spike, then he protested that I had a better wrapping than he and that his hands hurt. I swopped wraps with him, confident that I could still beat him and we started again. I would love to say that I did win, but unfortunately due to the double effort on top of my previous exertions, he just pipped me. It isn't all beer and skittles, as they say, you can't win 'em all.

I bowed out with my finale, the stone breaking stunt already described. As the sledgehammer crashed down repeatedly on the stone, the commère, lovely actress Betty Gillin, exclaimed, "He's mad!" The Swedish papers picked up the comment and reported " . . . a lovely Scottish show with a crazy strongman." That was me . . . *a crazy strongman!*

This was not the only occasion on which I had to fill in for others. Although more and more I turned to organisation and administration of strength events, occasionally I had to strip for action. One such occasion was in 1969 at the Toshimaen pleasure garden complex in Tokyo.

Due to unavoidable circumstances, I had the misfortune to wrestle Clayton Thomson, one of the greatest middleweights of the time, before a 20,000-strong crowd which included Princess Chichibu, sister of Emperor Hirohito. This fabulous professional had a long run in which he never lost a fall, let alone lose a bout. A real nice guy, he could have disposed of me very quickly, but he gave the crowd their money's worth before ending the bout with me very definitely in second place.

In 1989 I took a team of Highland Games athletes to Wilhelmshaven, Germany, a former Prussian naval port, which was celebrating a special festival. Our kilted heavies were a popular group, full of fun and good humour—especially when kept well-fed and watered! We did personal appearances and demonstrations of Highland games, participated in radio and TV shows and provided lots of copy for newspapers, one of which stated that the strongmen stole the show.

The organisers also arranged some indoor appearances including a daily stint with the Circus Lauenburger from East Friesland. There was not enough room for our traditional throwing events so we devised a strongman act with open challenges, which went down very well. However in spite of the sawdust and spangled circus atmosphere, I just could not persuade the lads to wear spangles on their kilts. Our presentations were headlined in newspapers "Die Schau der starken Schotten," saying our show charmed the public and was a high point of the festival.

Once again I was amazed and delighted at the versatility of circus families, for in this outfit a few resident performers did everything—horse-riding, trapeze, fire eating, animal training, acrobatics and even a strongman act. The highlight of the latter presentation featured the slender Joachim Lauenburger lifting and balancing fifteen kitchen chairs on his chin. It was very impressive indeed, as there were many more chairs than can be seen in pictures of the act.

To keep the record straight, I coached weightlifting at the highest level until the late 1970s, then, having been involved with the Empire and Commonwealth Games since 1958, I extended my activities until I became chairman of the Commonwealth Games Council for Scotland in 1990 and led a happy, successful team of nearly 130 people to the Games in Victoria in 1994.

I Win the Toss

Although I dearly loved Scottish Highland Games, I was never big enough to be successful against the heavies. I competed at Banchory Highland Games and was surprised at the serious approach taken even in obstacle races and pillow fights. Later I competed at amateur games in Coatbridge, Kirkintilloch, the Laminer Games, Dam Park and other such events. My most important appearance was tossing the caber for the Council of Europe projects in Lamego, Portugal in 1982. My competitive career ended at the Brodick Games on the beautiful island of Arran.

I had really only gone to watch but during the Games, Jack Carson, a well-known politician, encouraged me to enter, and after a couple of good tosses of the caber, I can remember my intention to put every possible effort into my third throw. The soles of my brogues (Highland shoes) had polished on the dry grass and my feet slipped from under me. The caber dropped fast and as I was going down, it bounced up and hit me on the side of the face and head—a double blow which knocked me clean out. I awoke on the way to hospital, suffering from loss of memory. It was a strange experience but gradually I was able to piece together where I was and what had happened although I could never recall that final toss.

Although it was my last Highland Games competition, years later in 1994 I was challenged once more

David Webster, center, and the Circus Lauenburger in Germany.

David Webster winning his first caber prize.

to toss the caber. Grampian Region, in Scotland's northeast, is the home of some of the greatest Highland Games and heavy athletes, and the regional council decided to support the Commonwealth Games team preparing to go to Canada. Being canny Scots, they decided that it was not a good thing to give something for nothing so they announced the world's heaviest caber—"2,400 pounds." However this simply meant that they had a real caber made into a bank cheque worth £2,400, which they would present to the Commonwealth Games fund only if I, as Scotland's team manager, could turn it correctly in a good throw.

It had been a long time since I had tossed the caber, but I borrowed spikes, and highly motivated due to my good friends' presence there and the importance of such a generous sum to the Games fund, I did two throws. Both were good and one was a perfect 12 o'clock. I had won the toss—and the money for the Scottish team; it was a good time to retire as an active athlete.

In 1996 I am still training with weights, in addition to some fitness workouts. Although I do not train with as heavy weights as I did in the past, I still feel fit and strong. At the time of writing I decided to see if I could still do some strongman stunts, although it's more than twenty years since I hung up my leopardskin. I was pleased to find I am still able to bend and, with a bit of effort, *break* six-inch nails. There's life in the old dog yet!

After appearing in "Power and Strength," a documentary by Wayne Gallasch, Australian video producer, Wayne made and distributed in 1996 a full length documentary about my collection of strength artefacts and photographs. My sporting interests have widened over the years and as chairman of the Commonwealth Games Council for Scotland from 1990-1995, I was able to make many important changes I felt to be necessary as we approached the millennium. After widespread consultation with sports governing bodies, selection processes were significantly improved and permitted pre-selection of international top-liners; a proactive stance was adopted, and training camps with an input of sports medicine and sports sciences were organised. Open government policies were introduced and a code of conduct was produced with the help of athletes in the team. These are but a few examples of innovations.

The press were most kind to the council in general and myself in particular. This was greatly appreciated as it helped the morale of our splendid team. It was one of the proudest moments of my life when as general team manager I led Scotland's biggest and best ever team into the great sporting arena at Victoria, Canada. The great roar which greeted our tartan-clad athletes still rings in my ears as I think of this. I am now looking forward to the 1998 Commonwealth Games in Malaysia in the capacity of chief of mission.

I thought my days of winning sporting trophies were over, but I was wrong:

"The National Sports Awards are given annually to those who have or are making an outstanding contribution in a voluntary capacity to Scottish sport at a national level. The winners exhibit certain special qualities and have been involved at a level well beyond that demanded of them in terms of their official designations."

This is an extract from a press release when I was honoured by the Scottish Sports Council and presented with a magnificent Caithness glass sculpture. The heavy crystal-like trophy has colours shining through and in the sunlight it is quite stunning. I had often wished for a crystal ball to foresee the future—this award, unique though it is, may not do that but it certainly gives me many magical memories of the past, but the best had yet to come.

Her Majesty the Queen thought fit to include me in her 1995 Birthday Honours List, and on 14 December 1995 at the investiture in Buckingham Palace, Her Royal Highness personally bestowed me with the OBE for my services to sport. The signed parchment accompanying the honour has all the dignity and ceremonial impact one might expect, nominating and appointing me to the Most Excellent Order of the British Empire. It begins:

"Elizabeth the Second, by the Grace of God of the United Kingdom of Great Britain and Northern Ireland and of Her other Realms and Territories Queen, Head of the Commonwealth, Defender of the Faith and Sovereign of the Most Excellent Order of the British Empire to Our trusty and well beloved David Pirie Webster Esquire"

It continues in similar style to nominate and appoint me to the Order and is signed by the Queen and Prince Philip.

As I left the beautiful palace and entered the courtyard with representatives of my family, I contemplated the lifelong journey which began in Leeds railway station in 1943 when my father bought me a copy of *Health and Strength* magazine to read in the train during our long trip to Scotland:

"A pebble on the streamlet scant
Has turned the course of many a river:
A dewdrop on the plant
Has warped the giant oak forever."

I have never believed that success in life revolves simply around material possessions and wealth. Of more importance to me is the quality of life with family and friends and the joy of sport, leisure, arts and travel—these elevate and enrich my life. The pleasure, happiness and fulfilment I have enjoyed over the years is due in no small measure to the company I have kept.

CHAPTER 1

Meeting the Strongmen:
The Company I Have Kept

For as long as I can remember I have been fascinated by physical strength and even as a small boy, I would pester my parents to take me to see every strongman who appeared in our town and to allow me to attend the popular professional wrestling shows of the late 1930s. Thanks to their encouragement, I had an early start in acquiring knowledge about these subjects, and I had the opportunity to see and sometimes meet some of the now legendary strength stars.

Over the years I have probably met more notable strength athletes than anyone else living today: Alexander Zass at a circus on the Links, Aberdeen; Mario Maciste in Yorkshire; Milo Steinborn in Florida; Thomas Inch and George Hackenschmidt many times in London; Sig Klein in New York; André Rolet in France; John Moriarty in Dublin and another Irish Hercules in Leeds; Joe Falzon in Malta; and also Ivan Karl, Jim Schofield, Magnus, Jimmy Evans, and Monohar Aich of India. I just love the meetings of the Oldetime Barbell and Strongmen in New York where many greats past and present meet annually. Many of these and others have become lifelong friends and correspondents; I count myself lucky to know eminent strongmen of today, like Peter Lindop, Ronnie Tait and Brian Varley.

Being closely involved with TVs World's Strongest Man contests since the late 1970s, I have met, and still meet, most of the astonishing modern athletes who compete in World's Strongest Man and World Muscle Power events: Jon Pall Sigmarsson, Jamie Reeves, Geoff Capes, Bill Kazmaier, Ab Wolders, Charlie van den Bosch, O.D. Wilson, Dan Markovic, Tom Magee, Grizzly Brown, Chris Okonkwo—all these and many more have been closely associated with our competitions in Scotland and elsewhere.

Add to this the world's most prominent strandpullers with whom I competed or officiated and all my weightlifting and powerlifting buddies, and you can see that my fascination for physical strength became something of an obsession. I make no apology for this, it has enriched my life immeasurably in terms of interest and friendships. Nor should we forget the artistic artistes like the Tovarichs, the Edwardos and Les Trios des Milles led by our late dear friend Reub Martin.

Without more ado, let me introduce you to some of these marvellous musclemen.

Zass, "the Amazing Samson"

At Old Aberdeen School in the mid-1930s, I regularly listened to a contemporary, Cliff, who seemed expert in all aspects of entertainment from cinema to circus. One day he told of a strongman who was appearing at a circus on the Links and how the town's leading boxers were invited to try to fell him with their punches to his torso. I pestered my parents to take me and we all enjoyed the experience.

I well remember how he lifted and carried a small horse on a little contraption on his shoulders and caught a girl shot from a cannon. At another stage he lifted a 227 kg (500 lb.) girder with his teeth in an audience participation contest. Actually the girder was set on supports and he had to lift it clear and lower it rather than lift it on to the supports, which the contestants tried to do with a dead lift.

He was not a large man, about 163 cm (5' 4"-5' 5") and around 70-73 kg (155-160 lb.), but he had a superb upper body, particularly his deltoids and chest, which was 122 cm (48") and he looked extremely powerful. The strongman was Alexander Zass, who although born in Vilna, Poland in 1888, lived most of his early years in Russia (Vilna or Vilnus is now in Lithuania). He eventually arrived in Britain in October 1924 and from then on looked upon this as his home base. His life was full of interest, adventure and even intrigue—he had been a prisoner with many escapes to his credit and had worked with military intelligence in Russia and latterly with a colleague who was a secret service agent in England!

Zass was one of a family of five, three boys and two girls. Their father, born about 1845, was in charge of five large estates in Turkestan, Russia, and was a very strong man still able to perform feats of strength at over eighty years of age. Alexander inherited some of his father's abilities as did one of his brothers and a sister, who were both exceptionally strong. Although the head of the family held considerable responsibility, the young folks had initially to labour hard in the fields, but they were always assured of an abundance of food.

As he grew up, Alexander Zass acquired a horse and a big wolfhound and, loving animals as he did, he taught them many tricks. He developed and used these skills until the end of his days, becoming a trainer of wild beasts when his strongman days were over. Growing into a fine young lad, Zass spent a lot of time in the saddle acting under his father as agent for the estates. This meant travelling around the country, and on his journeys he saw many circuses. One day Alex and his father travelled from Seransk where they lived, to sell horses in a town fifteen miles away. After their business was over, they visited a large circus, and later Alexander slipped away and went back to the circus to spend the night there. As a result he was whiplashed by his father and for a time was fed only on bread and water, such was family discipline at that time and place.

Being out of favour for worrying his dad so much, he was sent to a more remote part of the estates to tend 400 cows, 300 horses and 200 camels, assisted in his work by a pack of dogs. With little or no recreational distractions Zass spent most of his free time performing feats of horsemanship, training for strength and learning to become a good marksman with a rifle.

Back home after his temporary exile, he studied one of Sandow's books, which were translated into several languages, and with makeshift dumbbells, he practised the various exercises. Becoming more and more interested, he contacted the greatest Russian teachers of physical culture, Krecov, Demetrioff and Anokhin, who had been particularly helpful to George Lurich. When young Zass became more proficient in tests of strength, a competition was arranged against a nearby rival Ivan Petroff; Zass's father backed his son for twenty head of cattle and all the roubles he could muster.

Alexander duplicated the feats set by Petroff, which included bending a short iron bar one inch wide and a half-inch thick into horseshoe shape, bending a longer and thicker bar and straightening it, and standing on trestles to lift a huge stone by a handle lashed by wire to the boulder.

Zass then broke a chain with his fingers and challenged Petroff to do the same and as he failed, Zass claimed victory, but this was a little premature. Petroff suggested one more feat, the bending of an iron bar round the neck; however this time the bar had file marks along it to make sharp edges which cut into the flesh as the bar was bent. The ends were also sharpened making it painful to hold. Petroff's method was clearly unfair, but Zass accepted and Ivan bent the bar round *both their necks, crossing the ends behind Zass's head*. It was a difficult position to reach and full force could not be exerted by the younger man in trying to release himself. Spurred on by his supporters and bleeding profusely, he finally succeeded to stand free and exultant. As he said later, "Every fibre in my body was pulsing with fierce joy."

Soon after this he set off for Orenburg to a locomotive yard, engaged as a general worker, but he saw adverts for Anderjievsky's Circus, and he opted to join this outfit instead of eventually becoming an engine driver. The life was hard but he enjoyed the fellowship of the big top, particularly the company of the wrestlers and Kuratkin the Mighty, their 114 kg (18 st./252 lb.) strongman, whose speciality was the destruction of horseshoes with his bare hands. Zass was able to save Kuratkin embarrassment during one of the shows and in reward was given a place in the act.

He then switched to the Upatov Circus, a crack show with star artistes, in every way superior to Anderjievsky's. Here Zass acted as assistant to Duroff a famous trainer of domestic animals and birds, then in a Cossack equestrian act with swords and lances; he went on next to the flying trapeze and overhead rings, and performed in a wild animal act and with the wrestlers. It certainly was an educational experience for the young circus artiste. There at the Upatov Circus he collected from the 140 kg (22 st./308 lb.) wrestling leader Sergius Nicholavski, the cauliflower ear he sported for the rest of his days.

It was also with this show that he performed his first solo strongman act with bar bending; chain breaking; handstand walking over sharp nails; allowing the wrestling troupe to walk over a platform he supported on his body; balancing heavy objects on his forehead; and hoisting the heaviest men in a teeth lift. His act kept improving, and eighteen months after joining this circus, he was a respected and established performer. It was then that the circus was burned to ashes, a fate suffered by many such shows using primitive rush lights with whale oil lighting.

Joining with Sergius Nicholavski and five other wrestlers, Zass travelled the country, barely scraping a living from their challenges, until at Ashabad they met up with the Hoizeff Circus. Sergius and Alexander quickly disposed of the Hoizeff's two best wrestlers and were invited to join the circus which they accepted, providing all seven in their band were given jobs. Zass stayed with this circus until the draft caught up with him and he was conscripted into the Russian Army. His many fighting skills made him suitable for promotion, and he became a sergeant major in the twelfth Turkestan Rifle Brigade and was posted to the Persian (later Iranian) Border.

During his stint in the army, he became one of the gymnastic staff chiefs at the School of Physical Training and champion wrestler of this section of the Russian Military Command. For a time after this he trained woman wrestlers and managed a cinema at Krasnoslobsdk, and when this failed, he again became a professional strongman.

The outbreak of the Great War saw him drafted to the 180th Vindavski Cavalry Regiment and allocated intelligence duties at Kublin on the Austrian Front; it was invaluable training for later in life. Moving some 180 miles into Austria, a great battle took place in which Zass's horse was blown from under him. His legs were badly damaged by shrapnel and he was captured by Hungarians siding with the Austrians. After several operations, his limbs were saved, and he was put on construction work for a year, during which time he tried to escape on several occasions, once remaining free for seven days. Being a big security risk, he was transferred to Toraksentiniklosh where he escaped for ten weeks before recapture. As punishment, Alex and his fellow escapee Iamesh were shackled for four hours daily in an underground cell, but when put on parole

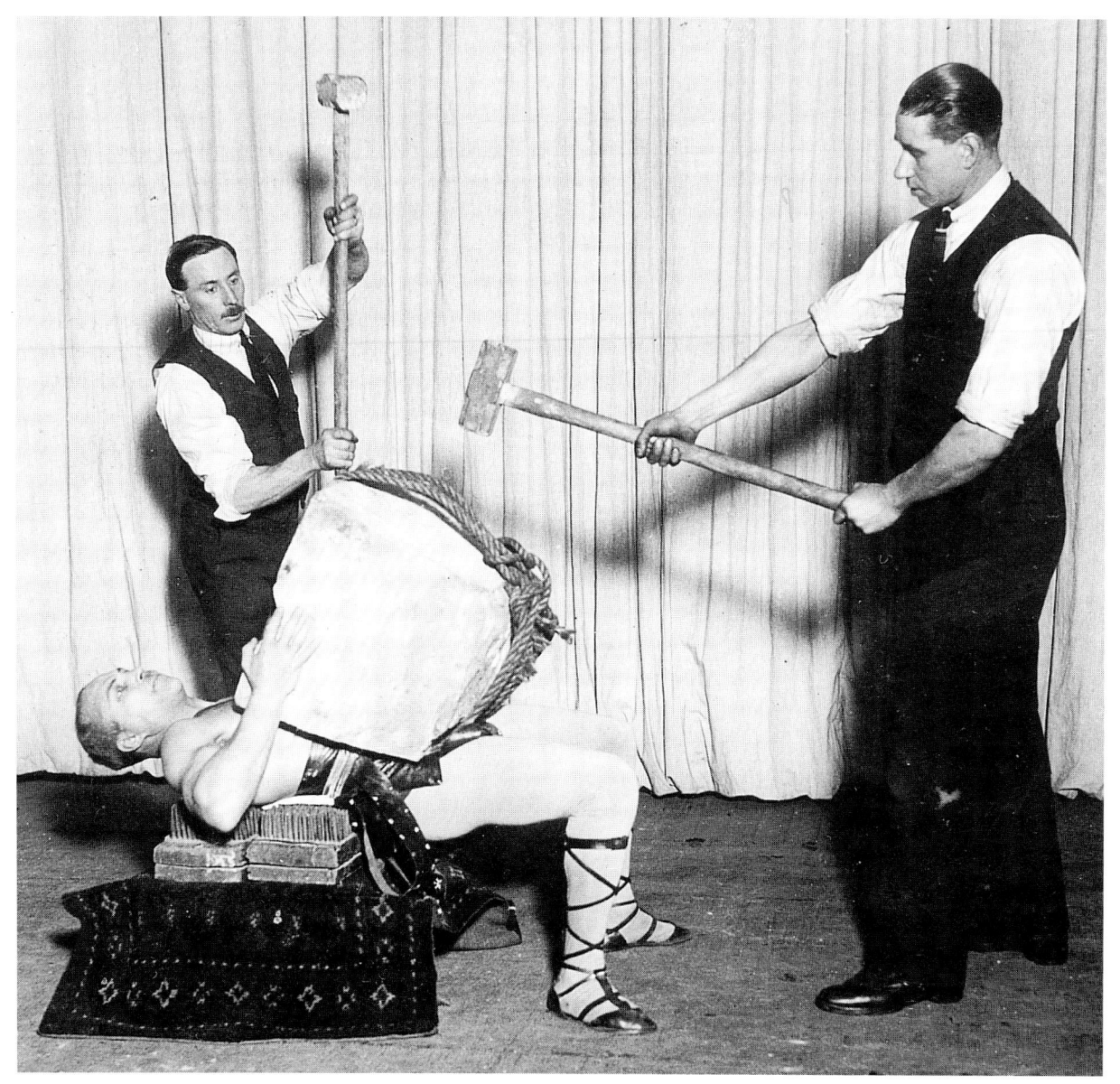

Zass, "the Amazing Samson."

he escaped yet again, and this time he knew to head for Kalashuar and Schmidt's Circus where he could obtain work. There for the first time he was billed as "The World's Strongest Man." Unfortunately the authorities were interested in how such a splendid athlete was not serving in the Austrian army and their investigations led to Zass's recapture.

The strongman said respectfully that the Austrians and Hungarians were in general considerate to their captives, but because of his record he was increasingly secured and eventually put in chains. With his physique deteriorating as a result of inactivity it was then that he devised the system of exercises which he eventually marketed in Britain. He worked the muscles against each other, pulling on the chains at different lengths and in different positions. This is one of the earliest examples (if not the earliest) of systematic isometric exercising, and in the process he regained his depleted strength and recovered his development.

The determined and dedicated Alexander Zass escaped yet again, and this time he reached Budapest and got a job loading ships and later joined a circus owned by Zaiaianosh, a former wrestling champion. In this show Zass was first a wrestler and then presenter of a dog act. Bill Pullum Jr., who knew Zass personally, told me that Zass was very fond of the ladies and always had a girl accompanying him in his caravan when Bill visited him in various places. Miss Kitty, a balancer, entered Zass's life and joined his dog act, and they presented their attractive show first at the Kasino in Budapest and then in Serbia. While there he received an intriguing message from Herr Schmidt who wanted him back for a special reason and, unable to resist the mysterious call, Zass returned to Budapest.

On arriving at the Hungarian capital, the reason for Schmidt's message became clear. Breitbart, the noted strongman, was packing them in at every appearance with a rival outfit and they were scheduled for Budapest. Schmidt felt that Zass was better than Breitbart and they could cash in on this current interest. He also wanted to steal a march on his opponents on his own ground; Schmidt was simply guarding his own patch. Zass listened carefully to all that Schmidt told him and they discussed at length a challenge to Breitbart. Zass was not at his best after the trials and tribulations of the recent past and thought he needed a month to train on Breitbart's specific feats. Alexander bought some chains of varying thicknesses and gradually increased his breaking powers and practised driving nails through planks. Training secretly, he resisted men pulling against his arms in opposite directions, and he lay on beds of nails supporting a stone on his chest while assistants thumped this with large sledgehammers.

After a month had passed, Zass was ready to meet his rival so Schmidt's Circus opened in Budapest, topping the bill with the name suggested by Frau Schmidt, "Samson—The World's Strongest Man," and timing the opening to coincide exactly with Breitbart's appearance. The opposition never materialised, which is a pity for it would have been a classic confrontation, but Schmidt still got very rich pickings with full houses for several shows each day. He was well-pleased.

Samson now got higher salaries than ever before, and he got three unrequested rises in pay during this period. While he was performing with Schmidt and gaining rapidly in international reputation, Director Devre of the Novi Circus of Paris saw him and offered him a salary much in excess of his current income. When Schmidt, his kindly boss, willingly released the strongman, he sent for Miss Kitty and the dogs and off they went to Paris on 22 October 1923. After a short season in the French capital, Zass moved to Switzerland and then wintered in Italy touring variety halls. It was while he was there that an invitation arrived on behalf of Sir Oswald Stohl to play the halls in Great Britain; as the necessary tickets were enclosed with the invitation, Samson immediately embarked for the country he eventually came to call "home."

The offer had been closed by Spadoni acting as Zass's agent, and he told the strongman he would appear at the Coliseum. "Coliseum" was thus the only word known to the strongman when he arrived at Victoria Station early in 1924. There were misunderstandings and complications on arrival for it was actually at Hackney that Samson opened on 4 February 1924 and from then onwards he had a very full engagement book: Shepherds Bush, then the Alhambra, Manchester, Bristol, Chatham, back to London for the Coliseum, Chiswick and Clapham, a week at Leicester and another five weeks in London—all with great success.

As was common at that time an audience participation contest was a popular feature and in Samson's case he first introduced a bar bending competition with £5 for the winner, the next best winning £3 and £2 respectively. Very handsome prizes indeed during the years of the great depression. In the early thirties he introduced a girder lifting contest and the stomach punch. There was no shortage of volunteers.

At the 1933 Annual Health & Strength League Display at the Holborn Empire, London, Samson's act consisted of the following feats:
- Driving a six-inch nail through a three-inch plank with his bare hand
- Lifting an iron girder weighing 302 kg (666 lb.) with his finger tips
- Breaking a heavy chain by chest expansion

• Twisting an iron bar six feet long by one and one-quarter inches by seven-sixteenths of an inch
• Tearing a sheet of iron with his bare hands
• Lifting and carrying a horse weighing 290.5 kg (640 lb.)
• Performing the human anvil: Resting on a pedestal with no support for his back, an iron plate one inch thick and six inches wide was placed on his body whilst two assistants hammered upon it with heavy sledgehammers.

The following year this sawn-off Hercules had a new stunt. He placed two thick pieces of wood on his head and had an assistant split the blocks with a big, sharp axe.

While assembling material and researching for this book, I advertised extensively for information on great strongmen. One of the responses came from Ron Townsend, better known as "Smokey the Clown," a musical, magical entertainer now based in Surrey, England. He told me that in the early 1950s when he was appearing in the Californian Circus, Workington, Berks, *Pathe Gazette* wanted their newsreel team to film Zass and persuaded Smokey to cooperate. He was required to drive his 7 cwt. van with five passengers over Samson who reclined behind a small ramp. The total weight going over Zass must have been nearly 772 kg (1,700 lb.) but it did not appear to perturb him one little bit. Indeed the feat had to be repeated three times for the cameras before the producer was satisfied. On the final run, the exhaust pipe of Smokey's van caught on the strongman's chest, causing injury, but it did not worry Zass, who was so pleased with Smokey's help that he gave the clown a fine performing dog.

Smokey greatly admired Alexander Zass and his bravery in different circumstances. One feat which particularly impressed him was when Samson resisted the pull of an army "duck." Zass attached himself to the back of the amphibious vessel which was filled with holiday-makers. He held on to a tree and signalled to the driver to give the boat full throttle. This he did, but Zass maintained his hold and resisted the terrific force to the amazement of all concerned. The incredible thing is that he did not do this as a regular stunt or work up to it over a long period of time, it was simply an idea he had to give a unique demonstration of his lasting strength. Yet again he lived up to his billing, the Amazing Samson.

Another clown, Coco, had a tale to tell of how Zass changed his act. At one stage of his career Samson had a shell-catching feat similar to that developed by Captain Henry Smith, "the Human Armour Plate." Four men lifted a huge shell into a cannon sited by the edge of the ring while the strongman stood at the other side and caught the shell in midair when it was fired.

Zass, "the Amazing Samson."

During a move from one town to another, the shell went missing, said to be inadvertently left behind. Samson immediately sacked the man responsible but was left with the problem of how to fill the gap in the act. A brave circus girl was called in to take the place of the shell which created a sensation, and for a long time it remained as a highlight of a fine show. I am pleased that this was one of his feats I witnessed; I have never seen it since.

While performing in Duffy's Circus, Ireland, in the 1930s, Zass's assistant Lil did a moonlight flit with one of the grooms. The strongman was in a fix, but an attractive young lady, Doris O'Hagan, came to his rescue. Without asking her parents, who were performers with Duffy's, Doris volunteered for the vacant position. When the cannon was fired she, being much lighter than Lil, went right over Samson's head and landed in the gallery. Her angry mother gave Zass an earful of verbal abuse.

An exceptional feat which he sometimes included was holding a pianist and a piano with his teeth while he was hanging upside down suspended by one foot! P.W. Arden, a dentist who was also the 76 kg (12 st./168 lb.) weightlifting champion, was called upon to do some dental work on Zass. It took him thirty minutes to draw one tooth and later said that Zass's teeth locked inwards, which made them very difficult to dislodge. It is not known if this was as a result of strength feats or maybe it was a natural assistance to him in this type of work.

During Samson's first British tour when he reached Penge, he met Edward Aston, Britain's strongest man, who said Zass was the best he had ever seen, and I understand these two ran a mail order business together for a short time. In South London Zass met W.A. Pullum, the little "Wizard of Weights," who thought equally highly of Samson and kept in touch throughout his life; after Zass finished with Aston, W.A. Pullum kept Zass's postal course available until the 1940s. Pullum also wrote a book on Samson's life, and this was translated into several languages, including Russian. He had long lost touch with his family, but his sister's son read the book and wrote to the publisher; Zass learned that his father was still alive, aged 103 years old.

This takes us to a fascinating aspect of "the Amazing Samson," as Zass came to be known. As already mentioned briefly, Zass had done intelligence work for Russia during the Great War, a matter about which he was very discreet and it was always assumed that this was more or less battlefield intelligence work. Although Samson was always freelance, using various agents, when he came to Britain he soon acquired a manager: Captain A.S. Howard, who always played a very low key role, was an Englishman, born in Russia, who had acted as interpreter when Zass first came to this country. When Howard died just before the Second World War, Zass was grief-stricken and, in an emotional state, he told his close friend Pullum that the Captain was a wonderful man to whom he owed a great deal in a non-monetary way. He elaborated that the Captain was much more than he appeared, and it was years later that old Bill Pullum was contacted by a gentleman who was writing of his experiences as an intelligence agent, and he wanted to check on the activities of Zass and Captain Howard who had been in the same business as himself! Bill met the author and learned a great deal about his colleagues that he had not known before. It appeared that Zass was a form of cover, and as Pullum said, "Zass would also have made a great bodyguard."

Both Howard and Zass knew many languages, and their show business background was a wonderful excuse for international travel. There has already been quite a lot of speculation amongst the small group remaining who knew Zass but the full story is unlikely ever to be told. Strangely enough when I was searching my files for illustrations for this section I came upon a nice pre-war letterheading and communication about Zass's course; the signature on the letter is "A.S. Howard, The Directing Secretary."

After retiring as a stage and circus strongman, the Amazing Samson resumed his role as an animal trainer, worked in Surrey, then moved to Devon where he presented an act at Paignton Zoo. He had no fear of beasts, large or small, and I remember reading of an escapade at the Waverley Market, Edinburgh where Zass was appearing. A French lion tamer was mauled by two young lions, and Zass rushed to the scene, totally confident he could handle these enraged kings of the jungle. I was not at all surprised to read this for I will always remember his piercing, almost hypnotic eyes. They seemed to bore right into you, even from some of his photographs. He would fix the animals with his stare and hold their gaze, immobilizing them, letting them know he felt no fear. As quite an old man he would lie on his back and leg press two lions on a seesaw, bending and straightening one leg at a time to make them rise and fall.

Alexander Zass spent some years in Essex and finally settled down in a little bungalow in Hockley with five acres of land. To those in the locality the broad-chested old man was just another neighbour—they did not know he had been the Amazing Samson, an adventurous, fascinating character who considerably enriched the strength scene over a long period of time. He died in 1962 at the age of seventy-five, and in his will he left to a lady the sum of £2,263. I understand this was to Mrs. Betty Tilsbury, who with her husband tended Zass's bungalow while he was away working as an animal trainer. Betty had assisted Samson in his act, sitting on a piano suspended from his teeth.

Alexander kept his sense of humour to the end: He pushed his old Cossack hat back on his head and said, "When I was building sheds on my land I was asked if I used a hammer. Of course I use a hammer—unless I am in a hurry, then I use my fists again!"

More Wartime Encounters—and Beyond

One memorable show during the war years I spent in Yorkshire was that of Tony Garcia and Harry Smith who were appearing at a gala in Dewsbury, Yorkshire. These were professional wrestlers and were doing their bit for a wartime charity. The part I admired most was their ability to balance huge weights on their head or chin. Harry balanced a barbell on his forehead, and Tony did a very spectacular stunt balancing a very long workman's ladder on his chin. He got a member of the audience to put up the ladder vertically, and the efforts of this man left us in no doubt that this was a very heavy ladder. Lifting it from the ground on to his chin was a feat in itself and then to balance it on one upright of the ladder still remains as one of the most outstanding feats I have witnessed.

I have on different occasions met two different strongmen calling themselves "the Irish Hercules." The first of these was on 1 May 1945, when I set my very first strandpulling record, at Tom Sinclair's Achilles Club, Leeds, Yorkshire. On the same programme was the then current Irish Hercules, Fred Walters.

Fred, a broad-shouldered, handsome lad with a fine physique, posed in leopardskin trunks and did a number of grip feats: card and directory tearing, breaking six-inch nails and resisting members of the audience in a tug of war with himself as a connecting link.

A couple of years later I went to Dublin to represent Scotland in an international strandpulling competition, in the process breaking the world record in the right arm upward push. On that occasion in 1947 while visiting the Hercules, Apollo and Premier Clubs I met John Moriarty who had toured the halls as a strongman after the First World War. John and I became good friends and, a cultured man, he wrote me very interesting letters which touched on his Celtic tastes in music and poetry.

Born on 9 May 1895 at Tralee, Co. Kerry, he began reading *Health and Strength* magazine in 1907. Inspired by this and by seeing a circus strongman in 1909, he trained not only for strength, but also practised juggling among other things. In 1913 another travelling circus came to Tralee, and John accepted the challenge of Hassan, the strongman topping the bill. The challenge was a one-hand lift of a formidable globe barbell with a two-and-one-half-inch diameter shaft. To everybody's surprise John succeeded—the actual weight was 90.8 kg (200 lb.). In 1917 Moriarty joined the renowned Irish circus of John Duffy and sons for seven seasons. He tented with John Swallow's in Britain and appeared again at the Royal Agricultural Hall in 1931-32. He also travelled with several other circuses such as Lynton's, Shaw's, Wilson's and Corvenieo's. During 1941-42 he was with the Royal Hippodrome Circus in Belfast and on tour with Fossett's during the war years.

It has been said that he beat Edward Aston in competition but this was not true; what happened was that when John was appearing at the Empire, Belfast in 1918, Aston, who was stationed there at the time, came on stage and failed to lift John's challenge barbell. Moriarty was a master of the bent press and acquired this weight from Arthur Saxon, and it was extremely difficult to lift for, apart from being very heavy, it was three and one-half inches thick! John told me that Reg Park had also tried without success to lift this weight, but by that time the bent press was well out of fashion and not practised by the top men. I saw Moriarty bent press around 109 kg (240 lb.) when he was well past his best, and in 1932 he did 120 kg (265 lb.) at 66 kg (10 st. 5 lb./145 lb.) bodyweight. I believe his best ever at a heavier bodyweight was in the region of 127 kg (280 lb.).

John became "Ireland's Strongest Man" in 1919, beating Alexander McAlpine of Bangor, Co. Down, who appeared as "Hassan," the man he had met in his first public appearance. At twenty-five years of age, John weighed 76 kg (12 st./168 lb.) but at eighty years of age he had gone down to 57 kg (9 st./126 lb.). He spent some thirty years as a professional on stage and in circus. In 1941 Moriarty enlisted his son William into the act which added scope as a double. It only lasted a few years before another son, Frank, took William's place and continued until 1949.

For many years John lived at York Street, Dublin with his wife Ruby, who was from a circus family. He lived there and trained until he died in 1978 at the age of eighty-three.

In between meeting the two Irish strongmen I met another two noteworthy entertainers, Mario Maciste of Italy and "the Amazing Briton."

Mario Maciste

The war years put an end to most of the remaining strength acts as able-bodied men joined the armed forces of their respective countries, but tradition dies hard and a few fairs and carnivals carried on to boost morale in those grim years.

These entertainments provided a welcome respite from the nightly ordeal of air raids and the claustrophobic atmosphere of the shelters. My father had survived the evacuation of France, and in the early 1940s he was in a British army unit stationed in Yorkshire; my mother, brother and I travelled hundreds of miles to join him there, thus keeping the family intact in spite of continuing hostilities.

One day we heard of a carnival at Ravensthorpe, near Dewsbury, and my father was told of a sideshow which he knew would interest me and my brother. One of the attractions was a strongman called Maciste who challenged all comers to wrestle him. There was a handsome cash prize for those who could stay the distance with him, and there was an even larger sum to anyone who could beat him.

It was with a great deal of excitement that we travelled to Ravensthorpe, and the medley of sounds and the mixture of smells which greeted us are with me now as I recall meandering amongst the booths, stands and stalls of flapping canvas. Food peddlers offered toffee apples, popcorn and candy floss, their aromas blending subtly with the less attractive smells of diesel oil, paraffin and the elephant house. A raucous spieler gathered a crowd with his ballyhoo about "Nature's mistakes," as he termed the physical abnormalities in the rather distasteful freak show, although I must confess I did not see it in this light at the time. I urged my father on as a hustler goaded him into trying his strength on what I now know to be a leg and back dynamometer, while nearby a hefty young millhand swung a heavy wooden mallet to make a bell ring. The

Mario Maciste.

screams from the Big Dipper, or Scenic Railway, as the thrilling ride was sometimes called, synchronised with the clanging of the bell to complete the turbulent cacophony of the carnival.

Eventually we found the booth we were looking for and on a little catwalk or bally platform outside the tent, standing with feet wide astride and arms folded across his chest, was the strongman clad in a long dressing gown.

As his manager made his pitch about Mario Maciste's past exploits, the athlete lifted a couple of weights and lowered them with a clatter thus attracting more attention. It was said that Maciste had served France with honour and was awaiting a posting to the Free French army. As he was only booked for a short season this would be the only opportunity to see him.

During Mario's circus career, said the announcer, Maciste had travelled the world and could speak seven languages fluently. He claimed several records and championships, and now as a wrestler he had an open challenge to anyone in his own bodyweight category, and although he was at present only a light-heavyweight, he would at this time accept any opponent regardless of bodyweight. There would of course be no refunds regardless of how long or short the bout may be.

A local rough-houser was quick to respond, and we paid our money as around a hundred people filed into the large tent which contained an unpadded wrestling ring. There was applause for both contestants and a few good-natured jeers and comments from the spectators who were already enjoying themselves. The challenger was more enthusiastic than competent, and Maciste had little difficulty with him although he took a few throws and allowed holds to be applied before breaking them, mainly by brute strength. He also demonstrated his ability by lifting and throwing his adversary as if he were a baby and then pinned him just before the expiry time for the challenge purse.

After the remainder of the crowd had departed, we stayed behind for a short chat with Maciste who, after telling us a bit about himself, encouraged us to "train hard, learn all you can, respect your parents and be guided by them." This man with the broken nose and cauliflower ears was quite a philosopher.

Wilfred Hegginson, "the Amazing Briton"

Wilfred Hegginson, who was professionally known as "The Amazing Briton," appeared in *Health and Strength* in 1937 pulling a big bus by his teeth. It was hauled in each direction to ensure that the feat was on the level. Trained by Jack Lewis, the expander specialist, Wilfred Briton at this time claimed the title "World's Strongest Youth." Nine years later I went to see him. What's more, although I was not in any way a writer at that time, I recorded my impressions in an exercise book which I still have and although I have since learned a great deal and realise that Wilf didn't rate as a world beater, it does indicate that good presentation can be very effective and evoke a considerable response from a young impressionable lad.

Here virtually unedited is what I penned on 8 March 1946:

"Wilfred Briton, or as he is known on screen and stage, 'the Amazing Briton,' was at the Tivoli, Aberdeen from 3-9 March 1946. The bills claimed him to be the "World's Strongest Man," but don't they all like that title? I went along hoping that he would be good, for he was a Health and Strength League member like myself and had been an instructor at the Northern Command School of Physical Training, York, which I had attended as an army cadet. I was not disappointed, his presentation was superb.

"His show started very impressively with the curtain rising to soft music revealing the Amazing Briton in an artistic pose on a pedestal and with his three female assistants on the side of the stage. I did not notice if they were also posing but I rather think they were. The poseur cast his cloak, a magnificent red and white garment, and gave a short demonstration of muscle control which showed his splendid physique to best advantage.

"After this he asked for four men to come from the audience to examine his equipment and to see that the feats he performed were definitely genuine, and I was first on stage. My father said I must have had starting blocks under my seat. Briton tore a pack of cards (unbaked), and it was obvious to me that they were not fanned. Bar bending and breaking came next, and this was also done very quickly and without effort.

"Those on stage then got to try his expanders. He let the three other men try his light strands but he would not let me try, commenting on the Health and Strength badge which I wore [I had already made my name as a champion strandpuller in spite of my tender years]. I think this set of strands would be about 175 lb. and I could have done that very easily, but he gave me the heavy ones which would be about 500 lb. rubbers because of the different way they test those made of elastic instead of steel. Furthermore they had huge globe dumbbell handles weighing about 30 lb. each, like those used by Tom Inch. When I was attempting to stretch the strands, he took me by the hips and lifted me clear of the ground and walked to the front of the stage holding me at arm's length in front of him, so easy!

"I failed the pull but put up a good enough show. He supported two girls on a swing-like contraption suspended from his shoulders and at the same time, back pressed the larger expander, and with the smaller set he stood on one handle and put a toothpiece attachment to the other end and with this held in his mouth, he stood erect to pull these strands with his teeth. His final feat was a supporting one: He had a platform on which there was fitted a big drum and two stationary bicycles, all of which was placed on his chest while he supported himself by his hands and feet—the Tomb of Hercules position. Two of the girl assistants mounted the bikes and pedalled away

Wilfred Hegginson, "the Amazing Briton," when he appeared with Tom Arnold's Harringey Circus in 1951-52.

merrily while the third girl got on top of the big drum and tap-danced energetically.

"This show of strength was on the whole too short but the reason is not that it was all Briton could do. Certainly not. Later I talked for about half an hour to Wilfred in his dressing room, and he told me of some of his other feats. The one which I liked best was when he donned roller skates and lifted a 60 lb. dumbbell overhead with one hand and skated off with it. The weight had been a present from Sig Klein.

"He said that the best method of training was the Army system of PT, and he believed rope climbing to be a great muscle builder. On his dressing table lay a three-quarter inch bar the shape of a horseshoe or magnet, and he explained that it was the one which he had bent in front of Adolf Hitler after thirty Strength Through Joy athletes had failed to make any impression on it. Before I left, the Amazing Briton gave me one of the bars which he had broken and also a large autographed photograph of himself. He did this of his own accord, I did not ask him for such souvenirs.

"His partner before the war was Jack Lewis, the expander expert, and as Briton was going to be in London after the Aberdeen show, he hoped to get in touch with him again.

"It is of interest to note that the rubber strands used in the performance were made from parachute rubber by the Sandow Appliance Co. These are only some of the things told to me by whom I consider one of the world's strongest men, the Amazing Briton."

Forty years later, I look back with the same enthusiasm and even now, although tempered by experience, I still find much to admire in this glittering and well-staged act.

Al Murray, "the Benefactor"

It would not surprise anybody to learn that the barrel-chested director of London's City Gym had in his earlier days been a strongman. What is harder to imagine is that a stage athlete like this would one day develop a system which would help defend the nation and become a world renowned expert in cardiac rehabilitation, working closely with the British Medical Research Council and other august bodies.

The multi-faceted career of Alistair Murray, MCSP is a revelation to those who may have believed that strength artistes were muscle-bound between the ears, for throughout his colourful and varied life this garrulous Scot has loved to confound "armchair experts." Now eighty-one at the time of writing, this doyen of the gym is still very active and rising to challenges in developing his sphere of influence in physical health, strength and fitness.

Al Murray first saw the light of day on 10 January 1916 in Thornton, Fife, and this small town boy has by his own tremendous efforts, literally pulled himself up by his own bootstrings. One of my closest associates, Al, with an aggressive and determined approach, has furrowed a path to the top of every field in which he has participated. At twelve years of age he formed his own sports' club to enable him to box, ice skate and play golf with his pals. This was no ordinary schoolboy, he was a leader in and out of school, and his teachers recognised his physical abilities by making him captain of several sports teams.

Soon becoming hooked on "iron pills," as weightlifting discs were called, Al declared that he was going to become a champion weightlifter; a *champion* weightlifter, mark you, not just a competition weightlifter. That typifies Al Murray's positive outlook, and he was as good as his word. Married at eighteen to his wee sweetheart Belle, who has shared his life for more than half a century, he won his first national weightlifting title a year later.

About this time Tony Byrne of Glasgow claimed to be "Scotland's Strongest Youth," and Al, coveting the title, realised that to gain credibility he would personally have to widen his repertoire. He quickly mastered a number of excellent feats used by professional strongmen and issued a similar title claim in major national daily newspapers. The match with Tony never materialised as the other young Scot embarked on a professional wrestling career and became a top-liner under the name of Tony Baer. Al Murray, on the other hand, worked on his stage presentation and was soon travelling with his act as Scotland's Strongest Youth.

During the 1930s a new mode of entertainment was sweeping Scotland and other less affluent parts of the UK. Known as "Go As You Please" contests, these gave opportunities to full- or part-time entertainers in those economically bleak years. Al and his pals were regular competitors in these events, especially in the east of Scotland as they had other daytime employment, and occasionally they ventured to Glasgow or Edinburgh for the biggest events.

The average working man's weekly wage at that time was around £2-10, and the Go As You Please prizes were usually £3, £2 and £1 for first, second and third. Area finals or those in larger venues were sometimes £25, £15 and £10, so competing in these provided excellent supplementary income for Al who rarely, if ever, placed lower than third. As Al's reputation increased, he was also able to command appearance money or travelling expenses in addition to prize money.

Competition was keen and a high standard of variety acts played the church halls, town halls and civic centres where these entertainments were held. Many national and international entertainers of pre-war years cut their teeth in such surroundings. Singers, dancers and comedians were plentiful but speciality acts like Al's were less common and he was popular with promoters and audiences. While large towns and cities could support theatres, Go As You Please competitions were a cost-effective way of providing smaller catchment areas with good live entertainment providing a boom for business.

Ever improving standards and the limited geographical area in which he operated ensured that Al had always to work hard improving, changing and updating his act. He brought in his friend "Porky" Bruce as master of ceremonies, and the humorous Porky hammed it up like a nineteenth-century chairman in an old-time Music Hall by linking each of Al's feats in comic, corny rhyme:

"Another of his strongman tricks
He'll let a man jump five feet six
On to his stomach—that says a lot
While Al, good lad, he flinches not!"

Corn, straight from the cob, and the crowds loved it!

Opening his act, Al would stride on to the stage in a velvet cloak with a large Cairngorm jewel in a clasp on his shoulder. He wore matching velvet trunks, gladiator boots and those long wrist straps with points which made the forearms look shorter and thicker. Casting aside his cloak with a flourish, the strongman began with sixty seconds only of muscular posing and then some fast abdominal retractions, single and central isolations, which had the girls in the audience shrieking. He would then crush an apple to pulp in one hand, and on one occasion Porky stood too close and had his evening dress sprayed with apple juice, much to the amusement of the crowd.

Al would tear a new pack of cards *while they were still in the box*, then he would remove them from the box and tear one half again, making two quarters. He has an affidavit dated 12 December 1935 from the Church of Scotland clergy certifying that he tore in public a standard pack of cards into sixteenths, and this was claimed as a world record. This feat was widely publicised in newspapers at the time. Al encouraged people to bring their own packs of cards for him to tear, telling them this proved there was no trickery. In fact he was a typical Scot trying to save himself the cost of buying his own playing cards! On one occasion somebody passing a box of cards on to the stage had inserted between the cards a piece of tin, like a sardine tin lid, and Al did not know why tearing was so hard until blood started to flow from his cut hand. He still completed the task but suffered as a result. Like all strongmen, he had to practise endlessly to be able to do such feats. The local paper mill provided him with "brock," cuttings trimmed to the required size, and he would tear these dummy cards three times daily.

Al would bend a poker by striking it across his forearm and, placing a rope around his neck, would allow people to pull on each end in an attempt to strangle him! He admits there was a gimmick or safety device worked into this stunt, the only one which was not entirely genuine—so it is definitely not to be tried by the uninitiated. Briefly, the rope is padded in the centre, not just to prevent chaffing the neck, but to bind against the padding on the opposite side so it can't be tightened any more—unless it slips.

Smashing a six-inch nail through a two-inch plank was another popular feat; Murray confided to me that he sharpened the nails to make it a little easier for himself. The only weightlifting in the act was a side press with two 25 kg (56 lb.) ringweights and a 13.5 kg (30 lb.) dumbbell, *all held in one hand*. He would press the two 56 lb. weights, one in each hand and drop back into a wrestler's bridge. For special shows, with transport available, Scotland's Strongest Youth would use a 86 kg (190 lb.) globe barbell for a bent press challenge. It should be kept in mind that he was lightweight and middleweight champion, not a heavyweight, so these were good stage performances.

Al's finale was always the Tomb of Hercules where he supported a piano, the pianist and two singers, all of them giving a rousing rendering of the Star Spangled Banner! Not all the feats they rehearsed went into the act. They tried to duplicate one of the stunts of the "hair artistes"; as Al was swinging one of his companions by his hair, he slipped out of Al's hand and both went flying, one of his pal's feet going through a nearby window.

On another occasion they went to see the act of a nearby strongman. One of his best items was beating a nail through wood with his bare hand. Badly presented, Pearson, for that was his name, carried the wood on to the stage well-wrapped up in brown paper. Unfortunately he could not get the string off the parcel and had to appeal to the audience for a knife!

By keeping up his specialist training, Al was vastly improving as a weightlifting champion when this sport suddenly had a devastating effect on his career as a professional strongman, bringing it to an abrupt halt. Someone complained to the British Amateur Weightlifting Association that Murray was infringing the rules by performing for cash. Al had to travel to London at his own expense to meet W.J. Lowry, BAWLA secretary, who explained that even if Al wasn't doing competition weightlifting in his act, BAWLA would prefer it if he would cut out the strongman act all together and concentrate on amateur lifting. Reluctantly Al agreed but, rankled by the jealousy of the individual reporting him, he simply turned to Herculean handbalancing, and soon the Milo Trio was appearing with great success at Go As You Please shows.

The trio consisted of Al, Joe Scappitticci, a former weightlifting champion of Italian extraction, and Arnie Shaw, who was awarded the Distinguished Flying Cross in the Royal Air Force during the war. Clad in black satin trousers with contrasting red inserts and stripes they made a splendid sight, stripped to the waist revealing their excellent physiques. The trio did all the standard balances and a few of their own invention, including one involving Joe doing a one-hand stand on Al's head, the strongman sinking into a deep, controlled squat to pick up a hanky from the floor.

The cash winnings had now to be split between the three partners so income was not as good for Al as his strongman act had been, but perhaps more important to a person of his temperament, he had not allowed himself to be beaten by the rival, who had hidden behind a cloak of anonymity.

With the onset of World War Two, Al immediately enlisted and had a meteoric rise, being promoted to a sergeant major in the elite Army Physical Training Corps. Typical of this inventive and innovative character he applied his analytical mind to a problem which had been causing great concern to the Ministry of Defence. The artillery guns, vital to defend the country in air raids, could be fired faster than gunners could load the shells. Using his own men, Murray devised a series of shell exercises which built strength, speed and stamina in appropriate muscle groups, and his artillery squad soon exceeded the speed of the guns. His training system was adopted by the British Army, booklets were published, and tremendous international publicity resulted. It was a vital defence factor in the Battle of Britain, and Al Murray's ingenuity was rewarded with the Diploma of Meritorious Service.

On release from the army, Al's heart was still very much in weightlifting and he quickly returned to his record-breaking activities, but it was a more thoughtful and caring individual than the happy-go-lucky strongman of the past. Convinced that his exceptional anatomical and physiological knowledge could be channelled to help his fellow man, he qualified as a remedial gymnast, and his activities as a state registered physiotherapist gained widespread recognition. It is relevant to note that Al's last full "oldetyme" strongman performance was given at a concert marking the graduation of selected army experts retraining for civilian rehabilitation professions.

Before long the Ministry of Education, recognising the importance of proper training in sport, appointed Al Murray as Britain's first full-time national coach and one of his early duties was to act as technical adviser to the BBC during the 1948 Olympic Games. Al stayed at the top of his profession in coaching at many world championships, Olympic and Commonwealth Games until 1970, on many occasions entertaining his teammates and others with his stunts. At one Maccabian Games, he had to give the American champion Frank Spellman a break between lifts in a demonstration. Al lay on his back, pulled over and pressed a barbell weighing 150 kg (331 lb.). This he then placed on his own feet and leg pressed it. Without taking it off his feet, he asked Spellman to sit on the bar and then pressed the lot for several repetitions, a performance which brought the house down.

As national coach Al Murray led a group of dedicated colleagues to gain public acceptance of weightlifting and weight training. He put such activities on a scientific basis and acted as consultant for widely differing bodies, from the Prison Commission to the Royal Ballet School. The latter, worried about stress factors on the spine, had Murray lecture to an eminent audience including such notables as Alicia Markova. They were so impressed they appointed him as the School's fitness and kinetic consultant.

Now entirely free of his competitive weightlifting commitments, Murray set to work with a vengeance to prove the value of scientific weight training, and as always, he believed that official recognition was essential. Teaming up with some of the greatest heart specialists, such as the late Dr Harold Lewis, the loquacious

Al Murray lifts Frank Spellman, USA weightlifting champion, in a show in Israel.

Scot soon convinced these coronary experts that he was on to something very special. Murray's method involved completely controllable work loading, with measurements and monitoring calculable to a single beat of the heart! The British Medical Research Council cooperated fully, financing some of the experiments and innovations at Murray's City Gym, and all this has helped lead to revolutionary changes in attitudes and practices relating to weight training.

The dark wavy hair of the weightlifting strongman I remember so well has now turned to grey, and two artificial knees have slowed his steps a little, but Al Murray still exudes vitality, and his drive and passion have not diminished with the passing of the years. Al at the age of eighty-one still has fire in his belly and is seeking fresh challenges. He passed over his gym, lock, stock and barrel, to Frank, his assistant for many years, but in the concluding stages of the transfer, the gym was totally destroyed by a bomb when the City of London was the target for a terrorist attack in April 1992.

His first gym in Scotland was devastated by a hurricane, his new gym by St. Pauls Cathedral was burned down on the eve of opening, and this third catastrophy was the end of the line. It would have been a good time to recognise his lifelong dedication to the nation's fitness in war and peace. He helped those with life threatening illnesses; he devised exercises for our gunners defending the country; he coached the sporting elite to victory, winning gold at world championships, Commonwealth and Olympic Games. It would have been nice to see one medal go *his* way at a time like this.

However now into his eighties, Al will not give up; he now concentrates on one-to-one teaching of the elderly and those suffering from heart disease. He may well produce a whole fund of new ideas for he always moves with the times. Al became involved in computer technology rather late in life, and largely because somebody said he was a bit old to consider such a modern high-tech approach. He hopes such advances will allow him to spend a little more time painting with water colours or enhancing his already well-developed linguistic abilities, but one thing is certain: Al Murray's unquenchable thirst for knowledge will be with him as long as he lives.

Among his best lifting feats are: official snatch 105 kg (231 lb.); clean 137.5 kg (303 lb.); jerk 132.5 kg (292 lb.); pull over, push on back and place on feet to leg press 191 kg (420 lb.). He also did the one arm swing with Gorner's kettlebell, doing 72.5 kg (160 lb.) with standard weights at that time.

Mighty Mac Batchelor

For some fifty years I have enjoyed globetrotting and regularly visiting the United States of America. Naturally I have always sought out strongmen, and I have met many great performers. One truly great character was Mac Batchelor. He died some years ago now, but I have always had a very special place in my heart for Mighty Mac.

In a sphere where there is an abundance of offbeat, interesting and unusual people, few deserve such adjectives as much as Ian Gordon Batchelor, affectionately known to millions as "Mac." This extrovert strongman weighed over 136 kg (300 lb.), and one of his contemporaries said that Mac's warm heart must occupy at least a third of his bodyweight. He was generous in the extreme as I discovered the first time I wrote to him back in the 1940s when we were setting up the Aberdeen Spartan Club. I had heard he was a Scot, although living in America, and I wrote asking him if he would allow us to appoint him an honourary member. By return we received a delightful letter with one of his hand-drawn cartoons and a few fine photographs of himself, which we framed to inspire our members. We kept in touch and after some thirty-five years, we eventually met and he was still the same generous-hearted soul, this time giving me a unique silver coin which I shall always treasure.

Although by this time he was virtually blind, his *in*sight into human nature was still laser sharp, and I recalled that Earle Liederman had said, "Mac's discernment penetrates any mask a guy may wear, instinctively enabling him to lay down the mat of welcome before the open door of his heart." Strongmen can be quite poetic at times.

Mac conversed at length on a very wide range of topics and was particularly enlightening on the theatre and strength performances. I had heard of his storytelling abilities using professional mimicry, but I was still very agreeably surprised at his skill in holding his audience in suspense as he described a dramatic feat of strength—yet a minute or two later he could have the crowd helpless with laughter with his keen sense of humour.

Mac told me that he had been born in Aberdeen on 24 May 1910, but although he had left Scotland at the age of five, he had remained true to his roots, hence the nickname "Mac." (Later research indicated that he may have been kidding about his place of birth.) He told of his early days in the Montrose-Arbroath area and how even at the height of his fame, he loved to wear the kilt. When Mac was young he showed considerable strength and stamina in rowing boats, and his physical abilities stood him in good stead when he once swam over a mile in choppy waters.

His professional career started in America where he was widely known as the barman who was "best in the West." People came from all over the world to meet Mac

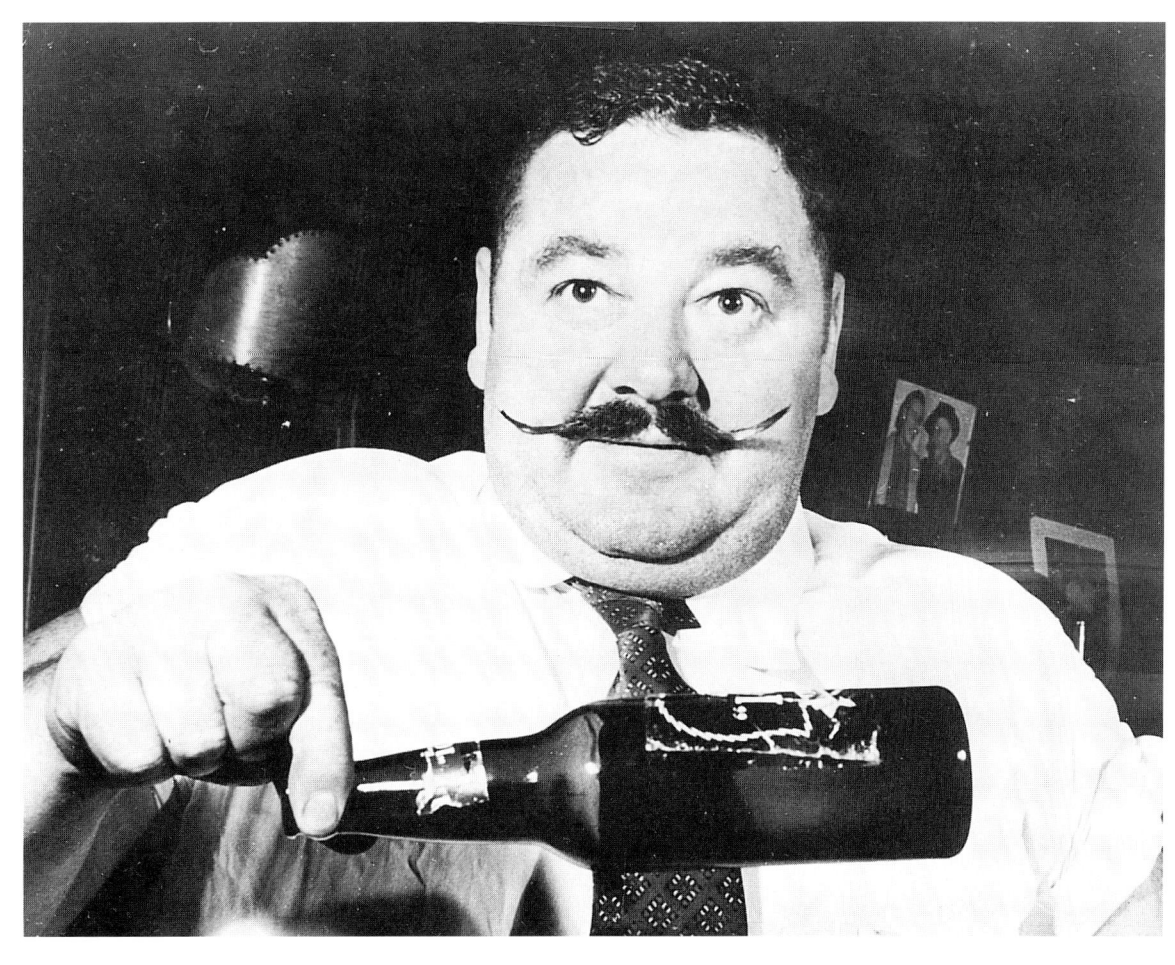

Mighty Mac Batchelor.

and see him in action at his bar in Hollywood. With his long waxed moustache he was a most distinctive figure, but much more than that, he was the undisputed king of wrist wrestlers. He competed with anybody at any time—no match-making or procrastination for Mac; if anybody thought they could beat him he would let them try immediately. If he felt the challenger was a "professional" or someone likely to try to capitalise on the competition, he would ensure a decent bet was placed, but he never allowed this to stand in the way of a match. Often he had five or six matches in one day, and on one occasion he took on a whole team of American football players, one after the other without a break, and as always he won.

He never lost a bout in his entire career, which lasted from 1931 until 1956, when he retired undefeated. He told us how just a few days earlier, a big and tough weightlifting plumber had been working in the house and had inveigled him into a match by boasting he had never been beaten in arm wrestling. Mac, in his seventies, had replied that neither had he, but he was always on the lookout for new experiences. The two ended up facing each other over the table with hands locked and Mac put the plumber down with ease. "Are you still strong?" he asked me, and when I told him I still trained regularly he cajoled, "Come on, try your strength against an old man." I accepted and like thousands of others, I fell victim to the old master. His hands were incredibly thick, and when he flexed his fingers, there seemed to be little "biceps" between the joints. It was an honour for me to oppose the man who at his best was considered unbeatable and I am not ashamed to say that try as I might, I could not budge that strong right arm and when he had finished his fun, he pressed my hand to the table.

Mac specialised in strength feats which could be performed in the bar, and this included bending large numbers of beer bottle tops between his fingers. He would bend threaded bottle tops between his forefinger and thumb only, *keeping both perfectly straight*. In another stunt he would place a beer cap between each finger of one hand and squeezing his fingers together he would crush all four caps at the same time. He had a whole series of tests with bottles and beer caps which he demonstrated in the tavern, and it was very good for business. He once bent 500 beer caps in 25 minutes, using the index finger and thumb of one hand only.

I am not acquainted with the measurements of American spikes, but Mac's publicity showed that he could bend all standard spikes into U shapes regardless of whether they were 60 or 120 gauge. His pinch gripping was phenomenal, and he claimed a record lift with 75 kg (165 lb.). On one occasion he picked up a pair of 36 kg (80 lb.) plates, one in each hand, and walked 30 feet with them. This type of work built him huge forearms, and he even had pads of muscle covering what is normally the bony part of the limb.

Mac Batchelor frequently featured in California shows, and he could always be relied upon to do something spectacular. Sometimes it would be a back lift with over 1,362 kg (3,000 lb.) or a hip lift—he liked the old-fashioned feats best. He welcomed publicity stunts, and both he and the Pacific Coast Telephone Company received many column inches in papers and magazines when in 1948, the big barman carried a 40-foot telephone pole for over 300 feet. The weight was calculated to be between 320-365 kg (700-800 lb.). Although he enjoyed these unusual strength stunts, he trained on more conventional lines, getting up at 6 A.M. to exercise. He began with numerous sets of squats with 159 kg (350 lb.), doing twenty very rapid reps in each set. Next he would do sets of dumbbell curls with 41 kg (90 lb.) in each hand and finish by doing a few rectangular fixes with the same weights. That does take a lot of strength. This of course was just the start of his workout.

Big Mac often appeared in movies and later on TV, although I don't know of him getting any major roles. I remember him being well-featured as a strongman in "Mighty Joe Young," and it was at a movie studio that he once carried a small horse on his back to duplicate the feats of Pagel of South Africa and Milo Barus. He carried the animal 20 feet on the flat and then climbed a 16-foot ladder with the estimated 295 kg (650 lb.) load.

One regret was that he had never competed in Scottish Highland Games as he felt he could have done very well; he came to this conclusion having thrown the 56 lb. (25 kg) weight a distance of 30 feet on his very first try. That is a very creditable performance.

The exiled Scot was game for any competition and would accept any challenge. Earle Liederman, the muscle magazine editor, once described a hilarious "belly bumping" contest between Mac and Cannonball Richards. The sight of these two pachyderms colliding must have been a vision to behold. The Earle of Hollywood neglected to say who won, but I suspect it's the kind of contest where there were no winners, only survivors.

At one time Mac was a great collector of strength memorabilia, and he had lots of pictures, books and stereoscopic slides on old-time strongmen and wrestlers. I obtained some of his collection through Harry Hill, and Tom Lincir got some, but I believe there was much more and I wonder what happened to such wonderful items.

In his heyday he was an impressive sight at 187 cm (6' 1½") with 49.5 cm (19½") arms, 21.5 cm (8½") wrists, 50 cm (20") neck, and well-defined 49 cm (19") calves. His thick fingers were very flexible and he was an accomplished violinist, fond of classical music. Mac's clever fingers were also used to advantage in painting and woodcarving, an activity in which he showed some skill. In the latter years of his life he became totally blind and sorely afflicted with diabetes, and when I last saw him he was living all alone with his dog Duffy. In spite of these tragic circumstances he could still laugh and joke, and our mutual friend Harry Hill told me that finally Mac had gone to a nursing home where he loved to make bawdy remarks to the ladies and yet was still the most popular person around.

On a rainy summer day in 1986, I received a letter from America telling me that the grim reaper had called on old Mac at 4 P.M. on 10 August 1986. As I sadly reread the letter, I recalled the words of Dick Tyler, who in 1967 had written, "Mac should be put in one of those time capsules. After all how else could anyone believe that someone like this great strongman ever existed."

Willie Beattie, "the Scottish Apollo"

On a hot evening in mid-June 1946, Alex Thomson and I were training at St. Katherine's Club, Aberdeen, when one of our pals came in excitedly telling us that there was a great strongman at the carnival. We finished our workout with all possible speed and hastened to Advocates Park. Full of anticipation we shouldered our way through the merry-making crowds until we saw a canvas-fronted booth with a garishly painted picture of a strongman doing a crucifix with big weights. Boldly emblazoned over this was the name "Apollo" and this puzzled us for the only Apollo we knew was William Bankier, now too old and too rich to be performing at a carnival.

Out came a bewhiskered, buckskin-clad spieler, looking like Buffalo Bill, who commenced to tell a colourful tale of how he discovered his mighty prodigy, whose feats would forever live in our minds. Rex Palmer, the gravel-voiced orator, said that as their caravans and trailers had been winding their way through southeast Scotland, the inhabitants of an agricultural area had paused in their tasks to watch the passing show. However it was the showmen's turn to stare when they saw one man who had not paused in his work handling heavy sacks of potatoes as though they were of thistledown. Palmer, a lean raw-boned Samson of another era, pulled his caravan off the road and headed for the indifferent farmhand.

Seeing that we were hanging on every word he spoke, the Buffalo Bill lookalike paused in his story to push his long straggly grey hair under his Stetson hat, then continued, "I said to this farmer, you make those sacks look very light. Who are you and could you lift that plough?" "I am Wullie Beattie and I am a weightlifter," replied the brawny fellow, and answering the second part of the query with actions rather than words, he grasped the handles of the plough and with a quick twisting pull of his

Willie Beattie pressing young Bill (W. S.) Pullum.

left hand and push with his right, he leaned back, counterbalancing the weight of the implement, and levered it until the blade pointed skywards. No wonder Rex Palmer gasped. I had seen Frankie Blair lever a heavy wheelbarrow in just such a way, and it is a beautiful, impressive feat requiring not only strength but superlative balance and skill.

Three months after meeting Palmer, Willie Beattie was no longer blushing unseen in a Kirkintilloch potato field but standing there in an Aberdeen showground with his arms folded across his chest challenging all comers to any weightlifting feat. They never had a more eager audience. Although it was an interesting narration we could hardly wait to pay our money and see this man in action.

We knew Willie (Wullie) Beattie as the greatest amateur weightlifter since the days of Launceston Elliot. The farmer's lad had taken up the sport in 1926 during the General Strike when some Glasgow policemen had been posted to his uncle's farm where he followed the plough. In those days police policy was to positively encourage strength athletics, and many of the best wrestlers and Highland Games heavies were members of "the Force." Strongmen of the Highlands and Islands flocked to Glasgow and Partick Police, and these men inspired young Willie, who was eighteen at the time, introducing him to barbells and dumbbells. His first proper coach was the knowledgeable but dour Bob Rice, who had competed against Jack Hayes for the 8-stone World Weightlifting Championship, and for a time Beattie trained at Rice's club.

After three years training, having beaten the best in Scotland, he went to London to tackle the greatest lifters in Britain. In his quest he was greatly assisted by W.A. Pullum, who had given up the stage to become the world's foremost competitive weightlifting coach. For six weeks Willie trained intensively under WAPs guidance and in spite of an injury, the Scottish farmhand won the 12-stone British Championship in 1929. His performance was a sensation for in winning the title, he also broke the famous T.W. Clarke's record in the clean and jerk, doing 118.84 kg (261 lb.), and the following Monday night exceeded C.F. Attenburgh's push record when he did 96.48 kg (212½ lb.). Willie actually weighed in at less than 69.9 kg (11 st./ 154.lb.) for these records.

Pullum told Willie countless tales of old-time strongmen and showed him the basics of the business, so when Beattie was "discovered" by Rex Palmer, he already had a fine repertoire of feats such as holding back two farm horses pulling in opposite directions. In the act which we saw in 1946, Willie lifted a 250 lb. (113.5 kg) barbell with his teeth, though sometimes he would lift 5 x 56 lb. block weights instead. He swung two 56 lb. weights with one hand and bent pressed them with his other. These were of the block and bar variety rather than with rings and, having such a wide grip, were hard to hold together. He also juggled with these same weights. The crucifix was done with 56 lb. held in each hand by the handle, rather than the much easier French style of laying it on the palm and reducing leverage by having it partly on the wrist.

After the show Alex and I bought photographs from Beattie (I still have mine and Alex had his until recently when he made a present to Willie's grandson, who was at that time Britain's best powerlifter at his weight). Willie Beattie was most modest and recounted his exploits with enthusiasm and said he would like to show us some of his other feats, but he had to reserve some of his strength as on Saturday he had to give around eighteen shows in the afternoon and evening. However if we wished to come on Sunday, then he would be glad to accommodate us. Here was a professional strongman willing to spend his only day off giving a free show to two young novice weight trainers. As good as his word, when we visited his caravan on Sunday (I believe it was 16 June 1946) he spent time showing us how to spin and juggle 56 lb. weights and when lifting, how to turn them on their ends, making the grip easier. It would have not been surprising if after such a busy Saturday he had declined to do anything difficult, but he also agreed to try my steel strands which I had brought along. Although Willie could not duplicate the specialised high poundage pulls, he was excellent at front chest pulls and earned our undying admiration for his efforts.

Willie left the fairground for the circus and he added to his appeal with his trio handbalancing act, The Almadas. In 1956 when I again met up with the Apollos in Pinders Circus, Willie was then accompanied by his daughter Jean (whom everybody called Sheena) and his oldest son Sandy, who had become a bodybuilder and strongman of note. In this show Willie did a leg press with a plank on which were seated fifteen men, and Sandy pressed two 56 lb. block weights with another 56 lb. balanced on top of it. Not many people could do that.

Willie and I kept in touch by mail until 1959-1960. Much later I met up with young John Maxwell, Sheena's son, a marvellous wee, record-breaking powerlifter, and I think he was quite surprised to be told by someone outside the family what a great strongman his grandfather had been. With a pedigree like his, it is not surprising young Maxwell won so many championships. I understand that Sandy went to Australia and died there prematurely. Willie Beattie's profile: height 5' 6"; weight 65.8 kg (10 st. 4 lb./145 lb.); chest 112 cm (44"); upper arm 40.6 cm (16").

Stefan Siatowski

On Blackpool's Golden Mile back in the swinging sixties, I saw a typical showground performer of considerable interest. Polish-born Stefan Siatowski was billed, predictably, as "Samson, the World's Strongest Man." Sounds a bit familiar doesn't it? Although it was an ambitious, not to say unimaginative billing, Stefan was a good strongman and he had some crisp Bank of England pound notes ready to give to any and all who could equal the "simple" weightlifting part of his act. This was not with an awkward dumbbell, not a mighty barbell or even an ancient kettlebell; it was with an ordinary bent wooden kitchen chair. His challenge was to do a lateral raise with the seat held horizontally at the finish, a mechanically disadvantaged position. He told me he never had to pay out, although many weightlifters and bodybuilders tried.

Joe Kirby, his spieler, drew audiences past the cash desk, and a lovely presenter stage-named Delilah assisted Samson, who also did quite a lot of talking about his feats. In his act Siatowski concentrated on bar and nail bending and the way he twisted and screwed six-inch nails around each other was quite unique. It is the only time I have seen this done. I also enjoyed seeing him hammer with his bare hand a six-inch nail through a three-inch tough wood plank. How do I know the wood was tough? I tried to duplicate the feat and failed, finishing with a very sore hand. Doing this sort of thing seven days a week, in as many as 30-40 shows daily, had built a pad of hard flesh on Stefan's hand.

Almost as impressive was the hard flesh on the side of his jaw where an excited assistant had struck him with a sledgehammer while trying to hit an anvil resting on Stefan's chest. The hammer swinger missed his target and the full force of the blow landed on the strongman's unprotected jaw. When he came out of hospital, the Pole had an iron frame made to protect his face from further accidents and as it turned out, it was a wise precaution which saved him from further grief. I often wondered how long he continued to perform, for he was not a young man when we met.

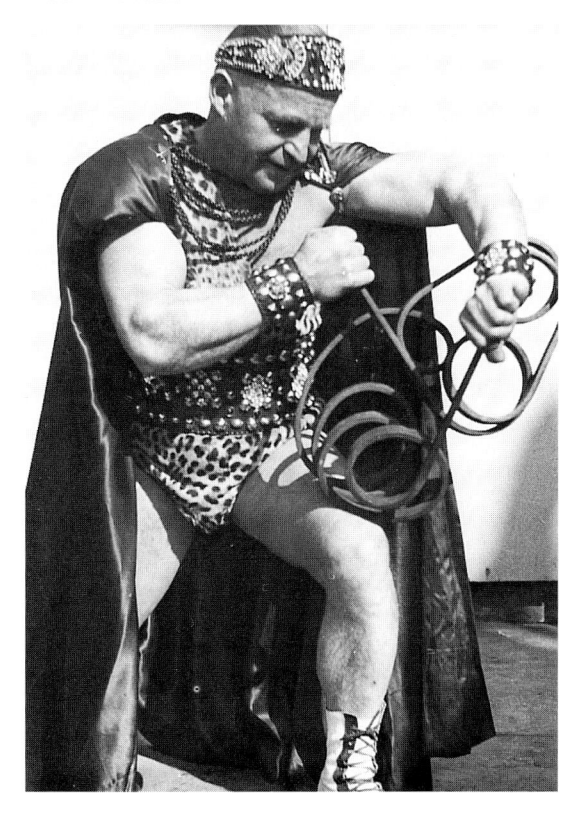

Stefan Siatowski.

Reub Martin, Strength Athlete Supreme

At the British amateur weightlifting championships of 1945, Oscar State announced a surprise item not included in the printed programme. As a break from lifting there would be a Herculean balancing act by Reuben Martin and Len Kippax. When the curtain went up there was a gasp of astonishment from the audience, for Reub Martin's physique was like nothing they had ever seen before. Just back in the country after about five and a half years, most of it spent in India, he had huge, very clearly defined and well-tanned muscles. What's more, the act showed he could use them extremely well.

Kippax weighed 61-63.5 kg (135-140 lb.), and the ease with which he was handled resulted in a prolonged standing ovation. Reub pressed Len in one hand, balanced him on his forearm, pulled him over with straight arms and so on, all without any sign of effort. The likeable young Samson did not consider himself a strongman at that time. That was to come later. He had been a Sergeant Physical Training Instructor in the Royal Air Force, excelling in gymnastics, stunt diving, basketball, hockey, acrobatics, Herculean handbalancing and weightlifting, often with human weights.

Reuben Joseph Martin was only 2 kg (4½ lb.) in weight when he was born on 15 March 1921 in Rosalind Road, South Tottenham, London, N15. By the time he was ten years old he had read Voltaire, Plutarch's *Lives*, most of the works of Guy de Maupassant and many other classics, thoroughly understanding them too. All this reading badly affected his eyes, and by thirteen he had to wear thick glasses; in later years we had lots of laughs about his apparent blindness, which I am sure he exaggerated purely for our amusement. It was his readings of the Viking sagas and *The Iliad* of Homer which led him to strength and physical culture activities, and he gave up his apprenticeship as a tailor and took to much more physical work, such as timber humping to lay a foundation of strength. When he was only seventeen, he could outcarry any man on the River Lea, carrying 363 kg (800 lb.) blocks of mahogany as positive proof of his capabilities.

Although his parents were small, at around 168 cm (5' 6"), Reub grew to a strapping six feet, with the broadest shoulders I had ever seen. When he sat in the bus, which was the usual mode of transport in those days before any of us could afford cars, Reub needed a double seat to himself - there wasn't room even for a kid. On joining the RAF there was not a jacket to fit him, and one had to be specially made for his tremendous width.

As a junior he pressed 87.5 kg (193 lb.), snatched 92.5 kg (204 lb.) and clean and jerked 110 kg (242½ lb.). It would be tempting with the passing of time for him to claim more, but he was always very honest, and all the lifts

Les Trois de Mille: bearer Reub Martin, planche Len Talbot, and balance Rusty Sellers.

I quote were done in good style before official referees, and long before drug-enhanced performances. In his second weightlifting contest he won the 1942 All India Olympic title with a 310 kg (683 lb.) total at 83 kg (13 st./183 lb.) bodyweight with no specialised training. In the third contest of his life in 1947, he won the British Heavyweight title, lifting 343 kg (755 lb.), and in his fourth he represented Britain against France, beating his opponent Perquier and performing his handbalancing act in the same programme. Can you imagine that happening nowadays? In the return match in France he won again. If ever there was a "natural" lifter it was Reub. Two weeks before he won the All India Championships in weightlifting, he won the All India Open Boxing Championships, again with minimal training as he was a dedicated all-rounder. He also did some wrestling in India, and in service competitions he ran 100 yards in 10.3 seconds and swam 100 yards in 60 seconds, although in his own estimation he was neither a runner or a swimmer. These were remarkable achievements considering the heat, disease and lack of good equipment and facilities.

In his early twenties some of his best stunts reflected his varied training: one-hand pull up with either hand; crucifix on Roman rings; front and back planches; and *a vertical chin of the bar with the body held horizontally in the flag position.* He would sometimes clown by doing a leg kick as in the breast stroke and bend and stretch his arms while holding a "flag." Later he did three chins with either hand; right-hand swings with partners 61-63.5 kg (135-140 lb.); straight arm pullovers with 91 kg (200 lb.); curls with 86 kg (190 lb.); pull-ups to the back of the neck with 68 kg (150 lb.) round his waist; fifteen handstand press-ups; fourteen consecutive tiger bends; and twelve reps seal ups.

In the early 1960s he was considered the greatest personality in British physical culture circles, and I met Reub on many occasions at contests, club visits and backstage. He was always a delightful, happy-go-lucky fellow, full of fun and telling anecdotes galore. In spite of the many successes going his way, he remained one of the boys, a role model of the age. Reub won top honours not just in British weightlifting, but also as a physique star, taking the Best Developed Man in the Services 1946 and Mr. London 1947, and was second to Steve Reeves in the tall class of Mr. Universe 1948. In all he competed in at least eleven Mr. Universe competitions, taking many second and third places. Unfortunately his massive proportions were not too popular with some of the judges at that time. He competed first as an amateur then turned full-time professional and remained so ever since in a long career as a fine stage artist and then gym owner who trained many well-known personalities.

I recall "the Four Martinis" he formed with the pals he had met in pre-war days, Len Talbot, Horry Berryman and Sam Perkins. Horry, "Mr. Abdominals," was one of the biggest top men in the business at 183 cm (6 ft.) and 79.5 kg (12½ st./175 lb.), but all three were very strong and bodyweights were of little importance to them. Horry was the first to leave the act so the name was changed to "the Three Martinis." Taking their agent's advice they again changed this to "Michael, George and Alan," but later it was simply "the Martinis," and they appeared in cabaret at the Dorchester and the Savoy and in Blackpool Tower Circus.

In 1949 they joined the Folies Bergères and became internationally known under the name "Les Trios des Milles." Sammy had to leave because of domestic problems, and Bill Green, better known as the photographer Vince and the man who started the fashion boom in Carnaby Street, introduced Reub to Rusty Sellers from the famous Foresters Club. Rusty had done a lot of balancing and gymnastics in the army with the phenomenal Nick Stuart, who became national gymnastics coach. Apart from being a superb balancer, Rusty was very strong, able to do a steady press on back with the 91 kg (14 st. 4 lb./200 lb.) Reub in a handbalance. It was a tremendously talented trio as Len was a wonderful middle man who made many terrific stunts possible. Reub's bearing goes without saying, it was truly herculean. There wasn't a similar act of such quality in the world at that time. They worked for over five years continuously without even a one week break.

Eventually the act broke up, and Rusty formed "the Duo Russmar" with the lovely Margaret and played all the top venues for almost three years. Reub teamed up with a beautiful and charming Folies girl, Beryl, and presented an act which had some balancing, some strongman stunts and a bit of comedy. Gradually this changed when Reub married Beryl, who had twins Kevin and Michael in 1953, and the act became more of a strongman act with comedy. When playing night clubs the comedy element was emphasised even more. He also did a part-time balancing act with Albert Bevan as "the Duo Ruvane" in and around 1960. The last time I saw the strongman act, Reub's lovely daughter Leonie acted as his assistant. This big strong jester often appeared in TV adverts where his strength was shown to advantage, and his weightlifting gym in Tottenham, North London was for a long time known as one of the best hard-core, heavy-duty muscle factories in the capital. This was but one of his fine gyms. Reub took over Mickey Wood's gym, and for fourteen years he ran this establishment and the Tough Guys Film Stunts Agency.

Whenever I think of Reub Martin, I recall one of the greatest feats I have had the pleasure to witness. It was at one of the Mr. Universe contests, when Reub did some impromptu balancing with Andre Picavet of France. Reub lay on his back with his arms stretched at full length on the ground. Picavet balanced on Reub's hands and the big Cockney then did a straight arm pull over with Andre still in the balance! Picavet weighed over 82kg (12st 12lb/180lb).

Weird things frequently happen when there is a strong bond between people, and while I was in London on 22 December 1993 with Al Murray, the former Olympic Weightlifting Coach, we spoke frequently of Reub Martin, our much admired friend. His name cropped up in several of our conversations and I was writing down Reub's phone number, which I did not have with me, when Al's phone rang. It was Michael, Reub's son, and he had terrible news; the previous evening Reub's gym party had been held and a wonderful time had been had by all. However on returning home with Beryl, Reub had collapsed and died immediately. The news was shattering, for Reub was always in fantastic physical shape and still performing great feats.

Reub had seemed to be an indestructible character who would go on and outlive us all. Right up until his sudden death he radiated health and strength. His fantastic physical development was still very much in evidence, and earlier in the year he had told me he worked out regularly in the gym, did strength feats and still appeared occasionally on TV. Although Reub was around seventy-two years of age, neither he nor his wife Beryl looked anything like their years. He died as he had lived, active and boisterously happy to the very end. In all the time I knew him I never once heard him say a single derogatory word about anyone.

He was laid to rest at the Western Synagogue, Bullsmoor Lane, Cheshunt, on Christmas Eve 1993 but his spirit will remain like a beacon to guide all those who believe in all-round fitness and the linking of health and strength.

Although his weight and measurements fluctuated during his long career, these are his measurements when we consider he was at his best: height 183 cm (6'), weight 91 kg (14 st. 4 lb./200 lb.), chest 131 cm (51½") , waist 84 cm (33"), neck 46 cm (18"), biceps 44.5 cm (17½"), forearm 33 cm (13"), wrist 19 cm (7½"), hips 99 cm (39"), thigh 62 cm (24½"), calf 39 cm (15½"), ankle 24 cm (9½").

Rusty Sellers

Rusty Sellers began training for lifting and wrestling at the Foresters Club which was famous in those days. In "the Duo Russmar," Rusty balanced first on chairs then did a bit of block building and some leverage feats. Margaret, who had a balletic background, was very strong and did fine work as an understander. Like all Reub's partners Rusty had a very fine physique, his forearms being quite outstanding. Having done the rounds as a "stripped act," the Duo Russmar then changed the format completely and did an act on a cat theme with wall and alley props. Rusty appeared as an acrobatic Tom cat and Margaret a coquettish tabby. They were booked in many countries in cabaret, stage and in circus and finally left show business to buy some land and settle in Mepan, Kent.

Yorkshire Lads:
Brian Varley, "Britain's Funniest Strongman"

At Corby Highland Games in 1989 I was hard at work getting the McGlashen Stones into position before the competition when a voice behind me queried, "Do you remember me?" Looking round I saw a bearded fellow about the same size as myself, and to be truthful he did not look at all familiar, nor could I place his strong north of England accent. "At one time even your mother could not tell us apart," he continued with a twinkle in his eyes, and immediately I knew his identity although almost quarter of a century had passed since last we met.

The bearded chap appearing on the same show as ourselves was "Hercules, Britain's Funniest Strongman," but he had been billed as "the World's Strongest," which had caused him some embarrassment as our group consisted of Jon Pall Sigmarsson, Iain Murray, the Highlander, Adrian Smith, Dr. Doug Edmunds, Roland Hill, et al., all of whom considerably outweighed and outlifted him. He had come over to make his peace with the heavy gang, who greeted him amicably, well-understanding the capriciousness of publicists. On visiting the arena he saw me and recognised me immediately.

In the 1950s and 1960s, before he had so much hair on his face and more on his head, Brian Varley (his real name) and I had been great pals and competitors at the highest level in the esoteric sport of strandpulling, the art of stretching steel strand chest expanders; both of us won many championship titles and broke records galore. At that time Brian lived in Hebden Bridge.

Brian Varley, "Britain's Funniest Strongman."

Brian Varley, now domiciled in Exeter, gave me some details of his act, which unfortunately I could not watch as our competition lasted throughout the afternoon while he appeared in another arena. His turn, according to all accounts, consisted of forty minutes of riotous fun, laughter, audience participation and stand-up comedy, with many spontaneous gags from Brian. He told me he had been kept very busy with shows, fêtes, galas and holiday camps in the summer, plus clubs, discos' and functions in the winter.

He had appeared on "Opportunity Knocks," "Summer Diary," "Characters in Show Business," and even in "Sportsview." Brian was most proud of his successes in *New Faces* and appearing in the all-winners final of that series, achieving the highest marks ever awarded to a speciality act. Danny La Rue said, "very, very funny act . . . great send up of himself. Marvellous wit and fun . . . the Tommy Logan of strongmen." Brian himself thought Terry Wogan hit the nail on the head when he said that Brian has a great ability to laugh at himself. But along with the comedy there are genuine feats of strength and skill, with a £1,000 challenge to anybody who could follow him throughout the act.

Bearing in mind the importance of the comedy routines, the following genuine feats are usually also included:
- breaking six-inch nails
- putting his head on one chair, feet on another, having two women stand on his stomach whilst tearing a telephone directory in half
- bending and straightening a steel bar in his teeth
- balancing a 27 kg (60 lb.) weight on his chin whilst pulling a 51 kg (112 lb.) expander
- walking on broken glass
- balancing on a roller board while tearing a telephone directory into four
- bending two six-inch nails in his teeth
- having three men assist in lifting a chair with a woman seated on it into the air and putting the chair in his teeth, then supporting it alone
- challenging six men in a tug of war
- knocking a six-inch nail through a block of wood with his hands and then pulling it out with his teeth
- pulling a 159 kg (350 lb.) expander behind his back while picking up a cloth from the floor with his teeth

One can see that the influence of Jim Schofield in items such as balancing weights on his chin and his strandpulling abilities shows through very clearly, although he cleverly incorporates balance and mobility into these feats to perplex the specialists.

"I appear first in a daft hat and wellies," Brian told me, "the whole act is geared for entertainment rather than strength only, and being both visual and aural it works well in most locations."

I remember with pleasure the many happy hours I spent in Brian's company at contests and shows. He was always good for a laugh, but he took his sport seriously and unlike many professional strongmen who simply claim titles and have never competed, Brian Varley had a fine record which nobody can take away, even with the passing of the years. He was exceptionally good at the downward pull knuckles and broke several records in this pull. Born on 24 April 1936 he won his first British Championships twenty years later, taking the middleweight title. In his eleven years as an amateur he won and lost championships at middle, 76 kg (12 st./168 lb.) and lightheavy. Brian Varley is a man with a social conscience, and the Duke of Edinburgh commended him on his fine work with delinquent children and for his work with the blind. This strongman's track record shows him to be a survivor and an achiever.

Jim Schofield

When I was very active in the strength field as a competitor rather than a writer, the little town of Hebden Bridge in the North of England was a hotbed of physical culture activity. Yorkshire had produced Tom Inch, Edward Aston, Ronald Walker, J.C. Tolson, Nat Thewlis and many other top lifters, strandpullers and professional strongmen. Another outstanding example of all these activities was J.W. Schofield, the granddaddy of the strength fraternity in Hebden Bridge.

Brian Varley introduced me to Jim, who told me he was born in 1889 and had been in the British Professional Weightlifting Championships in 1914. Well into his sixties when I saw him in action, he greatly impressed me with his abilities, and I judged him by his performance, not by his age.

Soon after the division of weightlifting competitions into amateur and professional sections, Schofield was backed and guided by Monte Saldo in his quest for championship honours. The combination was a good one, and Jim defeated Edwin Hawkin for the 11-stone British Professional Championships (70 kg/154 lb.). Army service in World War One put an end to many of his ambitions but he resumed lifting on his release from the army, and photos showed he had a very fine physique in those days. When the Second World War came along in 1939 he put away his barbells and concentrated on the war effort, and even when hostilities ceased, this time he did not resume training. The rusting equipment saddened him, and in 1952 the successes of local young bloods stirred him into action, for he did

Jim Schofield.

not feel a "has-been" and refused to accept that he could be beaten by advancing years. Jim started on a bold experiment to regain his health and strength.

His coordination, strength and mobility were all considerably impaired and the weights felt almost unliftable, but he persevered with a progressive schedule, increasing a repetition here and a few pounds there. To improve his coordination and balance he tried to copy a few of the simple stunts of stage artists he had known in this field, and soon there was a marked improvement. He enroled in the International Steel Strand Association and set some veteran records, this recognition stimulating him to further activity.

Soon he had put together an amazing act that defied copying. His lifting usually beat the strandpullers and his strandpulling beat the lifters—and if you were good enough to equal or beat him in these, he would combine his feats with juggling and club swinging!

For example a single-hand press of 68 kg (150 lb.) was good by any standards, and for a sixty-three year old it was great, but that was only stage one. Once the weight was aloft he would juggle two tennis balls with his left hand and challenge you to "beat that!" Another of his favourites was to do a two-hands anyhow with barbell and ringweight and support a "cannonball" on the end of a rod balanced on his chin. On lowering the weights he would knock away the rod and catch the cannonball on the back of his neck. He gave Paul Cinquevalli credit for being the originator of the idea but stated that Paul could not have used such heavy weights as he did.

I teased a little about the lightness of the cannonball, and he responded by using a longer pole and on the end of this he placed an old-fashioned gramophone with a horn. As a scratchy tune was ground out, he lifted the pole and gramophone to balance the lot on his forehead and then began to swing a pair of Indian clubs. Laying down the clubs he indicated that he was not finished yet and he lay down on the floor and stood up again, all the while balancing the gramophone on the pole on his head. The record was still playing so he did a few muscle controls to the music until the tune ended. It was a marathon feat of balance, control and endurance. At one club room show I saw him vary this by balancing the pole and gramophone as he stood on a roller while pulling an expander. "Stick a brush up my arse and I will sweep the stage as well," he boasted.

One of Jim Schofield's challenges was to balance a 45 kg (100 lb.) barbell on the chin and pull an expander at the same time. He was good at the front chest pull so he used strands quite close to record poundages, although he did let the cables rise more than rules would permit in a competition—but that is splitting hairs, it was a fine feat.

Jim used barbells with spherical weights, and one of these would be lifted *vertically*, by holding one of the ends and balancing it as it was pressed. Once his arm was locked and with the weight still vertical he did what he called the "cast-away," giving it a little push to change its position causing the barbell to fall horizontally and be caught in the crook of his arms. Without pause he would heave the weight backward over his head and catch it in his hands before it fell. It was a neat routine.

To display his strength and mobility, standing with legs very wide apart, he back pressed a heavy expander and at the same time bent forward until his head touched the floor; he then recovered to the upright position, only his feet and head having contacted the ground. He lay on his back in another stunt and lifted a 41 kg (90 lb.) weight on to one foot. Having got a little applause for this he then used his free foot to rotate the weight until he had it spinning quickly.

Jim presented his act in a very unassuming, matter-of-fact way. There was no hype or flourishes to encourage applause. I think the show suffered as a result, for the feats were extraordinary and should have been presented as such to obtain well-merited applause. To reach this degree of fitness, strength and skill at sixty-three years of age and after nearly twenty-five years of lay-off entailed Jim working out five or six times a week and sometimes even twice a day. It was a wonderful achievement and gave ample testimony to the high degree of dedication so often seen in this field of endeavour.

He continued his act until over seventy years of age and he was still fit and strong until the end of his days when he died in his eighties.

Keith Cockcroft, "the Amazing Magnus"

I had heard and read a good deal about the Amazing Magnus, but had never seen him in action, or even a photograph of him, so when I was booked to do a show at Bradford and saw that he was on the same bill I was very pleased. When we met there was immediate mutual recognition, for it was none other than an old strandpulling colleague, Keith Cockcroft, from Hebden Bridge.

Keith was somewhat limited in his allocation of time at that show in Bradford and could only feature a small selection of his feats; he can however put on a completely self-contained forty minutes of visual entertainment with audience participation for all ages.

His full show includes fire eating, bed of nails, karate and of course his feats of strength. Now much huskier than when he was in competition, Keith still includes strandpulling in his act. Other feats include the strangle, with a rope round his neck and people pulling on each end, bar bending, and a number of martial arts stunts including smashing wood and tiles.

In addition to performing in cabaret he takes part in many outdoor spectaculars organised by an excellent company, Jeff Brownhut Promotions, working from Leeds, and has appeared on the "Russell Harty Show," "Late Late Breakfast Show," and several others. The highlight of Keith's career was winning the top award at the Outdoor Show World Championships in 1981.

Arthur Robin

During the 1950s I was judge at many Mr. Britain and Mr. Universe competitions, and on one of these occasions I had the opportunity to see and talk at length with Arthur Robin, professional Mr. Universe 1957. This very pleasant individual originally came from Guadeloupe and then lived in France. He was a full-time professional working in theatres, cabaret, outdoor shows and circuses.

Robin had at least two acts, and as Tarzan and Pongo he had a male acrobatic partner dressed as an ape and so realistic that most of the audience believed it was a real animal. Arthur also appeared with an attractive woman called Lily. His solo strength act was also very popular and when appearing in Belle Vue Circus, Manchester, strandpulling was strongly featured; he back pressed the largest single strand expander I have ever seen. He also did some shell catching and posing. I last heard of him when he was performing with Zirkus Franz Althoff in 1965.

Arthur was 84 kg (13 st. 3 lb./185 lb.) at 169 cm (5' 6'") in height, his expanded chest was 128 cm (50½"), which looked massive with a 72 cm (28½") bodybuilder's waistline. He had genuine 44 cm (17") biceps, and 42 cm (16½") neck and calves. Arthur Robin had one of the finest physiques ever seen on a strongman, and I believe that he was born in 1927.

Jimmy Evans

Brian Varley, Jim Schofield, Keith Cockcroft, Arthur Robin and I were all strandpullers, competing with steel springs, mainly under the jurisdiction of the International Strandpulling Association, which is still in existence and keeping the sport alive. We always included some item with the strands in our annual shows, and in 1954 the star of our show was little Jimmy Evans.

Born in 1904 he was quite a veteran and we selected him because of his versatility as a strongman, handbalancer and entertainer. Only 160 cm (5' 3") in height, he had a good physique with superb control, having beaten Don Dorans, Mr. Britain 1943, in a unique muscle control competition at one of the *Health and Strength* annual shows soon after the war. He had also won an important contest for the title "Britain's Most Versatile Physical Culturist & Strength Athlete."

As an amateur in the 1930s Evans, a Scot, broke twenty strandpulling records at the Kings Cross Strandpulling Club in London. He was also a good weightlifter capable of a 91 kg (200 lb.) bent press and 107 kg (235 lb.) two-hands anyhow in the lightweight division. To demonstrate his muscular endurance he did a public workout at Portobello Pool, near Edinburgh, doing a cumulative workout total of 40 tons in presses and other overhead lifts and squats—unheard of at that time, regardless of bodyweight. Doctors monitored him and found not the slightest sign of strain, which helped change British lifters ideas on volume and intensity of training.

In Lubbock, Texas, USA, there was another strongman called James Evans, who also published a little physical culture magazine. Having identical names and interests, the two Jimmys became penpals. When war engulfed Europe in 1939 the British strongman sent his three children, George, Lois and Maureen, to Lubbock to live with his namesake.

After serving in the army and finishing college, I met up with Jimmy presenting his act on Rhyl Pier in North Wales. He did a lot of Herculean balancing, ring work, weightlifting and strandpulling. He also revolved, and looped the loop on a wheel contraption. It was a long act, well-interspersed with wisecracks and humour which were an integral part of all his turns.

At this time I was the number one strandpuller and, observing the unwritten code, I did not "jump his stage" but instead told him I was sure I could pull his strands and said that we would invite him to the Spartan Club show in Aberdeen at an appropriate time where I would like to attempt his strands, in private or in public, whichever he wished. Furthermore, I said I didn't want the money he offered to anybody duplicating his feats. We had become good friends so I was determined not to let rivalry spoil this. "How can it be a bet if there is nothing at stake?" asked Jim. To cut a long story short, he said that he could not go on performing for ever and I was much younger than he so if I could do what nobody else except himself had ever done and pull the challenge strands, then he would give them to me. We then changed the terms of his challenge, and this was published by Aberdeen journals.

In his pre-show visit to our club he was most impressed with my own challenge strands and failed to pull them in an upward push or back press. He did not bring his own expander at that time but said that at the show next day, I would have to pull it as he did. I was very confident of success, but Jimmy was a crafty customer, and in his act he let a few from the audience try to pull his strands in any way they wished and all failed. When it came to the open challenge, which included me, he said he would now demonstrate the feat as per open challenge, and producing a roller with board he balanced on this very volatile base and back pressed the expander. I knew I could pull the strands, but never having been on a roller it would have been beyond me, so I postponed the attempt.

When I moved to work in Glasgow, I booked the Amazing Evans for a west coast summer tour of resorts, and meantime I had been practising roller board balancing. At Dunoon I made a bet with Jimmy that I could duplicate anything he could do with his challenge expander, I managed without too much difficulty, indeed I managed a few repetitions and Jimmy, although a trifle disconsolate, was exceedingly sporting in his congratulations. It was a very proud day for me as I was, and still am, the only person ever to duplicate the challenge feat of the Amazing Evans.

I agreed he could keep the expanders for as long as he was performing, and he would let me know when he was finished with them. Although we then lost touch with each other over the years, he never forgot his promise and when I was coaching the great Louis Martin, World and Commonwealth Games Champion lifter, at an event in Yorkshire, Jim came to the show and we resumed correspondence. I got the impression that he was rather lonely, his children were in Australia and he had gone to Sheffield to look after his ninety-three-year-old sister.

We eventually arranged that he would come to my home and spend some time with me and, in keeping with the promise he had made years earlier, he would deliver the strands and some photographs at the same time. As he did not turn up on 18 December 1977 as we had arranged, and there were no phone calls I became quite worried, as he was now in his mid-seventies. Later he explained that he had been on his way when the car broke down and the problems surrounding this had been depressing. Summer being my busiest time for shows, we delayed our meeting, much to my regret as Jim died on 4 November 1978 after two vascular cerebral strokes. His relatives had never heard of our old bet so the challenge expander

Jimmy Evans.

never came to my personal museum of strength where it belongs.

Jim claimed a bent press of 91 kg (200 lb.) and a two-hands anyhow of 107 kg (235 lb.), and I believe he was capable of these lifts at his best.

Monohar Aich

From personal experience I can say that Monohar Aich, India's greatest small strongman, was a wonderful person. He lived a fascinating life, he was humorous, thoughtful, fair and a superb showman. He first came to prominence in Britain at the Mr. Universe contest in 1951 when he and his compatriot Monotosh Roy created a sensation. He was a mature bodybuilder and yogi at this time, yet more than thirty years later he was still performing daily with his strength act in an Indian circus.

Monohar Aich was born about 1913 and began training at the age of fifteen, when he weighed only 44.5 kg (7 st./98 lb.) at 137 cm (4' 6") in height. At his best he weighed about 67 kg (10½ st./147 lb.), and he only grew to 150 cm (4' 11"). Starting with a typical Indian schedule of free exercises including deep knee bends and circular press-ups, he eventually graduated to weights and strands or expanders. He served in the Indian Air Force 1943-48, and in 1950 he won the professional title "Hercules of India."

When he came to London I badly wanted to compete against him in strandpulling and to have him appear in one of my shows, so I travelled to London to meet up with him at the *Health and Strength* dance after the annual League display. After successful negotiations, little Monohar, who had presented his unique act at the *Health and Strength* show, left carrying his sports bag containing some of his props.

It was a dark, dismal night and I noticed some young louts loitering in a dark corner near the underground. These hooligans surrounded the little Indian and demanded to see what he had in his bag. Unperturbed, the diminutive strongman laid it down and slowly reached inside. Suddenly the scene changed, for in his hand, as he pulled it out of the bag, was a wicked looking spear head and razor sharp sword used in his show. He brandished these with great confidence, emitting a loud yell as he faced the tough guys. There was a sudden scatter, and they fled into the night as Aich calmly packed his bag and unhurriedly continued to the subway.

He was a multi-talented wee fellow, and I saw further evidence of this at Bell's Hotel, Aberdeen, where all the stars stayed while appearing in our shows. Monohar passed the time manipulating a pack of cards like a conjurer or gambler. He was most adroit with them, and when I asked where he had learned such skills, he laconically replied "in jail." It transpired that for a time he had been a political prisoner and picked up some unusual knowledge while behind bars.

His act was certainly different from those we had been accustomed to seeing in Britain. Divided into two spots, one consisted of very unusual posing, a quite original routine ranging from poses where he stood high on the toes of one foot like a ballerina and flexed his upper arm and back muscles to weird muscle controls, enhanced by the fact that he had tremendous muscular density. In the second part of the programme, he did various feats of strength. He had a big globe barbell, his tiny frame making this look immense, strands with which he excelled, and some "mind over matter" yoga stunts which usually horrified the audience. His favourite was to place the end of a long iron rod in his eye and then walk forward until the bar bent!

If this was thought to be too horrendous, then he would fix the spear head on to the iron rod and the sharp point would be placed on the soft part of his throat, just under the Adam's apple, and raising his hands in the air he would walk forward step by step as the orchestra drum

Monohar Aich.

beat out the time and the half-inch iron bar slowly bent under the pressure.

The sharp sword already mentioned was tested for sharpness by members of the audience who would cut a silk ribbon and sharpen a piece of wood with the weapon. Two assistants would then hold the sabre horizontally, and Monohar would rub his flesh over the blade and lie horizontally on the keen knife edge. Although marks could be seen on his body I never once saw him draw blood.

From time to time, tales of my friend Monohar filtered back from India, mainly from the Calcutta area. He was touring year after year, as a circus strongman. The last I heard was in 1981 when he turned up at the All India Best Physique contest, and my correspondent, the chief judge S.S. Jeerige, wrote to tell me that Aich, then sixty-six years of age, still had a physique as good as it had been thirty years earlier. Mighty Monohar Aich was then based in the South Dum-Dum area. In 1997 Monohar's picture was published in a bodybuilding magazine flexing his biceps and displaying a superb physique at the age of eighty-four! I always remember him with pride and pleasure, his friendly grin and puckish sense of humour etched in my memory. We kidded each other a lot, I would say he was so small he had to have turn-ups in his Y-fronts, but he would always top my gags by saying something funnier, which, come to think of it, wasn't too difficult!

Monohar Aich's profile: height 150 cm (4' 11"); weight 66 kg (10 st. 5 lb./145 lb.); chest 112 cm (44"); biceps 41 cm (16"); Olympic three lift total 250 kg (550 lb.).

Peter Lindop

Another champion strandpuller currently active is Peter Lindop, who has made his mark with an entertaining strength act. In addition to being billed under his own name, he has also been seen as Lindberg, Linberg, and with a musical partner as "the Odd Couple."

Peter was born in the north west town of Bury, Lancashire on 8 March 1935, "which makes me younger than Joan Collins," he quipped. Peter started strandpulling in 1967 with a splendid performance of nineteen out of twenty first class pulls, giving a hint of the great things to come. He went on to win many championships and broke numerous records, becoming the first under 12 stone to succeed with a 227 kg (500 lb.) right arm push. Peter also led the way by being the first man in Britain to blow up and burst a hot water bottle on a TV show, when he appeared on "The David Frost Programme," a feat which has often been copied since.

In the late 1960s he trained with the veteran strongman Geoff Morris of Stockport (1903-1977), who was still performing publicly at that time. The pair teamed up to make things easier for Geoff, who in spite of his advanced age still broke nails, and pulled a giant expander while doing the splits at the same time, showing he was supple as well as strong. Peter and Geoff did many shows together, including numerous appearances at wrestling spectaculars in the Midlands and North. When Geoff literally died with his boots on at the age of seventy-seven, Peter carried on, appearing solo at pubs, clubs and summer galas until in 1978, a very bad attack of arthritis in his lower back, legs, arms and shoulders put paid to his plans, and he lost a great deal of strength.

Over the years Peter did a considerable amount of wrestling, first as an amateur for some three and a half years at the Manchester Police Club, then from 1960 as a professional. By the late 1970s he had featured in over 1,200 bouts, mainly on a part-time basis as he did not like leaving his family (wife, son and two daughters) for long, although he did do tours of Germany, Belgium, Scotland, Northern and Southern Ireland and other parts of the UK.

Part of his success, Peter explains modestly, was that he was a handy weight of 86 kg (13½ st./189 lb.) and able to go into battle with the lighter heavies, middles and even sometimes top lightweights. He has been in the ring with Steve Vidor, Achmed the Turk, Hans Sieger, Karl Von Kramer, Gentleman Jim Lewis, Jackie TV Pallo and Bert and Vic Royal, the champion tag team. Peter says the strongest wrestler he ever met was Ernie Saxon Smith, one of the famous wrestlers from Wigan, who could lift him overhead *with one hand*.

Towards the end of his wrestling career, working under very varied conditions, he became increasingly afflicted with arthritis, a complaint well-known amongst professional grapplers. It got so bad he just had to cease wrestling and I can well remember the obvious pain he endured when walking. Being a believer in alternative medicine concepts, Peter took New Zealand green-lipped mussel capsules and stepped up his vitamin intake. Gradually after about a year, he regained his power and got back on stage again.

His strandpulling performances soared, and looking for a new angle, he teamed up with singer and multi-instrumentalist Ray Collins; known as "the Odd Couple," they injected a lot of humour into the act, Ray heckling from the audience before being invited on stage. This proved very popular, and bookings rolled in.

Peter Lindop has kept in the public eye with a series of record-breaking feats, often linked with charitable fund raising efforts or TV appearances. He broke 56 six-inch nails in one hour in 1985 and in 1987 in the market-place at Hyde, he towed a 1907 Peugeot using his teeth. A distance of 70 yards was covered, which is all the more commendable since the 14-stone, old-time music hall singer Miss Nancy was a passenger in the heavy old car.

In January 1989 he pulled an even heavier 1920 veteran car in the same fashion, this time with a delectable Page Three girl, Ginnette Sterling, as passenger, and immediately on completion of the towing feat, he broke 56 six-inch nails in one hour. "I was just a little tired," said Peter, "but it was in a good cause, the re-building of St. George's Church at Hyde." On a much publicised television event he broke 20 six-inch nails in 15 minutes, a feat made much harder as a determined young lady kept interrupting in order to interview him; otherwise he feels he could have done more.

Peter Lindop.

His 1994-5 act lasted some 35 minutes and included a human tug of war with several men pulling at each side; he pulled a giant expander (once belonging to Jim Evans), while displaying great mobility by bending forward to pick up a chiffon scarf in his teeth as he pulled the strands. Next he chose an attractive young lady from the audience and after asking her name, he attached a 32 kg (70 lb.) weight to his wrist and proceed to write her name on a blackboard.

A dangerous stunt then added some tension to the proceedings when he placed a razor sharp knife on his stomach and bent a flat iron bar round the handle of the weapon, similar to the feat which landed Scottish strongman Ronnie Tait in hospital. Breaking nails and bending iron bars with his teeth are all included, and as part of the comedy routine, Peter bent a bar round Ray Collins neck, a feat the crowds just love. Blowing up and bursting a hot water bottle is also often included in his well-rounded show.

In addition to his strength act, Lindberg is kept busy with TV work as an extra and walk-on artist and is often seen in soap operas, serials and plays. His trade is actually as a self-employed interior decorator of distinction, but it must be difficult to keep his hand in with such a busy show business schedule.

As a hobby he enjoys collecting strength memorabilia and is interested in everything related to physical power. As time goes on there is no sign of any reduction of activity or interest, for Peter Lindop is one of that rare breed that ploughs a lot back into the pastime which has given him so much pleasure over the years. In March 1993 Peter dropped me a line to tell me that he had sclerosis, and the hip problem which had been bothering him for so long had been a symptom of this. As a result he reduced his strength acts and stopped appearing on TV, which had included roles in "Chalk Face" and "Young Indiana Jones." Some four years later Peter is back of TV and still shows amazing strength, considerable drive, unbounded enthusiasm for life, family, friends and anything to do with physical power.

Ronnie Tait—Dicing with Death

Strongman acts and modern strength athletics competitions are always hazardous, and those who participate are well-aware of the dangers involved. Often the performers have to sign disclaimers stating they are aware of the unusual demands and dangerous nature of such activities, and the master of ceremonies or announcer will go to great lengths to point out that nobody, under any circumstances, should try to copy such feats. The audience may think it is just hype, but when you have been around the strength scene for as long as myself you know that it is brutally true and many of my close friends have suffered grave injuries over the years. Torn and permanently shortened biceps are common, badly injured joints are an occupational hazard, but sometimes there are bad accidents such as in 1990 when Jamie Barr, a powerlifter and strongman of international standard dropped the biggest McGlashen Stone on his leg and was incapacitated for several months. The gallant Jamie was soon back training and in competitive action again the following season. A year later a Finnish strongman dropped a car which fell on him, pinning him down until he was released to reveal horrific injuries.

One of the frightening strongman acts over the years has been that of Ronnie Tait of Edinburgh, whose career spanned from the 1940s through to the 1980s. I could hardly bear to watch when Ronnie bent mild steel bars; in order to thrill the audience he introduced an element of danger by placing a razor sharp dagger on his naked stomach and would then bend the mild steel bar over the end of the dagger, having to be extremely careful of the direction in which pressure was exerted. He had to apply just enough to hold the wicked-looking eleven-inch knife in position without pulling hard enough to stab himself—the force had to be applied *inwards* to bend the bar.

During a performance at Penicuik Athletic Club on a cold January night in 1976, Ronnie had a horrendous accident. While bending a fourteen-inch mild steel bar in the manner described, his concentration—and the knife—slipped. The weapon plunged into his stomach. Let Ronnie Tait take up the tale: "I thought something was wrong when I felt a jab. I looked down and saw the damned knife sticking in my body. I pulled it out and there was blood all

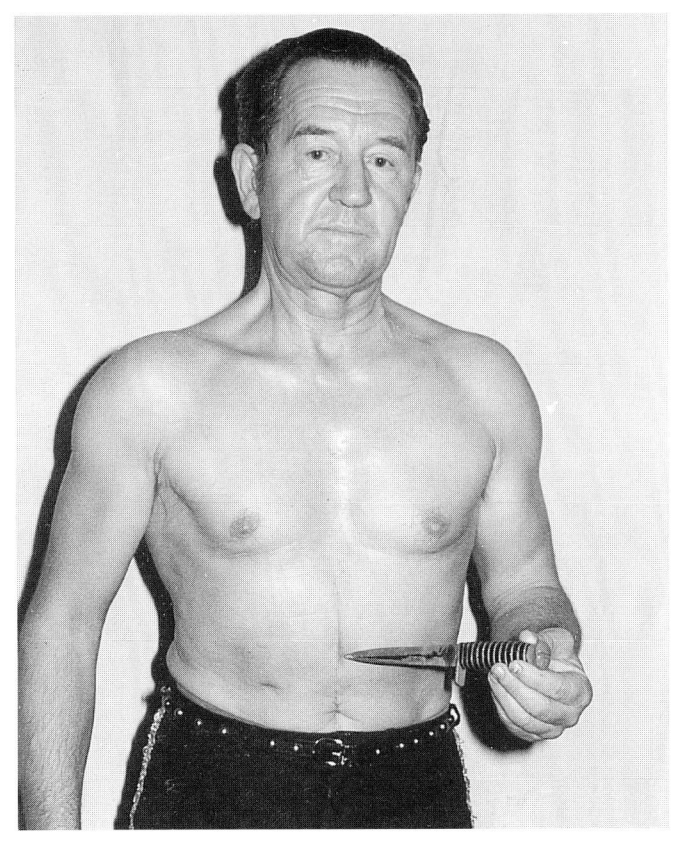

Ronnie Tait shows the spot where the knife went through his liver and pancreas.

over the place, but I managed to finish my act before I hit the deck."

The prompt action of a policemen saved his life, rushing him by car to the Royal Infirmary where he had to have an emergency operation and a blood transfusion; the twisting knife pierced 4½" into the liver. Typically Ronnie made light of the incident, "My knife act took a new twist and it had me in stitches!" True to his declaration at the time, he was soon back in show business with his £100 challenge to anybody who could duplicate his feats.

It would be crazy even to attempt to duplicate this act, and I urge readers to discourage any such attempts, particularly by the young who, lacking in experience, may not have as sound judgment. Peary Rader of America's *Iron Man* magazine refused to publish pictures of Ronnie Tait's feats, not wishing to prompt anybody to try them.

After his accident, the only change Ronnie made was to make the bar bending stunts even more exciting. Sometimes he would bend the bar round a dagger placed between his eyes on the bridge of his nose! At other times he would do a kind of wrestler's bridge with his head precariously balanced on a cola can and, with the dagger placed in the middle of his back, he would bend bars or six-inch nails.

The act started in the 1940s when he was a pupil of J.C. Tolson, "the Mighty Apollon," and as Sgt. Tait, Army Physical Training Corps, Ronnie did many charity shows, a custom he maintained throughout his career. On leaving the army he obtained a post of PTI at Edinburgh University. He also taught boxing at Cargilfield School, Edinburgh, but show business beckoned, and his act became the focal point of his life. Ronnie Tait appeared at many social and working mens' clubs in the east of Scotland but also loved going to wrestling and physical culture events to challenge the very best to attempt his speciality feat, that of lifting a special homemade lever bell, which defied everybody's efforts except his own. Ronnie offered a fine antique cup valued at £200 to the first person to succeed, but he has never had to part with his trophy.

This virtually unliftable object illustrates the effectiveness of specialised progressive training. Basically it required a pinch grip lift of a brick on to which various discs were added by Ronnie until it eventually weighed 41 kg (90 lb.); he could lift and balance this on a cola bottle resting on a stand, total height about sixteen inches. It required strength of fingers, coordination, control and balance. In his act Ronnie lifted the lever bell with his right hand, placed it on top of the bottle and took away his hand for twenty seconds, which required perfect balance. He then lifted the bell downwards but stopped six inches from the floor and held it there steadily for ten seconds before replacing it gently on the stage. He could do this for two repetitions. Ron gave me this apparatus for my wee museum, but it still resists all efforts to duplicate Ronnie's feat.

He has always liked unusual stunts such as hanging from behind his neck while holding a dumbbell in each hand. He could also do a one-hand chin while holding a dumbbell in his free hand.

Tait's grip strength was phenomenal. He could break no. 5 grade six-inch nails in seven seconds. He was the only man I ever saw breaking nails *held behind his back,* and for special challenges he would saw one and one-half inches off the six-inch nails and still break them in this awkward position. In another showy stunt he would lie on a bed of nails and break several nails in succession. Other items included some fine club swinging displays, in which he replaced the clubs with sharp machetes which could easily slice off a limb.

At sixty-five years of age Ronnie entered a night club "Search for a Star" contest and took first place over a host of pop groups, comedians, singers and speciality acts. With typical generosity for which he is well-known in strength circles, Ronnie gave his total winnings to the Disabled Society. Sadly in August 1986 Ronnie was diagnosed as having myeloma, i.e., bone cancer, and a trip arranged to the United States had to be cancelled. I have medical evidence to confirm this, yet amazingly he totally got over the problem and for some years continued to present his act.

Probably the best indication of Ronnie Tait's abilities and character is the respect in which he is held in his own strength circles.

Graham Brown, "the Highland Hercules"

During the 1950s the Aberdeen Spartan Club's tremendous physical culture shows encouraged many great champions. The term "physical culture" is used correctly, as the presentations contained bodybuilding for men and women, weightlifting, strandpulling, handbalancing, muscle control, fitness, fun and, of course, strength acts.

Always one of the first entries for these competitions was Graham Brown, a very fit looking young man from Arbroath. Born in 1931 his dark tan was from the sun, not from a lamp, bottle or pills, as are so many tans today. He greatly impressed fellow competitors and officials, and as originator of these shows I became close friends with Graham, doing my best to encourage him in his hobby and what became his vocation as a professional strongman, known as the Highland Hercules.

The "Highland" tag was useful even then, as it still is today: I was taking Highland Games to the furthest corners of the earth and my sponsors were McVitie's Biscuits and we cooperated with British Week export drives in conjunction with the British government. First I organised five events in Sweden (1968), with Princess Alexandra as Guest of Honour at the final; I then made arrangements for even more ambitious projects in Tokyo, Japan in 1969, where Prince William of Gloucester was our Chieftain and Princess Chichibu, the Emperor's sister, was our Guest of Honour, and then in 1971 at Golden Gate Park, San Francisco, where the Princess was accompanied by her husband, the Right Hon. Angus Ogilvie.

I included Graham and his strongman act in the line-up, for in addition to the games, we had to appear in halls and stores in America and on rooftop gardens in Japan. In his act the Highland Hercules pulled a large expander; broke two six-inch nails in quick succession (best time nine seconds each nail); bent a household poker over his bare forearm; crashed a five-inch nail through a plank of wood with his bare hand; and in the "Spear of Death," placed the sharp point of a spear against his throat and pressed forward until the metal shaft bent under the pressure. Other stunts included spinning and carrying three persons on his shoulders and allowing a large boulder (up to 113.5 kg/250 lb.), or a concrete block to be smashed on his chest while in the Tomb of Hercules position. In all, Graham had some sixty such items at his disposal, so he could do repeat shows at venues and still introduce changes.

As an amateur the Arbroath strongboy was one of the pioneers of the local YMCA's weight-training section and he did national service in Cyprus before his main successes as a bodybuilder. He won the Mr. Hercules title, run in conjunction with the Steve Reeves film *Hercules in Chains* while it was being promoted in Scotland. His handsome good looks, with dark wavy hair and gleaming white teeth, made him a hit with the ladies as well as the men in the audience. Wherever English was spoken his humorous line of patter supplemented his feats. Graham was always immaculately dressed, appearing in athletic singlet and kilt for his act and in full Highland dress for finales.

In Scotland he toured the halls and clubs, mainly in the 1960s and early 70s, and one of the highlights was on 20-21 July 1967 when he established a World marathon record in nail breaking, snapping 1,060 six-inch nails in 35 hours and 10 minutes, a feat still unbroken after all these years; few records have lasted so long.

A week after his marathon nail breaking record Graham again hit the headlines; three-year-old Margaret Dye got her head stuck between railings on the High Road Bridge, Arbroath. Two burly policemen strained to get her free and a dozen fishermen heaved on ropes. They said the bars would have to be cut. Emergency services were called but before they arrived, a quick-thinking bystander rushed for Graham Brown, and the strongman was quickly on the scene. Gripping the iron bars, as Apollon did in his act, Graham strained with all his might. The railings slowly yielded before his adrenalin-induced force, and the frightened youngster was pulled free. Pictures of the rescued kid and the herculean hero adorned the national newspapers the following day. Isobel Dye, Margaret's mother was loud in her praise, "I don't know how I can thank you enough." Modestly Graham replied, "It was just luck really. I suppose I am better trained than other men to do things like this."

Back From the Dead

In 1974 fate played a dirty trick on this popular personality. Between shows, like so many other artistes, Graham Brown supplemented his income and filled his time with other work. One day he was at the top of a tower wagon, doing maintenance work on a high lamp standard, when a passing vehicle hit the protruding stabiliser, and the unfortunate Graham was catapulted out of the platform. His headlong dive to the hard street far below was a catastrophe, and he all but died. Indeed many friends were told he was dead and letters of sympathy were written to his wife Sadie. For many months he was in a coma; the doctors said a lesser mortal would undoubtedly have died. For years he was in hospital having treatment and physiotherapy, but eventually the Highland Hercules lived up to his name and overcame seemingly impossible obstacles.

His struggle to recapture and retain his faculties was long and arduous, and although he could never again be the world record-breaking strongman he once was, he again took an active interest in training and fitness, advising the marines in such matters.

I cannot let this opportunity pass to recall a couple of favourite incidents on one of our overseas tours together. One night in Tokyo we were getting a little bored and Ian Campbell, the giant bearded wrestler who had often fought in Japan, contacted a local traditional doll maker, asking him to bring a supply of his wares for us to buy as souvenirs. In tandem with this and with no intended connection, I set up a jape to tease Ian and fellow wrestler Clayton Thomson, the unbeatable middleweight. I had arranged with the hotel receptionist to telephone us to say a Japanese wrestler had arrived wishing to challenge our men for a large sum.

The phone call came when the doll maker was with us, and Graham was up to his tricks. The Highland Hercules offered me a razor blade to eat and noting they were my favourite "Blue Gillette," we each took one and put it in our mouth, crunching away noisily much to the consternation of the doll vendor. Our companions, having seen it all before, never turned a hair, not even when Graham retired to a corner and began one of his stunts which I did not allow in my own shows. *With a small mallet he tapped a five-inch nail up one of his nostrils.* The doll man's face changed colour, but he was too polite to say anything.

Graham Brown, "the Highland Hercules."

At this stage the fake Japanese wrestler, suitably masked, came to our door and started talking gibberish with me, with just a sprinkling of Japanese words to make it sound authentic. I told our wrestlers he was insulting them, saying they were not real fighters but merely show-acting performers. This was too much for Clayton Thomson, a truly great wrestler, and he made a dive for the intruder who, unknown to all except myself, was Doug Duncan, the Highland dancer, in disguise. At this point the friendly neighbourhood doll dealer packed his wares rapidly and prepared to depart, a picture of perplexity. "Is something wrong?" I queried innocently. He pointed to Graham, "He puts a spike up his nose, razor blades are eaten, strange people talk rubbish and chase each other, and YOU ask ME if anything is wrong!"

We collapsed laughing, but he was happier when we bought all his dolls, one of which decorates my home to this day. Because of the commotion this had caused, the following night we got a lounge in the hotel for our socialising. A Japanese wedding in the neighbouring room spilled into our place, and we all had a great night, ending with an exchange of presents, the ones given to us beautifully beribboned. Later that night there was much laughter and general hilarity in and around the room Graham Brown shared with a very large member of our team who had imbibed a considerable amount of Japanese rice wine at the wedding and was now very fast asleep on top of his bed, stark naked, except for one of the large ribbons tied to a prominent part of his anatomy. Graham denied all knowledge of the decoration, but I for one never believed him; the prank was much in keeping with his sense of humour.

During his career as a strongman he had several appearances on TV including Grampian, the North East station. There he met Watt Nicoll, an entertainer who is now a mystic practitioner of alternative applied psychology. Very impressed with his new colleague, the talented Watt composed "The Ballad of Graham Brown—a Friend" and recorded this a few programmes later.

Graham Brown has another claim to fame—he is a talented artist and often amused us with his cartoons of funny wee bodybuilders. He provided the Spartan Club with its popular logo "Sparty," a humorous and never-aging muscleman still much admired on tank tops and sweat shirts. I also got Graham to illustrate my first book *Modern Strandpulling,* the model he drew starting skinny at the top of the first page and gradually developing as the exercises were illustrated. I persuaded D.G. Johnstone, the editor of *Health and Strength* to use Graham to illustrate the famous *Health and Strength Annual,* a task he handled admirably, and later he provided many drawings for the magazine itself.

The denizens of muscledom are invariably interesting, but Graham Brown, "the Highland Hercules," has the edge on most others, for he lived life to the full, cheated death, and came back once more to life and laughter.

Joe Falzon, "the Maltese Falzon"

The attractive island of Malta has produced a remarkable number of strong, well-built men, out of all proportion to its size and population. When I went there for the Commonwealth Weightlifting Championships in February 1983, I was pleased to be able to meet a number of their distinguished personalities. I had long known Charlie Mifsud, a weightlifting pub owner, and he was of considerable assistance in providing information and arranging interviews.

Born into a well-known acrobatic family, Joe Falzon started bodybuilding at the age of nine and soon became skilled in trapeze and tightrope work. By the time I met him, he was recognised as the George Cross Island's strongest man. Amongst the brawny, bearded performer's favourite feats was leg pressing the heavy end of a car, pulling a large car 100 feet by his hair, and allowing a large Oldsmobile car to be run over his forearm or his chest at 50 miles an hour. Other popular tests of his power included pulling an eight-ton truck a distance of 200 feet by neck strength alone; bar bending; using only his teeth to support a man sitting on a chair; and supporting weights while lying on a bed of nails, or supported only by his shoulders and heels.

On 29 January 1976, Joe pushed a 21-ton locomotive for 70 yards. Falzon has dragged a Boeing 727 aeroplane a distance of 30 feet, and he pulled an American saloon car a distance of 100 feet *with his hair.* Finally, he pulled an 8-ton charabanc a distance of 100 feet by a rope tied round his neck. Not content with blowing up and bursting hot water bottles, Joe did the same with the inner tube of a truck, which really tested his lungs.

In an unusual stunt, he hammered a large nail into a plank and then grasping the nail with his teeth, he would bend it backwards and forwards and from side to side until the nail broke, without ever having been touched by hand. An outdoor stunt which goes down well with audiences is when he resists two great stallions pulling him apart as he links their harness in the crooks of his arms. In what he considers the greatest feat of his life, Joe supported the front end of a car on his shoulders, the back wheels being blocked to prevent them moving.

Joe is also a competent handbalancer, regularly appearing with his family billed as "the Magnificent Seven." He was a well-built and trim middleweight around 70 kg (11 st./155 lb.) when we met, and he looked very smart and

Joe Falzon of Malta, with six men in a diesel engine car passing over his forearm. Photo by C. Gauci.

fit at over fifty years of age. I estimated his height to be about 170 cm (5' 7"). I expect nowadays he will be devoting more time to his gym in Zejtun, where he was born.

Charles Saliba, "the Iron Man of Malta"

Charles Saliba (1929-1982) lived in St Julian's and was known as "the Iron Man of Malta." He first came to the public eye as a boxer but changed to become a professional strongman, and for many years he performed standard strength feats in various towns and villages throughout the island and appeared on Maltese TV. Highlights of his career were bookings in Melbourne and in Singapore.

One of his interesting feats was to bend an iron bar 7' x 3" x ¼" over the bridge of his nose until it formed a right angle. He would then continue the bend using his thighs and chest until he had it bent into some six or seven circles. To vary this he would sometimes make the initial bend with the bar held in his teeth. He would balance an 82 kg (180 lb.) barbell across the bridge of his nose, break six-inch nails, and drive four-inch nails through a three-inch plank. In another feat which went down well with audiences, he would lie on a bed of 462 nails and lift an 82 kg (180 lb.) weight while his daughter Juliana would stand on his chest to make things a little bit harder. In later years Juliana would do the bar bending on the bridge of her nose and against the teeth, while Charles specialized more on pain resisting stunts such as pulling cars long distances with the vehicles attached to his long gray tresses. In his declining years Saliba also sported a huge white beard.

He last performed in 1981 and had a heart attack on 19 July 1982 and died almost immediately at St. Luke's Hospital, aged fifty-three.

Manjit Singh

During a TV strongman show with Geoff Capes, I met little Manjit Singh, "the Iron Man from Leicester." His stunts were of a *mind over matter* variety rather than the raw power of Capes, so there was no clashing of skills.

Born in India around 1950 he spent his formative years learning about yoga and other esoteric systems. By his early twenties he had formed his own ideas and would practise meditation in graveyards where he found the atmosphere calm and peaceful.

In Britain of the 1980s he discovered that a mixture of strength and death-defying yogi type activities went down well, and included in his acts are the following feats:

• lying on broken glass and letting a transit van drive over his chest
• pulling a five-ton truck with his teeth

• stopping two cars pulling in opposite directions

• leg pressing one end of a Mercedes while lying on broken glass

• bending an eight-foot iron bar, with one end placed against his throat

• lying on a bed of nails with another bed of nails on top of him, forming a human sandwich, while allowing a 13-stone man to stand on top

• pulling a car with five passengers by his neck

Not by any means a heavyweight, Manjit Singh is only 168 cm (5' 6") tall and weighs around 70 kg (11 st./154 lb.).

Siegmund Klein

To be in Siegmund Klein's town house in old New York was like being in a museum of strength. A huge gilt-framed oil painting of Prof. Attila looked down from the wall, weightlifting beer steins and Attila's press cuttings lay around and of course Grace, Sig's charming wife and Attila's youngest daughter, was there giving first-hand tales of days of yore. Alex Godo, an old friend who seems to have walked right out of one of Damon Runyon's books, had first brought Sig to my hotel to meet me. Like nearly every strongman I have ever met, Mr Klein loved the taste of haggis we had specially prepared, and after a most sociable meal partaking of this mysterious Scottish delicacy, he invited me to his home. The details given here and in other sections were provided by Siegmund Klein in writing and taped recording.

Sieg, more often written as Sig, and sometimes even as Ziggy, was born in Thorn, West Prussia, Germany 10 April 1902. His family left Germany and settled in Cleveland, Ohio in 1903. He was one of those rare strongmen who never claimed to have started as a weakling; he said he was always much stronger than his school mates. His mother never tired of telling how at the age of six she wanted to buy him a pair of shoes, but Sig insisted that they be gym slippers. He became very proficient at handbalancing and at seventeen started systematic weightlifting.

By the age of twenty he was internationally known in strongman circles. Siegmund Klein made his first public appearance in weightlifting and balancing at Luna Park, Cleveland in 1921 and three years later he went to New York to meet his hero Prof. Attila, the dean of strongmen. Unfortunately he was a few months too late, as the professor had recently died at the age of eighty. The enterprising Sig made an agreement with Madame Attila allowing him to operate the gym, and in 1927 he married Attila's youngest daughter, Grace.

Sig's gym became the best known haunt of bodybuilders and strongmen, and Bob Kennedy wrote, "Sig Klein's gym is one of the only modern equipped gymnasiums with a genuine atmosphere of old world chivalry and integrity. Somehow its walls had absorbed some of the very essence of those famed visitors of the past, lending a unique atmosphere of purpose and nostalgia." Klein, its owner, was featured ten times in Ripley's "Believe It or Not!" cartoons—more than any other person.

Sig did some vaudeville work and appeared at a great many physical culture shows, some of which he organised himself, but he also found time to publish his own magazine *Klein's Bell*, and he wrote for many others. The gym membership was very varied; he had labourers, professional strongmen, well-known actors and politicians,

Left: A concrete block is being broken on Manjit Singh's head at the National Exhibition Centre in Birmingham.

Right: Siegmund Klein performing "planche," York, Pennsylvania, 9 August 1937.

and it was the mecca for all strength athletes and fans visiting New York.

One of Sig's best stunts was performed in 1947 when he did a hollow back press-up into a handstand *with a 75 lb. globe dumbbell strapped to his back.*

Klein retained his strength throughout his life, and in 1969 at sixty-seven years of age this very pleasant character could still do twelve to thirteen handstand push-ups. Sig was 164 cm (5' 4 ½") in height; he usually claimed 5' 5" and wrote to me in March 1982 explaining why he had added one-half inch, the reason being that he was self-conscious about being short and tended to exaggerate his height, but knowing my strong desire for accuracy, he felt he should set the record straight. His bodyweight remained between 67-68 kg (c. 10½ st./148-150 lb.) for sixty years, and his profile was: chest 110 cm (43"); waist 78 cm (31"); neck 41 cm (16"); upper arm 39 cm (15½"); forearm 32 cm (12½"); calf 37 cm (14½"). This great hero of musclemen died in the early hours of 24 May 1987 at the age of eighty-four.

One of Sig's great joys was attending the annual reunions of the Association of Oldtime Barbell and Strongmen. The fraternal gathering with acts and presentations were the highlight of his year, and it's a sentiment shared by many others.

A classic photo of Siegmund Klein.

CHAPTER 2

The Association of Oldetime Barbell and Strongmen

Faith Lift

If you ever needed your faith lifting on the value of "Iron Pills," then the evidence is right here. Very virile, active guys are all around looking tanned and as fit as fleas, telling whoppers of the lifts that got away and what they are lifting in their current workouts. The great thing is that many are in their seventies and some in their eighties, and they look decades younger. John Grimek the first Mr. Universe and competitor in the 1936 Berlin Olympics, was a centre of attraction; he lives up to his old nickname "the Glow," although he is now well into his eighties.

Here I have met numerous Mr. Americas and Mr. Universe prize winners and multi-title holders in their chosen activities such as weightlifting and powerlifting: Reg Park, Joe Abbenda, Marvin Eder, Elmo Santiago, Leo Rosa, Red Lerille, Tommy Kono, Dave Shepherd, Terry Robinson, George Eiferman, Bill Pearl, Bob Delmonteque, Leo Stern, Gene Jantzen, Mabel Rader, Pudgy and Les Stockton, Jan and Terry Todd, Ray (Thunder) Stern and a

New York! New York! Whichever way you slice it, the Big Apple makes a bounteous feast. There's tremendous tension, vitality and hurry-scurry amongst the stark skyscrapers and it seems light years away from the more familiar Californian surf and sand I enjoy so much. Some parts of America harbour visceral antagonism for its biggest, most exciting and most feared city, but for me there is a very special attraction. Here in the Downtown Athletic Club, overlooking the Statue of Liberty, it is a dream come true. It's not a show or competition, it's the reunion of the Association of Oldetime Barbell and Strongmen.

In September 1990 I achieved a long held ambition when, for the first time, I was able to accept an invitation from Vic Boff to attend this wonderful event. There was not an oiled body or leopardskin in sight, but a glance at the bull necks and barrel chests told all—that this was no convention of floral arrangers or cake decorators. I have been back many times since and it simply gets better as time goes by.

Vic Boff at 19.

whole lot more. I have met and often seen in action lots of professional strongmen such as Slim Farman, Joe Ponder and the Great Joe Rollino, who although now in his nineties still works out almost every day. He and those like him are a real inspiration.

Presiding over the festivities are Boff and Biff, Vic Boff and Johnny Mandel; at that 1990 reunion they were sprightly seventy-eight year olds who had found the fountain of youth, and judging by their current display of energy they still drink copiously at that well.

Vic, a valued old friend, was a professional boxer, assistant to Joe Bonomo and George Jowett, and is a physical culture expert in his own right. A writer of note,

Johnny Mandel—"Biff."

he has over the years given me a great deal of inside information about strongmen. Vic is a really fine person, although he does have a strange habit; as President of the Iceberg Club he swims in the sea summer and winter, sometimes breaking the ice to get to the water underneath; otherwise he seems very sane. Something of a strongman in his younger days, he now does a great job as president of the Oldetimers.

Although it was in the dead of winter, Mr Iceberg, as he is known, invited me to join him for a dip in the Atlantic. Reluctantly (liar!) I declined his invitation, much preferring the state-of-the-art gym at the Downtown Athletic Club and their excellent *warm* swimming pool halfway up the skyscraper. It gave me a new idea for one of those disaster movies—can you imagine the chaos if the pool burst and you had to swim down eight floors to reach safety!

Biff (Johnny Mandel) is as mad as his pal. This former wrestler has had a very colourful and productive life. He was an artist's model and runner-up to Buster Crabbe when they were trying to find someone to take over from Johnny Weissmuller as Tarzan in the movies. He loaded trucks on the New York waterfront, was a construction hod carrier and got promoted to sandhog foreman, working beneath the ground constructing tunnels for the underground. Mandel became a policeman and then a detective with New York's finest and had so many adventures, a very fine book about him was published in 1997. In line with all this he became a wrestling champion and then a well-travelled international official. Now he has his own busy security agency, and while I was there, he was working as technical adviser on a film about Rocky Aoki, the popular Japanese wrestler, and would you believe it, he had Rocky himself present at this wonderful function for dedicated barbell men.

Strong to the End

At the March 1991 dinner, there amongst all these strongmen who radiated good health and strength, was a man in a wheelchair being fed from a drip and hooked to an oxygen tube to help him breathe. In spite of that, Al Leroux was in some ways the strongest man present.

Formerly a national weightlifting champion, Al suffered from a degenerative muscle and nerve disorder known as Lou Gehrig's disease. He knew he was deteriorating, but it was his remaining ambition to be with his old pals just one more time. Al's former firefighting colleagues rallied round and raised over $1,500 for the costs of transport, hotel for Al and his wife Donna and a physiotherapist to attend him. Roland Desrosiers, owner of a company specialising in wheelchair transportation, personally drove the vehicle, and with all this generous help Al was able to make the sentimental journey.

He sat quietly in a corner watching the strength acts and listening to the tall tales of big lifts; mighty men from all parts of the country, and some from abroad, shook his hand and wished him well. It was my first meeting with Al and although he could barely speak, his face was most expressive and when I introduced myself his eyebrows went up, apparently surprised that someone from across the Atlantic knew all about him. It was a touching and personal encounter which I shall treasure.

As he left the following day, legendary figures in the world of strength showered him with good wishes: "Hang in there, Al," "Good luck," "Glad you made it, old buddy." "Goodbye, guys," mouthed Al, barely able to whisper as he entered the lift. There were many glistening eyes as the doors closed behind him. Al, with the determination for which lifters are famous, had achieved his remaining wish. It was his last day on earth, he died the next day.

In 1993 that superb periodical *Iron Game History* (Vol. 11, No. 3) took me very much by surprise as it stated that the eleventh annual reunion dinner at the prestigious Downtown Athletic Club, New York, would have as its guests of honour Terry Robinson, the physique star who has lived a Technicolour life, and . . . wait for it—yours truly! I was astounded. I revel in these events where I can rejoin old pals and meet heroes of the past, but to be selected for major honours had never entered my mind.

I was accompanied by my old pal Alex Thomson, my former handbalancing and strongman partner of the Aberdeen Spartan Club. On our visits to New York we shock some folks by refusing to be intimidated by "no-go" areas, but go everywhere, walking for five to seven hours each day seeing the sights (and speaking to some of them!).

Of course the eleventh nostalgic banquet was the highlight of the trip. My natural modesty prevents me from saying too much but I was very touched as Prof Terry Todd, former powerlifting champion and director of the world-famous Todd/McLean Library, looked back on my activities at Commonwealth Games, Olympic Games, Highland Games, TV strength competitions, my lifting days and literary efforts. Then President Vic Boff presented me with a lovely big plaque, with what used to be called an illuminated address, summarising various achievements. That wasn't all; the noted and talented artist Jim Sanders came forward and there was an appreciative gasp as he revealed a skilfully produced full-colour painting of myself in national costume, with a much earlier physique pose monochromed in the background. It will be a treasured memento of a wonderful occasion. The same treatment was of course given to Terry Robinson my fellow guest.

A Gripping Show

Of course there has to be appropriate entertainment and the strength cabaret often has unique demonstrations of strong hands. As these performances deserve more space, I will describe some of the stars and acts in detail.

On what I will always remember as that special night of the presentation, the first performer to leave a big impression was John Brookfield from Pinehurst, North Carolina, who bends large nails and having mutilated enough of these, he then forms them into a chain. Dennis Rogers, who often appears with Brookfield, also put on a fine performance which included phone directory tearing and bar bending. Rogers and Brookfield so impressed me that I have written about them further in the later section entitled "Ironfists."

Russ Testo, arguably the world's best poseur, was also there to entertain us with his unique routines. With its robotic miming, this is an innovative and classy item for any programme. We were spellbound with Russ's encore, an original piece in honour of this special occasion, mimed in impeccable style to the music "Over the Rainbow." His natural physique was shown to advantage without any straining for effect, indeed it was a sensitive presentation—an unusual way to describe muscular posing.

Joe Rollino

Thoroughly enjoying these strength cabarets and vociferous in encouraging the performers was the oldest of the professional strongmen present, one of my favourite characters, the lovable Joe Rollino, born 19 March 1906. Of Italian stock, his father was very strong at 183 cm (6 ft.) and 136 kg (21 st. 6 lb./300 lb.). Joseph inherited his strength but not his size, remaining at 163 cm (5' 4") and 68 kg (10 st. 10 lb./150 lb.).

Young Joe, inspired by W.L. Travis, became assistant to this great personality, and later in the 1920s Rollino produced his own act on Coney Island, which once abounded with strongmen. In his show Joe bent spikes in his teeth by sticking one end on top of a stand, like a microphone stand, wrapping a cloth round the other end of the spike, and applying pressure to bend the nail. His claims included a teeth lift with 204 kg (450 lb.), one-finger lift 288 kg (635 lb.), hand and thigh lift 681 kg (1,500 lb.), dead lift 266 kg (585 lb.), back lift 1453 kg (3,200 lb.), bench

The Great Joe Rollino.

press 170 kg (375 lb.), and curl 84 kg (185 lb.), all at 79.5 kg (12½ st./175 lb.) bodyweight.

His photos showed he had been an accomplished handbalancer and understander and he was proud to have worked out with Otto Arco. Joe gave me a photograph of himself doing a fine right-hand straight arm planche on his bearer Frank Affronti; this was taken in 1947 when they were managed by Max Tishman of New York.

I found the Great Rollino to be a very modest, extremely pleasant and happy person. He was most polite and always referred to WLT as "*Mr.* Travis." A real credit to the strength fraternity, at eighty-nine he was very sprightly, still working parttime packing flowers and enjoying regular light exercise.

Steven Sadicario, "the Mighty Stefan"

At the first Oldetimers reunion I attended in New York, I was greatly impressed by the act of Steven Sadicario appearing as "the Mighty Stefan." The feat which appealed to me most involved Stefan hammering a six-inch nail into a two-inch thick wooden plank, *then pulling it out with his teeth!* I was very close and therefore could observe clearly that it was totally genuine—and he had other excellent items. At this time Steve was thirty-one years of age and was doing shows at clubs in New Jersey and the Big Apple.

The Mighty Stefan told me that he was born in Brooklyn, New Jersey on 23 December 1957; his mother's father came from Russia and her mother from Romania. His father's parents came from Monastir, then part of Turkey, and their ancestors had emigrated from Spain at the time of the inquisition. Stefan has a special affection for Coney Island strongmen as his mother lived near the part of the boardwalk which was a musclemen's mecca for many years. Apart from the Atom, and Travis it was also the haunt of Bonomo, Buster Crabbe, Tony Sansone and in more recent times Vic Boff and the Iceberg Club. Stefan's grandfather was one of the Mighty Atom's customers, and little Stefan would listen with awe to the wonderful tales about the strongman.

Sadicario recalled, "Many years later, at Vic Boff's 1987 reunion of Oldetime Barbell and Strongmen, I met a towering figure in black who was introduced as a protégé of the Mighty Atom. He performed amazing feats of strength, and I was inspired by this man, Slim the Hammerman. He was extremely helpful and encouraged me to meet the sons of Joe Greenstein, the Mighty Atom. In turn they told me of their father's feats and made suggestions on how best to build up my act."

He gave his first public performance on 8 February 1988 at the Chameleon Club in Greenwich Village before a crowd consisting largely of bikers, purple-haired "punks" and tattooed East Villagers. Steve grinned at the recollection, "They proved to be a great audience and at the end gave me a standing ovation. . . . I knew then that I could perform anywhere." Successful appearances in Bangkok confirmed this belief.

By the time I witnessed Steve's performance he had a fine and varied repertoire of spike and bar bending, chain breaking, pinch gripping, hammer levering, muscle control and card tearing. After tearing a full pack of cards into quarters he gave me one of the portions for my little strength museum where it has stayed on view ever since.

Steven Sadicario, "the Mighty Stefan."

Mighty Stefan has also appeared on TV and in several films including "Total Panic" and "Shadows in the City." This likeable fellow has earned himself a good reputation in his native city with his anti-drug campaign particularly aimed at influencing young people. One police liaison officer, Bernie Anderson, who administers the campaign said, "The Mighty Stefan has a truly dynamic programme and has the kids amazed. He is a good representation of what we are doing. We are selling integrity and honesty. Nothing here is a fake." I will personally endorse that view.

Steven Sadicario's profile: height 168 cm (5' 6"); weight 86 kg (13 st. 8 lb./190 lb.); chest 122 cm (48"); waist 88 cm (34½"); neck 44 cm (17¼").

Slim "the Hammerman" Farman

Lawrence Farman, a powerful stoneworker in Pottstown, Pennsylvania, USA, was at Zern's Market in Gilbertsville when he saw Joe Greenstein, the Mighty Atom, perform his act, which invariably included advice to the audience. The Atom seemed to look straight at Lawrie, whose rangy physique did not indicate his true power, and proceeded to

Slim "the Hammerman" Farman.

criticise the poor physical condition of the average American. Slim, as Farman was widely known, did not like the insinuation and growled, "Don't look at me when you say things like that." He was fiercely proud of his strength and so needed little encouragement to step up on to the platform with Joe, who could not fail to be impressed when Slim bent one of the steel spikes. It was the beginning of a long and mutually beneficial friendship which lasted over thirty years until Joe's death and even after that, Slim has continued to perpetuate the memory of his friend by promoting the book on the life and times of Joe and publicising whenever he can the "mind over matter" theories of the Mighty Atom.

Slim "the Hammerman" maintains that, like Joe L. Greenstein, his world record feats are the product of self power through mind control. He has been aided not only by Joe Greenstein but in later years by Ed Spielman, the multi-faceted creator of the *Kung-Fu* TV series. With their assistance Lawrence Farman has utilised untapped energy and potential which most people possess but do not employ.

Born at Niagara Falls, New York circa 1931, Slim grew to 198 cm (6' 6") in height and at his heaviest bodyweight, he was around 109 kg (17 st. 2 lb./240 lb.), a marked contrast to his diminutive strongman mentor. He began performing in 1960 and was still securing a considerable amount of bookings in 1987 when he was honoured by an invitation to perform for the connoisseurs of the Oldetime Strongman Association in New York. For many years Lawrence held down three jobs; he was a stonecutter, a supervisor for Gill Quarries, Fairview Village, Collegeville, and of course a professional strongman.

"I cut stone fourteen to sixteen hours a day with a 16 lb. hammer for eighteen years. At one time I was breaking and lifting one hundred tons of stone a day," he recalls. It was this regime which built him his great and specialised strength, and contributed to his lean, functional physique, with very well-defined upper body muscles. He never missed a single day's work until one traumatic February day when he was buried in the quarry under thirty tons of stone, escaping being completely crushed but almost suffocating to death. In spite of the shock, a broken rib and a bout of flu he had only two days off work and is now sorry that such an incident broke an otherwise unblemished record. "Knowing what I do now, I think I could have gone to work," he mused.

Slim's performances include scrolling, bending iron into exotic shapes, and driving a 40-penny spike through a two-inch plank of wood with his hand; he also bends and breaks spikes or horseshoes when he can obtain them. Of course his pièce de résistance is hammer lifting, which has made him world famous as Slim "the Hammerman." He is unbeaten in such challenges and says he has never been tested to the full. His challenge hammers are in excess of 13.5 kg (30 lb.), but he won't divulge the exact weight as he is still active. In the finale of his exhibitions Farman splits four heavy steel chains in rapid succession.

Slim lifts and levers hammers in every conceivable position; the tools are sometimes at arm's length forward, horizontally in line with the shoulders or alternatively in the crucifix position sideways. He holds them by the very ends and allows them to lower slowly towards his face or head, taking a long time to do this, and as the tension mounts a pin could be heard to drop. Having lightly touched his forehead, nose or lips, he then levers them back until the shafts are vertical; his arms have been as straight as possible throughout.

Probably his hardest challenge is when he lifts his hammers from the horizontal position on the floor. He kneels down and places his hand on the very end of a regulation-sized sledgehammer, with his hammer heads adapted so that varying weights can be used. He then pivots the hammer upright while his hand remains on the floor. The best performance of this type I have ever personally witnessed was in 1987 when Bill Kazmaier challenged Jon Pall Sigmarsson to an impromptu competition between events at Huntly, and both succeeded with what I believe was a 10 kg (22 lb.) hammer. There was not any bigger one present but nobody else could duplicate the stunt.

As a variation the Hammerman sometimes uses two hammers at the same time, using a total of 19.5 kg (43 lb.). According to an article in the *Reading Times*, in 1979 Slim raised two hammers, with 31-inch handles, weighing 24 kg (52½ lb.) each, "The strain causing Farman's eyes to bulge while his biceps shuddered and threatened to pop their oiled casing . . . but the thick, cable-like arms responded to a test as much mind control as brute force." To add a special thrill and variety to his act the strongman often uses razor sharp axes for his leverage stunts, but as with his hammers, he strongly advises his audiences against trying such feats.

A father of five children, Slim Farman thinks age should be judged by the condition of the body rather than by years, and he is devoted to physical fitness, working out 340 days of the year. He has a regular diet supplemented by trace minerals and multiple vitamins, but he adamantly refuses medicines of any type.

Slim Farman is convinced that mind control is a major factor in his performances. In the decades of tutelage by Greenstein he learned of self-hypnosis, unlocking the mind to summon inner power and overcoming the subconscious which normally protects the body. He is aware of physiological as well as psychological factors, stating that he uses the emotions to stimulate the flow of adrenalin, and in his talks to youth and community organisations, he gives some examples of how he does this.

I saw Slim perform his act for the Oldetimers in 1994 and found it most impressive, executed in his own inimitable style and with considerable panache. The Hammerman, one of that now rare fraternity, the professional strongman, has also savoured success at Madison Square Garden, New York, scene of many strength exhibitions more than half a century ago. There a standing room only crowd witnessed a five hour show promoted by Aaron Banks which included Slim Farman and his dearest friend the Mighty Atom. In later years in his solo performances the Hammerman dressed all in black with "Slim" embroidered on his chest over a gold star of David. This was not a religious statement but an act of respect and remembrance for the man who had taught him so much. The Mighty Atom's influence is noticeable even in interviews a decade after Joe's death.

"Strongmen are a thing of the past," he said with a faraway look in his deep-set, piercing eyes, "I am best at what I do and I'll keep doing it. When I can't do this any longer, then I will soon be seeing my old friend the Atom."

Ironfists: Dennis Rogers and John Brookfield

The names of Dennis Rogers and John Brookfield keep cropping up at international strength festivals. They often appear together but also have their own independent acts. The first of these strongmen, Dennis Rogers, was born in Bethseda, Maryland on 11 September 1956 and lived for a time in Fredericksburg, Virginia and more recently in Houston, Texas. Between 1975 and 1988 he won the US Championships and over sixty awards in arm wrestling. He is 175 cm (5' 9"), and his bodyweight in the mid-nineties fluctuated around 66-67 kg (10½ st./145-148 lb.).

He now has a strongman act which demonstrates extremely powerful hands and arms, his feats including bending spikes, ripping decks of cards into halves and quarters, breaking official police handcuffs and driving nails through planks with his bare hands. In my view his best weightlifting feat is a single arm curl of 53 kg (117 lb.) at 67 kg (10½ st./148 lb.) bodyweight. He also did 48 kg

(105 lb.) at 58 kg (128 lb.) bodyweight; these are tremendous poundages.

Most extraordinary of all his performances was early in 1994 when he teamed up with the Texas Air Aces, who specialise in air combat missions, to raise money for DARE (Drug Abuse Resistance Education). At Hooks Airport, Houston, "Mighty Might," as Dennis calls himself, established a new world record by holding back two T-34 high performance military planes, preventing them from taking off. The planes totalled 570 horsepower and close to 2,725 kg (6,000 lb.) exerting plus-545 kg (1,200 lb.) of force on Dennis's comparatively light frame. I had a certificate supplied with the technical details, and the feat was witnessed by my respected friends Vic Boff and Professor Terry Todd. The integrity of these experts in human strength is beyond reproach.

The feats of Dennis Rogers have been watched on many TV shows including "The Late Show" with David Letterman. I have also seen Dennis's act on several occasions and never cease to be amazed at the hand strength he demonstrates. I have several nice mementos indicating his prowess and an artistic one is a little sculpture he made from a fork which he bent into the shape of a cobra showing its fangs. He did this one night as we sat at dinner; it's not often the strength cabaret takes place right on your own table.

Often Dennis Rogers appears with his friend John Brookfield. When they combine forces John will lie with his head on one chair and heels on another while Dennis stands on John's unsupported midriff performing his breaking and tearing feats.

John Brookfield was born in 1959 in Wayne, Indiana, but now lives in Pinehurst, North Carolina and is recognised as the current world's best at spike bending. Many consider him the best ever and he has bent forty 60-penny spikes in one minute. He bends very short steel bars, one being 5" long and ½" x ¼" thick. The other size bent in his act is usually 7" long and ¾" x ¼" thick; these require around 261 kg (575 lb.) of pressure to bend. Amongst my memorabilia I have chisels and files which he has broken under our close scrutiny at the Oldetime Strongman banquets in New York. Another noteworthy feat is his record 20 sit-ups with 181.5 kg (400 lb.) at his chest. One stunt which beats all challengers is the way he raises and lowers a 23 lb. sledgehammer by walking up and down the handle using only his finger tips. I understand that when pushed he can do this with a 36 lb. hammer. His card tearing feats are legendary, and as an unusual variation to more standard feats he can tear the corner off a full deck of plastic coated cards, which are much harder than the older and cheaper packs.

John's introduction to the world of strength came at the age of sixteen when he was fortunate to meet nail bender Charlie Leary, a local man who could bend nails beyond the capability of the strongest guys in the neighbourhood. Inspired by this, John practised hard and two years later could bend 60-penny nails and knock nails through wood with his hands.

At an early stage he discovered for himself some things which many experienced strength entertainers have overlooked. He realised that the apparently static feats of bending and breaking metal objects were made possible by dynamic, even explosive effort. It was something I had to be taught by old Geoff Morris, one of Britain's best ever nail breakers and I am ashamed that although I put his advice into practice and it became second nature to me, I failed to realise that it was a key factor to success in this sphere. Each and every bend and straighten should be done with maximum effort to get the greatest range of movement.

Dennis Rogers rips a paperback book behind his back while standing on a bed of nails—2" apart, not a standard bed of nails—supported by John Brookfield.

Furthermore, the movements should be repeated at speed to build up heat and break down the molecules. This led John Brookfield to realise that to improve his power (power being a combination of strength applied with speed) he should improve his cardiovascular efficiency. He is the only stage strongman I have ever met who accords *top priority* to such stamina and strength training, it is a major part of his training regime. Full marks to John Brookfield for revealing these two secrets of his phenomenal ability: firstly, explosive efforts and secondly, progressive cardiovascular and muscular endurance training.

There is another driving force in the life of Mr Brookfield. In the early '80s the Christian faith began to figure more prominently in his life, and he decided that the teachings of the Bible could be conveyed and perhaps remembered through his feats of strength. John will bend a horseshoe into an S for salvation and refer his audience to Psalms. Another classic example of his evangelical approach is in linking playing cards with the sin of gambling and symbolically tearing two packs asunder while quoting appropriately.

Significantly, the Pinehurst strongman works in a hospital and is very aware of the need for us all to work hard to create a better world. This he does in some unusual ways: His very first strongman show, back in 1985, was for an audience of convicts in Carolina State Prison.

Bending and breaking horseshoes is reserved for the elite amongst strongmen and this Captain of Crush™ claims his place with the very best by mutilating them *two at a time*. John demonstrates a great sense of balance when he puts a jug of water on top of an 8' length of 2" x 4" timber, which he then balances on his chin while he tears a pack of cards in half. Alternatively he will balance a heavy sledgehammer on his chin as he bends a thick nail. The audience quiets down apprehensively, aware of the possible damage if there is a slip.

John Brookfield and Dennis Rogers first started performing together in August 1992 and no matter how many times I see their acts, they always have a range of interesting feats in store. Last time I saw them I was particularly impressed with John's bending of a brand new file, breaking a cold steel chisel and wrapping a plastic coated deck of cards with tape and then tearing them *inside their box*. No fanning the cards there. Dennis did some terrific directory tearing, ripping six Manhattan phone books in half lengthwise, wearing oven gloves for some of the tearing to make it harder.

Vic Boff, president of the Oldetime Strongmen, provided new directories still wrapped in the manufacturer's packing so they were not prepared in any way. Dennis also bent a ½" thick and 18" long iron bar around his neck and tore a small section out of a pack of cards for me to put in my little strength museum. It's a feat beyond all but the greatest grip artists who ever lived. I once saw a photo of a similar pack from which Paul von Boeckman had torn a piece like it, but I now had one for myself.

Dennis Rogers and John Brookfield have more than physical strength, they also have strength of character, and every year they do dozens of shows of an inspirational and motivational nature. These strongmen are always willing to help church groups, raise money for good causes, or help children in need. We could do with a lot more people like these.

Joe Ponder

Some people might say that Joe Ponder is lucky to be alive, having broken twenty-seven bones in a sensational "Slide of Death" accident in 1978. On the other hand it was a serious vehicle collision which had earlier put him on the right road to fame as one of the greatest jaw strength artists of all time. I was fortunate enough to meet Joe in October 1990 and confirm many fascinating facts gleaned from correspondence and news cuttings received from him over the years. A truly remarkable performer, and although then in his late sixties, he was still active professionally, showing continuing ambition and enthusiasm.

Born on 7 June 1923 Joe took up professional boxing at a very early age in Phoenix, Arizona, learning the rudiments of exercise and nutrition. His career was interrupted on 24 February 1942 when he enlisted for the Navy, but some three years later a painful leg and back injury led to his release with a 10 percent disability on 31 January 1945. A gradual and progressive training regime enabled him to run ten miles a day by the end of the year, and he was right back to fighting fitness, ready for the ring in California where he was now residing.

In 1949 he moved to North Carolina and became involved with the first health club in Greensboro, operated by Bill Piephoff. Again fate struck and in the aforementioned collision, Joe was thrown through the windscreen and on to the road, sustaining multiple injuries, including a fractured neck. Incapacitated for many months, Joe was in constant pain until he constructed a bench in his leather shop and used weights for traction. In this way he also began to build neck strength and to add some mobility exercises. Later for a challenging variation he hung a bed sheet over the rafters, and gripping it with his teeth, lifted his feet off the ground!

Once fully recovered, he experimented to find out just how strong his neck and jaw strength had developed, and to his amazement he found he could pull a pick-up truck using a simple teeth hold. This encouraged him to do some specialized training, and two years after his horrendous accident he could lift heavy barbells and pull railway boxcars with his teeth, and in a couple of cunning stunts which got nationwide publicity he lifted pretty girls from the Miss Nude World and Miss Nude America 1974 contests.

Since that time his amazing feats have become world famous through the magazines, *Guinness Records* and Ripley's *Believe It or Not*, whose drawings featured him on many occasions, including showing Joe lifting a 259 kg (570 lb.) racing car engine using only his teeth whilst hanging from a helicopter. He pulled a 24,970 kg (55,000 lb.) truck with his teeth on 6 July 1973, and a 41,859 kg (92,200 lb.) boxcar for a world record on 19 August 1973. In 1974 he bent a half-inch 10/20 hot roll steel bar using his teeth and jaw as levers, and a year later he did a 100-foot death slide hanging by his teeth.

It was this stunt which caused his most serious accident. From a 35-feet high platform stretched a wire sloping to a lower platform, which could be anything from 50-100 feet away depending on the location and the importance of the event. A pulley wheel with a mouthpiece was suspended from the wire and having taken his teeth grip, Joe would slide down at speed. He often wore a long robe with a cross on the chest and up there in space, with arms outstretched sideways, he resembled an angel in flight as he zoomed through the air supported only by his teeth. On the fateful occasion on Mother's Day, 1978 Joe pushed off the platform as usual and rapidly accelerated as he slid down the wire until there was an ominous crack like the report of a gun, and the gear separated from the wire. The assembled crowd of some 1,500 people knew instantly there was trouble but Joe's recollection is of the sensation that he was flying!

That quickly came to an end when with a sickening jar he hit the ground, his legs buckling and feet twisting beneath him. There was a stunned silence as Joe's assistant Andy made the strongman's broken body as comfortable as possible without causing further damage. Ponder recovered his usual composure and joked to cheer up the shocked group around him. "Call the hospital and make sure there are loads of pretty nurses on duty," he quipped; he was still putting on a brave face when they wheeled him into the operating theatre that evening.

There were compound fractures of both ankles and badly torn leg ligaments. Joe wrote telling me that there were twenty-seven breaks in all, and he spent many weeks in hospital before he was allowed to transfer to a hospital bed in his gym in the picturesquely-named Love Valley where he has lived and operated the Ponder Leather Company since 1963.

He has been a pillar of society there and was one of the first town councillors and police commissioners; his community spirit makes him prefer shows at churches, schools, dinners and fairs to those in circus and theatres. He does enjoy TV work and travel, and one of his greatest memories is of spending his sixty-fourth birthday in Tokyo doing work for Japanese TV, teeth lifting, amongst other things, a large fridge-freezer.

At 175 cm (5' 9") in height, Joe Ponder's bodyweight has fluctuated over the years. He was a neat 97 kg (15 st. 4 lb./214 lb.) or thereabouts when we met, but he has been as high as 104 kg (16 st. 6 lb./230 lb.), sporting a

Joe Ponder.

61 cm (24") neck at that time, although it is usually around the 49 cm (19") mark.

Joe is forever dreaming up new and spectacular feats: He has held a machine gun in his teeth and fired off thousands of rounds. In his mighty mouth he wields a 9 kg. (20 lb.) sledgehammer to smash concrete blocks, with the hammer travelling at an estimated 65 miles an hour at the moment of impact. Appearing at various pumpkin shows, he lifts with his molars the largest pumpkins available, which may not sound too impressive until you realise that some American pumpkins weigh over 182 kg (400 lb.)—the biggest ever lifted by Joe was at the Circleville Pumpkin Show in 1985 when the monster fruit is said to have weighed 275 kg (606 lb.)!

At other times Ponder has lifted a "cat lady" and her leopard in a large cage with heavy steel bars, and sometimes he teeth lifted a partner, Galen Shinkle, an expert archer. While hanging upside down, Shinkle shot ten arrows at a conventional target, always hitting their mark, and this combined show of strength and skill invariably scored a bullseye with audiences. As a little party piece Joe would put a golf club in his teeth and putt better than many people can using their hands.

Strangely enough Joe never has teeth problems, but his neck muscles often suffer from an abundance of heavy lifting—I can imagine that would be a real pain in the neck!

Along the way I have encountered many more Sons of Samson although some were old-timers by the time we met and I did not see their acts. However they were only too willing to tell me many tales of their activities, best feats and incidents in their fascinating lives. Their anecdotes and memories are too good to keep to myself; it seems to me more appropriate to deal with them within their own era rather than amongst the more modern strongmen, the main subject of this book, and I very much look forward to sharing with readers in a future volume the information I have gathered from men such as W.A. Pullum and his son Billy, Thomas Inch, George Hackenschmidt, Edward Aston and his son Ted.

Meantime the next sections in *this* publication will deal with my associates in TV strongman competitions, with which I have been actively associated since the late 1970s as a consultant and as a referee.

The Competitors

PART 2
Sons of Samson

CHAPTER 3

A Sport is Born:
The Development of Modern Strength Athletics

Strength literature is full of claimants to the title "World's Strongest Man," and hundreds of professional circus and stage performers have used variations of this, such as "the Strongest Man on Earth." The vast majority of these had never appeared in competition other than their own specialised challenges to the audience as part of their act. Even today in spite of the many independent competitions open to them, we still have the occasional brazen deceiver who lays claim to the title without any foundation whatsoever. There is one like this in Britain who has been invited and challenged time and again but never accepts for very obvious reasons—he would not stand a chance against the genuine sportsman—and therein lies the difference. Some strongmen have just an act while nowadays we have a whole legion of strength athletes competing in a wide range of events at different levels.

In our Spartan physical culture shows as far back as the 1940s, we usually included audience participation strength competitions. I also had these in the outdoor and indoor Highland Games which I organised at home and abroad. Many physical culture shows did this, it was nothing new. However my historical interests led me to investigate classical and traditional feats of strength and my in-depth investigations to bring old tests to new audiences led to recognition of the Stones of Strength and the Inch dumbbells, to mention but two, resulting in a new era. Between 1952 and 1955 these largely long-forgotten relics were obtained, publicised and adapted for active participation in competition rather than exhibition. The press highly acclaimed these efforts, and our shows invariably sold out.

A few years later I established links and athletic exchanges with Gotland, a little island off the Swedish coast, where they have island games not unlike our Highland Games. *Stangstortning*, or caber tossing, was and still is their major event. I was enthralled with their *femkamp* and personally entered this event, which consists of a battery of five varied athletic tests, including running, jumping, wrestling and two throwing events. It is a splendid concept where a huge entry begins the contest with a race over rough terrain, finishing with a sprint to the finish. The fastest 50 percent of the runners go on to the next test and the slower runners (50 percent of the entry) are eliminated. So it goes on, the numbers reducing after every event. I mulled over the similarities to our Highland Games where we have a battery of five throwing events with stone, hammer, caber and throwing weights for height and distance.

In the 1960s I was organising a great many big indoor shows in the Kelvin Hall, Glasgow and other major venues, always featuring strength competitions by invitation in addtion to open events. I was also working for four different TV stations in Scotland and England. I had a regular fitness show on Border TV and a sports series with Grampian TV and often did "easy-when-you-know-how" type shows with the BBC. In the latter, for example, we had various people try tests of strength and skill, followed by an expert who would make it look very simple. Naturally I used this opportunity to feature my favourites, such as the Stones of Strength.

There was a growing acceptance that this sort of thing was good for the mass media. In the 1970s a number of things happened which significantly changed strength sports and entertainment. They happened around the same time and were not perceived then as being revolutionary.

Chronologically, I legally registered the concept of World Heavy Events Championships with a battery of tests giving points per event and a cumulative total to decide places. The date of registration was 23 May 1973, registration no. 28203.

In 1977 Mark McCormack's Trans World International organised a TV programme in America to decide who was the world's strongest man. It was described as "a quirky little contest with good entertainment potential." Dyed-in-the-wool strength enthusiasts liked the idea but not some of the tests or the lack of international contenders. Behind the scenes, the late Oscar State, International Weightlifting Federation secretary, was consulted and Dr. Terry Todd, USA, became more involved. Both were extremely knowledgable and experienced in strength sports, and both were valued friends of mine.

Oscar contacted me first for information and points of view and later introduced me to Margo Green and Ken Hawkes, a wonderful old journalist, both directly involved in setting up such programmes for Trans World International (TWI). Apart from my previous informal advisory role, I now had to referee Britain's Strongest Man and consult contenders. When the competition became more truly international, I was appointed World's Strongest Man referee, a position I filled for more than ten years.

In parallel with these developments, but completely unassociated, were significant changes in my own activities when Dr. Douglas Edmunds and I began organising Highland Games on a regular and professional basis. We set out to make these into multinational events and with the influx of top-line foreign stars from powerlifting and weightlifting, we included several strength events especially with them in mind so they could have a guaranteed income.

With a little standardisation of equipment and regular competition, the main men became very good, and the popularity of the open strength competitions led Doug and me to regularly include these in our international circuit of Highland Games. We perceived a need for a development of the concept in parallel with the throwing events, and therefore invited the best Scottish strongmen and some foreign guests to compete in a battery of five strength tests between and alongside the throwers, who maintained their traditional competitions with cabers, hammers etc. Our motivations were many and all intertwined. We liked strength athletics and this alone was justification enough, but we also wanted to retain an element of ethnic distinctiveness to challenge the levelling effect of mass media and other twentieth century influences. These frequent live competitions performed before large audiences were by necessity very different in character from the once-a-year TV competitions, made over a period of days and edited to suit a home audience. Our shows were a big hit. Soon we had an impressive following of knowledgeable fans and athletes who were prepared to specialise, train and compete with our contests as their main sporting activity.

The progressive development of events was crucial to success. We spent, and still spend, a good deal of time on new ideas and discussing improvements which will make good items even better. The Scottish traditional *clach cuid fir* (manhood stones) provides a great example. In ancient times a young man would seek to lift such a stone on to a wall at waist height to prove his manhood. He would then be allowed to wear the eagle's feather in his bonnet. It could well be the origin of the saying "it was a feather in his cap," to indicate a notable success.

In 1953 when I resuscitated this test with the legendary Inver Stone from the valley of the Dee, my Spartan colleagues and I were content to offer prizes to those who could lift it on to a table at waist height. Henry Downs, Mr. Britain 1956 was the winner of the first big competition. A few years later, for much more sophisticated shows with Archie McCulloch, the show biz impresario, we had the arena of Glasgow's Kelvin Hall made like a castle forecourt and the Inver Stone was lifted on to a mock wall. This was also adapted for high-class Scottish hotel *ceilidhs* for many years.

Now that Doug and I were developing this new sport, we had to make the traditional feats and tests into scoring events. The result was well beyond our initial expectations. Instead of one Inver Stone we needed *a set of stones* and so Doug contacted the McGlashens' stonemasons, whose forbearers had been responsible for some of Edinburgh New Town's most prestigious building in Georgian times. The company's master craftsman made a beautifully graded set of smooth perfectly round stones from 90 kg (198 lb.) upwards; to match them we had a set of equally spaced whisky casks, on to which the stones had to be lifted in sequence while being timed. The mixture of movements, fast runs between stones, contrasting lifts, and the struggles with the heaviest boulder always rouses the crowd, who enthusiastically encourage the athletes to greater efforts.

Great though that was, development was still a priority, and in 1993, double sets of stones were introduced at Doug's suggestion, thus creating a very visual race to add to the existing exciting ingredients. Having so many stones gave me the idea that records could now be broken with six, seven, eight or more stones, so in 1995, a whole new era began. With our ideas being widely copied, sometimes with concrete and metal sub-standard equipment, we like to keep ahead of the field and we now have a unique array of fifteen graded McGlashen Stones. It is emphasised that these are the only such McGlashen Stones in existence, and we have to be constantly on the lookout for those who try to copy our event name as well as our ideas.

The farmer's walk was another great addition to multi-discipline competitions. It requires little or no skill but it does demand strength, muscular and cardiovascular endurance. In olden times strong farm lads would carry heavy milk churns in their hands instead of on a wooden yoke, but now in competitions specially adapted oxygen cylinders bring the event up to date.

Such strength tests sometimes develop in parallel, and in 1965 my friend Joe Weider, America's Baron of Bodybuilding, provided information which may otherwise have been lost. When rural society got together at America's county fairs, there was good-natured competition, securing the well-earned admiration of one's neighbours. Early settlers had a healthy respect for physical power, and no strength test was more individual and gruelling than the farmer's walk. In the West, the walk was sometimes done with a heavy sack of silver dollars, the prize for the winner. I would very much like to have more details of such bygone events and hope some readers may be able to provide any information.

The walk had long died out at Scottish Highland Games, but was reinstated when John Bridges, an ex-Royal Marine, introduced it at Burlington Highland Games in Canada in 1969. The event was adopted by Fergus Games, Ontario, where it became known as the Fergus walk; 200 lb. were carried in each hand (total 181.5 kg/400 lb.), and the record of 131.38 metres was established by Dan Markovic, a tough undercover cop of Yugoslav origin. This is currently held by Warren Trask, a local hero in Ontario. On my annual visits as commentator at Fergus Games I was enthralled by the walk and the audience reactions it evoked. I pestered Ken Hawkes, TWI's producer of the World's Strongest Man, to add it to the battery of tests, and since he had more money for equipment than we had, he should have it *as a race* for all the competitors at the same time. He liked the idea and used it in the 1983 competition, but with the competitors racing in pairs carrying a 175 lb. log in each hand.

Originally in our Scottish shows we had little solid cylinders which did not look too heavy; then we used huge logs but these scoured the competitors' thighs. Doug then had some superb oxygen cylinders converted, which

Dr. Douglas Edmunds, left, with Arnold Schwarzenegger, center, and Jon Pall Sigmarsson, right.

were as heavy as they looked and did not impede movement. These became standard and can be filled and weighted according to the level of the competition; they have been as heavy as 91 kg (200 lb.) each.

The world record walk with 136.2 kg total, 68 kg each hand (300 lb., 150 lb. each hand) was broken by Jon Pall Sigmarsson before 7,000 spectators at the Galloway Games in 1986 when he covered more than 270 metres. For a while we continued to call it the Fergus walk when done for distance and used the name farmer's walk when the event was done against the clock. Now the term farmer's walk has become widely used for all variations.

Although we have always adapted or devised most of the tests ourselves, refining them until they work well, we also have friends in the business making their own contributions. The first of these is Alex Thomson who introduced us to the arm-over-arm pull which is now a standard event. I learned of the car carry when I refereed Nummisto and Suonenvirta's big Finnish competition in 1989. The opposing Finnish promoters were the first we heard of doing a car turnover, and Jon Pall and our other Icelandic pals introduced us to car rolling over and over, from wheels back to wheels. Charlie van den Bosch told me of the car train when he claimed a world record in the late 1980s.

I got the idea of caber toss for height from observing the best heavies tossing the caber, and before it become a competition event, I would wander across the line of throw and the crowd would roar a warning to me as the caber sailed over my head. Of course the heavies concerned knew what I was doing. I did the first caber for height event at Garnock International Games in 1989, and the first dead lift hold for time was done there in May 1995. To give credit where it is due, I had previously seen Ray Nobile do a lengthy hold with the end of a car back in the early 1970s. Conan's wheel was inspired by an early sequence in the film *Conan the Barbarian*.

The crucifix is one of the hardest events to judge owing to the poor arm locks of competitors with elbow and biceps injuries, but it was much loved by TV companies because of facial expressions, timing and general appeal. Doug and I analysed the factors which gave the crucifix its appeal to the viewing audience and the factors required of a good strength test. We then reviewed possibilities *which eliminated the aspects causing controversy in the crucifix*, and the Hercules hold was the result of these deliberations.

Discussions and *deliberations* are bland words for our intense brain-storming sessions, but it's a great partnership with well-balanced results. I tend to worry about the severity of events and things like competition conditions, gradients and underfoot surfaces. Big Doug has a special talent when he gets hold of an idea and makes it into an awesome event which tests the strongest men who ever lived. A good example of this was when I suggested a variation of a barrow push. I had seen a car on a small trailer, and the fact that the engine was a little in front of the wheels made it possible for one man to lift the back and push the car and trailer. We discussed this and Douglas thought it was too easy. The outcome of our discussion was Doug's lorry push, where the end of his truck is lifted and then it has to be pushed like a wheelbarrow! It gives a whole new meaning to the term "pick-up truck." It is one of the toughest events ever devised.

Dr. Douglas Edmunds, Scotland

Over the years Douglas has become the world's most experienced strength athletics referee. Each year from May to September he spends weekends refereeing strongman competitions and Highland games. In one season he does more major events than many officials do in a lifetime.

Like many others at the top of this field Dr. Edmunds was a very good all-rounder, a schoolboy athletics champion, and as an adult he won four Scottish shot-putting championships—he was the first Scottish amateur to exceed 50 feet in putting the shot. Tony Chapman, the national athletic coach, told me about the strength of the schoolboys, Doug and his pal George McHugh, and I invited them to enter the Scottish Junior Weightlifting Championships. Doug accepted, winning the title with ease, and went on to win two Scottish senior weightlifting titles at superheavyweight when Scotland had its biggest and best ever competitions in this class.

A graduate of Strathclyde University, he represented Scotland on several occasions and then began his travels, boxing in the West Indies, rugby in Kenya, competing along with me in the Femkamp in Sweden, Highland Games in America and so on. The ubiquitous Scot even competed in the very first World's Powerlifting Championships in Pennsylvania, USA, not for his homeland but for Zambia!

Back home he twice won the World Caber Tossing Championship and became the fourth man to toss the big Braemar caber. An important managerial position took him to Nigeria for several years, and in 1980 he established the Lagos Highland Games to which he invited his pals from different countries. This is typical of the man; for him sport is about having fun, and he works as hard in enjoying himself as he does in achieving success in sport and business.

Douglas is managing director of the family's huge and still expanding milk and juice business, which in 1993 developed a massive new plant and enlarged fleet of vehicles. His business acumen has been a decided asset in our strength athletics operations and usually his intimidating size and appearance is in our favour in negotiating deals!

Although advising them since the late 1970s, it was in 1981 that TWI booked me to referee World's Strongest Man (WSM) events. I continued in this role until 1991 when Douglas was supposed to take over, but some external politics delayed this for one year so Doug began as WSM referee in 1993 and has done well since then. When I look back to that young school-kid I first met all those years ago, I am happy with all I see in the way our friendship and business partnership developed. His exterior may at times be rough and tough, but this is more than matched by his basic honesty and loyalty to his friends and associates.

Since 1981 we have built up competitions throughout the season from May until September ranging from what we called Local Heroes (after the popular Scottish film) to Muscle Power Championships at various levels—Scottish, British, European—and in 1985 we had our first World Muscle Power Championships. Held at the Country Fair in Calderglen Country Park, East Kilbride, this premier title was won by Jon Pall Sigmarsson. Two years later we introduced the first World Team Championships, a pairs competition won by England, represented by 6' 5" Geoff Capes and 6' 9" Mark Higgins.

It was at this stage we agreed that we had now achieved what we had set out to do, we had created a structure for strength athletics as a new participation sport, and we formed an association, the International Federation of Strength Athletes (IFSA), to promote the activity. Dr. Edmunds and I would like to put on record our thanks to all who contributed to this development by their encouragement and support in staging competitions. Particularly in mind are local authorities such as Cunninghame, North Ayrshire, East Kilbride, Wigton, Eastwood, Inverness and Glasgow.

Most of the Muscle Power Championships have been staged in Scotland, but in 1991 the World Muscle Power Championships were held in North America for the very first time, and this seventh championship was probably the most enjoyable of this very successful series. This particular competition is described in more detail in the section headed "It's Tough at the Top": It is a fine illustration of the hazards faced and the physical and mental stamina needed to participate in this type of competition.

While undoubtedly Scotland was in the vanguard of live strength athletics competitions, there followed similar developments in other countries. Around 1984 in Quebec, another cradle of strongmen, French-Canadians showed great interest when Jean-Claude Arsenault promoted his competition, the Louis Cyr Tournament, commemorating Louis Cyr (1863-1912), the world's

Defi Mark Ten 1986 winners Tom Magee, center, Jon Pall Sigmarsson, left, and Mark Higgins, right.

strongest man of his time. With the initial show proving an attraction, Arsenault was sponsored in 1984-5 by a cigarette company, and the title was changed to Défi Mark Ten; he arranged several provincial and annual shows, the Canadian Championships being held in Quebec City's Colisee and the finals moving to Montreal's Forum in 1987.

There was a bit of a sour note and some controversy with one newspaper heading claiming "Nationalism marred contest." The writer protested, "It was evident that separatist policies were touted at the . . . Louis Cyr Challenge. The name Quebec was boldly painted on the huge backdrop but separate from Canada and was listed with France, the United States and Great Britain. The latter team had Irish, Scot and English representatives but were merely labelled as 'England' over the pubic address system all day." The writer was a Canadian from Montreal itself, and he had other gripes but commended the camaraderie of the athletes. It is a pity that politics sometimes intrude into sport.

Tom Magee of Canada was the most popular winner of these contests, with Bill Kazmaier a close second. Jon Pall Sigmarsson was always a favourite; he loved the crowds there but found the events rather mundane. His pal Hjalti Arnason broke records in Montreal, and I believe Mark Higgins of England was the final winner in this Défi Mark Ten series of contests, which seemed to disappear on the completion of the cigarette company contract.

The events included a throw for distance, usually done backwards over the head, a heavy wheelbarrow push, a race carrying a sack, and a very static push on a platform or rack; the competitors would sometimes black out in this last event, according to my informants, who competed there.

In the far-off Soviet Union, weightlifter and shipping magnate Bronius Vysniauskas visited his friend Valentinas Dikulis, strongman of the Russian State Circus, and from him learned of these competitions. Finding the concept a fascinating one, Bronius spoke with sports authorities in Vilnius and on 11-12 November 1989 arranged the first Lithuanian Mighty Man competition. The Mighty Man title was one being used in South Africa where Monty Brett was the main strength entrepreneur.

Fifteen participants took part in the first Lithuanian competition, including three Finns and an Estonian. The results were first, R. Zenkevicius (Klaipeda); second, Kestutis Cenhus (Kursenai); and third, Arunas Vitlevicius (Kaunas).

On 9 August 1990 the second Lithuanian competition was held in Vingis Park in Vilnius, again with fifteen competitors. In one event Romas Kunca (Lazdjai) pulled a five-ton cart 15 metres in 12.4 seconds. My old friend Arvydas Svegzda (Kursenai) threw a 35 kg stump 6.12 metres to win that event. Overall winner was E. Karskis (Joniskis), second was R. Zenkevicius (Klaipeda), and third E. Kvetinskas.

Lithuania was represented in Canada in 1990 by Zenkevicius and Svegzda. Mark Higgins beat Bill Kazmaier for top place, and Zenkevicius took sixth place. Mark Higgins also won the international competition on the 31 July 1993 in Klaipeda, Lithuania.

Lithuanian contests became more successful over the years and then in 1995, still under the leadership of Bronius Vysniauskas, a major breakthrough was made by linking up with the International Federation of Strength Athletes (IFSA). This resulted in a truly world-class field at their event with Dr. Douglas Edmunds, the IFSA President as a guest of honour. The contest result was first, Gary Taylor and second, Forbes Cowan. Stasys Mecius (Klaipeda), the highest placed Lithuanian, was selected to compete in the televised World's Strongest Man competition. There in the Bahamas where the TV contest was held, historic meetings took place resulting in agreement to grant full IFSA membership to the Lithuanian Federation. In 1996 they organised a splendid World Grand Prix in Lithuania's three main towns, and the cream of international strength athletes supported the event. Bronius and his colleague, President Zenonas Janavicius, deserve hearty congratulations for all the hard work they have done to reach this stage of development.

Finland has been represented in many World's Strongest Man competitions, with the most successful being Ilkka Nummisto and a little later Riku Kiri and Marko Varalahti. Marku Suonenvirta, Ilkka Kinnunen and Roger Ekstrom have been other excellent representatives. Messrs Nummisto and Suonenvirta formed their own company, Suomen Vahvin Mies R.Y. (Strongest Man of Finland Co.) in 1987 and have organised many fine competitions, with world-class entrants such as Sigmarsson, Kazmaier, O.D. Wilson, and athletes from the former Soviet Union.

Strongman events have proved very popular in Finland and several other organisations have entered the field. In these events Aarre Kapyla was probably the greatest. He was 188 cm (6' 2") and 125 kg (19 st. 10 lb./276 lb.); Aarre had been World Junior Powerlifting champ at 100 kg (15 st. 10½ lb./220½ lb.) in 1987 and as a senior at 110 kg (17½ st./243 lb.) in 1991. I am told he had also three European titles to his credit before he succumbed to a drugs ban. For a time there was a need to rationalise the Finnish situation as it has become quite confusing with claims and counterclaims. Ilkka Kinnunen became IFSA's representative in 1995 and organised a TVs Strongest Man In Europe event in 1996, and internal agreement was reached with Suomen Vahin Mies doing national TV titles.

Modern strength athletics flourished in the Netherlands thanks to the influence of Avro TV and freelance producer Job Klinkenberg with his trusty presenter Jack Van Der Voorn. To encourage live presentations and competitions, Dr. Edmunds and I did some events at Pony Park and other venues in Holland, and we have both refereed European and Netherlands' Strongest Man contests on Dutch TV. There have been many excellent competitors from this area, including the seven-foot giant Ted Van der Parre who won WSM in 1992, and Ab Wolders, second in '84 and '89 and third in '86. The top men Cees De Vreugd and Siem Wulfse ("Simon the Wolf") became famous and infamous, while other good competitors have included Gerard du Prie, Huub Van Eck, Berend Veneberg, Marc Daalman, 6' 3" and 25 st. (350 lb.) arm wrestling and powerlifting champion, and Tjalling van den Bosch, a popular figure on the European strength circuit and now a promoter in his own right.

These strongmen from different lands are the true modern gladiators, willing to compete against all comers in any feats of strength. They are not show athletes but contestants and challengers in an exciting new live sport with standard tests and frequent innovations. We are proud to have been there at the conception, its birth and during its very rapid development.

The World's Strongest Man TV Competitions

Trans World International first introduced the now famous series of competitions in 1977 when the inaugural event was held in the United States. The title was not truly accurate as the entrants were solely Americans. It is a pity this limitation spoiled the credibility of the title as the top three were of a high standard.

The best known competitor in the lineup was Lou Ferrigno, a prominent bodybuilder who had become enormously popular for his portrayal of the TV character, "the Incredible Hulk." Ferrigno placed fourth, which is contrary to the list published by TWI and which I quoted in *Sons of Samson, Volume 1*. The winner was Bruce Wilhelm, America's great superheavyweight Olympic lifter; second was Robert Young, offensive tackle for the St. Louis Cardinals of the National Football League, and third place went to former Olympic weightlifter Ken Patera, who became a professional wrestler. For six years the competition remained based in America, with the vast majority of contestants coming from within its boundaries.

Unaccustomed as strength devotees were to the rather strange blend of tests which made up these invitational tournaments, there was at first a mixed reception, but as various aspects became more refined by trial and error, there was a noticeable increase in credibility and interest.

Vehicle pulls became an almost permanent inclusion, and muscle-tearing feats, such as bar bending, were eliminated as they seemed to result in injury. Scoring too has been changed to give closer results, with now only one point differences between placings, as opposed to the early days when there could be twelve points difference between the first and third men in any one event. Competition could be spread over four days, giving greater recovery periods for the athletes.

With diversity, first to New Zealand then to various parts of Europe, there was a development of the concept to show a range of athletic backgrounds, and efforts were made to capture the atmosphere of the countries visited. This sometimes involved competitors having lengthy periods of transportation; for example, in Tenerife, from sea level to the top of a high, extinct volcano and back again for consecutive tests. There was sometimes isolation and at other times large crowds—variety was the name of the game. In 1992 Iceland provided the most unique settings of all, ranging from a naturally heated lagoon and boiling geysers to inhospitable, exposed and bitterly cold waterfalls. It was not only man against man, but also man against the elements.

An ancient and beautiful Roman arena, the kind of place where professional strength athletics events first thrived, was the venue in 1994 and there was another change of direction, with a big crowd seeing the world's strongest men compete in this ancient setting but under modern lighting and with special effects. Difficult though it may have been, this was surpassed in 1995 when the contest moved to the legendary Lost Kingdom in Southern Africa's Sun City. Here the contenders had to cope not only with the scorching sun but also with high altitude. In the Bahamas, soft sandy beaches provided nature's handicap for the competitors.

Over the years the tests became more demanding to the point where the participants turned cars completely over and even carried a real car complete with engine! There are combat events, boulder lifting races, events supporting two chest-high whisky barrels, and a whole lot more.

Competitors from all over the world have been interesting, with blonde Vikings contrasting with black champions from America, Africa, and Polynesia; entrants have included a champion powerlifter, Iron Bear Collins who entered with full feathered headdress and Native American Indian apparel, and a tattooed Samoan chief. These and other colourful characters are all genuine, not pro-wrestling type hype. They come from varied backgrounds with powerlifters in the majority, but also Olympic athletes, shot-putters, hammer throwers, American football players, Highland Games heavies, bodybuilders and judoka.

Although not involved at the conceptual stage I was brought in at a very early date in an advisory capacity along with Oscar State. I was therefore delighted in 1980 when Trans World International invited me to become involved with the organisation and refereeing of TV's Britain's Strongest Man and, having proved myself there, went on to the main World's Strongest Man annual competition. I refereed for TWI from 1981 until 1991, a record which will be hard to beat. My business colleague, Dr. Douglas Edmunds, was involved in some events on a voluntary basis until 1992 and, since then, together we have officially acted as consultants. We now also had the responsibility of providing most of the equipment, which was an important breakthrough. Doug became referee in 1993, and his dynamic personality has been a feature ever since. It has never been an easy event, but the competitors and their efforts have given us great joy over the years, just as they have entertained countless millions on television.

TWI's World's Strongest Man has developed beyond recognition with many more competitors, qualifying heats and an improved structure.

CHAPTER 4

The Contestants

Many competitive weightlifters, powerlifters, bodybuilders and sundry heavy labourers envy the exposure given to these strongmen of the modern media, but they should believe Bill Kazmaier when he said it was not an easy way to earn a few bucks.

In the comfort of your home, sitting in front of the TV after Christmas dinner and a glass or two of wine, it's not too difficult to indulge in some wishful thinking that you or one of your training mates could equal or beat the established champions. Just somewhere out there may be an unsung hero who could surprise us all, so if you think you know of someone like this we want to hear from you.

The physique profile of a typical good world-class competitor is 6' 2½" (187 cm), 133.5 kg (21 st./294 lb.) with a high proportion of functional muscle as opposed to obesity. As the years go on competitors get bigger and bigger. The tallest winner was over seven feet and in the most recent *WSM* there were athletes of 6' 10", 6' 9", 6' 7" and the others very little less.

To convince the selectors, those chosen must have authentic achievements which can be readily checked, and preferably have performed in public before accepted officials. Powerlifting and weightlifting records are admirable and many in the past have come via these routes. However the battery of tests are not of a static nature but cover all kinds of strength from muscular endurance to dynamic, explosive power. Others require great strength combined with cardiovascular fitness, which is alien to some training regimes. There should be an ability to cope with strange equipment and unusual feats for which there has been little, if any, specialised practice.

It is not generally appreciated that TV competition conditions can influence and adversely affect performances. There may be unexpected breaks for technical reasons, film changes, etc., and it is here that the calm, controlled competitor has the advantage. The same applies to weather conditions on TV locations. In one show there may be beautiful sun and strength-sapping humidity, and at the next show zero temperatures and a chilling breeze. In 1993 these were combined when competitors had to carry 200 lb. kegs from a thermally heated lake into a biting wind! It's not easy to cope with such external influences.

A firm lifting platform or solid gym floor is *very* different from working on a beach where the more you put into a lift the more the sand yields! In 1995 the finalists had to run off the beach and into the waves to toss a log over a bar.

Another important factor in comparing performances and records with those seen on TV is to keep in mind that after pulling a huge truck up the slightest gradient, perhaps on a road with weird cambers, competitors' lungs feel fit to burst, trembling legs feel like jelly—every muscle and joint screams for mercy! Yet there is no time for a much needed rest, it's probably on to the bus and off to another location for the dead lift with some weird contraption straight from the Spanish Inquisition. A personal best? Forget it!

If a week of such torture doesn't scare the living daylights out of you then you may be the very person to figure in the next World's Strongest Man contest.

The Vikings of Iceland

The harsh volcanic terrain and lunar-like landscapes of Iceland, with its inhospitable winter climate has spawned some of the toughest and strongest men who have ever lived. In former times, from the late eighth to the eleventh centuries, marauding Vikings travelled along the coastlines of Northern Europe, known and feared for their ferocity and physical might. They sailed in their distinctive dragon-prowed longboats powered not only by the wind, but by mighty oarsmen who sat in places according to their strength. To determine their respective abilities, oarsmen had to lift huge graded rocks, very like the McGlashen Stones, and the larger that they lifted, the more prestigious a place they had in the longship.

In this land of ice and fire inhabited by fierce sea warriors, only the strong survived, and their lifestyles and death tolls produced a process of selective breeding which is inherited by the purebred inhabitants of today, producing more genetically gifted strength athletes per head of population than any other country in the world.

Magnus Ver Magnusson, Hjalti Arnason, Andreas and Peter Gudmundsson, Torvi Olafsson, and the greatest of them all, Jon Pall Sigmarsson, are classic examples of direct descendants of the Vikings who are immortalised in the Norse sagas and art, noted worldwide for their dynamic vitality. The Viking legacy goes far beyond physical attributes; there is a distinctive psychology and mental attitude which is easily recognisable amongst Norse strength athletes. In my view this is attributable to the sagas which these men learn and know by heart from an early age, for the tales of heroism, and adventure are potent medicine in a boy's formative years.

Jon Pall most of all had the Vikings' Homeric sense of chivalry, fortitude and endurance, and although I did not know it at the time, he had the same outlook as his forbearers. A born winner, he believed that his own efforts, and not fate, decided his destiny, and he accepted with little comment the inevitable ups and downs of life. Like ancient Vikings he feared nobody and nothing, he even faced death without a qualm, but we are getting a little ahead of the fascinating story of the man most respected and popular amongst his peers, the strongest men in the world.

The Iceman Cometh: Jon Pall Sigmarsson

Born in Hafnarfjorour on 28 April 1960, Jon Pall from his earliest years was destined to become a strength star, and at the tender age of five he was introduced to Glima, traditional Icelandic wrestling. His foster father Sveinn Gudmundsson was champion, holder of the Grettisbelti, and exhorted Jon Pall to achieve greatness in the field of sport. Although to the youngster it was simply his favourite game, it gave him the basis for several sports in which he later became renowned. Sometimes when participating in other combat sports such as karate, sumo or Cumberland wrestling he found himself reverting to the old fundamental skills which had became instinctive.

As a happy youth with attentive and dependable parents, he grew up in the company of five siblings, becoming a dedicated sportsman with a well-rounded programme, including swimming, handball and middle distance running. However, he was also a very enthusiastic and skilful soccer player, and it was with some reluctance that he gave up team sports to plough a solitary furrow when he took up karate at the age of sixteen and Olympic lifting at the age of seventeen.

Soon he was winning championships, and just as he began to set his sights on the Olympic Games, he had to seek medical attention for a recurring elbow injury. The doctor advised him that if he persisted with maximum training loads the dynamic nature of snatching and jerking might permanently damage the joint. Loath to give up lifting he switched, temporarily he thought, to powerlifting and, not surprisingly, won the national championships in 1978 and was prizewinner at the Nordic Games in 1979. He became the Scandinavian superheavyweight champion in 1980 and 1981—no easy task when the activity is so popular in these Northern lands. Entering his first European championships, he confounded the experts by winning the silver medal at 125 kg (275½ lb.) and went on to the world

Jon Pall Sigmarsson.

championships in Calcutta, where he took the bronze medal while he still considered himself a relative newcomer to the sport.

Jon Pall Sigmarsson was now becoming a national hero in Iceland and winning many honours in international competition, where he was extremely popular because of his colourful personality. The young Viking was quite an enigma, appearing to be two completely different characters; he was quiet, gentle and mannerly at all times away from the competition area, but when the adrenalin started to flow, he became a supercharged superhuman, shouting for assistance from Odin, Thor or others from their generous allowance of Norse gods.

He displayed phenomenal energy which, it seemed, if harnessed would light up all the space around him. After successes he would leap in exultation, and he beat the ground in anger if he failed. He was a raging inferno in competition and when it was all over he accepted the plaudits of the crowd with genuine appreciation.

Jon Pall, or Palli as his friends called him, was Iceland's greatest ever bodybuilder and in top shape he could not be outclassed in major international competition, for his muscle density had quality which was immediately obvious, even to the uninitiated. He looked as if his muscles were hewn out of Iceland's volcanic rocks, and the observer was left in no doubt that those were not mirror muscles but very functional ones.

At 192 cm (6' 3½"), he was one of the few top bodybuilders to allow himself to be taped, and even when cut to ribbons, (as bodybuilders described the low fat state), he sported genuine 52 cm (20½") biceps and 75 cm (29½") thighs. Sigmarsson studied bodybuilding and strength training for some time giving him a wealth of experience and knowledge which he utilised to great effect when he began competing in bodybuilding competitions, and in his first major competition, he won the Mr. Iceland 90 kg and overall categories.

This physical phenomenon fluctuated his bodyweight between 113-141 kg, a 28 kg differential (250-310 lb., a 60 lb. differential), depending on whether he was in ripped bodybuilding condition winning the Mr. Iceland competition or in strength contests against pachyderms such as Geoff Capes, then weighing around 165 kg (26 st./364 lb.), or Californian Grizzly Brown, who could be as heavy as 172 kg (27 st./378 lb.). Even at 141 kg (22 st. 3 lb./310 lb.), Palli was giving away a lot of bodyweight. Although he could go heavier, he preferred to maintain a good appearance. His public image meant a lot to him.

"I may be the strongest man, but I am no dumbbell. I don't just want to be strong, I also want to be well-built, healthy and happy," declared this likeable young giant. He was blessed with a combination of splendid facial and physical appearance, abounding good health and fine demeanour. This made the so-called "Iceman" a very hot property in Europe and a great ambassador for whichever activity he represented or whichever product or firm he was promoting. His quiet approach initially made him seem shy or even slightly aloof, but that initial impression rapidly disappeared when his successes as a bodybuilder, lifter, strongman and businessman gave him more self-confidence, although he did not flaunt this self-assurance—except when on the competition platform.

The experiences and awards of the European and world championships made Jon Pall train like a fiend for the next world title to be held in Dallas, Texas, for he longed to see America. Being a very patriotic Icelander he desperately wanted to win the powerlifting championship for his homeland; therefore it was a great blow when his sports association could not afford to send him. He had left school at seventeen years of age to earn a living and at that time could not personally afford to pay the airfare. He first worked with his father as a carpenter and was later employed as a bouncer in the toughest night spot in Reykjavik.

Actually soon after Jon Pall arrived on the scene, it became one of the best conducted clubs in town but not until he had emphatically proved he could handle himself as and when necessary. He was probably something unique in the "profession" in those days for he was no bow-tied gorilla with the red knuckles then signifying his trade; he preferred to verbally persuade people to behave in an orderly manner, and it was with great reluctance, and only when absolutely essential, that he used force. Again, unlike many bouncers, he despatched wrong-doers almost gently, even although they were doing everything in their power to provoke him.

He didn't care for the bouncing business but accepted a kind offer from Job Josefsson, an Icelandic wrestling champ who became rich as a professional and returned home to open a nice hotel. Denied the world powerlifting title, Jon Pall Sigmarsson was despondent and frustrated, for what was the point of being the strongest man alive if he did not get the opportunity to demonstrate this? But his Norse gods had not forgotten him.

I had seen the powerlifting results—official squat 357.5 kg (788 lb.), bench press 232.5 kg (512½ lb.), dead lift 367.5 kg (810 lb.)—and heard of Sigmarsson's extrovert performances; being a consultant for TWI, I discussed this with Ken Hawkes, the very experienced and competitor-friendly TV producer who for many years put together the "World's Strongest Man" programme. Wasting no time, Ken booked JPS for the 1983 European and World's Strongest Man events. In the latter JPS won the Fergus (farmer's) walk, lorry loading and wool hoist—to the best of my knowledge it was the first time Geoff Capes had been beaten in a pulley event. The very experienced Capes placed first overall and Sigmarsson, the new boy, second.

My business partner Doug Edmunds then wrote to Jon Pall, inviting him to compete in the Scottish Highland Games circuit, and on 3 April 1984 Jon Pall replied, accepting. The very first games was the International Games which I organised in Kilbirnie for some fourteen years and has always been known for the policy of encouraging new talent. Many famous names have "cut their teeth" there in the Garnock Valley.

Like Bill Kazmaier, Geoff Capes and other notable strongmen, Jon Pall loved Scottish Highland Games, and he competed regularly, his best events being

Jon Pall Sigmarsson.

tossing the caber and throwing the 25 kg/56 lb. weight for height. As a professional athlete and strongman he relished all such competitions, although he knew he could not always expect to beat experts at their highly technical specialities.

As a guest at Finland's Strongest Man competition in 1989 it took Sigmarsson only 15.66 secs to run a 30-metre course and overturn three standard cars during his sprint! As referee I could hardly keep up with him and I didn't turn any cars. The cars still had engines and seats fitted, there was no faking. This new Finnish all-comer's record beat Geoff Capes's time of 17.7 secs at Nice in 1986, but the Finnish course was 30 m long compared to the 40 m course in Nice. These are two of the greatest feats ever seen.

Jon Pall Sigmarsson's new gym in Iceland did great business but it did not detract from his energies and his earning capacity in the highly competitive field of strength athletics. He was a regular winner of World's Strongest Man competitions and World Muscle Power championships. He won major events in many countries, particularly in Scandinavia. He landed fine contracts with Ambrosia, the creamed rice people, and with Joe Weider, the world's greatest muscle mogul.

"Pow-er, Viking Pow-er!"
This was Jon Pall's favourite battle cry, indeed "pow-er"—that's how he said it—was a favourite word of his, and he used it as an adjective to describe anything he did with great enthusiasm. You were always conscious of Jon Pall's physical power, a power which he seemed to generate within his inner self, and perhaps even he did not know its inward, deep source, its real nature or the extent of his boundaries. There was a fusing of the physical and mental which amounted to a certain kind of genius.

Don't just take my word for it, ask Jamie Reeves, Forbes Cowan, Adrian Smith, Walter Weir, Jock Reeves, Doug Edmunds and any of those closely associated with Jon Pall over the years. Not only the competitors and officials loved Jon Pall, Jim Pollock, our technical and equipment man at hundreds of shows and on TV, demonstrated his feelings by naming his own newborn son Jon Pall.

Sigmarsson's physical robustness was almost always confined to the competitive arena, not often indulging in boisterous horseplay common amongst some young athletes. He was a well-balanced individual, who had hammered out his personal philosophy of life on the unyielding anvil of experience as if he had used Thor's hammer. He invested much of his winnings in the founding of Gym 80 in Iceland's capital, in partnership with his friend, dentist Johann Moller. It was here that he spent his last hours.

I vividly recall that during the competition, the Ultimate Challenge, with Geoff Capes and Bill Kazmaier, Jon Pall was taking lift for lift with Bill, who had broken world records in the dead lift, a variation of which they were now performing. They were nearing the limits of human capability when Jon Pall approached the weight. "Easy meat!" he scorned, glaring at the huge loaded cartwheels. He then lifted the weight and before lowering startled everybody with a dynamic statement aimed, I think, at psyching out his opponent, "There's no reason to be alive if you can't do the *dead* lift!" He won the event and the competition.

However, those words were to be prophetic, for on 16 January 1993, not fully recovered from injuries and a long, hard professional schedule, he was working out on heavy dead lifts, doing repetitions with a 300 kg (661½ lb.) barbell, when he had a sudden and massive heart attack, dying immediately. The volcano was exhausted.

Reflecting on his last season, 1992, I can now perceive some changes in Jon Pall. He brought his son with him for the very first time, and as we drove around Scotland to the games, the great champion took time to tell young Sigmar (born 1983) why the grass was so much greener in Scotland and told him about Glamis Castle and other things of interest we encountered. At the games he was not the totally focused athlete we knew, but between events kicked a ball and larked with his lad. He won most events but not all. It seemed as if the severe injuries which he had suffered had taken their toll, but with his uncommon tenacity he came back to win again, and in his last contest, the main annual open competition in Finland, he won decisively although he collected more injuries which kept him out of the *WSM* competition of 1992 in his own homeland.

Soon afterwards came the fatal workout.

Our hero's funeral was on a very grand scale at the Hallgrimskikja, Reykjavik's beautiful cathedral, which was packed from the altar to its huge doors. The interior was decorated with the historic banners of Iceland's sports' associations while a band and large choir was supplemented by the country's greatest singers. A poignant and dignified ceremony was conducted by the Rev Jon Porsteinsson whose sensitive yet inspiring choice of words in relating Jon Pall's career were reminiscent of the sagas. He concluded by reminding us that Jon Pall had been born with many good qualities which he had developed further to the benefit of himself and his companions:

"By nature he was a quiet man, who managed his considerable temper with mature consideration, pitting it against the challenges inherent in his sport. He was a fine looking man, whose countenance betrayed a gentle heart. But above all he was a gentleman, a man of high integrity, full of goodwill towards everyone. His feats turned him into a world celebrity, but fame never went to his head. He was happy for the victories he brought here, but his friendly and modest disposition towards his fellows remained the same as always. His whole conduct was exemplary—exceedingly temperate, striving first and foremost to further health and efficiency. His compatriots adored him, he carried with him an air of catching joy—a vigour and optimism. He was a natural joker, whose gift for words allowed him to crack many a witty remark. He was also well-read and well-informed, a joy to talk with, and a popular friend and teammate.

"Let us remember this stout and trusted gentleman, the illustrious sportsman, the pride of his country let us remember his warm smile, the wink in his eye, the sunshine in his heart."

This is a much abbreviated extract from a wonderful and well-deserved, eulogy.

There has been talk of erecting a memorial to Jon Pall, and I hope that one day this materialises. If not I hope that readers, researchers and writers will pass on to posterity the fact that at this time his contemporaries, the majority of practising international strength athletes, still consider Jon Pall Sigmarsson the all-time greatest of the genre.

Hjalti Arnason, the Great "Ursus"

Country:	Iceland
Sport:	Pro Strongman
Born:	Reykjavik, Iceland, 1963
1989 stats:	
Height:	188 cm (6'2")
Weight:	146 kg (23 st./322 lb.)
Chest:	142 cm (56")
Waist:	101 cm (40")
Biceps:	53 cm (21")
Thigh:	79 cm (31")

An observant Russian writer astutely noted that the harsh, mountainous regions of the world produced some of the toughest strongest men on this earth. He pointed out that where there was little flat, level ground, team games and sports often gave way to strength activities where men would lift and throw boulders and tree trunks or wrestle with each other. Our subject now, the formidable Hjalti Arnason, long known and feared in the realms of strength and nicknamed "Ursus" ("the Bear"), came from just such an area.

Hjalti competed internationally from 1983, when he shot to fame as a junior powerlifter representing his country in major events, and after taking a computer course, finished the major part of his career by competing in the World's Strongest Man of 1996. Hjalti won the Scandinavian gold when powerlifting was very healthy in Sweden, Norway, Finland and Denmark as well as Iceland. Even as a junior he earned a place in the senior national team, and I was most impressed when I saw him in action in 1984: He was like a raging bull of a lifter, without any mental barriers.

That year he took part in some small Highland games but made the mistake of totally ignoring technique

Hjalti Arnason, "Ursus."

and relied only on his tremendous strength. He quickly learned that even in power sports, strength can sometimes be the enemy of the strong—the skill factor just cannot be overlooked.

Hjalti came back to Britain for many years, improving on each occasion and showing the potential to become truly great if he could harness his strength and have proper, regular coaching. It is however in all-round strength events that Arnason excelled, and in such competitions he was world-class, proving this at the World Muscle Power championships in Britain and in the Défi Mark Ten in Canada, where he broke the world record in the platform lift.

Hjalti had an animalistic approach to competition, going in with all barrels firing; there were no half measures. This was shown in Iceland's Strongest Man when he was arm wrestling, and on the signal to begin, Hjalti exerted all his strength and there was an ominous crack as his opponent's arm broke and Arnason forced it down to win. Again, this time at Bellahouston, a particularly demanding sponsor insisted on something spectacular for the TV cameras; Hjalti grabbed him by an arm and leg and after spinning him around, actually threw the sponsor a considerable distance as startled bystanders rushed to catch the poor, bewildered, and thereafter very subdued, executive!

There was yet another example at Earlshall where he opposed Bill Kazmaier in a wrestling final, the greatest match of the season. At our events wrestling is totally genuine, no fixing whatsoever, and honour as well as prizes are at stake. Most of the heavies dislike wrestling—the fear of injury and the knock-on effect of missing important events is always very much in evidence so we seldom include this sport. Neither the American nor the Icelander had lost a match up until that time, so it was of tremendous interest to all concerned. The best of three falls was contested and we had no submissions. Strange as it may seen to those accustomed to TV wrestling, such real bouts as ours are almost always over very quickly.

Hjalti went immediately on the offensive in his usual all-out (or should I say all-in?) fashion and rapidly he took the first fall. Bill was thunderstruck, another fall would break his unbeaten run. In the next round he fought like a man possessed and equalised by taking a brilliant fall. The tension was terrific as the two grapplers squared up for the final fall, and everything else stopped—even the stall holders round the perimeter of the ground ceased trading to witness this classic battle, for by this time it was clear that this was something very special.

Well, the action was certainly fast and furious, and this is not a cliché, the bout was both furious and fast. Finally Bill used a skilful variation of a suplex to fell the massive Icelander, and in triumph he jumped to his feet, punching the air in exaltation. But was the action over? Not on your life!

Arnason scrambled upright and took a mighty leap on to the victor's back, and there they were again attacking each other like wildcats. The remainder of the heavies rushed in to separate them, and I was in the thick of it; in the midst of all the excitement I forgot to switch off my microphone so the fascinated crowd, enjoying every minute of it, heard each word uttered in the melee, including Hjalti's apologetic, "Only a little bit of fun, Dave." He meant it—that's his idea of fun.

The tough Icelander also trained in karate, and on one auspicious occasion a screen opponent of "Rambo" Stallone sought out Hjalti as a sparring partner. Naturally Hjalti obliged and went through the required regime, but when the opportunity occurred a few days later, Arnason gleefully indulged in a proper bout, fighting and defeating the star, "Mind you I haven't had any other bookings since that time," he told me ruefully.

He seems to enjoy nothing better than a "legitimate" punch-up. I well remember the time in central Europe when an irate competitor seemed poised to tear me limb from limb in front of the TV cameras, Hjalti moved in and gently but firmly got rid of the offender. Afterwards in his perfect but heavily accented English he told me, "I hoped he would try to punch, I wanted to take him!"

Ursus has been tester at World's Strongest Man contests including those held in France, Hungary, Iceland, and also at Huntly Castle for the Ultimate Challenge. He was a great tester, for his ability and expertise were invaluable in these difficult circumstances where the possibilities and limits in the various feats are virtually unknown. When we were in Nice, we had to use a boat for the dead lift. It was not the one we wanted, so there had to be lots of experimentation on the eve of the event. Hjalti did lift after lift, each heavier than the last, and as it turned out his testing poundages exceeded the top efforts of many of the competitors.

His companion in testing was invariably Mark Higgins, and the two were firm friends and keen rivals. When they met in various internationals in different parts of the globe they had little personal duels as well as the

Hjalti Arnason, left, gives Bill Kazmaier a bear hug.

overall prizes in mind, and this kind of rivalry, backed with friendship, represents the best in sport.

In private life Ursus has had a chequered career. He was a much feared bar bouncer, a caring supervisor in a psychiatric hospital, security agent, an occasional events promoter and a debt collector—who could refuse *him*? More recently he went back to college to qualify in computer technology. He is married to Margaret, a big strong woman. On the other hand I found Hjalti's dad to be a much smaller, gentle man, and Hjalti's brother an accomplished musician amongst the top of the pops in Iceland.

It is a pity that Hjalti Arnason has lived in the shadow of Jon Pall, after all he was undoubtedly one of the world's strongest men.

Andreas Gudmundsson

Born in 1965, Andreas Gudmundsson, 192 cm (6' 3½") and 126 kg (19 st. 12 lb./278 lb.) was essentially an international field athlete but could not overlook the success and

Magnus Ver Magnusson, left, in competition, and above, at ease.

pleasure his strength compatriots were having. He gave the activity a try and did extremely well, especially in 1994 where he even had a victory over Manfred Hoeberl, when the Austrian was at his peak. Andreas won many fine prizes but suffered some injuries in the process and was unable to compete in 1995 or 1996. He greatly misses the sport and hopes he may make a comeback.

Magnus Ver Magnusson

Country:	Iceland
Sport:	Pro strongman
Born:	23 April 1963
	Egilsstaðir, Iceland
Resides:	Reykjavik
1996 stats:	
Height:	190 cm (6'3")
Weight:	130 kg (20 st 7 lb./287 lb.)
Chest:	145 cm (57")
Waist:	105 cm (41")
Biceps:	52 cm (20½")
Thigh:	82 cm (32")

Of all the great champions in the lineups for the 1995 and 1996 World's Strongest Man title, Magnus Ver had the most impressive record in past events. He won the title in 1991 when the competition was held in Tenerife and was runner-up in 1992 and 1993. He regained the title in 1994 in

South Africa and after winning the 1995 World Muscle Power championships in Scotland, he went to the Bahamas and won the World's Strongest Man title for the third time; he won again in 1996 in Mauritius, equalling Sigmarsson's record of winning the title four times. He is a worthy representative of Iceland's superb "heavy" athletes. In a country of mighty men and numerous champions out of all proportion to the size of the population—even in such company—Magnusson is classed as one of the all-time greats.

After indulging in a wide range of sporting activities Magnus Ver, an engineer by profession, began powerlifting in 1984 and in 1985 won medals in the European and world championships. A few years later, in 1989, and again in 1990, he won Senior European titles in the 125 kg category. His totals often exceeded those of everybody else in the competition regardless of bodyweight, and as a result he has gained several "Best Lifter" awards. Notable lifts include squat 400 kg (882 lb.), bench press 274.5 kg (605 lb.), dead lift 375 kg (827 lb.) and total 1015 kg (2231 lb.).

The proud Norseman's sportsmanship in the face of adversity has considerably impressed his colleagues. His dedicated professionalism always ensures maximum effort in his quest to beat the record of his hero, Jon Pall Sigmarsson.

Torvi Olafsson

Country:	Iceland
Sport:	Powerlifting
Born:	13 April 1965
Resides:	Reykjavik
1995 stats:	
Height:	200 cm (6'7")
Weight:	160 kg (25 st. 3 lb./353 lb.)
Chest:	165 cm (65")
Biceps:	55 cm (21½")

Torvi is a superb powerlifter with many championships and records to his credit. This huge man was Icelandic champion as well as being one of their most successful strongmen. Particularly good at weight carrying, such as the Husafell Stone, he was hampered by a chest injury at the end of 1995 season.

I make no apology for devoting this proportion of space to the competitors of one small country, for in the world of strength it is a very special place and these are exceptional people. Take the top five men from any other country and I guarantee that they would be outshone by these modern Icelandic Vikings. Of course the Norsemen came from more than one country, and likewise these same countries have produced strength athletes demonstrating the same traits. Is it not significant that we have had competitors like Riku Kiri, Ilkka Nummisto, Lars Hedlund, Markku Varalahti, Henning Thorsen, Henrik Ravn, Magnus Samuelsson, Markku Suonenvirta and Ilkka Kinnunen? It is one of the patterns in strength lore which cannot be overlooked.

Gerrit Badenhorst

Country:	South Africa
Sport:	Rugby, powerlifting, weightlifting
Born:	10 October 1962 De Aar, Orange Free State, South Africa
Resides:	Bloemfontein
1992 stats:	
Height:	186 cm (6'1")
Weight:	138 kg (21 st. 10 lb./304 lb.)
Chest:	128 cm (50")
Biceps:	55 cm (22")
Thigh:	87 cm (34")

In 1992 Gerrit became the first South African to compete in modern strongman competitions; he entered several

Gerrit Badenhorst.

important contests in Britain and Finland, then finally the World's Strongest Man in Iceland. He is the most successful African and has won the Mighty Man tournament in South Africa, and in his younger days he represented his nation in lifting weights.

Between 1988 and 1990 Gerrit won three world powerlifting titles (1988, 1989 and 1990) and broke world records in the squat 450 kg (992 lb.), dead lift 402 kg (886 lb.) and total 1102.5 kg (2431 lb.). He was one of the elite totalling over 1100 kg in the three lifts. Having beaten the totals of Lars Noren, Don Reinhoudt and Bill Kazmaier, he was hailed as the greatest ever powerlifter, and at that stage he retired from the sport as there was no financial incentive.

In 1993 in his quest for the World's Strongest Man title, he sustained an injury in a clash of the titans, the Pole Push. Gerrit was forced to retire from the competition but vowed he would be back to make amends. The following year, with many home supporters to back him up, he placed fourth in the finals, winning the dead lifting event in the process.

In 1995 he improved his placing still further, taking second place overall to Magnusson in spite of suffering bad injury in the Bavarian stone lift. This caused a huge black bruise which eventually covered the whole of his stomach, but it did not prevent him from giving 100 percent in every event.

Brian Bell

Born:	4 February 1967	
Country:	Scotland	
Occupation:	PSV driver	
Resides:	Dundee	
1996 stats:		
Height:	185 cm	(6'1")
Weight:	127 kg	(20 st./280 lb.)
Chest:	147 cm	(58")
Biceps:	53 cm	(21")

One of Scotland's leading powerlifters, Brian has won many international titles and broken world records in the sport. He travelled to Mauritius to be a tester in the 1996 WSM and ended up competing due to the withdrawal of Leonid Tarenenko.

Raimonds Bergmanis

Born:	25 July 1965	
Country:	Latvia	
Resides:	Riga	
1996 stats:		
Height:	190 cm	(6'3")
Weight:	130 kg	(20 st. 7 lb./287 lb.)
Chest:	122 cm	(48")
Biceps:	45 cm	(18")

This powerful and athletic young man competed in the weightlifting events at Barcelona and Atlanta before becoming a finalist in the 1996 WSM. Four times champion of Latvia, Raimonds set no less than fifteen weightlifting records. He has a serious approach to all competitions and even learned English to overcome language difficulties at such events.

Tjalling van den Bosch

Country:	The Netherlands	
Sport:	Pro strongman	
Born:	28 June 1958	
	Achlum, Holland	
1990 stats:		
Height:	191 cm	(6'3")
Weight:	140 kg	(22 st./308 lb.)
Chest:	139 cm	(55")
Waist:	105 cm	(41")
Biceps:	50 cm	(20")
Thigh:	85 cm	(33½")

Tjalling finally made his debut in the World's Strongest Man contest in 1990. In 1989 he had beaten the rest of the Netherlands' top strongmen to win their national Strongest Man competition thus qualifying for the international event to be held in Spain, but had to withdraw at the last minute with a torn Achilles tendon. Ab Wolders, who was in San Sebastian to watch the competition, found himself competing again instead, having been joint second to Tjalling in their national event.

Popularly known as "Charlie" on the strongman circuit, van den Bosch earned an entry in the *Guinness Book of Records* by pulling a total of eighteen cars. He held Strongest Man titles in his native province of Friesland and also in North and South Netherlands.

His unlikely introduction to sport as a youngster was via draughts, in which he competed at top level. He also played soccer and a Friesian sport, Kaatsen, which is similar to lawn tennis. He took up powerlifting, where his best figures were: squat 365 kg (804 lb.), bench press 227 kg (500 lb.), dead lift 350 kg (771 lb.). On the advice of Geoff Capes, he switched to professional Highland Games in 1986 and found he liked its "happy-go-lucky" atmosphere; he has held several Dutch records.

Anton Boucher

Country:	Namibia
Sport:	Pro strongman
Born:	7 March 1973
Resides:	Keelmanshoop, Namibia

1994 stats:
Height:	180 cm	(5' 11")
Weight:	136 kg	(21 st. 6 lb./300 lb.)
Chest:	145 cm	(57")
Biceps:	58 cm	(23")
Thigh:	82 cm	(32")

At only twenty-one years of age, Anton was the youngest competitor ever to be selected for the World's Strongest Man event. Already one of the strongest men in Africa, he made a very good impression on his first European tour in 1994, placing in the top three in every competition he entered.

He began competing in strength athletics in 1992 and came fourth in the Johannesburg Jamboree Strongman contest of 1993. Anton then placed second in the 1994 South African Strongman competition and was selected for a number of prime overseas competitions, including the World Muscle Power and TWI's World's Strongest Man.

Boucher's all-round ability was first seen in track and field events in which he won many prizes as a junior and set an under-15s' record in the shot put with an official 20.62 metres. In powerlifting he claims a 300 kg squat (661° lb.) and a phenomenal 600 kg (1,320 lb.) in the dead lift. Clearly this was not the standard lift, but it could have been a high, partial movement with straps. He has lifted a 170 kg log (375 lb.) overhead, and in training he uses 265 kg (584 lb.) in bent forward rowing.

Young Anton has a very pleasant personality, is keen to learn all he can from more experienced competitors and officials, and is determined to become the World's Strongest Man; some of his supporters think he may achieve this ambition.

Derek Boyer

Born:	*Ca. 1970*
Country:	*Fiji*
Occupation:	*Professional strongman*
Resides:	*WSW, Australia*

1996 stats:
Height:	194 cm	(6' 4½")
Weight:	151 kg	(23 st. 11 lb./333 lb.)
Chest:	152 cm	(60")

Derek's mother is a sixth generation descendant of the king of Rotuma, a Pacific Island. His father has an equally colourful background, his family stemming from the famous pirate, Bully Hayes.

Nicknamed "the Island Warrior," Derek is a fearsome sight when he dons his decorated Tarpa cloth round his waist and puts on his warpaint for important occasions. Sometimes he does an interesting, storytelling war dance related to Polynesian power.

His sporting background includes martial arts, Australian rules football and professional tough guy competitions. He won the Australian Drug-Free Powerlifting Championships and placed third and second in their world championships in England 1992 and Canada 1993, when he narrowly missed a world record in the deadlift. Although he had appeared in some lesser competitions in Australia, Derek Boyer's first appearance in major international competitions was in 1996 when he toured Europe and qualified for the World finals.

Rick "Grizzly" Brown

Country:	*USA*
Sport:	*Wrestling, pro strongman*
Born:	*4 April 1960*
	Berkeley, California

1986 stats:
Height:	180 cm	(5'11")
Weight:	171 kg	(26 st. 13 lb./377 lb.)
Chest:	165 cm	(65")
Waist:	130 cm	(51")
Biceps:	63.5 cm	(25")
Thigh:	84 cm	(33")

Apart from the above measurements, Grizzly boasts a shoulder span of 89 cm (35"), deltoid to deltoid. With shoulders just under a yard wide, a chest equal to the height of a 5' 5" person and biceps more than two feet in girth, this meant that TWI had to book two seats, not one, for his transatlantic flight from San Francisco when he made his first appearance in the 1985 World's Strongest Man contest in Cascais, Portugal.

His most impressive result in that year's competition was winning the crucifix with a record time of 1 minute 4.8 seconds; this event involved holding 12.5 kg (27° lb.) weights suspended from hands outstretched at either side for the greatest possible time.

Brown's size is matched by his strongman feats. The mass-circulation US magazine *National Enquirer* published pictures of him holding back two large motorcycles as they accelerated at full power on dry concrete. Wearing arm harnesses, he held them for a full minute, with the equivalent of a 295 kg (650 lb.) pull on each arm. Using only his little finger, he has pressed overhead a man weighing 72.5 kg (11 st. 6 lb./160 lb.), and he has been attributed with the following lifts: squat 453 kg (1,000 lb.), bench press 299 kg (659 lb.), dead lift 366 kg (807 lb.) and inclined press 249 kg (549 lb.).

One of my articles about his feats led to him receiving an invitation to compete in the World's Strongest Man competition. He then competed on the British circuit in 1986, including Highland Games. Indeed when Grizzly was presented to the Queen during one such event at the

Rick "Grizzly" Brown.

1986 Commonwealth Games in Edinburgh, it was reported that the Queen asked Grizzly how he managed to practise caber tossing in California, to which he replied, "I just cut me a redwood tree, ma'am."

He was an amateur wrestler and powerlifter from the age of fifteen and won a version of the US heavyweight wrestling crown in 1981, having retired from powerlifting a year earlier. He then concentrated on muscle power, with parttime involvement as a professional wrestler.

Outside the power game he works as a youth counsellor on drug abuse, which he says has reached frightening proportions in California. He claims never to have used steroids to aid muscular development.

Jean-Pierre Brulois

Country:	*France*
Sport:	*Powerlifting*
Born:	*18 April 1957*
	Lille, France
1985 stats:	
Height:	*180 cm (5' 11")*
Weight:	*110 kg (17 st. 5 lb./243 lb.)*
Chest:	*125 cm (49")*
Waist:	*97 cm (38")*
Biceps:	*50 cm (20")*
Thigh:	*75 cm (29½")*

Brulois' sporting life has centred on the two strongman disciplines of Olympic lifting and powerlifting. He began as an Olympic lifter at age seventeen and collected the national title for the 110 kg (242½ lb.) class in the first year of competition. He later switched to powerlifting as a knee injury made the two Olympic lifts difficult.

In 1980 he collected the first of four national powerlifting titles, again in the 110 kg class. His increasing weight put him in the 125 kg (275½ lb.) class the following year, and again he was champion, a feat he repeated in 1983 and 1984, when he was silver medallist at the world championships in Dallas.

His best competition lifts were: squat 352 kg (776 lb.), bench press 220 kg (485 lb.), dead lift 340 kg (750 lb.), best total 892 kg (1,967 lb.).

Jean-Pierre Brulois.

Geoff Capes

Country: *Great Britain*
Sport: *Pro Highland Games*
Born: *22 August 1949*
Holbeach, Lincs

1985 stats:
Height: *198 cm* *(6'6")*
Weight: *146 kg* *(23 st./322 lb.)*
Chest: *135 cm* *(53")*
Waist: *107 cm* *(42")*
Biceps: *50 cm* *(20")*
Thigh: *79 cm* *(31")*

Geoff won Europe's Strongest Man in 1980 (London), 1982 (Amsterdam) and 1984 (Marken); and Britain's Strongest Man titles in 1979, 1981 and 1983. In the World's Strongest Man competition he was the winner in 1983 and 1985, runner-up to Bill Kazmaier in 1981, runner-up to Jon Pall Sigmarsson in 1986, third in 1980 and 1984, and fourth in 1982. In short he held eight Strongest Man titles—two World, three European and three British—which, in thirteen appearances from 1979-1985, is a formidable achievement. Two World Muscle Power championships must also be chalked up amongst the major titles held by this remarkable man.

He has also had great success in professional Highland Games and took the World Heavy Events title in Lagos, Nigeria, in 1981, winning four out of five events. He has set world records in events such as 56 lb. weight over the bar, brick lifting and racing over an upgraded 100 ft. (30 m) course with a 190 kg (420 lb.) refrigerator on his back. He again won the title in 1983, 1985, 1986 and 1987.

In his prime Geoff was one of the best caber tossers, but before turning professional his main event was putting the shot; as Britain's greatest shot-putter he came fourth in the 1970 Commonwealth Games in Edinburgh, then at the next two Games won gold medals. He was also first in the European Indoor Championships of 1974 and 1976 and fifth in the 1980 Olympic Games. He set the UK all-comers record at 21.68 m.

Voted Britain's best ever field events athlete in 1983, this all-round sportsman represented Lincolnshire at basketball, soccer and cross-country, besides being a useful sprinter. He is also a great believer in star performers giving something back to sport, and has coached many youngsters at athletics and strength events.

An ex-policeman, he ran a sportswear retail shop at Holbeach in his native Lincolnshire, but now lives in Spalding where he does TV and promotional work for a wide variety of commercial products. His hobbies include breeding parakeets and other birds, travel and eating.

Geoff Capes throwing the 56 lb. weight.

Forbes Cowan, Scotland's Strongest Man 1992-96

Country: *Scotland*
Sport: *Pro strongman and Highland Games*
Born: *16 October 1964*
Kilwinning, Ayrshire, Scotland
Resides: *Kilwinning*

1995 stats:
Height: *194 cm* *(6' 4½")*
Weight: *130 kg* *(20 st. 7 lb./287 lb.)*
Chest: *142 cm* *(56")*
Waist: *91 cm* *(36")*
Biceps: *51 cm* *(20")*
Thigh: *74 cm* *(29")*

Forbes Cowan entered and won his first strongman competition, Cunninghame's Strongest Man, in May 1990 and repeating this win the following year moved into the professional ranks. A year later he won Scotland's Strongest Man and was joint first with Gary Taylor in Europe's

Strongest Man. In 1993 he took the British Muscle Power championship, and was the competition tester and British reserve for the 1993 World's Strongest Man competition in France.

This very determined Scot has had a meteoric career in the professional ranks, competing whenever possible, not just in strongman competitions but also in Highland Games where he excelled in caber tossing and throwing the 56 lb. weight for height. His throws of 16' 6" in the latter put him in world rankings.

Forbes Cowan placed fourth in the World Muscle Power championships of 1993 and 1994 and won the European Muscle Power title in 1995, beating the great Magnus Ver Magnusson and other famous title holders.

In the World's Strongest Man competition in South Africa 1994, he created a sensation when he won his heat against tough opposition, including the current title holder, and entered the final in great style. During a sensational pole push where he beat the eventual overall winner, Forbes sustained an agonizing rib injury. True to his reputation for toughness, he battled on to finish fourth in the competition although in great pain. He also had to have a hernia operation, having continued to compete after nipping his abdomen lifting a heavy log on top of his lifting belt. The operation left him without a navel.

Forbes won the World Muscle Power championship 1996 just four months after major shoulder surgery and two slipped discs. He was outstanding in his heat of the World's Strongest Man in Mauritius; however, back injuries recurred and he placed fifth in the final. Over the years in spite of a hectic strength itinerary, he still managed to fit in many Highland Games between May and September each year.

Away from the competitive arena he enjoys a quiet life and do-it-yourself activities and has rebuilt an old cottage on the outskirts of the small town in which he lives. Fond of flora and fauna, the secluded location allows him to enjoy the wildlife which abounds in Scotland.

Colin Cox

Country: *New Zealand*
Sport: *Powerlifting*
Born: *17 January 1962*
Resides: *Napier, New Zealand*
1996 stats:
Height: *183 cm   (6')*
Weight: *133 kg   (20 st. 13 lb./293 lb.)*
Biceps: *51 cm   (20")*

Of Maori extraction, Colin is a colourful contestant with his tattooed armband and Polynesian chant of war or welcome (*haka*), depending on the occasion. Over the years he has realised his fine physical potential by participation in various strength-related sports. Training at his own gym in Napier, he won three New Zealand powerlifting championships before taking up professional strongman events in 1994.

His first season in the big time was 1995 when he competed at Callander, next in the World Muscle Power championships and two months later, the World's Strongest Man in the Bahamas. In this competition New Zealand's strongest man used his very powerful legs to particularly good effect in the wheel flip, where massive tractor wheels were turned over and over, not rolled, over a soft, sandy beach course.

His next competition was in Denmark and weeks later, still looking for fresh fields to conquer, Colin entered the New Zealand Highland Games championships before a very large crowd in Waipu and led most of the way. Just when he looked certain to win, the title slipped from his grasp in the last two events. It was a great debut and only inexperience in the activities stood between him and first place. In just five months as an international strongman, Colin Cox had shown great strength, stamina,

Forbes Cowan.

versatility and motivation of the highest order. He went on to win six of the ten events in the 1996 New Zealand's Strongest Man, beating the hefty Aucklander and Highland Games champion, Pouri Rackete-Stones, and Invercargill's Craig Young, into second and third places.

Roger Ekstrom

Country: *Finland*
Sport: *Powerlifting*
Born: *11 March 1947*
Teppo, Finland
1985 stats:
Height: *190 cm* *(6'3")*
Weight: *130 kg* *(20½ st./287 lb.)*
Chest: *140 cm* *(55")*
Waist: *100 cm* *(39")*
Biceps: *49 cm* *(19")*
Thigh: *70 cm* *(27½")*

Ekstrom was third in Europe's Strongest Man in 1982, competing for Sweden where he now lives; he was reserve in the World's Strongest Man 1984 and a competitor in the 1985 event, on that occasion competing for his native Finland, which his family left when he was three years old.

His main sporting interests as a schoolboy were running and the high jump, and he did not start lifting until he was twenty-seven. Two years later he won his first powerlifting competition and in the same year, placed eleventh in the Swedish championships. By 1978 he had moved up to third in national rankings, and he took the first of his three Nordic championships in 1980, and the European 125 kg (275½ lb.) at Parma, Italy in 1981. During 1982 he came fourth in the 125 kg world championship. Injury kept him out of competition for a long time, but he made a successful return in 1984.

Roger has lived in Sweden for most of his life, where he has worked at a school for the mentally handicapped and enjoys angling, his main hobby.

His best competition lifts are: squat 342.5 kg (755 lb.), bench press 232.5 kg (513 lb.), dead lift 350 kg (772 lb.), best total 912.5 kg (2,012 lb.).

Gregg Ernst

Country: *Canada*
Sport: *Pro strongman*
Born: *30 September 1961*
Lunenburg, Nova Scotia
1992 stats:
Height: *183 cm* *(6')*
Weight: *148 kg* *(23 st. 4 lb./326 lb.)*
Chest: *149 cm* *(58½")*
Waist: *124 cm* *(49")*
Biceps: *56 cm* *(22")*
Thigh: *84 cm* *(33")*

Born into a Nova Scotia farming family, when he was twelve Gregg's father gave him a set of weights for Christmas, which were intended to build him up for haymaking.

Gregg Ernst.

This gave Gregg a passion for strength sports, which has been with him ever since.

By the time he was twenty-one, Gregg had begun collecting strength titles. He was Atlantic Powerlifting Champion in 1982 and again in 1983; also in 1983 he became arm wrestling champion of Lunenburg. In 1990 he collected the Canadian Professional Strongman title, and he won the Nova Scotia Farmer's Walk in 1988 and 1989. His best lifts are: squat 340 kg (750 lb.), bench press 231 kg (510 lb.) and dead lift 362.5 kg (800 lb.).

He achieved one sporting ambition in the summer of 1991 by back lifting a team of oxen weighing 2004.5 kg (4420 lb.), breaking the biggest live weight back lift previously achieved. Another ambition is to dead lift the magic 435.5 kg (1000 lb.) and to break the legendary French Canadian Louis Cyr's record for the dumbbell press. He appeared in the World's Strongest Man for the first time in 1991 when he won the "Best Personality" award and finished in fifth place.

An active churchman and family man, Gregg plays several instruments, writes songs and is a beef and dairy farmer in Lunenburg.

Laszlo Fekete

Country: Hungary
Sport: Millstone lifting
Born: 28 January 1958
Osi, Hungary
1994 stats:
Height: 192 cm (6'3")
Weight: 135 kg (21 st. 4 lb.)/298 lb.)
Chest: 138 cm (54")
Biceps: 52 cm (20½")

Laszlo has competed in several World's Strongest Man competitions, in Hungary, Tenerife, Finland and South Africa. In Finland he won the stone lifting event, creating a new record. After that he gained more bodyweight and strength, winning a number of international contests held in his own country. He is always very keen to be matched with young contenders as he feels his experience, matched with his physical attributes, gives him an edge.

Often very extroverted and laughing loudly when things are going his way, he is equally well-known for the steely look in his striking electric blue eyes when he faces tough opposition. His intensity on such occasions can be disconcerting to his opponents. His forte is millstone lifting, and for many years he has been the foremost exhibitor of this test of strength

Lou Ferrigno, "the Incredible Hulk"

A whole generation of youngsters, including my own kids, grew up with weekly episodes of *The Incredible Hulk*, a TV adaption of the Marvel Comic character. The story related episodes in the life of a young scientist played by Bill Bixby, who is exposed to massive doses of gamma rays; afterwards, whenever under great stress and angry, he would temporarily develop superhuman strength. Fortunately the story line showed that the man and his monster were dedicated to the triumph of good over evil, and the popularity of the series was phenomenal. The Hulk was soon a household name with an instantly recognisable image and identity.

The bodybuilder fortunate enough to play this leading role was Lou Ferrigno, whose real life story is worthy of television exposure. Although Lou eventually won Mr. Universe titles and is one of the best known bodybuilders in the history of the activity, he started life as a small underdeveloped child badly handicapped by deafness.

He was dominated by his father, a New York cop who featured prominently in the 1977 cult documentary *Pumping Iron*. Long after, in a series of interviews, Lou revealed that their relationship had been a stormy one, not all that it appeared in his early publicity.

At 6' 5" and sometimes over 136 kg (21 st. 6 lb./300 lb.), Lou was one of the biggest and most muscular competitors in a sport full of big men. He was, and still is, outstanding. He had turned to bodybuilding as an escape from many of the negative aspects of his life and immediately found it suited his needs. As a baby he suffered an ear infection, which led to deafness. Unfortunately, the damage was not discovered until he was four years old and he could barely talk; he was just thought to be a backward child. Wearing a hearing aid improved things, but in some ways set him apart from other kids, who called him "deaf Louie" or "tin ear." They punched him on the chest where the device was housed to create a cacophony of sound, which threatened to burst his eardrums.

He was part of an Italian family with old-fashioned values, and the hard work ethic was top of their strict code of conduct. It was a lesson he learned well but it was not at all easy. Big Louie was taught by nuns, and when seated at the back of the class, he had difficulty in lip-reading so performed poorly. He was still wrongly thought to be a little stupid. As a teenager he was thin as a beanpole and he lived in the scary urban jungle which is Brooklyn. It was said that a frontline soldier had a better chance of surviving World War Two than a skinny, quiet lad had of surviving New York.

On taking up regular weight training, Lou embraced the "no pain no gain" concept with alacrity, and avoiding the hustle and bustle of the gyms, he isolated himself in the privacy of his room and worked hard with the weights. Later with heavier loads he moved to the

Lou Ferrigno, "the Incredible Hulk."

basement. There he devoted more time and energy getting rid of accumulated frustration and visualising the self-attained physical improvement he would achieve when his dream became a reality. His father's weights had been around the house since he was a kid, but he got his own gear and exchanged a pile of quite valuable comics for some muscle mags and made rapid progress with his training. Like many young beginners he worked mainly on his arms and shoulders, but this was enough to impress schoolmates, and for the first time he saw a little respect directed towards himself. Unfortunately, his euphoria was short-lived.

Concentration on bodybuilding badly affected his grades at school, and his father was extremely annoyed when he received Lou's report. He got a chain and padlock and immobilised the weight training apparatus so that it could not be used. Naturally young Ferrigno was despondent, but he was also determined and he got a hacksaw and released the weights, worked out, then chained them up again. It took his dad a week to discover the ruse, and again there was hell to pay.

His mother's steadying influence was once more called into play and a deal was struck. It was agreed that Lou could spend as much time as he wanted working out in the basement—as long as he spent an equal amount of time studying in his room. It paid off and Lou Ferrigno earned passing marks once more. He confesses that more than once his studying was not entirely confined to academic subjects, but included slipping his monthly muscle magazine between the pages of his lesson book.

With dedication and self-discipline he improved beyond all bounds. For a once gawky lad it was an impossible dream come true. This spurred him to greater efforts and his progress accelerated. No longer did he feel like an "elephant man." Faith in himself with weights as his medium had been the key elements in his survival in a hostile environment.

Now a fully-fledged bodybuilder, Louie went to shows and watched top-liners like his first idol, Larry Scott at the Brooklyn Academy of Music in 1965. He also saw Arnold Schwarzenegger win the IFBB Mr. Universe, but lose in the Mr. Olympia to Sergio Oliva. It was Lou's whole life. He didn't want a fancy car or electronic musical entertainment centres, "There is nothing I loved more than the feel of the knurled handhold on a seven-foot Olympic bar."

While bodybuilding was his priority, it is also clear that he was very interested in strength and ability. He still got into occasional fights when people tried to bully him. "I never enjoyed fighting but by then I was winning and trouble seemed to diminish soon after that." He also took a joy in arm wrestling competitions, in which he was unbeaten. There was a very revealing incident when he was nineteen years of age, at the station when travelling to see Sergio Oliva. The ticket seller was not in his booth as the train arrived, and the little group couldn't get in, so Louie ran to the railings, grabbing two of them to try to pull them apart. At first they didn't move but as his companions shouted encouragement, "Sergio, think of Sergio," the bars slowly yielded enough for them to squeeze through and catch the train. He confessed he felt uneasy about the incident, but he was determined not to miss the show, and the adrenalin was flowing fast.

On another occasion at an Olympia Health Club, before Dennis Tinnerino and some of the best known bodybuilders, he beat a self-acclaimed pinch grip champion of the world by lifting 120 lb. (2 x 60 lb. discs) using finger strength alone; the champion had lifted two 50 lb. discs.

Ferrigno began bodybuilding contests at nineteen and was then 6' 5" and 97.6 kg (15 st. 5 lb./215 lb.). His first was the Mr. New Jersey Open Hercules competition in Trenton, New Jersey. In his second competition, he came second in the tall class of the Mr Wagner. contest, with Steve Michalik the overall winner. Lou won the Mr. Teenage Eastern America and the Teenage Mr. America, came second in his first Mr. America competition, and came first on his second attempt. In the NABBA Mr. Universe in London, he placed fourth, and at twenty-one he was the youngest person ever to win the IFBB Mr. Universe, a title he took for the second time in Verona, Italy. Another highlight was winning Schwarzenegger's Mr. International, but he came second to Arnold in the Mr. Olympia. A cabinet of gleaming trophies confirmed his new identity.

Golden opportunities came with a major appearance in the film *Pumping Iron* and in 1976 ABC's *TV Superstars*, for which he reduced from 125 to 102 kg (275 to 224 lb.). His excellent performance, where he won $13,900, was a boost for bodybuilding and resulted in an offer to play professional football. Needless to say he refused. Soon after this he moved to California, with the sponsorship of Joe Weider.

Invited to compete in the first World's Strongest Man competition in 1977, he placed fourth overall. With some specialisation and experience he could have gone much further in strength athletics but then a part in a regular TV series came along, with a starring role as "the Incredible Hulk," alongside Bill Bixby. Richard Keel, who was "Jaws," a famous villain in a James Bond movie, was initially spoken of for the part of the Hulk, but Lou had a great audition, acting and crying in a totally natural, uninhibited way, and got the part.

It is planned that this aspect of his life and other relevant details will be covered appropriately in a future volume of *Sons of Samson* dealing specifically with strongmen stars of the big and small screen.

Lou Ferrigno's quest for physical perfection and strength had been realised but his deeply poignant and sensitive account of the hardships along the way cannot be easily forgotten.

John Gamble

Country:	United States
Sport:	Powerlifting
Born:	26 June 1957
1983 stats:	
Height:	181 cm (5'11")
Weight:	136 kg (21 st. 6 lb./300 lb.)

John placed third to Bill Kazmaier and Tom Magee in World's Strongest Man 1982 when he won the battery lift, came second to Geoff Capes in bar bending and shared third place with Tom Magee in the dead lift. He starred at American football, wrestling and track at high school and challenged Kazmaier for preeminence as the United States' top powerlifter.

His impressive list of victories include junior national 125 kg in 1981, senior national in 1982 and 1983, YMCA national in 1982 and 1983, and World 125kg in 1982. He retained the world 125 kg title in Gothenburg, Sweden in 1983, with a total of 967 kg (2,132 lb.), only 7 kg less than Kazmaier in the superheavy class. His best ever squat, bench press and dead lift—done at various times—total 1,030 kg (2,271 lb.), which was more than the world record.

John was assistant strength and conditioning coach at the University of Virginia and also coached weight throwers on the track team.

Yngve Gustavsson

Born:	30 March 1959	
Country:	Sweden	
1984 stats:		
Height:	176 cm	(5'9")
Weight:	131 kg	(20 st. 9 lb./289 lb.)
Chest:	130 cm	(51")
Biceps:	49 cm	(19")
Thigh:	79 cm	(31")

This Nordic and Sweden powerlifting champion ranked third in Europe and fifth in the world when he competed in the 1984 World's Strongest Man. Yngve was a useful sprinter, and soccer and ice hockey player before turning to bodybuilding at the age of twenty-one. He worked as a security guard in the lovely new town of Solna near Stockholm, where he racked up a squat of 355 kg (783 lb.), bench press 232.5 kg (513 lb.) and dead lift 320 kg (706 lb.).

Allan Hallberg

Country:	New Zealand	
Sport:	Powerlifting	
Born:	28 March 1955	
1983 stats:		
Height:	189 cm	(6' 2½")
Weight:	122.2 kg	(19 st. 3 lb./269 lb.)

Hallberg's sporting career began at the age of twelve on joining Leith Harriers and AA Club. He broke the Otago record in his first competition and has won provincial titles for shot and discus in addition to setting records in the shot. He won the national shot title in 1982, was third in 1979 and 1983, and fourth in 1980.

He began weight training in 1978 and entered his first powerlifting competition a fortnight later, totalling 475kg (1,047 lb.)—"Nothing sensational, but it hooked me on weights." He has competed nationally since 1979 and attained the following results: 1979 third 110 kg (247½ lb.) class; 1980 and 1981 first over 110 kg (275½ lb.) class; 1982,

1983 first 125 kg class. He held national records for squat 302.5 kg (667 lb.), dead lift 320 kg (706 lb.) and total 792.5 kg (1,747 lb.) plus all provincial records for 125 kg. He competed for New Zealand against Australia in 1981 and took second place.

George Hechter

Country:	United States
Sport:	Powerlifting
Born:	14 August 1961
	Baltimore, Maryland, USA
1985 stats:	
Height:	180 cm (5'11")
Weight:	155 kg (24 st. 6 lb./342 lb.)
Chest:	152 cm (60")
Waist:	112 cm (44")
Biceps:	53 cm (21")
Thigh:	86 cm (34")

Like Cees de Vreugd, Hechter went to Cascais, Portugal direct from the World Powerlifting Championships in Helsinki in order to compete in the 1985 World's Strongest Man event. De Vreugd and Hechter were in opposition in the superheavy class (over 125 kg/275½ lb.).

Born in Baltimore, Maryland, at high school he played American football and took part "with fair success," he says, in wrestling and gymnastics. He began lifting weights in 1978 as part of conditioning training, became hooked and started powerlifting seriously the following year, after he graduated. Two years later he became the American teenage champion in the superheavy class, and went on to win the US YMCA title in 1982 and 1983. He collected the world junior crown at Perth, Australia in 1984; in 1985, in successive months, he won US national and US senior titles, the latter event being open to previous winners of national championships.

His best competition lifts are: squat 442 kg (974 lb.), bench press 265 kg (584 lb.), dead lift 372 kg (820 lb.), best total 1,074 kg (2,368 lb.).

Lars Hedlund

Country:	Sweden
Sport:	Powerlifting
Height:	192 cm (6'3")
Weight:	145 kg (22 st. 12 lb./320 lb.)

Scandinavian strongmen have been highly respected for more than 100 years, professionals such as August Johnson, Caspari, Hjalmar Lundin, Adolph and Joe Nordquest coming readily to mind. Lars Hedlund of Sweden is of much more recent vintage, and he was one of the first foreign TV strength athletes to be invited to the American competition World's Strongest Man.

As a youth he became known as a competent shot-putter, hammer and discus thrower. He enjoyed weight training and turned to Olympic lifting, smashing 64 junior records before taking up powerlifting in 1969. He soon became well-known to hardcore enthusiasts, but it was eight years later before he became an international star, competing in the 1977 world championships in Perth, Australia.

Hedlund's official lifts include (lb.):

1977:	SQ 639	BP 573	DL 705
1978:	727	600	717
1979:	837½	600	683
1980:	903	629 WR	793

During this time his training was interrupted for military service. He became army shot-put champion and was also given leave to compete in the World's Strongest Man competition of 1980. This same year he badly injured the quadriceps of both legs while squatting with 380 kg (837 lb.) in the Nordic championships.

The bench press was his best lift, and Lars did ten repetitions with 272.4 kg (600 lb.), six reps with 300 kg (660 lb.), and a single with 318 kg (700 lb.). The last two feats were without a significant pause at the chest, he simply touched and pressed.

In World's Strongest Man competitions the big Swede placed third in 1978, second in 1979 and second again in 1980. On each occasion this superbly built athlete made a very good impression.

Manfred Hoeberl

Country:	Austria
Sport:	Bodybuilding
Born:	12 May 1964
	Graz, Austria
Resides:	Munich, Germany
1994 stats:	
Height:	194 cm (6' 4½")
Weight:	135 kg (21 st. 4 lb./298 lb.)
Chest:	145 cm (57")
Waist:	105 cm (41")
Biceps:	63 cm (25")
Thigh:	82 cm (32")

Manfred Hoeberl had developed the biggest muscular arms in the world; they were larger than the waist of many women, and he was not afraid to have them measured. At the Mr. Olympic competition on 10 September 1994, Joe Roark, respected journalist and historian, measured Manfred backstage and onstage. He recorded the following: wrist 8.37" (21.3 cm); forearm straight 16" (40.6 cm); gooseneck (right-angled) 17.5" (44.5 cm); upper arm 25.75" (65.4 cm)—*cold*; after five repetitions in the one-arm curl with a 150 lb. dumbbell 26" (66 cm). He also showed

Manfred's arm to be wider than two Pepsi cans placed one on top of the other, standing 9.25" (23.5 cm) tall.

Immediately after the World's Strongest Man in Tenerife, 1991, I wrote an article about this young Austrian, who went to Munich, Germany, learned to speak good English, wanted to get into films and is a really nice guy. It sounds like a resumé of Arnold Schwarzenegger and the subject of my article did seem to be following in Arnold's footsteps:

"The name will not ring a bell just yet," I wrote, "but mark my words this man is destined for greatness. At 6' 4", he makes an immediate impact with his broad shoulders and his unusual mode of dress, which usually allows him to reveal a pair of 24-inch arms! Yes, 24 in., 61 cm, no misprint.

"As if this isn't enough the man is fantastically strong, having caused a sensation on Austrian TV by overturning ten cars, each 1,874 lb., in 3½ minutes. Manfred's feats earned him a place in the World's Strongest Man competition and he is sure to gain a lot of new fans as a result." This was Manfred's first major international exposure and he certainly lived up to my expectations.

He grew up with the exploits and rise to fame of Arnold Schwarzenegger ringing in his ears but was quick to dispel any desire to trade on the accomplishments of his illustrious townsman. Hoeberl's supporters pointed out that their hero was taller, had bigger muscles and was stronger than Schwarzenegger, but Manfred shunned comparisons, preferring to be assessed on his own personal merits and accomplishments.

As a very young man he participated in a few competitions, winning the Mr. Bavaria title, but at the same time he was a fine all-round strength athlete, having done a

Manfred Hoeberl.

250 kg (551 lb.) bench press, 360 kg (794 lb.) squat and a 320 kg (705 lb.) dead lift.

Few competitors do well in their first WSM competition, and Manfred was no exception. He suffered a back injury, and while he was not selected for the 1992 competition, Douglas Edmunds and I were convinced of his merits and invited him to major shows in Scotland. We felt he needed some experience of the big time contests, and make no mistake, such experience is important. His log lift of 150 kg (331 lb.) was miles ahead of most strongmen, but others at national level could equal or beat that. Hoeberl is far travelled and won the loading event in an important South African competition with 75 kg (165 lb.) objects. He showed a good turn of speed, although the 90 kg (198½ lb.) and 100 kg (220½ lb.) used in European and world-class events tested his back, legs and lungs a good deal more.

Apart from Manfred's enormous potential we saw in him considerable panache, which was sure to make him a great crowd puller. His happy disposition and relaxed company made him a welcome entry wherever he went, and the media welcomed him with open arms. The good-looking Austrian would throw double biceps and other poses for the cameras and sign autographs patiently for the fans, yet remain modest and relatively quiet when off the platform, belying his swashbuckling appearance.

This dashing image can partly be attributed to the bandanna which he always wears—travelling, competing, eating and socializing, and it has become quite a trademark. On very informal occasions he sometimes favours ripped jeans, and invariably those huge biceps are bursting from his sleeves. This mind-boggling display of muscularity immediately warns his opponents that he is "armed" and dangerous. Some jealous bodybuilders started a rumour that Manfred's muscles were synthetic, hinting at implants, a suggestion which has been treated with hilarity by those who have seen how well these muscles function in competitions. Silicone would never impart such raw power as he displayed.

Hoeberl has set world records in several events, including a single-hand throw of 18 feet with the 56 lb. weight for height, and he remains unbeaten in two-handed throwing of weights over the Trojan Wall. In a closely contested battle throughout the competition, Manfred came second to Magnus Ver Magnusson in the World's Strongest Man, 1994. The popular Austrian has won European and World Muscle Power championships, and a book has been written about him and his training methods; he has also appeared in many TV shows and films.

Sadly, after having come so close to victory in the 1994 WSM competition, his career in strength competitions would appear to be over. He was involved in a horrendous car accident in which he broke limbs in addition to fracturing his hip in eight places. Manfred's 84-page book, *10 Minutes To Massive Arms,* has enjoyed great sales, the many photographs being particularly popular.

Nathan Jones

Country: Australia
Sport: Pro strongman
Born: 21 August 1969
Resides: Gold Coast, Queensland
1995 stats:
Height: 208 cm (6' 10")
Weight: 155 kg (24 st. 5 lb./341 lb.)
Chest: 145 cm (57")
Biceps: 56 cm (22")
Thigh: 82 cm (32")

Universally known as "Megaman," Nathan began lifting weights in 1988. He soon broke junior Australian records in the bench press (210 kg/463 lb.) and dead lift (315 kg/694 lb.), but youthful follies on the wrong side of the law put him out of competition for some time. In 1994 he made his debut as a strongman on the Scottish circuit and had a convincing win in the worldwide strength competition in Callander against tough international opposition, including Gary Taylor, Torvi Olafsson, Wayne Price, Joe Onasai, Phil Martin, Colin Cox and Canadian Chuck Hasse. It was a most impressive start to his new career.

The next big event in that first season was the World Muscle Power championships and again he was a superb competitor, highly popular with the huge crowd. Magnus Magnusson won but Megaman was close behind. On then to the Bahamas for the World's Strongest Man event and, as described in the competition report, Nathan suffered a very bad spiral fracture of the arm in his bout with Samuelsson of Sweden, a specialist and champion in arm wrestling. Jones took it very philosophically: "It has happened, and there is nothing else I can do," but he promised he would be back the next year and would be all out to win.

Svend Karlsen

Born: 6 October 1967
Norway
Sport: Bodybuilding, gym owner
1996 stats:
Height: 188 cm (6' 2")
Weight: 145 kg (22 st. 12 lb./320 lb.)
Chest: 155 cm (61")
Biceps: 58 cm (23")

Karlsen was junior world record holder in the dead lift and won several bodybuilding titles before selection for the 1996 WSM. An outdoor enthusiast, he enjoys walking his dogs, hunting and fishing.

Bill Kazmaier

Country:	USA
Sport:	Pro strongman
Born:	30 December 1953
	Wisconsin, USA
Resides:	Auburn, Alabama
1990 stats:	
Height:	191 cm (6'3")
Weight:	146 kg (23 st./322 lb.)
Chest:	142 cm (56")
Waist:	101 cm (40")
Biceps:	53 cm (21")
Thigh:	81 cm (32")

It is my considered opinion that Bill Kazmaier is the greatest American strength athlete ever known. Let me be quite specific: In reviewing amateurs in weightlifting, powerlifting, field events, stage and circus professionals or modern TV competition strongmen, I vote Bill Kazmaier the best, not just of the United States but of the whole American continent, and certainly one of the best in the world as well. I do this with good reason, and I am totally aware that many American enthusiasts, perhaps most, name one comparatively modern favourite and one old-timer as being ahead of Kaz. I argue that the facts don't match up with their theories.

Kazmaier has a long record of being a *competition* strongman, facing the best from many parts of the world. He competed in world powerlifting championships, breaking world records in the process and winning the World's Strongest Man competition. He did not specialise in a few chosen feats at which he excelled, but travelled the world trying ethnic tests of strength and meeting all comers. He was sometimes beaten, but that's no disgrace in open competition; if he had stuck to structured, unofficial situations, with his own equipment, used under his own terms that would have been a completely different story. None of the former entertainers claiming to be the world's strongest man could equal Bill Kazmaier in all-round tests of strength.

Ever since the 1940s, I recorded immediately my impressions of the strongmen I met, and thanks to my friends Jan and Terry Todd, I met Bill Kazmaier *before* he had been featured in magazines or on TV. Here is what I wrote back in mid 1979 for a bodybuilding magazine. I met them at Prestwick Airport when they arrived from America, and their little group made a huge impression: "I could hardly believe my eyes. I had seen the world's greatest physiques as a Mr. Universe judge, and the world's top lifters for four decades, but there before my eyes was a human being who could outbulk the hulk, outmuscle Mr. Universe's and outlift world champions. The vast majority of readers will not have heard of Bill Kazmaier, but mark my words, before long his name will become famous, and I want you to remember who first turned the spotlight on this amazing physical specimen. First a physique profile, height 6' 2", weight 320 lb., chest 60" and waist a mere 40" after a big meal." (It was hard to find a time to measure him otherwise, as he ate quite a lot!)

We went to a High and Mighty shop for large menswear, and I saw him taped by disbelieving assistants who just couldn't find anything to fit such differentials between chest and waist. Bill's upper arms were 22" and forearms 17", the biggest muscular arms of that time. Thighs stretched the tape to 32" and calves were 20.5". Glasgow wit was much in evidence, and one guy said, "Those are not calves, they are cows!" One Scots lassie pointed out his thighs were the same as her bust measurement. To round off this statistical review, we found his neck was too large for a 22" collar, the largest in the store. The good news was that we found a tie to fit him. The bad news was that he never wore a tie.

Bill Kazmaier.

There were many things that measurements alone did not reveal. I had never seen such density of muscle. He seemed to have muscles in places that other people didn't have places. The normally flattish muscles of the upper back, the lower portions of the trapezius, and the rhomboids were extremely thick and rounded, looking as though there were inches of thick layers of muscle. His hands were huge and in the palms, muscles as large as pigeons' eggs bulged when he brought his fingers and thumb together. Kazmaier's deltoids were the largest I had seen, and I swear you could set a teacup on his anterior deltoid and another on the posterior part of the muscle. The coraco-brachialis in his elbow was as large as some biceps, and his forearms seemed to insert well up the humerus.

So much for the physical appearance of the man—could he use these muscle to good effect? He certainly could. He had recently won the national powerlifting championship, and Prof. Todd hotly tipped him to become America's greatest powerlifter. Kaz proved him to be correct. On that visit to Scotland, I personally witnessed him set records in events he had never tried before. His first powerlifting contest was in November 1976, and he made phenomenal progress to beat the legendary and hitherto unbeatable Don Reinhoudt, the world record holder in the dead lift.

On his first visit to Scotland, we headed for Royal Deeside in the beautiful Highlands where for centuries the Stones of Dee have been a challenge for the most powerful of men. Of the various boulders, I targeted the *clach cuid fir* (manhood stone) at Inver for Kaz. To succeed with this, the stone has to be lifted waist high, preferably on to a wall or pillar so there is no doubt about the result. There was no doubt about Bill's lifts being high enough. He scorned using a wall and initially lifted it easily. He repeated the feat so I could take photographs, and this mighty man had his own ideas on how it should be lifted.

He was even more ambitious the second time; having taken it to his waist he muscled it up his body little by little until he had it resting on his chest. Breathing noisily, he gradually rotated his hands until they were comfortably under the stone, and slowly he push pressed the Inver Stone overhead until his arms were fully extended.

I wrote at the time that this would probably end the challenge of the manhood stone, for would any strongman wish to follow such an exhibition of raw power? I was wrong (again)! Bill's performance inspired other people and set new horizons. Some years later Highland games heavies Hamish Davidson and Francis Brebner duplicated the full lift, and some well-known Americans have tried their hands. Steve Jeck and Randy Strossen, the popular editor of *MILO* magazine, have lifted with distinction, the former taking the stone to his shoulders and the latter completing the traditional lift. IronMind Enterprises produced a fine illustrated T-shirt to commemorate the feat.

Next stop was the famous Braemar Gathering, the annual event attended by the Royal Family and up to 32,000 people. Bill entered most of the heavy events. He did well with the stones, had problems with the caber, and really came into his own in throwing the 56 lb. weight for height. There were 25,000 people there that day, and they cheered enthusiastically as his first efforts soared over the bar with several feet to spare.

Sensing something unusual, many spectators flocked to that part of the lovely arena set amongst heather-covered hills. Sure enough an extraordinary event developed, and as the bar gradually went higher, many top-line athletes had to admit defeat. Incidentally one of those seeing Bill for the first time was young, trim, fresh-faced Douglas Edmunds. For years the Braemar record had stood at 15 feet and Bill Kazmaier beat this with ease and went on to tackle the world record, held by Grant Anderson, Scottish weightlifting champion and Commonwealth Games medallist. The bar was raised to 16' 1", giving everyone cricks in their neck as they gazed up at the slender bar, which would fall at the slightest touch of the weight.

The bronzed American was equal to the task, and with a deep breath, a long strong pull and a final grunt of exertion, he projected the missile upwards to cross the bar with inches to spare. The roar of the spectators echoed through the great glen, drowning the skirl of the bagpipes and startling the stags grazing on the nearby mountain tops.

Bill was quietly ecstatic and an hour later as Terry, Jan, Bill and I bathed in the tumbling river overlooking the valley, he told me he would never forget the experience. In later years and in many countries, I have noted that when Bill is ready to psych up, he blocks out distractions by putting on his walkman and plays his favourite "battle music" from the soul stirring, adrenalin producing bagpipes. It is the same music which the clansmen used in days of old and, sadly, the great music which spurred on thousands of Scottish soldiers to their gallant deaths on the Western Front (1914-1918). The Germans called these fearless, kilted men "the ladies from Hell," such was the effect of the bagpipes, and Bill Kazmaier used it to his advantage. If you have seen Kaz compete you may have seen him use the walkman and noticed his Highlander T-shirt with the slogan "There can be only one."

He has told me many wonderful stories which illustrate his competitive instincts, and I have witnessed some amazing things in his company. Bill recalled as a

Bill Kazmaier.

young man being short of funds and entering the World Goldfish Eating championship, for which there was a cash prize as well as the title. The fish were live and swimming about in bowls as the competitors lined up at the tables. On the signal, his rivals picked up fish singly and holding them by the tails, dropped them into their mouths. Not our Bill. He had his own approach, for he badly wanted the prize. He lifted a bowl at a time, with many fish in each, and draining off the water through his fingers he gulped down the goldfish in huge mouthfuls, swallowing them so fast they hardly touched the sides of his throat!

Statistics show that he swallowed an all-time record of 1,000 goldfish, 500 more than his nearest rival that day. In addition to his substantial cash prize, they gave him a tank of goldfish, but I am certainly not going to tell you what he did with them. He is a naturally quiet man but is not slow to speak his mind emphatically when the situation warrants it.

I recall an incident in an airport lounge on a trip to Africa. Bill joined colleagues at a table, and because the chairs had been filled, he pulled over a bar stool and went to get drinks. A waiter put the stool back when Bill was at the bar. Bill returned and looked a bit puzzled as he regained the stool. To the amusement of the group, every time Bill rose for a drink, to phone or go to the toilet, the waiter quickly took the stool back to the bar. Eventually an exasperated Bill quietly snarled at the man, "Move this seat again and I will take your arm off and beat you to death with it!" After that the waiter kept his distance.

Kaz won the 1979 world powerlifting championship in Dayton, Ohio with a 1,041 kg total (2,293 lb.). In the process he benched a new world record 282 kg (622 lb.), and although he improved on this, he could have gone a great deal further had it not been for an anterior deltoid/pectoral injury sustained in bar bending. He tried a world record in the dead lift that day and missed, but he made no mistake on that African trip in 1981.

Doug Edmunds had been living in Africa and pining for his old pals and heroes, so he organised Lagos Highland Games. Part of the proceedings was a world record attempt on the dead lift by Bill Kazmaier. The American had recently broken the world record with 402.5 kg (886° lb.) and was confident of more. Unfortunately the only bar big Doug could muster was a horrible, rusty, slightly bent 1-inch plain bar without sleeves. I would not have had it as a training bar let alone for a record attempt. Some of the discs were home-made, and all of them were thin, making them wobbly, not a flanged plate amongst them.

There were some 4,500 people watching as Bill elected to warm up with 300 lb. He then did 202, 263, 322 and 368 kg (445, 580, 710 and 810 lb.). These were done very easily, but the lousy bar put paid to his hopes of a record. Instead he asked that all the weights be loaded and he would attempt this wearing handstraps. The weight was given as 415 kg (914 lb.), but for the sake of accuracy, my count of the discs from my announcing position made it approximately 404 kg (890 lb.). I could have been wrong of course, but the idea was to go beyond the world record and he did; he lifted it in good style. Bearing in mind the humidity, lack of acclimatization and the impoverished equipment, it was a superb demonstration. I believe the only men ever to better Kazmaier's official dead lift record have been Doyle Kenady with 410 kg (903 lb.) in 1986 and Gary Heisey with 420 kg (925 lb.) in 1992. I believe our big pal O.D. Wilson may have broken the 900 lb. barrier but not officially or in competition.

We all celebrated after the games. Some big money had been won, and the boys were in good spirits as they met the sponsors. One guest however was a bit of a nuisance, bothering the competitors to lift him and his wife for photographs. He had not been a sponsor but having seen the publicity and goodwill generated for these generous benefactors, he now wanted a slice of the action. "Let's have an arm wrestling competition for $500," he suggested. "Buzz off," was the gist of the reply from the tired but happy strongmen, unwilling to put their arms at risk.

"Each of you lift me up, and I will give a prize to the best," was his next idea. Bill felt that the timing was bad and said later that this sort of thing was a prostitution of his talents. Noticing an electric fan whirling overhead and circulating a cooling breeze, he addressed the annoying tormentor, "OK, man, I don't want your money but I'll tell you what I will do," he explained in a gentle voice, "I will lift you overhead with one hand . . ." he paused, moving his face closer to the provoker, and his eyes took on that steely look reserved for special occasions, "I will lift you right up . . . *and put your nuts in the fan!*"

The pest paled as he shrunk away and missed Bill's wink to the folks round the table, and the party proceeded pleasantly.

Bill Kazmaier and Jon Pall Sigmarsson disagreed about many things, notably on who was the World's Strongest Man, but until 1990 they shared a unique distinction: Each had won the title three times. Kaz was the conqueror in 1980, 1981 and 1982; Jon Pall provided an irresistible Viking assault in 1984, 1986 and 1988, when they met in the event for the first time. In 1990, however, Jon Pall went one up on Kazmaier and won the event for the fourth time. Bill was seriously injured at the 1981 World's Strongest Man competition, and if examined closely a gap in his huge chest muscles can be seen.

Bill was the football hero at Burlington High School, Wisconsin Southern Lakes and won a sports scholarship at the University of Wisconsin 1973-74, where he starred as a fullback. Then Bill discovered weights and decided to become supremo with them, an ambition he achieved at the age of twenty-five in 1979. That year he won the American powerlifting championships in Mississippi, lifting 280 kg (617 lb.) for his first American record, and as already mentioned, at the world championships the same year, he won the super-heavyweight class and set a new world record bench press.

In the intervening years he had toughened up as an oil rig roughneck, strip club bouncer and lumberjack in Alaska. Although he suffered a serious quadriceps injury, he still retained his title in 1980 and increased the world bench press to 287 kg (633 lb.). Then he increased this slowly until in 1983 he again took the title when he broke the 300 kg barrier (661 lb.). He also set world records for the dead lift 410 kg (904 lb.) and combined total for the three lifts of 1,100 kg (2,425 lb.). His best squat was 420 kg (926 lb.). These achievements gave his motto "Conceive, believe, achieve" further credibility. Through cooperation with Auburn University's National Strength Research Centre, he has become probably the most scientifically evaluated strength athlete.

He made a brief return to football full-time in 1985, but turned down contract offers from the Green Bay Packers and Jacksonville. As previously mentioned, he was introduced to Highland Games by me and went to Braemar and broke the world record in throwing the weight for height in his very first games. He later increased this at the Lagos Highland Games. He also broke the world record at Airth Games and for this won himself a car! An additional feat of strength is his ability to hold a 56 lb. (25 kg) weight sideways on his pinky.

A formidable athlete with a highly explosive temperament, Kazmaier has described himself as "the strongest man who ever lived."

Doyle Kenady

Country: USA
Sport: Powerlifting
Born: 29 August 1948
1983 stats:
Height: 178 cm (5'10")
Weight: 136 kg (21 st. 6 lb./300 lb.)

Doyle was a newcomer to Strongest Man competition in 1983, and he came to it with one of the most impressive powerlifting records in North America. He has won the world superheavy title twice (1978, 1980), world series (1979), world games (1981) and in 1983 he set a world record of 403.6 kg (890 lb.) for the dead lift. Other victories include the Hawaiian international (three times), senior national (1978, 1980) and the junior national.

One of the States' most highly rated teachers in the strength game, he was coach to the US men's team at the world championships in Sweden, 1983 and also coached the national women's team.

He entered competitive lifting after using weights to build himself for shot and discus at high school, where he also played fullback at American football. He began as an Olympic lifter, but from 1969 concentrated on powerlifting.

Ilkka Kinnunen

Country: Finland
Sport: Pro strongman
Born: 13 November 1964
       Joensuu, Finland
1992 stats:
Height: 190 cm (6'3")
Weight: 133 kg (20 st. 13 lb./293 lb.)

In 1983 Ilkka won the European Muscle Power championship and appears on the European *Gladiators* TV series as "Barbarian." His best powerlifts are: squat 310 kg (683 lb.), bench press 240 kg (529 lb.), dead lift 350 kg (772 lb.) and overall total 910 kg (2,006 lb.).

Riku Kiri

Country:	Finland
Sport:	Pro strongman
Born:	5 April 1963
	Kotka, Finland
Resides:	Helsinki
1993 stats:	
Height:	193 cm (6'4")
Weight:	145 kg (22 st. 12 lb./320 lb.)
Chest:	150 cm (59")
Waist:	101 cm (40")
Biceps:	54 cm (21")
Thigh:	80 cm (31½")

Riku Kiri was one of a long line of Finnish strength athletes selected for the World's Strongest Man competition. The many contests in his homeland have nurtured greats such as Ilkka Nummisto, Markku Suonenvirta and Ilkka Kinnunen, and in open competitions valuable prizes have attracted the cream of international competitors to Finland.

Kiri has been remarkably successful in beating off all opposition whether from home or abroad and finished third in the World's Strongest Man competitions

Riku Kiri.

From left, Gerrit Badenhorst (South Africa), Ilkka Kinnunen (Finland), and Berend Veneberg (The Netherlands) at World's Strongest Man in Orange, France, 1993.

of 1993 and 1994, having entered these competitions as one of the favourites. In the early part of the 1996 season he won every contest he entered, most notably Europe's Strongest Man and the World Grand Prix in a three competition tour of Lithuania. In the WSM of 1996 Riku started very strongly and looked a likely winner, but two injuries sustained during the contest took their toll, and he finished in second place.

Coming from a powerlifting background and security work, this professional strongman is particularly noted for his excellent bench press of 302.5 kg (667 lb.) and for the strength of his grip; he set the first world record in the Hercules Hold.

Rudi Küster

Country:	Germany	
Sport:	Weightlifting	
Born:	7 April 1955	
	Ellenberg, German Federal Republic	
1989 stats:		
Height:	188 cm	(6'2")
Weight:	130 kg	(20 st. 7 lb./287 lb.)
Chest:	130 cm	(51")
Waist:	110 cm	(43")
Biceps:	47 cm	(18½")
Thigh:	77 cm	(30")

Rudi made his Strongest Man bow at the European Strongest Man in Marken, Holland in 1984. He won his very first event, a similar one to the churn carry, and went on to finish an impressive second equal with the formidable Ab Wolders, just two points behind Geoff Capes. In the World's Strongest Man at Mora, Sweden four months later he took fourth place.

Küster has won eight German titles in weightlifting, three times as powerlifting champion and five times in the Olympic disciplines, in which he snatched 158 kg (348 lb.) and clean and jerked 210 kg (463 lb.). His best international results were as a powerlifter. He was gold medallist in the superheavy class at the 1988 European championships and runner-up in the world. He has also won silver and bronze medals at the European level.

His best lifts in powerlifting are: squat 380 kg (838 lb.), bench press 205 kg (452 lb.), dead lift 400 kg (882 lb.), combined lifts 967.5 kg (2,133 lb.).

Rudi has worked as a TV technician with the post office; away from weights his main leisure interest is electronics, and he has taught himself English with the aid of a minicomputer.

Curtis Leffler

Country:	Hawaii	
Sport:	Bodybuilding	
Born:	26 January 1962	
1995 stats:		
Height:	185 cm	(6'1")
Weight:	124 kg	(19˚ st./273 lb.)
Chest:	143 cm	(56")
Biceps:	54.5 cm	(21½")

World-class bodybuilder Curtis Leffler came straight from the 1995 national championships at the last minute to compete for the first time in the World's Strongest Man contest, held that year in the Bahamas. Although essentially a modest, quiet man, his sensational physique made him a high-profile contestant, and he was probably the most photographed man in the event. A fitness consultant, he practises what he preaches and has a well-balanced, high level of all-round physical fitness.

Pavel Lepik

Born:	13 March 1968	
Country:	Estonia	
Occupation:	Property manager	
Resides:	OK Falls, Vancouver, Canada	
1996 stats:		
Height:	191 cm	(6'3")
Weight:	132 kg	(20 st. 11 lb./219 lb.)
Chest:	135 cm	(53")
Biceps:	56 cm	(22")

Now known as Paul, rather than Pavel, this quiet man is one of the best powerlifters ever to compete in the World's Strongest Man. His exciting squatting competition, which he won against Magnus Ver Magnusson, Megaman Jones and other topliners, was one of the highlights of the qualifying heats of 1996.

Paul is married to Natasha, a lovely girl of Russian and Japanese descent, and they have a little son Paul.

William (Bill) Miles Lyndon

Country:	Australia	
Sport:	American football, powerlifting	
Born:	30 January 1964	
	Doncaster, Australia	
1993 stats:		
Height:	191 cm	(6'3")
Weight:	138 kg	(21 st. 10 lb./304 lb.)
Chest:	147 cm	(58")
Biceps:	53 cm	(21")

Bill made his debut as an international competitor in strength events in 1993. A keen all-round sportsman, he has participated in many individual and team sports, particularly enjoying American football, where he played for top Australian teams and in which he was twice voted "Player of the Year." Bill's robust play has also proved popular in the rugby league.

In his holistic approach to fitness, Bill Lyndon has a passion for healthy outdoor recreation and takes great pleasure in walking in the Australian bush, hence his nickname, "Koala Bill."

As a powerlifter, he has won three Australian national titles and a second in the wider-based Pacific championships. An indication of Bill Lyndon's strength can be judged from his best lifts: squat 350 kg (771½ lb.), bench press 235 kg (518 lb.), dead lift 350 kg (771½ lb.).

Tom Magee

Country:	*Canada*	
Sport:	*Wrestling, pro strongman*	
Born:	*1 July 1958*	
	Manitoba, Canada	
1985 stats:		
Height:	*194 cm*	*(6' 4½")*
Weight:	*125 kg*	*(19 st. 10 lb./276 lb.)*
Chest:	*121 cm*	*(48")*
Waist:	*86 cm*	*(34")*
Biceps:	*51 cm*	*(20")*
Thigh:	*71 cm*	*(28")*

Tom won the Défi Louis Cyr tournament in Quebec in 1984 and 1985, beating Jon Pall Sigmarsson into third place in 1985. He came second to Bill Kazmaier in the World's Strongest Man 1982 and fourth to Geoff Capes in 1983.

He won the world superheavy powerlifting championships in Munich in 1982 and was second in Calcutta in 1981. He was the first Canadian to total more than 2,000 lb. for the three powerlifts and held the title Canadian Champion of Champions in 1982. He has set twenty-three British Columbian records and also the British Columbian record for the clean and jerk in Olympic lifting.

Born in Manitoba, Magee has been successful at gymnastics, wrestling and track and field events at high school, before taking up lifting seriously. Other interests include swimming, diving, tennis, kick boxing and music. Tom came second in the 1980 North American tug-of-war championship. He became a professional wrestler on the western Canadian circuit and held the Mr. British Columbia title in bodybuilding in 1984.

He eventually left his home in Vancouver to go to California where he became an actor working in films and TV and starred in the documentary film *Man of Iron*.

Tom's best competition lifts are: squat 390 kg (860 lb.), bench press 260 kg (573 lb.), dead lift 367 kg (809 lb.), best total 1,011 kg (2,230 lb.).

Tom Magee.

Dusko Markovic

Country:	*Canada*	
Sport:	*Highland Games*	
Born:	*3 February 1956*	
	Tetovo, Yugoslavia	
Resides:	*Toronto, Canada*	
1986 stats:		
Height:	*189 cm*	*(6' 2½")*
Weight:	*127 kg*	*(20 st./280 lb.)*
Chest:	*137 cm*	*(54")*
Waist:	*96.5 cm*	*(38")*
Biceps:	*47 cm*	*(18½")*
Thigh:	*74 cm*	*(29")*

Barrel-chested Dusko Markovic, sometimes known as "Desperate Dan," charmed the big crowds at the 1986 World's Strongest Man in Nice, France, by greeting them with a cheerful *bonjour* and distributing handfuls of Toronto Police Department badges to his young admirers. He also collected fourth place, and the "Best Personality" award. Contracted to compete in Hungary in 1988, he had to pull out with a leg injury sustained while taking part in a Highland Games in Canada.

Born in Tetovo in the former Yugoslavia, Dusko now has Canadian nationality and has been a key member of Toronto's vice squad, working long stints as an undercover operator to break up the drug rings that plague that city. He has been awarded several recommendations. Colleagues call him "Mountain Man," when he grows a bushy black beard as disguise.

At high school in Canada he set records for discus and javelin. He played Canadian football for the collegiate champions and soccer for Scarborough Rangers. He became a powerlifter, and after enroling with the police in 1977, joined their tug-of-war team for five years. Turning his strength to professional Highland Games, he eventually took over from Dave Harrington as the sport's number one in Canada and represented his country in the World Series of Heavy Events and World Championships. In 1985 he set a world record in the farmer's walk, a similar event to the churn carry, by carrying two objects weighing 91 kg (200 lb.) each a distance of 130 m (427 ft.) at Keswick, Ontario.

Dusko's enormous chest was built mainly by the bench press, where he uses over 225 kg (496 lb.). He is indeed a formidable competitor and very friendly character.

Phil Martin

Country:	USA
Sport:	Highland Games
Born:	27 October 1964
Resides:	Modesto, California
1995 stats:	
Height:	196 cm (6'5")
Weight:	164 kg (25 st. 9 lb./362 lb.)
Chest:	147 cm (58")
Biceps:	52 cm (20½")

Working in the construction industry, and training for and competing in professional Highland Games have given Phil enormous strength. His athletic background has stood him in good stead in strength athletics, and in his first season, he reached the finals of the World's Strongest Man competition, placing third in the maritime medley, a loading event.

One of his first sporting passions was rock climbing, and he has some fantastic achievements in this sphere, having completed the very technical 2,800 ft. climb up the Royal Arches in the beautiful Yosemite National Park, California.

Phil Martin was a outstanding athlete in junior college football for two years and in 1985 was introduced to Highland Games by his strength coach, Bob McKay. Phil continued his other athletic interests, entering occasional Highland Games until 1992, when he began competing regularly. In 1993 he won the North American amateur championship and two armfuls of trophies at Santa Rosa and turned professional the following season. He won the US 56 lb. weight for height championship in 1994 and was the world's best in this event in the 1995 season, with 17-foot throws to his credit.

He is a modest man, not given to exaggeration, and makes no claims to being a great lifter. He does not enter powerlifting competitions, as his training plan for his two other sports is already overloaded. However his 1995 gym lifts show him to be extremely powerful: bench press 500 lb. x 3-5 reps; dead lifts 600 lb. x 2-3 reps; squat 750 lb. x 2; power clean 365 lb. single.

Phil acquired the nickname "Stonehenge" at the time of the California earthquake a few years before these lifts were made, but he is shy of speaking about this. The big man simply says its because he can't pass a boulder without throwing, lifting or unending it.

Stasys Mecius

Country:	Lithuania
Sport:	Weightlifting
Born:	31 August 1956
1995 stats:	
Height:	188 cm (6'2")
Weight:	120 kg (18 st. 12½ lb./264½ lb.)
Biceps:	51 cm (20")

Over the years Stasys Mecius aspired to represent the Soviet Union in Olympic weightlifting. He won the junior championships of the USSR and as a senior competitor won several Lithuanian championships. Turning to strongman competitions, he has won major events in his country and as national champion was selected for the World's Strongest Man of 1995 and 1996.

Although he is a little on the light side to compete successfully with the superheavyweights of today, Stasys is a very determined athlete and constantly surprises with his splendid feats.

Ilkka Nummisto

Country:	Finland
Sport:	Pro strongman
Born:	24 April 1944
	Turku, Finland
1992 stats:	
Height:	186 cm (6' 1")
Weight:	125 kg (19 st 10 lb./276 lb.)
Chest:	134 cm (52.8")
Waist:	110 cm (43")
Biceps:	54 cm (21")
Thigh:	69 cm (27")

Ilkka Nummisto has an unlikely pedigree for a strongman, weighing 125 kg (nearly 20 stones), as he made his sporting name in canoeing, one of Finland's most popular sports; he represented his country in four Olympic Games, achieving a fifth place, his best result, in 1968.

Twenty-four years later and a grandfather, he competed in the 1992 World's Strongest Man for the fifth time at the age of forty-eight and was still one of Finland's most popular sportsmen as a professional strongman and a director of Finland's Strongest Man Company. Indeed, his immense good humour, sportsmanship and all-out endeavour won him the "Best Personality" award at the World's Strongest Man in 1988, in Hungary, where he finished in fifth place.

The ageless Ilkka Nummisto, winner of Finland's Strongest Man.

He missed some events due to tearing his biceps at Nice in 1986, an injury that sidelined him for many months. Before his injury he had impressed everyone by becoming the first man ever to place the five Stones of Strength, weighing from 95 to 140 kg (210-309 lb.), on top of their respective barrels.

In 1990 he regained the Finland's Strongest Man title by dethroning his friend and coach, Markku Suonenvirta, in their home town, Turku, although both had to give best to a guest competitor, Bill Kazmaier. In the same year Ilkka took third place in the World's Strongest Man when it was held in Joensuu in his home country.

After his canoeing career, Ilkka turned to powerlifting and became Finnish champion for the superheavy class in 1981, 1983 and 1985, also taking the Nordic (Inter-Scandinavian) title in 1983. His best competition lifts are: squat 350 kg (772 lb.), bench press 250 kg (551 lb.), dead lift 367.5 kg (810 lb.), combined total 950 kg (2,094 lb.).

Pius Ochieng

Born:	25 July 1960
	Nairobi, Kenya
Resides:	Koya
1984 stats:	
Height:	169 cm (5' 6½")
Weight:	99 kg (15 st. 8 lb./218 lb.)
Chest:	122 cm (48")
Biceps:	50 cm (20")
Thigh:	68 cm (27")

One of the very few Africans to compete in such events, Pius was the smallest man ever to try for the World Strongest Man title. I was very surprised when he was selected in 1984, for as a strongman he was not in the same class as the Nigerians, Okonkwo, Ironbar Bassey or the great Orok. However, he was Kenya's outstanding lifter and had won six national titles on the Olympic set and broke four powerlifting records in two months. At that time he had just won the Oceanic championship in Tahiti, was silver medal winner in American Cup competition and tenth in the Olympic Games.

Jorma Ojanaho

Born:	23 February 1968
	Finland
Occupation:	Doorman
Resides:	Lohja
1996 stats:	
Height:	191 cm (6'3")
Weight:	135 kg (21 st. 4 lb./298 lb.)
Chest:	148 cm (58")
Biceps:	55 cm (22")

Winner of the hotly contested 1996 Finland's Strongest Man, Jorma reached the World's Strongest Man six months later. Before turning to such events, he was a competent powerlifter. Jorma's career began as a junior bodybuilding champion, and he has greatly improved his physique since then. He enjoys reading—his favourite author is Stephen King and he relaxes to the music of Led Zeppelin.

Chris Okonkwo

Country:	Nigeria
Sport:	Field events

Born: 16 November 1946
Aianbra, Lagos, Nigeria
1983 stats:
Height: 190 cm (6'3")
Weight: 127 kg (20 st./280 lb.)

In the early 1980s, Okonkwo was the undisputed long-term holder of the Nigerian shot put and national hammer records, with a best put of 21 m (69 ft.). He competed in the shot at the 1972 Munich Olympics and won the bronze medal in 1973 in the All-African championships. He also did some Olympic lifting, mainly as part of his field events build-up.

Chris twice represented Nigeria in World Highland Games Heavy Events Championships at Lagos, and also competed with success at Highland Games meetings in Scotland, where he reached the World Championships in 1982. Travelling by car on the last lap of his journey to this latter event, he was in a car crash but arrived just in time for the opening competition. Although he must have been badly shaken up, he did not say anything about the crash until after the event and in spite of jet lag and trauma, he performed well. He admired the unrelated Scottish Highland Games stars Bill and Grant Anderson so much that he named his son Anderson after them. Bill and Grant both, incidentally, competed in the first Britain's Strongest Man competition in 1979, Bill finishing runner-up to Geoff Capes. In 1983 Chris competed in the WSM competition in New Zealand, suffering a very upset stomach, which depleted his strength.

Chris worked for the Nigerian police and also as a sports coach. One of his country's most popular sportsmen, outside field events and weight training he enjoys playing tennis.

Heinz Ollesch

Country: Germany
Sport: German Stonelifting
Born: 27 November 1966
Resides: Bavaria, Germany
1994 stats:
Height: 190 cm (6'2")
Weight: 145 kg (22 st. 12 lb./320 lb.)
Chest: 150 cm (59")
Biceps: 56 cm (22")

Heinz Ollesch is famous in the world of strength for his abilities in the traditional stone lifting competitions of Bavaria. It was there 125 years ago that strongman competition became popular in beer gardens, the centres of social activity from Bavaria right across the Austrian border to Vienna. Hans Ollesch finds that even today, particularly during beer festivals, there is still great interest in various kinds of stone lifting.

This broad-shouldered athlete is very easygoing until he gets into the athletic arena—then he becomes a human dynamo, giving one hundred percent effort in every event. This was his undoing during the summer of 1994 when, having placed at the top of the main German events and home internationals, he plied his trade overseas with the best in the world. His all-out approach, throwing caution to the wind, resulted in a calf injury which hindered him considerably in the tests involving running and carrying. Nevertheless he continued competing, without any cancellations, and his dogged determination was not overlooked by fellow competitors and fans who supported him every inch of the way. In 1994 and 1995 Heinz competed in the World Muscle Power championships and the World's Strongest Man contest; he placed fourth in WSM of 1995, second in Europe's Strongest Man 1996 and second in the 1996 World Grand Prix in Lithuania.

His knowledge of the English language is improving rapidly for, as in sport, Heinz Ollesch is a real trier.

Heinz Ollesch.

Joe Onasai.

Joe Onasai

Country:	Samoa
Sport:	Powerlifting
Born:	10 December 1965
	Seetage, Samoa
Resides:	Honolulu, Hawaii
1994 stats:	
Height:	194 cm (6' 4½")
Weight:	161 kg (25 st. 5 lb./355 lb.)
Chest:	143 cm (56")
Biceps:	57 cm (22½")
Thigh:	84 cm (33")

Ordained as a high chief of his mother's native village in Western Samoa, Joe Onasai's name as chief is "Amituana'i."

In Hawaii, Joe is better known for his football talents than his powerlifting, although he won two national championships of the American Drug Free Powerlifting Association. He was the biggest man in the 1994 World's Strongest Man, in which he won the sumo wrestling event. In 1995 at 174 kg (384 lb.) he was even more muscular and heavy. Joe, a very popular personality, has some big lifts to his credit, including a 370 kg (815 lb.) squat, 260 kg (573 lb.) bench press, and a 322 kg (710 lb.) dead lift.

In his senior year at college he was nominated Offensive Player of the Year and was team captain of the side winning the State Football Championship. He was enroled with the University of Hawaii's Rainbow Warrior Football Team and then played for the Dallas Cowboys in the National League. It was while he was playing with the Cowboys that he sustained a career-ending neck injury.

This accident left him paralysed from the waist up, and it took two years before he was fully recovered and able to participate once again in sporting activities. Regaining his strength via powerlifting, he found he had a natural aptitude and soared to the top, winning his first national title in his third major contest!

Both his father and mother come from royal lineages in the islands of Samoa and as a result of cultural custom, Joe has an extensive tattoo from waist to knees, and additional ones on his arms. His tattoo was done in the traditional manner by a skilled master tattooist, who used a specially designed hammer and sharpened boar tusks dipped in ink. It took ten days prior to his ordination as high chief to complete the whole painful process, and only then could the ceremony take place. Joe performed brilliantly in the WSM heats and placed ninth in the finals.

Joe married his high school sweetheart Ann. "She is my best friend and has given me unbelievable support," said Joe Onasai. They have three beautiful daughters, Tali, Careena and Shayna.

Ted van der Parre

Country:	The Netherlands
Sport:	Pro strongman
Born:	21 September 1955
	Amsterdam, Holland
1992 stats:	
Height:	213 cm (7')
Weight:	157 kg (24 st. 10 lb./346 lb.)
Chest:	145 cm (57")
Waist:	120 cm (47")
Biceps:	55 cm (22")
Thigh:	75 cm (30")

Ted, the popular Dutch giant, won the World's Strongest Man title in 1992. Formerly an American football player for the Hague Raiders, in the two years he played with the team he proved to be a formidable defender. During his training stints with the footballers it became clear that Ted was ideally suited to strength sports, and some minor contests soon indicated he had a great future as a competitive strongman.

Ted van der Parre won the Netherlands' Strongest Man titles in 1991 and again in 1992. After taking the latter national championship with a comfortable five point margin he went on to beat a tough line-up in Iceland and became the first Dutchman to win the world title. The competition in the "land of ice and fire" was featured worldwide on TV. Ted's success in this toughest of events paved the way for him to give up his job as a market gardener and become a full-time strength athlete.

Unfortunately a troublesome knee injury greatly hampered him in the 1993 season, but in 1994 he regained the Dutch title and was in good shape when the world's strongest men assembled in Sun City, South Africa. Ted made his way through the heats to the final but his suspect limb let him down again and he finished in plaster from toe to knee.

Ted speaks excellent English and is a very friendly, happy character, popular with the public, press, organisers and competitors.

Ted van der Parre.

Ken Patera

Country: USA
Sport: Pro wrestling
Born: 7 November 1944
Portland, Oregon, USA
Resides: Minnesota
1972 stats:
Height: 187 cm (6' 1¾")
Weight: 154 kg (24 st. 4 lb./340 lb.)
Chest: 149 cm (58¾")
Waist: 120 cm (47")
Biceps: 54.5 cm (21½") arm straight
Thigh: 89 cm (35")
Calf: 56 cm (22")

This awesome athlete was one of the best weightlifters America has ever produced, and he helped restore the pride of the United States team in international weightlifting. However he was not just a weightlifter, he was an exceptional all-rounder—world-class shot-putter, award winning wrestler, footballer and competent basketball player.

In spite of an injured back, Ken came third in the first World's Strongest Man competition back in 1977, although through an early mistake Lou Ferrigno's name went into many of the record books; Lou actually came fourth.

A superb high school and college athlete, Ken Patera was a candidate for a shot-putting place in the Olympic team of 1968, with over 64 ft. to his credit in official meets. His lifetime best competition put was just one-half inch off 66 ft. Bruce Wilhelm, the first TV WSM thought Ken was probably the world's strongest man of the late sixties and early seventies. Ken was second in the World Weightlifting Championships of 1971 and qualified for the Munich Olympics, pressing 229.5 kg (505½ lb.), snatching 176 kg (387½ lb.) and clean and jerking 229.5 kg (505½ lb.). This 635 kg (1,398½ lb.) total made him a hot tip for the gold medal at Munich.

Unfortunately for Ken, the vociferous German crowd was solidly behind young Rudolph Mang, and representing the USSR was Vasily Alexeev, one of the all-time greats. I was there in person and can confirm there were much greater stresses; indeed I vowed I would never go back to another Olympic Games and I have kept that promise. It was here that terrorists slaughtered innocent wrestlers and weightlifters in a murderous attack, one of the Israeli team being an American, David Berger. Believe me, nobody was left unmoved. Like everybody else, tough weightlifters wept when the news of the massacre swept through the Olympic village. There was an atmosphere

Ken Patera.

of doom and gloom affecting everything, not just performances. The superheavy competition had to be rescheduled, and Ken Patera was only one of those who did not meet previous expectations, bombing out on the snatch.

Perhaps in addition he had overtrained, and mistrained, for some of his lifting approaching the Games was absolutely phenomenal. For example in an excellent review of Patera's career (quite the best I have seen on this lifter), Bruce Wilhelm told how Ken had rack jerked 245 kg (540 lb.) seven or eight times before the competition *and missed a 167.6 kg (369¼ lb.) snatch 13 times in one session.*

Turning to professional wrestling, dying his hair blonde and completely changing his image, Ken Patera was nominated the Recruit of the Year and became one of the biggest attractions in this multi-million dollar business.

There was a downside, which maybe should be forgotten, but I have sometimes been accused of only glorifying strongmen and not always telling the full story.

According to newspaper reports in 1985, late one night after a bout, Patera and Mesanori Saito, his tag team partner, went to a McDonald's restaurant to eat. It was closed and the employee inside refused to let them in. Patera, with some choice words, threw a 10 kg rock through the window. Later police went to the motel where they were staying, and Saito answered the door. He told them to go away, but not exactly in those words, and threatened them. Patera then got into the act, and Mike Royko reported, "Patera and Saito took turns lifting and throwing one of the cops against the wall," going on to describe a knee drop and a horrific catalogue of injuries. The other cop sprayed Saito with a can of mace; "Saito just smiled and bashed him," wrote Royko. This policeman ended up with a broken leg, broken ribs and broken teeth. He pulled a gun, and Patera calmed down when other cops arrived, but Saito had to be clubbed.

Ken Patera paid his debt to society and went back to the hard life of worldwide pro wrestling with renewed success as a villain. On retiring he settled down and invested his earnings in Patera's Fitness Emporium in St. Paul, Minnesota, where he is in his element and much sought after for his advice on all related topics.

James Perry

Country:	USA	
Sport:	Powerlifting	
Born:	23 October 1961	
	Warren County, North Carolina	
1992 stats:		
Height:	183 cm	(6')
Weight:	196 kg	(29 st. 6 lb./412 lb.)
Chest:	160 cm	(63")
Waist:	140 cm	(55")
Biceps:	63.5 cm	(25")
Thigh:	86 cm	(34")

Weighing in at 196 kg (29½ st.), Perry was one of the heaviest men ever to enter the World's Strongest Man contest, and in the 1992 event he did so in memory of his training partner and close friend, fellow North Carolina giant, O.D. Wilson. They met in the summer of 1989 in Durham while using the same gym for weight training. It was a year after O.D. had taken the US national and world superheavy powerlifting titles, a feat James was to emulate for the Natural (drug-free) Athletes Strength Association in 1992.

Perry became hooked on the World's Strongest Man concept and vowed to earn selection. O.D.'s death in 1991 redoubled Perry's resolution, and he earned his invitation to the 1992 World's Strongest Man contest in Iceland with those national and world titles, in Maryland and Oklahoma respectively. "This will be for O.D.", he said when accepting.

James began his sporting career playing American football at college as a tackler and was three years team captain and the leading tackler in North Carolina. Two years in semi-professional ranks followed.

At the age of twenty-eight he switched to powerlifting, setting North Carolina records in his first year. He has set world records and his best performances are: squat 420 kg (926 lb), bench press 274 kg (604 lb.), dead lift 351.5 kg (775 lb.), best competition total 1,029 kg (2,269 lb.). He has recorded 465 kg (1,025 lb.) for the triple squat (repetitions) and pressed 204 kg (450 lb.) overhead.

Bill Pittuck

Country:	England
Sport:	Strength athletics
Born:	13 July 1963
Resides:	Northampton
1995 stats:	
Height:	180 cm (5'11")
Weight:	133 kg (20 st 13 lb./293 lb.)
Chest:	147 cm (58")
Biceps:	52 cm (20°")

One of the most experienced pro strongmen, Bill competed in many important contests for five years before finally being selected for the main TV event. His first experience at the WSM was in Finland, 1990 when he coached Britain's representative, Adrian Smith. He promised to come back in his own right and after winning two British titles to his credit, he received the coveted invitation. Coming from a country where the competition is very keen, he felt it was a great honour and he repaid this with 100% effort in difficult climatic conditions in 1995. Bill represented England again in 1996.

Evgeny Popov

Born:	28 June 1955
	Pernik, Bulgaria
Sport:	Strength athlete
Occupation:	Bank security manager
Resides:	Sofia
1996 stats:	
Height:	193 cm (6'4")
Weight:	150 kg (23 st. 9 lb./331 lb.)
Chest:	140 cm (55")

With a university degree in mechanical engineering technology, Evgueniy Stefanov Popov, to give him his full and correct name, is a brainy and brawny Bulgarian sports hero. After being an age group champion and Balkan champion in the shot put, he trained more with weights and became a world-class competitor in Olympic lifting, then powerlifting then changed after twenty years at the top, to strongman events.

A very precise man, he will tell you be began weightlifting on 10 January 1975 and eventually became second in European and in world championships and mounted the victors' rostrum along with lifters like Rakmanov of Russia and Gerd Bonk of Germany. Coached by the great coach Abadjev, for some time he lived in full-time training camps with full financial insurance and profound medical, physical and psychological monitoring. Shortly before the Moscow Olympics he was only 3 kg below the world record held by Alexeev of Russia.

Twenty-six days before the competition he was selected for the Games, and it was during a maximal training session when he was doing two repetition snatches with 195 kg, he lost control, badly sprained his shoulder and broke a piece off his scapula. His motivation was such that he still participated, wearing a plaster "corset," and saw medals won with less than he had been doing in the gym. He gave up this form of lifting because of the politics surrounding the 1984 Olympic boycott.

He began powerlifting in 1990 and has never had a powerlifting bar nor championship contenders as training partners. Eventually he ranked second in the world in the dead lift. Mr. Popov has risen to the top against all the odds. In spite of his late start and the very difficult circumstances which now exist in Bulgaria, his performances at the World Muscle Power championships and the 1996 World's Strongest Man show why he has become such a legendary and respected figure in strength sports.

Daniel Poulin

Born:	14 August 1952
Country;	St. Simon, Quebec, Canada
Occupation:	Bulldozer operator
1984 stats:	
Height:	186 cm (6'1")
Weight:	114 kg (17 st. 13 lb./251 lb.)
Chest:	122 cm (48")
Biceps:	43 cm (17")
Thigh:	66 cm (26")

Poulin was an outstanding competitor in the Canadian Louis Cyr memorial competitions in the mid-1980s, but apart from arm wrestling which he won, he did not shine in the 1984 WSM.

A naturally strong individual, he kept in shape through hard work from dawn until dusk and did not do any systematic training. Daniel held the Canadian record for pushing a heavy laden wheelbarrow.

Wayne Price

Country:	South Africa
Sport:	Pro strongman, rugby
Born:	25 March 1967
	Benoni, Transvaal, South Africa

1994 stats:

Height:	190 cm	(6'3")
Weight:	144 kg	(22 st. 10 lb./318 lb.)
Chest:	140 cm	(55")
Biceps:	54 cm	(21")
Thigh:	80 cm	(31½")
Calf:	50 cm	(20")

Wayne was South Africa's most active international representative in the 1994 and 1995 seasons, making several trips which covered many thousands of miles. With successes in Scandinavia and on his various trips to Britain, he was selected for the World's Strongest Man competition in 1994 and 1995. In 1995 he made the finals and placed eighth.

Wayne has a quiet, but friendly personality and a ready smile. His sense of humour was apparent on one of his visits Scotland where kilts must be worn in Highland Games events. Wayne got a great reception when he lined up to compete wearing a kilt—with leopardskin spots!

Formerly a police detective fond of rugby football, he took up weight-training as assistance work for this demanding sport. Wayne found he liked lifting weights and devoted more time to this type of training, although he resisted pleas from his colleagues to take up powerlifting. Instead he turned to strongman events and won the Johannesburg Jamboree Strongman tournament of 1993 and placed second to Gerrit Badenhorst in the South African championship.

Now operating a gym in Pretoria, he is recognised as one of the strongest men in Africa and receives many invitations to overseas events, for in addition to showing great talent as a strength athlete, his fine sportsmanship and pleasant demeanour makes him an excellent ambassador for his country. One of his fellow athletes described him as "the number one gentleman on the professional strongman circuit."

He is particularly good in pulling events and has pulled a 101-ton Boeing 707 for 20 metres; he has also pulled an electric train unit weighing 96 tons.

Wayne Price.

Steve Pulcinella

Country:	USA
Sport:	Highland Games
Born:	19 October 1965
	Philadelphia, USA
Resides:	Swarthmore, Pennsylvania, USA

1994 stats:

Height:	186 cm	(6'1")
Weight:	137 kg	(21 st. 8 lb./302 lb.)
Chest:	142 cm	(56")
Biceps:	50 cm	(20")
Thigh:	72 cm	(28")

This imposing professional strongman is undefeated in such contests in the United States of America, and he also won the North American strongman championships held in Toronto, Canada. In 1993 Steve tested himself in ethnic strength events and was eager to meet in open competition with champions from other lands.

Appearing on the American circuit of Scottish Games, Steve still managed to find time for his work with the family printing business, where he is actively engaged on the sales side. The highlight of his career was in 1994 when he competed in the WSM in Sun City.

In the many competitive strength events he has entered, Steve has always done well in throwing for height, weight carrying, truck pulling, log lifting and loading. He competed in powerlifting some years ago, squatting and dead lifting over 317.5 kg (700 lb.), but prefers the more dynamic movements of Olympic lifting. With his experience and versatility, Steve Pulcinella has the attributes of a champion and will work hard to reach the top.

Flemming Rasmussen

Country:	Denmark
Sport:	Powerlifting
Born:	12 March 1968
1995 stats:	
Height:	197 cm (6'5")
Weight:	155 kg (24 st. 6 lb./342 lb.)
Chest:	115 cm (45")
Biceps:	55 cm (22")

After becoming Danish powerlifting champion of 1993-94, Flemming also succeeded to the title of Denmark's Strongest Man, previously won by Henrik Ravn and Henning Thorsen, who had competed with some success in world-class competitions. Flemming's best powerlifts to date have been bench press 250 kg (551 lb.), squat 320 kg (705½ lb.) and dead lift 330 kg (727½ lb.). A blacksmith by trade, he is a rough, tough contender for titles and has good all-round abilities which makes him a hard man to beat.

Flemming Rasmussen, left, and Henrik Ravn, above.

Henrik Ravn

Country:	Denmark
Sport:	Pro strongman
Born:	27 May 1968, Karup, Denmark
Resides:	Viborg, Denmark
1994 stats:	
Height:	182 cm (6')
Weight:	130 kg (20st 7lb/287lb)
Chest:	125 cm (49")
Waist:	85 cm (33½")
Biceps:	53 cm (21")
Thigh:	85 cm (33½")

Denmark's Strongest Man of 1993 and 1994, he took over the title from Henning Thorsen, the powerful Dane who excelled in past World's Strongest Man competitions. Henrik began training to reduce his waistline and found he enjoyed using heavy weights. He decided to take up powerlifting and in 1990, at his very first attempt, he won the Danish championships. Increasing his weight to 125 kg (276 lb.) he entered Denmark's Strongest Man competition and placed fourth.

Each year his placings in this contest improved, and finally in 1993 he won the title from Thorsen. With this fine achievement came the opportunity to represent his country in the World's Strongest Man competition, which was televised in Orange, France in 1993.

His successful debut in the big event, coupled with the successful defence of his national title, resulted in an invitation to the 1994 competition in Sun City. Henrik Ravn had greatly increased his bodyweight and power since the previous year and was very confident of a much improved position. He pointed to a 380 kg (838 lb.) dead lift as an indicator of his ability, and his coach was extremely pleased with Henrik's form in the closing stages of training for this big event. Unfortunately a deltoid injury caused him great pain in the Viking axe hold, and he had to retire from the competition.

Jamie Reeves

Country:	Great Britain
Sport:	Pro strongman
Born:	3 May 1962
	Sheffield, Yorkshire
Resides:	Sheffield
1992 stats:	
Height:	192 cm (6'3")
Weight:	145 kg (22 st. 12 lb./320 lb.)
Chest:	152 cm (60")
Waist:	106 cm (42")
Biceps:	56 cm (22")
Thigh:	79 cm (31")

The retirement of Geoff Capes, twice World's Strongest Man, after he finished runner-up to Sigmarsson in 1986, threatened a weakening of the future British challenge. Then the arrival of a massive colliery blacksmith's welder, to win a national competition organised by Capes and me, redressed the balance.

In his teens at the City School in his native Sheffield, Jamie Reeves had been a swimmer at county level, played soccer as centre forward and rugby as No. 8 for the side that won the under-fifteens Yorkshire championships.

The turning point in his sporting life came in 1982 when he watched Bill Kazmaier winning his third World's Strongest Man title on BBC TV. Jamie made that title his own aim and took up weights; four years later he became powerlifting's Yorkshire and North East champion in the superheavy class. His best competition lifts in powerlifting were: squat 362.5 kg (800 lb.), bench press 245 kg (540 lb.), dead lift 367.5 kg (810 lb.).

He exceeded these limits before rupturing the biceps tendons of both arms. One was torn in competition in a car turnover. I was at the other end of the temporary arena in George Square, Glasgow when it happened and, like others, I heard a distinct snap when he sustained the injury. The other rupture was while attempting an 384 kg (845 lb.) dead lift in training. After consulting his local hospital, he was rushed at speed to Glasgow where he had another operation similar to the previous one. This time it was the other arm.

He won Britain's Strongest Man, and was British Muscle Power Champion, first rising to fame by winning the Midlands Strongest Man in 1987 and East Britain's Strongest Man 1988. In 1988 he also achieved his first national win in John Smith's Trial of Strength, for which heats had been held in various parts of Britain in order to find a successor to Geoff Capes. After clinching the title, in an exhibition he broke Tom Topham's 274-year-old record by harness-lifting three huge beer barrels weighing a total of 845 kg (1,862 lb.). These performances gained him selection to represent Britain in the World's Strongest Man in Hungary where he finished a creditable third to Jon Pall Sigmarsson and Bill Kazmaier. Seeing the prospects as an international professional, Jamie gave up his coal pit job as a blacksmith and now competes worldwide but particularly in Scotland, Iceland, Finland and other Scandinavian countries.

Jamie Reeves.

In San Sebastian, 1989 he won the World's Strongest Man at the second attempt, having come third in 1988. Due to injury he missed the event for the next two years, but still participated by assisting with commentaries. Jamie returned to compete in Iceland in 1992, to land second equal with Magnus Ver Magnusson of Iceland, the previous year's winner.

Don Reinhoudt

Country: USA
Sport: Powerlifting
Born: 6 March 1945
Dunkirk, N.Y. State
Resides: Brockton, Massachusetts, USA
1977 stats:
Height: 192 cm (6' 3½")
Weight: 163-172.5 kg
(25 st-27 st. 2 lb./360-380 lb.)
Chest: 152 cm (60")
Neck: 55 cm (22")
Biceps: 58 cm (22¾")
Forearms: 47 cm (18½")
Thigh: 86 cm (34")

In 1977, powerlifters were claiming Donald Reinhoudt had taken over from Paul Anderson as the strongest man in the world. They pointed out that at his best, the much respected Paul Anderson was perhaps the strongest of his time but Paul was now forty-four years of age, and most Olympic lifters agreed that Vlasov, Zhabotinski and now the great Alexeev were more worthy claimants to that title. Reinhoudt was better than all of them and not just the strongest in the world, the strongest man of all time, claimed powerlifters.

Prof. Terry Todd, a great authority on strength sports, pointed out that the dead lift was the most basic and simple test of overall strength, and at that time nobody had done as much as Don. He had officially lifted 402 kg (885 lb.), and in November 1976, he pulled 410 kg (904 lb.) above knee high, coming close to completing the pull. Reinhoudt was four times world powerlifting champion (1973 until 1976) and held world records in the squat, dead lift and total.

He came into sport via basketball, football and athletics. In all of these he played to win and was in a winning varsity basketball team, an All Conference player in football, and put the 12 lb. shot (5.5 kg) 52' 6" (over 16 metres). This was without weight-training, which was still being discouraged in some badly informed academic circles. When he went to Parsons College in Iowa and was granted a track and field scholarship, things changed. There were now more enlightened coaches who introduced him to weight-training and he improved rapidly.

Don got hooked on weights and tried Olympic lifting but lacked a specialist coach to teach him good techniques. Nevertheless, he pressed 150 kg (330 lb.), snatched 113.5 kg (250 lb.) and clean and jerked 168 kg (370 lb.). Somewhere along the line he was coached by Larry Barnholth, who coached greats such as Pete George. At 112.6 kg (248 lb.), Reinhoudt competed in around six Olympic competitions, including the junior nationals of 1967.

Obtaining a degree in finance, Don was halted in his tracks when Cupid came along and he met the famous Cindy Wyatt, a world renowned strength athlete in her own right. Cindy majored in psychology and married Don in 1969 three years after they met. Cindy was national champion and international discus thrower and shot putter. She participated in the Pan-American Games and other notable events. Cindy also won accolades in Olympic lifting and could outlift many men of her own weight in the clean and jerk or powerlifts. She could squat 188, bench 102 and dead lift 175 kg (415, 225 and 385 lb.). Lifts like these earned her the American powerlifting championships in 1977-78. I make no apologies for introducing Cindy into this article, for Don and his statuesque and competent coach were a great, inseparable team throughout his lifting career. I well remember how she bewildered the officials and delighted fans when she alone handed Don weights close on 272 kg (600 lb.) for bench pressing!

In all Don Reinhoudt broke forty world powerlifting records. He was the first man ever to break the 2,400 lb. barrier (1,089.6 kg), and in 1975 he wiped out Jon Cole's total with 2,420 lb. (1,098.7 kg). Don's 2,400 lb. was in competition, but his individual, best ever lifts totalled much more. In his day he did more 900 lb. (408.6 kg) competition squats than any other competitor. It is very important to remember that all these were performed *without the bundling of the early years and without the supporting suits of the present.* Don even spurned knee wraps and thick lifting belt!

Having won four world titles, Reinhoudt began feeling a little bored and unchallenged and after the death of his dear father, he was despondent and decided to retire from powerlifting. But his strength career was not yet over. An invitation to compete in the World's Strongest Man competition revived his interest, but he declined as his bodyweight was down to around 113.5 kg (250 lb.), although he promised to enter the following year. By that time he was back to 154.4 kg (340 lb.) and feeling good.

The rest is history. He won the log lift with 122.6 kg (270 lb.), the girl lift (a partial squat with a number of girls on a platform), and the tram pull. Bruce Wilhelm, the title holder, and Don pulled in the tug of war for first place. According to Don's supporters, he had gained ground on Bruce when the referee blew his whistle a little too soon. Don relaxed, they said, and Bruce seized the initiative to win.

A year later Don Reinhoudt came back to the 1979 World's Strongest Man contest after months of dedicated training, and the records show that he went back home with the title and a $12,670 prize purse. The good citizens and civic fathers were proud of their favourite son and on the outskirts of town erected a sign for all to see: "Welcome to Brockton—Home of Don Reinhoudt—World's Strongest Man."

"Don was immensely popular with the fans, a true people's champion. Sometimes he seems almost too friendly, and his energy and concentration before a big meet are drained away by countless questions and requests for photographs from the hordes of fans who follow him wherever he goes." (Prof. Terry Todd, the first official US superheavyweight powerlifting champion)

"He is a true gentleman . . . His heart is as big as all outdoors. He is the last of the Leviathans." (Herb Glossbrenner, referee, writer, statistician)

"Not an ounce of the prima donna in him. He signed autographs during the competition . . . he was the perfect gentleman on and off the platform." (Clarence Bass, author and "Ripped" physique star)

These quotes are given to emphasise one of my most important lessons to young athletes: *Be a winner, become famous, and keep in mind, long after people have forgotten how much you lifted, they will remember what kind of man you were.* Don Reinhoudt was a great athlete and a great man.

Further reading on Don's training and accomplishments are to be found in *Inside Powerlifting* by Terry Todd and *Powerlifting USA*, March 1995 by H. Glossbrenner.

Bernard "Spinks" Rolle

Country: Bahamas
Sport: Powerlifting
Born: 28 December 1963
1995 stats:
Height: 190.5 cm (6' 3")
Weight: 134 kg (21 st. 1½ lb./295½ lb.)
Chest: 146 cm (57½")
Biceps: 57 cm (22½")

Spinks was the local hero and the best supported athlete of the 1995 World's Strongest Man competition. A security guard by profession, he had until that time never been beaten in any strength contest. He had started competing as a powerlifter in 1990, winning the national powerlifting championships that year in his first attempt, and never looked back until the World's Strongest Man came to Paradise Island. A talking point amongst his athletic colleagues is his unique hairstyle known as a "Bart Simpson" after the cartoon character.

Magnus Samuelsson

Country: Sweden
Sport: Arm wrestling
Born: 21 December 1969
1995 stats:
Height: 200 cm (6' 6½")
Weight: 123 kg (19 st. 5 lb./217 lb.)
Biceps: 53 cm (21")

In 1995 Magnus made a sensational entry in the World's Strongest Man. The fifth heat was contested by four

Magnus Samuelsson.

mighty men, namely 6' 10" Nathan Jones, 6' 6" Torvi Olafsson, 6' 5" Phil Martin, and Magnus, the lightest by far, the others ranging from 32-42 kg heavier! In spite of this, Magnus won the heat and made the finals. In doing so he put Nathan, one of the overall favourites, out of the competition during the arm wrestling competition. It was a sensational bout with Megaman Jones's arm breaking in the process. Samuelsson was most disappointed about this. He had been arm wrestling since he was seventeen years of age and had won five Swedish championships in addition to the European championships. Magnus said, "Nathan pulled hard from a position we call 'the arm breaker' and it is almost inevitable that in such a situation a break occurs. He is a really powerful and tough guy. He will be back."

Magnus and his brother have a farm in Sweden, and the athlete's lovely wife is also strong and fit; she is a blacksmith by profession.

Adrian Smith

Country: *Great Britain*
Sport: *Pro strongman*
Born: *18 March 1964*
Corby, Northants
1990 stats:
Height: *180 cm* *(5'11")*
Weight: *121 kg* *(19 st./266 lb.)*
Chest: *137 cm* *(54")*
Waist: *91 cm* *(36")*
Biceps: *53 cm* *(21")*
Thigh: *79 cm* *(31")*

The travelling reserve and tester in San Sebastian in 1989, Adrian then stepped into the 1990 line-up in the World's Strongest Man contest in place of the reigning champion, Jamie Reeves, who was recovering from a serious arm injury.

Coached by former World's Strongest Man, Geoff Capes, Smith had been doing well in competition. He had recently set a new world record for the brick lift, raising twenty-six 3kg (6½ lb.) bricks pressed side by side to an arms outstretched position, then returning them to the table. He was joint second, with Bill Kazmaier, to Tjalling van den Bosch in a strength competition at Shrewsbury organised by Capes; he took the same position behind Jon Pall Sigmarsson, with van den Bosch third, at a mixed Highland Games/strength contest in Scotland.

His introduction to muscle sport came via bodybuilding, and he won the Mr. East Midlands and Mr. Northants titles in 1985. He then turned to strength events, in which he made rapid progress. He has organised the large Highland gathering in Corby and worked in his father's licensed trade stocktaking company, where shifting barrels in pub cellars provided some useful training exercise.

Markku Suonenvirta

Country: *Finland*
Sport: *Pro strongman*
Born: *12 April 1955*
Salo, Finland
1991 stats:
Height: *184 cm* *(6' ½")*
Weight: *127 kg* *(20 st/280 lb)*
Chest: *136 cm* *(53½")*
Waist: *106 cm* *(42")*
Biceps: *53 cm* *(21")*
Thigh: *71 cm* *(28")*

A tester in 1990s World's Strongest Man contest, like Hjalti Arnason of Iceland, ex-policeman Markku has long been in the shadow of another strongman, the Finnish maestro and his close friend in Turku, Ilkka Nummisto. In 1990 he and the Finland's Strongest Man Company played an invaluable role in setting up the World's Strongest Man competition in Joensuu. Markku won the Finland's Strongest Man title in 1989 (behind guest competitor Jon Pall Sigmarsson) and was runner-up to Ilkka in 1990 (behind guest Bill Kazmaier).

In 1991 he tied with Ilkka on points for the title of Finland's Strongest Man, but lost on fewer first places. Ilkka, however, sportingly agreed to step down and let Markku represent their country in Tenerife for the World's Strongest Man contest, and to help him as coach—at a mere 20 stones, Markku was the lightest competitor in that year's competition.

He won the Finnish powerlifting championship in 1986 and has over a dozen other medals in that sport. His best lifts are: squat 320 kg (706 lb.), bench press 240 kg (529 lb.), dead lift 330 kg (727½ lb.), best competition total 850 kg (1,874 lb.).

Gary Taylor

Country: *Great Britain*
Sport: *Pro strongman*
Born: *14 October 1961*
Swansea, Wales
Resides: *London*
1992 stats:
Height: *183 cm* *(6')*
Weight: *130 kg* *(20 st. 7 lb./287 lb.)*
Chest: *137 cm* *(54")*
Waist: *91 cm* *(36")*
Biceps: *56 cm* *(22")*
Thigh: *79 cm* *(31")*

Taylor Made for Strength

The World's Strongest Man competition in Orange, France in 1993 was one of the best ever and culminated in a win for Gary Taylor, "the Welsh Dragon." A worthy winner, he further enhanced Britain's reputation established by such athletes as Geoff Capes and Jamie Reeves.

Gary first staked his claim for the World's Strongest Man title in Tenerife as he pulled himself up from last place to finally finish third, looking stronger after three demanding days than he did in the opening events.

At that time TV viewers saw Gary as a new star, but it had taken more than thirteen years of hard work for him to become an "overnight success," as he was then described. Over the years, however, he proved his versatility in no uncertain fashion. In Olympic lifting he took four Welsh titles and was a big hit at the Commonwealth Games

Gary Taylor.

in Brisbane, Australia when he broke several records, making him the Commonwealth's best ever in that specific discipline. More was yet to come, for lifting in the 110 kg category at the Los Angeles Olympics he placed second in the snatch.

"Heavy duty" training for the Olympics built him a tremendous physique, giving him a rock-hard appearance. A two-year excursion into bodybuilding filled his trophy cabinet to overflowing, winning the British intermediate title and being twice runner-up in the main British championships—the only person beating him was Dorian Yates, acclaimed as the world's number one.

Still accepting challenges, Gary Taylor took up powerlifting and has the following lifts to his credit: squat 355 kg (783 lb.), bench press 220 kg (485 lb.), dead lift 315 kg (695 lb.), totalling 890 kg (1,963 lb.). In training he has done more: His best squat is 385 kg (849 lb.) and dead lift 355 kg (783 lb.). Powerlifting gave him more trophies and more muscle, so much in fact he was selected for the AAU Mr. Universe in Tucson, Arizona. There he took fourth place, but in the prestigious East European Grand Prix, the Sandow Classic in Czechoslovakia he won hands down.

In modern strength athletics as seen in the TV competitions, he has won British and European championships and represented Britain with distinction in many overseas internationals.

Gary is a physical education instructor in the prison service and although he is as tough as they come, with his pleasant disposition and rugged involvement, he is very popular in strength circles, where he is usually very polite and humorous.

During 1994, Gary Taylor lifted 270 kg (595 lb.) overhead, a new world record, but fate was unkind and he suffered a severe biceps injury which kept him out of some major contests. However, the fighting spirit which thrilled his many supporters was very much in evidence as he continued to win major contests and establish new records. I have been asked to referee Gary attempting a jerk from behind neck with 272 kg (600 lb.) for the *Guinness Book of Records* programme. This is still awaited as two severe injuries to arm and abdomen have taken their toll, and surgery has been necessary. At this time he is training heavy power cleaning up to 200 kg and doing partial squats about 500kg for 15 reps! It looks likely that Gary will continue for quite some time giving pleasure to strength disciples the world over.

Henning Thorsen

Country:	Denmark	
Sport:	Pro strongman	
Born:	20 October 1959	
	Randers, Denmark	
1992 stats:		
Height:	193 cm	(6'4")
Weight:	137 kg	(21 st. 8 lb./302 lb.)
Chest:	140 cm	(55")
Waist:	100 cm	(39")
Biceps:	55 cm	(21½")
Thigh:	90 cm	(35½")

Five times Denmark's superheavyweight powerlifting champion (1984, 1985, 1986, 1989 and 1990), Henning has best competition lifts of: squat 340 kg (748 lb.), bench press 225 kg (495 lb.), dead lift 332.5 kg (731½ lb.). He has also competed successfully at the European level.

He was Denmark's Strongest Man in 1984, 1987, 1988 and 1989. In June 1990 he won the inaugural Hercules strength competition in Denmark and has competed with distinction in Scottish events. He was a reserve in 1990's World's Strongest Man contest and came into the competition at the eleventh hour when Kazmaier withdrew; and despite having only a week to prepare, finished in the prize money with fourth place, earning a repeat invitation for 1991. He repaid that by lifting himself to second place, winning the truck pull, Stones of Strength and arm-over-arm pull; in doing so he booked a 1992 ticket for Iceland, but not however with the same success.

Henning has spent many years as a construction worker and a part-time bouncer.

Henning Thorsen.

Vladimir Tourtchinski

Born:	*28 September 1963*	
	Russia	
Occupation:	*TV gladiator*	
Resides:	*Moscow*	
1996 stats:		
Height:	*173 cm*	*(5'8")*
Weight:	*110 kg*	*(17 st. 5 lb./243 lb.)*
Chest:	*130 cm*	*(51")*
Biceps:	*50 cm*	*(20")*

This good-humoured athlete played football for the Moscow Bears and the Moscow Giants. He loves weight training and built himself a fine physique which he puts to good use in many sports. One of the toughest European Gladiators on TV, he is appropriately known as "Dynamite."

Vladimir, a popular personality in the 1996 competition in Mauritius, is a keen collector of strength memorabilia and enjoys wood carving and music.

Ron Trottier

Country:	*Canada*	
Sport:	*Pro strongman*	
Born:	*1968*	
Resides:	*Canada*	
1994 stats:		
Height:	*190 cm*	*(6'3")*
Weight:	*136 kg*	*(21 st. 6 lb./300 lb.)*
Chest:	*139 cm*	*(55")*
Biceps:	*49 cm*	*(19")*

This French-Canadian strongman is little known outside his own area, preferring to compete in domestic competitions, rather than in the more high profile European events. Ron has however been tempted to some overseas events, such as a Japanese competition, where he gave a very good account of himself. The 1994 WSM contest in South Africa was his first opportunity to show his abilities to the vast legions of enthusiasts who follow strongman competitions worldwide.

Aap Uspenski

Country:	*Russia*	
Sport:	*Wrestling*	
Born:	*17 July 1966*	
	Tallinn, Estonia	
1990 stats:		
Height	*188 cm*	*(6'2")*
Weight:	*112 kg*	*(17 st. 8 lb./246 lb.)*
Chest:	*114 cm*	*(45")*
Waist:	*94 cm*	*(37")*
Biceps:	*44 cm*	*(17")*
Thigh:	*65 cm*	*(26")*

At 112 kg, Uspenski was easily the lightest competitor in the 1990 Worlds's Strongest Man contest; but his relative lack of poundage proved no handicap when he competed against much heavier competitors to win the title in Estonia's Strongest Man on 6 June 1990 in Tallinn.

Estonia, although one of the smallest republics of the former USSR, has a strongman tradition reaching back more than seven hundred years to sacrificial ceremonies in which competitors pulled against each other with ropes or poles on St. John's Day, the traditional beginning of summer.

In more recent times, Gustav Boesberg was a world famous wrestler and weightlifter towards the end of the last century, with George Lurich, George Hackenschmidt and Alex Aberg following him. Lurich had a strongman act in which he held back two camels pulling against him. In weightlifting, Jaan Talts won the mid-heavyweight class at the Munich Olympics of 1972, having been silver medallist in Mexico four years earlier.

Uspenski came to strongman sport from wrestling and has worked as a driver.

Regin Vagadal

Born: 22 March 1970
Country: Faroe Islands
Occupation: Studying as a ship captain
1996 stats:
Height: 186 cm (6'1")
Weight: 130 kg (20 st. 7 lb./287 lb.)
Chest: 130 cm (51")
Biceps: 52 cm (20½")

Vagadal is a very determined competitor who made his debut as a strongman in 1996. He has great potential although lacks opportunity in his homeland. Hobbies include football, swimming, powerlifting and darts.

Marko Varalahti

Country: Finland
Sport: Boxing and kick boxing
Born: 26 February 1968
1995 stats:
Height: 205 cm (6' 8½")
Weight: 140 kg (22 st./308 lb.)
Chest: 133 cm (52")
Biceps: 149 cm (58½")

After gradual improvement over some years Marko won the annual Finnish TV competition to find Finland's Strongest Man, and 1995 saw him in the WSM TV contest for the first time. Few have done as well as he did in that first attempt. He won two events in the heats and two of the most difficult events in the finals, the farmer's walk and the maritime medley loading event. Marko finished third overall, a very fine achievement for a first international appearance.

Berend Veneberg

Country: The Netherlands
Sport: Powerlifting
Born: 6 November 1963
Resides: Glefteren, Holland
1995 stats:
Height: 186 cm (6'1")
Weight: 133 kg (20 st. 13 lb./293 lb.)
Chest: 140 cm (55")
Biceps: 53 cm (21")

After winning the Netherlands' Strongest Man title in 1993, Berend made his WSM debut at Orange in France. This Dutch heavyweight powerlifting champion brought with him a horde of good-humoured, vociferous supporters who added considerably to the atmosphere of the occasion. Like most others in the competition for the first time, he did not perform up to his own expectations but promised he would be back to try again.

Although giant Ted van der Parre represented the Netherlands in 1994, Berend kept his promise and was selected again in 1995. In the first, tough heat, against the eventual winner Magnus Magnusson and Joe Onasai he gave a good account of himself, beating the hotly-fancied Anton Boucher.

Berend, who competed again in 1996, has a friendly, easy-going personality and earns his living by operating his own sports school and fitness equipment consultancy.

Cees de Vreugd

Country: The Netherlands
Sport: Powerlifting
Born: 9 March 1952
Katwijk, Netherlands
1985 stats:
Height: 186 cm (6'1")
Weight: 141 kg (22 st. 3 lb./311 lb.)
Chest: 157 cm (62")
Waist: 110 cm (43")
Biceps: 51 cm (20")
Thigh: 79 cm (31")

A butcher by trade, keen soccer player and judo black belt in his youth, Cees took up powerlifting in 1980 at Olympia Sports College. Under the influence of Gerard du Prie, he competed in the 1981 Netherlands championships, taking fourth place with a total of 635 kg (1,400 lb.).

In 1982 he moved up to the 125 kg class and took second place in the Netherlands championships with an 860 kg (1,896 lb.) total, second place in the European championships, and third in the world championships. In 1983 he became Netherlands champion with 890 kg (1,962½ lb.), exceeded 900 kg (1984½ lb.) for second place at the European championships in Finland, and a week later, smashed the Netherlands record with a total of 935 kg (2061½ lb.). His big ambition to exceed 1,000 kg (2,205 lb.) for the three main lifts was realised when the 1985 European championships were held in the Netherlands.

He competed in the 1982 Netherlands' Strongest Man event but had to withdraw due to injury. He was, however, runner-up to Ab Wolders in the 1984 event and also in that year he qualified for Europe's Strongest Man and led the competition at the halfway point, but snapped his shoulder tendon in steel bar bending; he could then take no further effective part but still achieved fourth place. In the 1985 World's Strongest Man event in Cascais, Portugal, he replaced Wolders who had been suffering from septicaemia in his arm. De Vreugd had come direct from Helsinki where he had just won the gold medal competing against George Hechter in the world championships, and despite

Cees de Vreugd.

his last minute entry into the World's Strongest Man, he won third place.

His best competition lifts are: squat 420 kg (926 lb.) European record, bench press 225 kg (496 lb.), dead lift 370 kg (816 lb.), best total 1,002.5 kg (2,210½ lb.).

Dave Waddington

Country:	USA
Born:	5 October 1952
	Sandusky, Ohio
Work:	Car part press operator
1984 stats:	
Height:	183 cm (6')
Weight:	138 kg (21 st. 10 lb./304 lb.)
Chest:	142 cm (56")
Biceps:	53 cm (21")
Thigh:	84 cm (33")

Dave was the first man ever to squat with 1,000 lb, and prior to his bid for the title in 1984, he had also bench pressed 267.5 kg (590 lb.) and dead lifted 360 kg (794 lb.). Away from strength sports he enjoyed fishing, softball and darts.

Bruce Wilhelm

There will always be a place in history for Bruce Wilhelm, winner of the very first TV World's Strongest Man. He won in 1977 and successfully defended his title the following year. Bruce had already a very good reputation as an all-round strength athlete, and this put the seal on a wonderful career.

Born on 13 July 1945, he first showed promise as a wrestler and quickly became fiercely competitive, winning many coveted awards before switching to more high-profile strength events in track and field. Bruce became internationally known as a discus thrower and shot putter, and it was in these capacities that I first became acquainted with his enthusiasm and abilities. While promoting Highland Games in San Francisco in 1971, one of the team, big Dave Prowse (later famous as Darth Vader of *Star Wars* movies) got an invitation from Bruce to train with him at his California home. Dave suggested I join them but, as always, I was on a tight schedule and missed a golden opportunity.

Bruce did a lot of weightlifitng as part of his athletic training, and became so good that he annexed the American superheavyweight title in Olympic lifting; he went on to participate in world championships and achieved the ultimate honor of competing with distinction in the Olympic Games. At Montreal in 1976, he lined up against the great Vasily Alexeev (USSR), and many others, including the noted East Germans Gerd Bonk and Helmut Losch. Only Alexeev, the defending champ, snatched more than Bruce Wilhelm's 172.5 kg, and American hopes were high. Had his clean and jerk been of this standard, he would have been high on the Olympic victory rostrum. His 215 kg was a good effort, and although the Germans did more, Bruce did America proud.

Bruce clearly enjoyed the World's Strongest Man events, appearing as an affable but totally confident competitor. At 6'3" and 326 lb., he lifted strongly and moved quickly, providing a good prototype for future contenders. His comments made it clear that he was a self-made strength athlete who appreciated the contribution which could be made by coaches, but he liked to think for himself. After retiring from these competitions, Bruce Wilhelm became commissioner for the event.

Over the years, Bruce has retained his interest in his favorite activities and has written, with authority, articles on his weightlifting contemporaries. Now lighter in weight than in his heyday and looking less than his age, he is a popular figure at reunions of the Oldtime Barbell and Strongman Association.

Bruce Wilhelm.

O.D. Wilson

Country:	USA
Sport:	Powerlifting
Born:	12 September 1954
	Winter Haven, Florida

1991 stats:
Height:	196 cm	(6'5")
Weight:	182 kg	(28 st. 8 lb./400 lb.)
Chest:	152 cm	(60")
Waist:	122 cm	(48")
Biceps:	60 cm	(23½")
Thigh:	86 cm	(34")

Nightmare No More

O.D. claimed that was how he was registered at birth and that was how he happily went through life, without a conventional Christian name—and who would argue with a professional bodyguard, 6'5" tall and weighing 29 stone! But despite his nickname, "Nightmare," Wilson was a genial character, who enjoyed life and got on well with people.

He spent twelve years of his adult life in the US Army, seeing eight years' service overseas in Germany, Japan and Korea. Before he started putting on weight, O.D. was a track athlete, specializing in 200 m. He was an all-American basketball player, boxed for two years while in the army and played a lot of racketball.

Powerlifting, however, was the sport at which he was most successful. He rose to fame in the 1980s by becoming five-times US Services champion, and five times US Army title-holder; he won the United States superheavyweight title in 1988 and went on to take the world crown as well. His best competition figures were: squat 462 kg (1,018 lb.), bench press 257 kg (567 lb.), dead lift 406 kg (895 lb.), highest total 1,102.5 kg (2,430 lb.).

A resident of North Carolina, O.D. was a high profile security officer, often looking after the rich and famous but occasionally he appeared in films and on TV. In his first strongman competition, he was a great success in the Scottish Power Challenge as part of the Capital City of Culture celebrations held in Glasgow.

The World's Strongest Man 1990 brought the most thrilling climax of the contest's thirteen-year history. O.D. Wilson went to the final event leading Jon Pall Sigmarsson by 5.5 points, with the knowledge that even if the blond Viking won it, he would need only sixth place to claim overall victory. The event involved carrying a hod of bricks weighing 100 kg (220½ lb.) over a 200 m course. The Estonian Uspenski had set the fastest time of 52.7 seconds in the earlier heats, when O.D. and Jon Pall went to the line for the last one.

In addition to the hods, Jon Pall was carrying his own bodyweight of 133 kg (21 st.); O.D. was 51 kg (8 st.) heavier. The weight handicap proved too much, and Jon Pall duly won, with O.D. in seventh place, taking second place overall by half a point. I believe that had there not been an emphasis on cardiovascular strength and endurance to suit the host country Finland, O.D. would have won the title.

In the 1991 World's Strongest Man event in Tenerife, hampered by a back injury said to be a prolapsed disc, O.D. dropped to fifth place. Returning home bitterly disappointed, a few weeks later on the morning of 29 October 1991, he participated in a radio show and, feeling chest pains, went outside for fresh air. Collapsing on the pavement, he was taken to hospital where he died, aged only thirty-seven years old; the cause of his death was diagnosed as cardiac arrest

O.D. was loved by spectators, organisers, TV personnel and fellow competitors. His awesome size and stern visage hid a heart of gold; he was a quiet but affable companion and received his fans willingly, taking time to answer their endless questions, give autographs or pose for photos.

O.D. Wilson was particularly good with children, and they loved this gentle giant who revelled in the nickname "the Nightmare" because he gave his opponents bad dreams. He was a charismatic character and a very sporting competitor, who always conducted himself with great dignity and is greatly missed in the world of strength.

Ab Wolders

Country:	The Netherlands	
Sport:	Powerlifting	
Born:	10 June 1951	
	Rotterdam, Holland	
1986 stats:		
Height:	182 cm	(6')
Weight:	125 kg	(19 st. 10 lb./276 lb.)
Chest:	130 cm	(51")
Waist:	100 cm	(39")
Biceps:	52 cm	(20½")
Thigh:	78 cm	(31")

Wolders, runner-up to Sigmarsson in the 1984 World's Strongest Man contest at Mora, Sweden, was the Netherlands' final choice for the 1985 competition in Portugal. He was already training for the contest when he ran into trouble during his night-time job as a club bouncer. Bitten in the arm by someone he had been trying to eject, he went to hospital for stitching. The wound then turned septic, and he spent many months under medical care. For some time it seemed probable that the arm would be amputated. Fortunately this proved unnecessary, but even when he finally left the hospital, his sporting career was in doubt.

O.D. Wilson.

Ab Wolders.

Ab is a very tough character, however, and fully fit, he returned to competition in time for the 1986 World's Strongest Man event in Nice where he finished in third place. Ab continued to be popular in WSM contests, and his best placing was in 1989, when he was second to Jamie Reeves.

His first sport was judo for twenty years between the ages of five and twenty-five; he switched to karate and bodybuilding, and then powerlifting. He has twice been a European gold medallist, was runner-up at the world championships and took the title at Dallas in 1984, only to be disqualified. Ab, who ran his own sports school for a while, ran into financial difficulties and was forced to turn to security work.

Simon Wulfse

Country: *The Netherlands*
Sport: *Powerlifting*

Born: *12 January 1952*
1983 stats:
Height: *181 cm (5'11")*
Weight: *110 kg (17 st. 5 lb./243 lb.)*

Runner-up to Geoff Capes in Europe's Strongest Man 1982, Simon lost only on the final event, when he took fourth place to Cape's first at Cumberland wrestling. He won the barrel loading, and shared first place in the truck pull with Capes and in the dead lift (370 kg/816 lb.) with Roger Ekstrom and Hamish Davidson.

Wulfse took up judo and karate as a young man when he worked on the docks in Rotterdam, and began powerlifting in 1979 at Adden Otter Sporting School in Zwijndrecht, where he trained four hours a day, four times a week. Within months he had taken third place in the Dutch championships at Alkmaar and won the first of his three national titles in 1980. He was seventh in the 1980 European championships and fifth in 1981.

Wulfse came third in the 1983 World's Strongest Man contest in New Zealand and won the £1,000 bonus for being leader after the first day's four events, but dropped out of the picture after being jailed for drug dealing.

The Contests

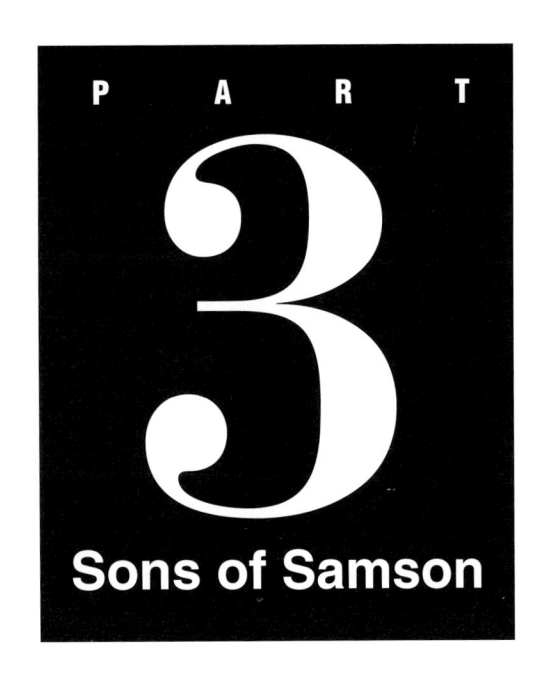

PART 3
Sons of Samson

CHAPTER 5

The Contests

Universal Studios, California, USA 1977

The very first competition in the series was held over three days in 1977 at Universal Studios in California. There were eight competitors and ten events to be shown on CBS on ten consecutive Saturdays during the winter TV season. According to reports, the top places got a total of $18,187, the bottom four got $2,000 each.

Bruce Wilhelm won the barrel lift (113.5 kg/250 lb.), wheelbarrow race, tram pull, fridge race and tug-of-war. It was an overwhelming victory. Robert Young won the girl lift (squat) and was consistently placed with points in seven of the ten events. Ken Patera, with an injured back, won the tyre toss, was second with the wheelbarrow and third in tug of war. Ferrigno "The Hulk," won the steel bar bend and a dead lift grasping the bumper of a car. Professional strongman and former champion bodybuilder Mike Dayton won the wrist roll, winding up 45.4 kg (100 lb.) on ten feet of rope.

Almost inevitably there are injuries, and this inaugural event was no exception. There were two bad incidents, first when George Frenn, a champion weight thrower tore his left biceps tendon, and later Franco Columbu, a future Mr. Olympia, dislocated a knee in the refrigerator race.

The event was not well reported, with a lack of information on performances and equipment, but it has

Bruce Wilhelm (USA) in the fridge race (top) and tug-of-war (bottom), WSM 1977.

been ascertained that the wheelbarrow race was with approximately 340.5 kg (750 lb.) up a 40-yard slope. A 28", 16 kg (35 lb.) tyre was thrown from a 10 ft. circle. In the tram pull, the vehicle weighed approximately 2,724 kg (6,000 lb.) and was pulled for 40 yards. The refrigerator and roll bars weighed 186 kg (410 lb.) and were carried for 40 yards.

There were some very well-known officials, including weightlifters Tommy Kono, Paul Anderson, John Terpak, Russ Knipp, and field athlete Harold Connolly, Olympic gold medallist.

Final Result

1. *Bruce Wilhelm*   5. *Franco Columbu*
2. *Robert Young*   6. *Jon Cole*
3. *Ken Patera*   7. *Mike Dayton*
4. *Lou Ferrigno*   8. *George Frenn*

Universal Tour Center, California, USA 1978

Bruce Wilhelm defended his title in the 1978 contest, which followed the same three day pattern at the Universal Tour Center, Hollywood. A single overseas representative, Lars Hedlund, a 142 kg Swedish powerlifter (22 st. 5 lb./313 lb.), was added to the line-up to help justify the "world" title.

Contestants vying with Wilhelm, 148 kg (23 st. 4 lb./326 lb.) also included professional wrestler Ivan Putski, 112.5 kg (17 st. 10 lb./248 lb.); Don Reinhoudt, 156 kg (24 st. 8 lb./344 lb.), four times world powerlifting champion; Gus Rethwisch, a powerlifter weighing in at 147 kg (23 st. 2 lb./324 lb.), who later appeared as the fearsome Buzzsaw in Arnold Schwarzenegger's *Running Man*; Brian Oldfield, 112.5 kg (17 st. 10 lb./248 lb.), former Olympic shot-putter; John Matuszak, 140 kg (22 st 1 lb/309 lb.), Oakland Raiders defence star; Jon Kolb 118.5 kg (18 st. 9 lb./261 lb.), Pittsburgh Steelers offensive linesman; Jack Wright, 109 kg (17 st. 2 lb./240 lb.), wrist wrestling champ; and Boris Djerassi 112.5 kg (17 st. 10 lb./248 lb.) hammer thrower.

There were hordes of well-known officials, including Terry Todd, (replacing Paul Anderson); Harold Connolly, 1956 Olympic gold in hammer throwing; and Bob Zuver; plus Olympic weightlifting champions, stars and officials Tommy Kono, John Terpak, Russ Knipp and Bob Hise.

Considering inflation, prizes compared very favourably with current winnings, with $500 to the winner of each event, $350 for second, $200 for third, $100 for fourth and $50 for fifth. That's not all: The overall winner got $10,000, second $7,000, third $5,000, fourth $3,000, fifth $2,000, and sixth $1,000. With place money, every contestant was guaranteed at least $2,000.

In my view, the points system of those early events was far from perfect, with points for the first five places only, and even then they were not geared to keep many competitors within striking distance of each other. The first got 10, second 7, third 4, fourth 2, fifth 1, remainder 0. In the tug-of-war, the final event, points were doubled and only the first four men competed. (Points in current competitions are now 10, 9, 8, 7, 6, 5, 4, 3, 2, 1.)

The barrel lift came first and showed an improved standard, with four men equal or better than the 113.5 kg (250 lb.) which won for Bruce Wilhelm the previous year. Reinhoudt registered 123 kg (270 lb.) to win the event, with Bruce doing 118 kg (260 lb.) for second.

In the steel bar bend, hot rolled construction steel bars were bent over the head or round the neck until the ends were within 8 inches of each other. Bars of increasing thickness were used in each round. Hedlund and Wilhelm tied for first, Reinhoudt was third, Kolb next and Rethwisch fifth.

The girl lift was a big favourite with the crowd. The platform and two girls used in the first lift weighed about 181.6 kg (400 lb.). Another girl was added after each round. Reinhoudt won; Wilhelm, Rethwisch and Djerassi were equal second, and Hedlund fifth.

Wrist rollers were used in the following event, with Mike Dayton's record (25.3 secs) well and truly smashed by Jon Kolb who rolled the 45.4 kg (100 lb.) weight on 10 ft. of rope in a fast 18.75 seconds. Hedlund was second, Putski third, Oldfield fourth and Wilhelm fifth.

The second day began with wheelbarrow racing, using 340.5 kg (750 lb.) over a 100 ft. course up a nine-degree incline. The result was Wilhelm, Rethwisch, Kolb, Hedlund, Djerassi.

The tyre toss was next, using a 28" tyre weighing 16 kg (35 lb.). One or two hands could be used but only one revolution of the body in a 10 ft. throwing circle was permitted. Those who know Brian "Crazy Horse" Oldfield were not surprised that this excellent all-round thrower came first, in spite of the general favourite being hammer thrower Djerassi, who finished a disappointed fourth. Oldfield made a new record of 42' 8½"; Reinhoudt was second, Wilhelm third.

A dead lift with the end of a car completed the second day. Various well-known cars were used. Jack Benny's old Maxwell, Paul Newman's car from the film *The Sting*, and finally Peter Falk's car from *Columbo*, which only Wilhelm and Reinhoudt could lift. After extra weight had been added, the decision went to Don. Five others tied for third place. Such ties were common in the American competitions, whereas later television producers have objected to any ties at all.

At this stage the leaders were Reinhoudt, Wilhelm, Hedlund, Kolb, and Rethwisch.

Next came a tram pull with passengers and vehicle weighing 4,358 kg (9,600 lb.) which was dragged over a 100 ft. course. Wilhelm was pretty confident, but Reinhoudt beat him, and with Hedlund in third place, the overall score of the first three remained unchanged.

A refrigerator was carried 100 ft. in the next timed event, the fridge weighing 190.6 kg (420 lb.). In some of the earlier heats, Bruce Wilhelm's record of 17.2 secs was broken so, paired with Don Reinhoudt, he entered the final heat in a rather worried frame of mind. He relaxed when he clocked 14.1 seconds for second place, Hedlund having done a new record of 13.4 secs. Kolb was third.

The bottom four men were now eliminated, and in the tug-of-war with a 1½" rope, Reinhoudt met Kolb and disposed of him in 10 seconds, while Wilhelm had a much tougher time with Lars Hedlund. It took Bruce a minute to win the bout, both finishing totally exhausted and requiring oxygen.

It appears that Don took some of Bruce's comments for the TV cameras a little too seriously, and there was a needle, and a somewhat controversial finish, which was eventually won by Bruce to give him the overall title. He had been the only competitor to gain points in all ten events.

The prize money for the victory was $12,715, approximately £9,537 at the time of writing. In 1995 after years of inflation, the first prize was £10,000. Don Reinhoudt got $9,550, Lars Hedlund $6,745, and Jon Kolb $3,120.

Universal Studios, California, USA 1979

The third annual event in 1979 had some really big guys, such as Cleve Dean strongman and wrist-wrestler from Marietta, Georgia, weighing 209 kg (32 st. 12 lb./460 lb.); Jerry Blackwell, a professional wrestler from Knoxville, Tennessee, weighing 191 kg (30 st./420 lb.); Don Reinhoudt from Brooklyn, New York, at 156.6 kg (24 st. 9 lb./345 lb.); Bill Kazmaier, at that time American powerlifting champion, at 145 kg (22 st. 12 lb./320 lb.); Lars Hedlund, world powerlifter from Sweden, at 143 kg (22 st. 10 lb/318 lb.); Joe Dube, former American weightlifting champ from Sanderson, Florida, 143 kg (22½ st./315 lb.); Bob Young, of the St. Louis Cardinals, 129 kg (20 st. 5 lb./285 lb.); Bill Anderson, Scottish Highland Games champion 127 kg (20 st./280 lb.); John Kolb, outstanding tackle of the Pittsburgh Steelers and comparatively a lightweight— 106.7 kg (16 st. 11 lb./235 lb.); and Dave Johns, 1977 Mr. America from Hollywood, California.

They followed the pattern of having nine events for the ten men and then the top four participating in tug-of-war heats; scoring was as before. The overall prizes were first $10,000, second $7,000, third $5,000, fourth $2,000, fifth $1,000. There was additional prize money for points in the individual events and a minimum guarantee of $2,000. In addition to the high prize money, another notable feature of these early competitions was the large number of top-level sporting officials to oversee the events.

The first event was a barrel lift, and Blackwell and Johns went out first. Young, Kolb and Anderson failed at 113.5 kg (250 lb.). Surprisingly Dube, who as an Olympic lifter should have been great in overhead work, went out at 4.5 kg (10 lb.) more. Reinhoudt alone succeeded with 136.2 kg (300 lb.) to beat Kazmaier and Hedlund.

In the bar bending, the first hot rolled steel bar to be bent was 3 ft. in length and one-half inch thick. They had to be bent until the ends were within 8 inches of touching. All except Blackwell bent the first. Dean, Kolb, Kazmaier, Hedlund and Reinhoudt bent the second bar of 3½ ft. in length and nine-sixteenths of an inch thick. Next came bars of 4 ft. and five-eighths of an inch thick; and then 4 ft. and eleven-sixteenths of an inch thick; and while none succeeded with the latter, Kolb came nearest to getting a complete bend, Dean was next, Kaz third, Hedlund fourth and Reinhoudt fifth.

In caber tossing, the log was tossed for distance, which suits strongmen much better than the Scottish method of giving a perfectly *straight* toss. The final caber was 14 ft. and 50 kg (110 lb.), and 7" in diameter at the top and 6" at the bottom. Kolb won again with a throw of 36' 8"; Bill Kazmaier was only 2" behind. Hedlund did 18' 11" on his first throw, then jumped to 35' ½" to snatch third place from the favourite Bill Anderson, who could not get out of the groove of Scottish style throwing. Kolb was now nearly three points ahead of Kazmaier.

Dead lifting the back of a car came next. Kaz edged out Reinhoudt for first place, Young was third. and five men shared fourth place.

In a wheelbarrow race, a 340.5 kg (750 lb.) wheelbarrow had to be pushed over a 100 ft. uphill course. Kazmaier increased his overall lead with a time of 12.25 seconds, and Reinhoudt's second place (12.99 seconds) put him second overall at this halfway stage. Young was third.

The girl lift, a sort of half squat with a girl-loaded platform, proved to be a popular event. In the first round, the apparatus and two girls weighed 210.2 kg (463 lb.). All succeeded, although Bill Anderson was injured in the process and was the second man to withdraw. The second round was with 275.6 kg (607 lb.), and the third with 328.2 kg (723 lb.) saw the elimination of Dean, Kolb and Johns. Dube failed with 350.9 kg (773 lb.) to place fifth, and Hedlund went out on next round at 384.5 kg (847 lb.).

Young, Reinhoudt and Kazmaier battled it out for the top three places. Amazingly, Bill had to give best to the footballer Bob Young when Bill failed with 416.3 kg (917 lb.), but Reinhoudt created a new record with 454 kg (1,000 lb.).

In the hoist lift, a washing machine had to be raised about 10 ft. within 30 seconds by a hand-over-hand pull. A wire and pulley contraption was used, and competitors sat on an adjustable bench with thighs locked. The weight of the washing machine was raised for each round. It started at 106.7 kg (235 lb.) and went on to 131.7 kg (290 lb.). Young failed at this weight, and all remaining except Kolb and Hedlund failed at 158.9 kg (350 lb.). These two stalwarts went on from here for other two rounds of 168 kg (370 lb.) and 177 kg (390 lb.) and split the points in a tie at that weight. This brought to a close the second day of the competition.

In those far-off days the athletes were given a rest day (a nice touch which was reintroduced in 1994 after a break of some years). During this there was a pleasant interlude for some feats of strength—Bill Pearl, former Mr. Universe and Mr. America blowing up and bursting a hot water bottle; Jan Todd driving a nail through a board with her bare hand; Jesse Wood, a 6' tall Texan breaking a 4" x 2" plank over his own head; and Tennessee evangelist Paul Wrenn, 150 kg (23 st. 8 lb./330 lb.), pulling a Universal Studio tram with his teeth. Eight-times world powerlifting champ Larry Pacifico was the connecting link in a 10-man tug-of-war. Clasping his hands in front of him, he resisted the efforts of five men each side pulling on ropes looped around his elbow joints.

Next day commenced with a tram pull. The vehicle and its passengers weighed approximately 3,541 kg (7,800 lb.) and had to be pulled over a 100 ft. course in a timed event. Pulling in pairs, and switching trams for a second round, Reinhoudt took first place, Hedlund second, Young third, Dean fourth, and Kolb fifth. Bill Kazmaier was a non-scorer, unusual for him in this event.

There was yet another race, this time with a refrigerator. Two such timed races as consecutive events would now be frowned upon as creating imbalance. The fridge and apparatus weighed approximately 190.7 kg (420 lb.) and had to be carried over a 100 ft. course. Dube and Johns failed to make the distance. One of Kolb's straps broke and he finished badly. In the final heat the Swede, Hedlund, recorded 13.73 sec. to come first overall, and his opponent Reinhoudt was second with 15.44. Mighty Cleve Dean placed third in 17.45 sec., great for a man of 6' 7", and 209 kg (460 lb.) Kaz did 18.13 sec. to finish fourth; Bob Young placed fifth, doing 19.46 sec.

Tug-of-war completed the competition with the points doubled for this event. The rope was fixed round the waist of competitors, and the contestant who had pulled his opponent nearest to the centre line at the end of the time limit won the bout. Kolb, the Pittsburgh Steeler beat Bill Kazmaier, and Hedlund beat Don Reinhoudt. In the semifinal Don defaulted, and so Bill was awarded third place.

In the final pull, Kolb beat Hedlund easily, thus gaining 20 points. My personal opinion is that this could well have distorted placings beyond recognition, but fortunately Reinhoudt had enough points in hand to retain his lead and take the title. The big Swede was second and Kazmaier third. Fourth was Kolb, Young fifth, Dean sixth, Dube seventh, Johns eighth.

Don's win netted him $12,670, Hedlund took $9,080 and Kazmaier $7,195.

Great Gorge, New Jersey, USA 1980

This was Playboy Club country and their Bunny girls were much in evidence, but every strongmen there had a really heavy date in his diary—to win the title of World's Strongest Man. Although still held in America there was now a decidedly British input, with the main sponsor awarding the British Meat Trophy and, of course, cash prizes. Furthermore my old TWI friends Margo Green and Brian Venner travelled from London to produce the programme, which incidently was shown on Thames TV, rather than BBC as in more recent years.

The lineup included Olympian Geoff Capes, Britain's superb international shot-put champion. He had won Europe's Strongest Man to earn this place, and at 143 kg (22 st. 7 lb./315 lb.), he looked very trim. Reports of the bodyweights vary greatly, but heaviest was the American arm wrestler Cleve Dean, who was upwards of 200 kg (31 st. 6 lb./440 lb.); and lightest was Netherlands' Strongest Man, Gerard Du Prie, at 114 kg (18 st. 8 lb./260 lb.). The only other European was Lars Hedlund, Sweden, European champion powerlifter, at 140 kg (22 st./308 lb.). Representing Canada was shot-putter Bishop Dolegiewicz, at 134 kg (21 st. 11 lb./305 lb.); the remainder were Americans.

Billy Graham, former professional world wrestling champion and footballer looked very strong at exactly the same weight as Geoff Capes, although not as tall. Jerry Hannan, of USA's Olympic weightlifting squad, weighed 152 kg (23 st. 13 lb./335 lb.); Larry Kidney, powerlifting champion, 128.5 kg (20 st. 3 lb./283 lb.); Bill Kazmaier, 147.5 kg (23 st. 3 lb./325 lb.); and the defending champion Don Reinhoudt, 145 kg (22 st. 12 lb./320 lb.).

Geoff Capes (Great Britain) in the log lift, WSM 1980.

The last three were powerlifters—Kidney and Kazmaier had also been professional footballers, the former for ten years.

The contest opened with the log lift. The logs were short and thick, with very big arm and handholes. The first weight taken was 113.5 kg (250 lb.). After lifting 137.1 kg (302 lb.), Geoff Capes failed at 148 kg (326 lb.), at which stage there were six left in the event. The other shot-putter, Bishop Dolegiewicz, also missed. Bill Kazmaier pulled the 326 lb. log from the hang and pressed it easily. Don Reinhoudt missed the clean twice then got it to his chest on his third attempt. It was still very tough, needing two heaves in the second part of the lift before getting it aloft. It was a great show of determination, but things looked ominous for the title holder. A potential winner, like Hannan he pulled a hamstring in this first event.

Jerry Hannan and Don Reinhoudt failed with the next log, which weighed 157 kg (346 lb.) and shared points as third equal. Kaz and Lars succeeded and shared first place. The competition element seemed to be under-played here, and the finish seemed very inconclusive. Lars had fallen and hit his head on the log, and Kaz was perhaps simply saving some energy, but it was unsatisfactory for enthusiasts.

Throwing the 56 lb. (25.4 kg) for height came next. Du Prie didn't get past 10 ft., Cleve Dean failed at 12 ft., but after that the standard was surprisingly good.

Reinhoudt easily did 14½ ft., which at that time was good in any company. Three men cleared 16 ft. with ease: Dolegiewicz, Capes and Kazmaier were superb—explosive and coordinated. I was particularly impressed with the smooth, controlled throwing of the Canadian, who had won a bronze medal in shot putting at the Commonwealth Games.

The height went to 16' 7", and here Geoff failed, but that was no disgrace; what is surprising is that his two opponents succeeded, Bill Kazmaier by a considerable margin—fantastic! The bar was raised to 17 ft.—a new world record. Kaz missed and Bishop succeeded, clearing the bar by about one foot. Ten points for Dolegiewicz, nine for Kaz, eight for Capes. In 1980 it was the best 56 lb. throwing ever seen.

Bill Kazmaier led by three points after two events, Capes and Hedlund followed.

Truck pulling (a 7,718 kg/17,000 lb. vehicle) was again a popular feature, with the 100 ft. course well marked and nicely laid out. In the first two man heat, Cleve Dean, with a time of 29.34 sec., soundly whacked Du Prie, who took 38.99 sec. Billy Graham was slower in the next heat—40.39, while Larry Kidney did 32.91 sec.

Reinhoudt seemed to rally, and his 29.40 sec. was excellent, considering the difference in bodyweight between him and Cleve Dean. Hedlund, on leave from the

Swedish army, had a time of 32.91 sec. Could nobody beat big Cleve, the arm wrestler? Capes was known as a great truck puller, *he* could be the man to do it. At the end of his pull he was desperate to know his time. He didn't make it; 30.30 sec. was slower than he had hoped. Jerry Hannan in the other lane failed to complete the course.

The final round could perhaps provide a great climax to the event. Bill Kazmaier was against the Canadian, Bishop Dolegiewicz, who was rapidly accumulating new fans. Kaz won with a disappointing 31.44 sec., so it was a well-deserved win for Cleve, with plucky Don Reinhoudt second. Geoff Capes was third, and Kaz, although only fourth in the truck pull, was still overall leader with 25.5 points, with Lars Hedlund and Geoff Capes second equal. British hopes were high.

A wheelbarrow push was next, using a motor engine mounted on wheels. (I remembered this in 1995 when the competitors *carried two engines* mounted on a pole held across their shoulders). The two lane course was up a slight gradient, but these running events are tough on the heavy men. Dolegiewicz kicked off with a time of 18.5 sec. Du Prie took 21.07. In the second heat, Hedlund showed a good turn of speed with 17.5 to Kidney's 21.94.

The best heat was Kazmaier versus Capes, with super-fast times of 14.4 and 15.37 sec. respectively. These were not beaten. Dean failed to complete the course, and Reinhoudt was injured. Billy Graham did 22.67 sec. (and some clowning) in the final heat. The winning order of the wheelbarrow push was Bill Kazmaier, Geoff Capes and Lars Hedlund—which exactly reflected the overall position at this stage of the competition.

Bar bending was once popular with stage strongmen, and the finalists in this test showed that with a little specialisation they could compare with the best. In the closing stages a 4' 6" iron bar, eleven-sixteenths of an inch thick, had to be bent as much as possible. It could be done round the neck, over the head, round the knee or in any such fashion. The final measurement put Bill Kazmaier first with the ends of the bar only 5 inches apart. Geoff Capes was second with 17-inch distance. Lars Hedlund, although next, had 38 inches between the ends. Cleve Dean was fourth.

A 190.7 kg (420 lb.) fridge-freezer had to be carried in the next event. It was supported on a frame which the competitors held on their backs as they ran down the course. It was a visually impressive feat. Don Reinhoudt finally retired due to injuries. He had come into the competition in good condition, having push pressed a 150 kg (330 lb.) barrel overhead in training, but in the log lift (a last minute switch) had torn a hamstring. Don also tore his biceps in the 56 lb. for height and made it worse in the wheelbarrow push. He persisted in spite of excruciating pain until the tendon finally came off the bone. Tough though he was, poor Don needed a month off work after the competition to allow his injuries to heal. He had been a good and much respected champion.

Superstar Billy Graham had long been a heavy weight trainer and as a result, sported a magnificent strongman's physique. Being well experienced in wrestling hype, he had established a great rapport with the crowd as seen in the fridge-freezer carry, when his time of 16.98 sec. received a fine ovation, although the experts knew it was not enough for a top place.

It was the gritty Brit, Geoff Capes, who filled the premier place with a remarkable 10.72 sec. time. Bill Kazmaier was second (11.38), and Lars Hedlund third.

The Bunny girls were much in evidence throughout and featured strongly in this next event. It was

Bill Kazmaier (USA) in the Bunny lift, WSM 1980. Photo by Bruce Klemens.

a girl lift in which they sat on apparatus based on a Smith machine. Competitors had to squat with the ever increasing load of Bunnies, who did not distract the athletes one little bit.

Geoff showed his inexperience for the first and only time. Having failed to recover immediately from the squat, he moved his feet and then managed to complete the lift. This was ruled out, but commissioner Bruce Wilhelm, well experienced in these contests and other strength sports, allowed him another attempt. It was to no avail, but Wilhelm's nice gesture made everybody feel good.

With 424 kg (934 lb.) on the platform, only Lars and Kaz remained in the competition. The former failed, the latter succeeded so the points were as follows: Bill Kazmaier 10 points, Lars Hedlund (387.7 kg/854 lb.) 9, Larry Kidney (337.8 kg/744 lb.) 8, and Bishop Dolegiewicz and Jerry Hannan were equal with 6.5 each. Lars now took over second place, but Geoff was only one point behind him.

Next came the silver dollar lift, a dead lift with a higher than standard bar. The first round started at 227 kg (500 lb.) and gradually increased to 411.3 kg (906 lb.), with which Jerry Hannan failed and Larry Kidney succeeded. Lars Hedlund, using a sumo-like stance, failed with 424 kg (934 lb.), and Kaz, the world record-holder, made an easy lift. The load was increased to $1,700 silver dollars, which weighed 434 kg (956 lb.). There was a (Larry) Kidney failure at this weight, and the aggressive Bill Kazmaier lifted it to win again. He looked unbeatable.

The battery hold provided another true strongman event, even more static than the dead lift. Some of the techniques looked decidedly suspect because of bent arms; I thought Jerry Hannan, Lars Hedlund and Bill Kazmaier used the best styles.

Being first in this event is always difficult, but Cleve Dean managed 22.29 sec. Geoff Capes, with shoulders intact in those days, did 31.64 sec. Bishop did a few seconds more, but his right arm in particular seemed rather bent. Gerard Du Prie held the battery horizontal for some 33 sec. Billy Graham contracted his pectorals and locked his arms on his lats for the best time so far, 45.5 sec. It was a short-lived lead, with Jerry Hannan coming next and taking over with 48.75 sec. in a fine hold. Lars Hedlund and Larry Kidney were around the 40 sec. bracket, and Kaz, using the best technique I have seen him employ, pushed up to the 43-second zone.

The end result saw some new high scorers, Hannan 10 points, Graham 9 and Kazmaier 8. Overall placings were now Kazmaier, Hedlund, Capes, Dolegiewicz.

These four went on to compete in tug-of-war for the final event. What I see as a crazy situation emerged as a result of a doubtful scoring system where double points were in effect for this last event. In spite of all his wins, if Kaz was beaten in the semifinals by Hedlund, who then went on to win the final, then the Swede would win the title. The draw for the first round matched Kazmaier against Hedlund, and Capes against Dolegiewicz.

Kaz and Geoff won their spirited bouts and then met up for the very last test. They faced each other along the rope, and I would love to say it was a great finish, but that's not the way I saw it. Both men dug in and played a waiting game. Four minutes passed and neither yielded. Six minutes and attention was beginning to wander. Seven minutes and it was like watching grass grow. Eight minutes and the camera crew were mentally calculating the possibilities of overtime. A little while later, it seemed like hours, Geoff suddenly conceded the pull and it was all over.

Bill Kazmaier had won his first World's Strongest Man title, and turned out to be a great champion. Sweden's Lars Hedlund was back in second place, as in the previous year, and the new kid on the block, Geoff Capes, did well in his debut to place third.

Great Gorge, New Jersey, USA 1981

The Playboy resort in Great Gorge, deep in the Pocono Mountains in upstate New Jersey was again the setting for the fifth World's Strongest Man competition. As is almost invariably the case over the years, there was doubt about where and when the competition would be staged, if it would be in 1981 or 1982, and whether indeed there would be a competition, even although TV ratings had been very good. The result was a major change with NBC taking over from CBS, which had covered the contest since its inception.

As far as the line-up was concerned, connoisseurs have not considered this a vintage year. There was no criticism of the powerlifters, but there were comments on the imbalance of three shot-putters, two football players and only one Olympic lifter, only one of these six from overseas. If the title was to have creditability there would have to be a proper international lineup.

The competitors were Bill Kazmaier, defending champion and legendary powerlifter; Keith Bishop, offensive linesman of the Denver Broncos and the smallest man in the competition at 191 cm (6' 3") and 120 kg (18 st. 13 lb./265 lb.)!; Geoff Capes, Olympic shot-putter and Britain's Strongest Man; Jerry Hannan, the 1981 U. S. senior national superheavyweight weightlifting champion; Durwin Piper, California powerlifting champion, who weighed between 197-204 kg (435-450 lb.); Staggo Piszko, Netherlands' Strongest Man and Dutch powerlifting champion; Dave Waddington, noted powerlifter who squatted with more than half a ton; Craig Wolfley, offensive guard of the Pittsburgh Steelers; Joe Zelezniak, a rapidly improving shot-putter; and Bishop Dolegiewicz, shot-putter who was fourth in the 1980 WSM competition.

There was but little change in the format around this time, and the log lift opened the competition, with a series of superb looking logs. Lifters were allowed as many lifts as they wished and could make as many attempts as required within 90 seconds. They were also allowed to pass if they did not wish to attempt a certain weight.

Dolegiewicz, whose performance the previous year had been very impressive, did 88.5 kg (195 lb.), passed on 104.4 kg (230 lb.), and failed at 125.3 kg (276 lb.). The previous year he did 137.1 kg (302 lb.) fairly easily, but an injury sustained in the WSM was still hindering him, and it seemed unwise to invite him in such circumstances. The Canadian had a rough ride this time.

Bishop, Capes and Zelezniak went out at 141.7 kg (312 lb.), and Piper and Waddington failed with 154.4 kg (340 lb.). The next stage, 163.4 kg (360 lb.) proved to be too much for Hannan, Piszko and Wolfley, but it was a breeze for Kaz. The passes and misses led to the following order: Kazmaier 10 points; Hannan, Wolfley, and Piszko 8 each; Waddington and Piper 5.5 each; Capes, Bishop and Zelezniak 3 each; Dolegiewicz 1.

In the 56 lb for height event, using one hand only, the weight was thrown over a crossbar between pole vaulting stands. Five men failed to go beyond the opening height of 12 ft., while Geoff Capes went on to win with 17 ft. Bill Kazmaier did a fine 16½ ft., throwing very consistently and up until the last, looking good enough to win. Dolegiewicz came third, after winning the event last time. Hannan did 15½ ft. to place fourth, and Bishop in fifth place did 14 ft.

There were to be two heats in the truck pull, as the event was done with two trucks. Since there are invariably differences, the fairer methods used in later contests had a second round where competitors switched trucks and averaged the time or else all used the same truck. On this occasion, the severity of the event, using 3,178 kg (7,000 lb.) trucks over a 100 ft. course, led to judging being done on a one pull only basis.

Geoff Capes won with 30.95 sec., which was close to Cleve Dean's record at that time. Staggo Piszko was close behind him with 31.20 sec. Kaz, who had raced with Capes, came third with 34.94 sec., but even his previous season's 31.44 would not have altered his placing. Bishop crossed the line at 35.95 sec. to gain fourth; then came Waddington (37 sec.), Hannan (39.79), Zelezniak (47.73), Dolegiewicz (47.98) and Piper (48.1). Wolfley failed to complete the course.

In a barrow push, a 336 kg (740 lb.) engine was mounted on two wheels and had to be pushed up an incline. Nowadays the competitors lift the back of a standard four-wheeled pick-up truck, complete with engine, and push the entire load about the same distance. The gargantuan competitors, not particularly suited to this event, had a tough time, but the results were good, the first seven all beating the previous year's best time. Bill Kazmaier steamed to a win (9.65 sec.) with Capes again in hot pursuit (10.04); Zelezniak was a commendable third with 10.61. Further placings were Bishop, Waddington, Hannan, Piszko, in that order—all up on the previous year's men—then came Dolegiewicz, Piper and Wolfley.

For the first, but certainly not the last time, there was beer keg loading. The 76.3 kg (168 lb.) kegs had to be lifted, carried and heaved on to a truck, with the nearest keg six feet from the vehicle. A very demanding event, many finished physically distressed and requiring oxygen. There were some good races and emotive performances when Bishop and Zelezniak ran out of steam with two barrels to go. Both took several attempts: Bishop finally clocked 1: 23.81 minutes while his opponent still persevered and finally completed the task but severely smashed one of his fingers in the process.

In the fastest heat Geoff Capes gave a striking demonstration of controlled, methodical precision and stormed through to a fine 57.08 sec. Bill Kazmaier gave a glimpse of his awesome power by simply standing and *throwing the kegs* on to the truck, taking a mere 48.11 sec. to win the event! The end result was Kazmaier, Capes, Waddington, Dolegiewicz, Piszko, Hannan, Wolfley, Bishop, Zelezniak, Piper.

The battery hold was repeated from the previous year, and while Olympic lifter Hannan had won then, this time powerlifters swept the board, with Piper and Waddington in the premier places. The first man is always at a disadvantage without any mark to beat, but on this occasion Durwin Piper was exceptional, producing a time which nobody else could achieve. He held the 27.2 kg (60 lb.) battery for 43.63 sec. Waddington was nearly two seconds slower. Hannan, suffering from an injury in the previous event, could not match his previous winning time which would have been good enough to win again; instead he placed third with 40.81 sec. Wolfley surprisingly edged out Kaz by a fraction of a second, and Piszko pushed Capes into seventh place, a blow for the big Brit; Bishop, Dolegiewicz and Zelezniak trailed.

Bar bending may be great to watch, but as already mentioned, it's not favoured by competitors owing to injury problems. Bars of varying lengths and thickness were used, the smallest being half-an-inch thick and 3' long. Hannan and Dolegiewicz went out at this stage. The next was 6" longer but was one-sixteenth thicker. Only Waddington and Piper failed to bend these completely. At five-eights inches thick and 4 ft. long, only Capes and Kazmaier succeeded. In a disturbing final, a one and one-sixteenth-inch bar was used, and Kazmaier was severely injured.

Kaz's biceps and deltoid soon showed multi-coloured bruising, with Geoff Capes suffering a similar fate. Frantically icing his shoulder between every attempt, Geoff made a brave show and it paid off. It was he who got the winning ten points, while Bill got nine. It was said that a change from hot rolled steel to cold rolled bars was the main cause of the problem. Hot rolled steel is favoured by competitors.

In the leg strength test, the services of the Playboy Bunnies was dispensed with as the contestants objected to their fidgeting and movement while the squat was being performed, and instead building blocks were used. They were less impressive as well as less attractive. "Bunnies should be mandatory," grunted one disenchanted chauvinist.

Kaz was well and truly annoyed at the announcer's continual comments regarding Dave Waddington's legs being the strongest in the world. The speaker, Hal Connolly, the champion field athlete, probably did Dave a disservice as Kaz got psyched up until his eyes seemed to bulge, and he won in convincing style, lifting 440 kg (969 lb.) with ease while Waddington failed. The latter's judgment seemed suspect when he passed on 380.5 kg (838 lb.), which left the big Piper playing a merry tune in second place. As was common in those days, there was a five-way draw with Capes, Hannan, Bishop, Zelezniak and Dolegiewicz bringing up the rear each getting three points. Bill Kazmaier was now 14 points ahead of Capes and 23 ahead of Waddington in third place, and for knowledgeable fans it was all over, bar the shouting—and there was plenty of this coming soon.

A silver dollar dead lift opened safely with nobody failing until 318 kg (700 lb.) when Bronco Bishop went out. Piszko failed with 60 lb. more, and Zelezniak and Dolegiewicz went out at 381.4 kg (840 lb.). Kaz went bananas when Geoff Capes' sumo-style dead lift of the same weight was passed, and even more when Bruce Wilhelm, the power commissioner, supported the decision. In true Kazmaier style, Bill let his feelings be known in front of the cameras as he finished his following lifts.

Since as chief referee I have been involved in such incidents, my behind-the-scenes comments may be of interest. Firstly, I can understand Bill's reactions in such circumstances. For a number of reasons I felt that the style used by Geoff, although within the rules of powerlifting, was not suitable for strength competitions. However for *one* main reason the rules were altered when I was brought in to officiate some years later. The bar is in a high position in the containers, not just a few inches from the ground as in powerlifting; the bar bends considerably, tilting the boxes and bringing them inward. With the very wide stance in sumo-style, the long legs of a 6' 5" lifter like Geoff Capes brings the toes of slippered feet close under the edge of the boxes. In these competitions there are often lost handholds and slips, and in another similar event in Scandinavia, a competitor had a toe amputated as a result of a lost hold.

There are quite different technical reasons why Kaz got a bit mad. He said Capes had not stood fully erect and pulled the shoulders back. There was doubt and I have some sympathy, but having said that, the commissioner is in a good position to see the lift and whether or not it was acceptable. I know Bruce Wilhelm to be a very experienced, honest man who knows his sport. The fact that he accepted a lift of a foreigner against an American opponent only serves to highlight his impartiality. Bill's record in powerlifting and strength competitions shows he quite often raged, much to the surprise of people who had a great admiration for him and would not wish to give him a raw deal. He was now 18 points ahead of Capes and 24.5 points ahead of Waddington, his nearest rivals. It would have done his popularity a lot of good if he had been less emotive at this stage.

On next to the caber toss—throwing a 100 lb. telephone pole (45.4 kg.), not in the traditional Scottish way, but for distance. Balancing this 14 ft. caber was hard enough without the crosswind with which the competitors had to contend. To run and throw it in these circumstances made it a real strongman sport. It was done in a series of qualifying rounds, a lengthy procedure, and the results were a little out of step with other events. Zelezniak with 40 ft. was tremendous. Waddington was a surprised second with a fine 38' 6". The very experienced Geoff Capes, a Highland Games champion, was third with 38' 4½", and Kaz was seventh.

Sumo wrestling was selected for the final, and it was an exceedingly popular choice, with the contestants in *mawashis*, the nappy-like garb of Japanese wrestlers. Wolfley beat Piszko, Hannan pushed Zelezniak out of the ring, Bishop threw Waddington. There was some confusion regarding as to who won between Dolegiewicz and Capes, and a rematch was ordered, in which Geoff Capes was a clear winner. Kaz withdrew after hurting his shoulder against Piper.

In this round robin format, Wolfley then met Hannan, and Bishop clashed with Piper, the former winning in each case. After a bye, Capes was beaten by Bishop, who went on to match Wolfley in the final. The two American football players produced a good bout, with

Keith Bishop of the Denver Broncos beating Pittsburgh Steelers defensive guard. The event was worth a bonus of $1,000 to Keith and 20 points instead of the usual 10. The points pulled up his score; he had placed low in several events, indeed nobody placed lower in the squat and in the dead lift. Again I think this highlights an anomaly in the old scoring system. Would it not be very unfair if the 20 points pulled a mediocre competitor into first place?

In the final analysis Bill Kazmaier, with 96 points, was a very worthy winner of the $20,000. Geoff Capes was also well ahead of his nearest rival with 88 points, and he took home $10,000. Dave Waddington was third and received $7,000, followed by Hannan who got $5,000, Wolfley $3,500, Bishop $4,000, Piszko $2,500, Piper $2,000 and Zelezniak and Dolegiewicz each $1,000.

Magic Mountain, Southern California, USA 1982

There was only one European, the rest were North American, but the 1982 entry was a good one, led by Bill Kazmaier, weighing 150 kg (23 st. 8 lb./330 lb.) and with two victories already under his belt. Others included Dave Waddington, the first to officially squat 454 kg (1,000 lb.) and third in the 1981 WSM event; Ernie Hackett, world 275 lb. powerlifting champ of 1981 and ex-world record holder in the squat; Big Bill Dunn, university strength coach and formidable powerlifter and athlete; John Gamble, the 275 lb. senior national champion; Russ Browner of the Cincinnati Bengals; Jim Hough of the Minnesota Vikings; Curt Marsh, a graduate of the University of Washington and at that time with the Los Angeles Raiders; and Tom Magee of Canada, the 1981 275 lb. world championship silver medallist. The sole European was Geoff Capes, the British shot put champion, third in 1980 and second in 1981.

There were none of the great Scandinavian strongmen or European powerlifters and nobody from the southern part of the globe, and while recognising the merit of Bill Kazmaier, there were rumblings from other parts of the world which laid claim to great traditions in strength.

The first event was the log lift, won by Kaz with Hackett, a former Olympic lifter, in second place. Four men placed equal third: Waddington, Capes, Gamble and Magee split the points.

The previous year's result in the 56 lb. throw for height was reversed when Bill Kazmaier took first and Geoff Capes second. Tom Magee placed third, and Hackett's fourth was enough for him to retain overall second place.

The ever-popular truck pull saw Kazmaier and Capes at the top again, and Geoff now took over the overall second place when a 7,718 kg (17,000 lb.) truck was pulled over a 100 ft. course. The football players had been doing quite well, and Marsh placed third, Waddington fourth, and Dunn fifth.

Bar bending, a pet hate of the competitors, has since been dropped because of the numerous injuries sustained during competition. Kaz and Capes had both been injured in 1981 and both adjusted their techniques for 1982. Geoff improved to win the event, but Bill dropped to fourth, and the gap between the two narrowed to 2.5 points. Gamble, however, improved his position by placing second and moved up to fourth overall, just behind Magee who was fifth in the bar bend. This proved to be the highlight of the competition for Hough, who placed third with the bars.

Tossing the caber for distance produced some surprises for experts when Dave Waddington won the event; Tom Magee was second and Bill Kazmaier third. Waddington had been tenth the previous year, and Geoff Capes and Bill Kazmaier later became amongst the best in the world in this event. Marsh was still hanging in and placed ahead of Gamble, who was beating him for the overall fourth place.

In the loading race, the athletic Tom Magee and Curt Marsh took the premier places in putting beer kegs onto a truck in the fastest possible time. Capes, Waddington and Kazmaier took the next three spots in this gruelling trial, which leaves the competitors gasping for breath. The superheavyweights Gamble and Dunn found their bodyweights a handicap rather than a help and finished last.

Gamble redeemed himself in the battery hold where a truck battery had to be held forward on extended arms for as long as possible. It was his best placing in the contest. Ernie Hackett did remarkably well for one with such a long reach and came second. Bill Dunn also liked this static event and took third place. Tom Magee was jubilant when his fourth place took him ahead of Capes overall. Geoff always hated this event and placed last. It was a major setback to his championship hopes. A fifth place eroded Bill Kazmaier's lead but he was still in a good position.

Powerlifters were comfortable with the next lift, a squat with a block on a sliding rack. It was three-way tie for first place with Magee, Waddington and Hackett sharing top spot. In this competition only one man *did not* tie, this was Hough in eighth place. There was a tie for Kaz and Gamble, then another draw with Capes and Dunn splitting sixth place.

In the dead lift there was yet another tie for first place, and indeed draws again all the way down except for the last place. Today's TV producers would probably have apoplexy. Placings were Kazmaier and Hackett, Magee and Gamble, Waddington and Dunn, Capes, Hough and Browner, then Marsh on his own.

The final event was a lengthy sumo wrestling tournament, and the points were doubled for this event, giving a very definite edge to contact or combat sportsmen. Marsh and Browning the football players did well, with Marsh getting a massive, and I believe, unfair, 20 points for first place. Kaz placed second and displayed considerable tactical skill in all his bouts. He first beat Waddington in a tough bout and disposed of John Gamble, a worthy competitor throughout the whole competition. Kaz even beat Marsh in the earlier rounds; therefore it was ironic that the Raider should best him in the final. I mention this as Tom Magee had gone into the sumo 10 points behind Kaz, yet because of the double points for one event could easily have emerged the winner. Fortunately it worked out O.K. In sumo, March won, Kaz was runner-up; Browner, the Bengal footballer, enjoyed 16 points as third (although last in the overall competition and in four other events), Gamble was fourth, and Magee and Capes tied in fifth place.

The final scoring saw Bill Kazmaier a worthy winner for the third time with the Canadian Adonis Tom Magee second, John Gamble third and the English shot-putter Geoff Capes fourth. Ernie Hackett came fifth, then Marsh, Waddington, Dunn, Hough and Browner.

Christchurch, New Zealand 1983

For the first time the competition moved from North America, and significant changes were seen in Christchurch, New Zealand. The United States had two representatives, John Gamble and Doyle Kenady, while Africa and the Antipodes were represented for the first time. From Scandinavia, Jon Pall Sigmarsson of Iceland made a startling debut in the competition, and from the European continent were Siem Wulfse (Netherlands) and Geoff Capes, again representing Britain.

Capes's previous experience stood him in good stead, and although hard pressed by Wulfse and the new boy Sigmarsson, who won three events to Geoff's two wins, the Briton won by virtue of a higher average.

The first event was steel bar bending. Siem Wulfse, a dour European powerlifting champion, won this event bending a bar 15 mm thick. He did a complete bend to get the ends of the bar within 20 cm (8 in.) of each other. Tom Magee, world powerlifting champion was second, bending the bar to 45 cm and Geoff Capes bent the steel to 85.7 cm. John Gamble and Sigmarsson followed next.

The Fergus walk provided the second event. Often known as the farmer's walk, this was my first innovation to the World's Strongest Man competition, and it has now become one of the standard tests all over the world. Thick, awkward logs which scraped the thighs, were carried, one in each hand, for as far as possible. Sigmarsson won by carrying this 158.9 kg (350 lb.) load for 176' 6". He remained virtually unbeaten in this event throughout his career, and his records still stand; he was seldom pressed to the limit, usually doing just enough to win. Geoff Capes was second, Wulfse third, and fourth was the huge Nigerian, Chris Okonkwo, who put the shot at the Olympic Games. Now the athletes usually carry oxygen cylinders with handles, filled up to as much as 95.3 kg (210 lb.) each for the toughest competitions.

I have great reservations about the procedure in the dead lift as conducted in this competition. It started at 246 kg (542 lb.), far too light for men of this calibre, and Okonkwo had eight attempts working up to 385 kg (849 lb.) before dropping out. A higher start would most likely have given better results to most lifters. Capes went up to 415 kg (915 lb.) before packing in, and Allan Hallberg, the homeland representative cheered by his own crowd, failed at 475 kg (1,047 lb.) after succeeding with 455 kg (1,003 lb.). Tom Magee and Sigmarsson fought it out for the top spot, the Icelander doing 525 kg (1,157½ lb.) and the Canadian doing 10 kg more to win. Kenady, Gamble and Wulfse followed in that order. Tom had 14 lifts, Jon Pall 15; there were 99 dead lifts in total, leaving the TV crew nearly as tired as the lifters—a marathon event.

In event four, a tractor pull had to be abandoned after the first competitors failed the test. We have always found negative results with this type of vehicle, and therefore do everything possible to avoid using them, even if sponsorship depends on the inclusion of tractors. Their name hints at the problem—too much traction. A lorry of nearly ten tons was substituted—the exact weight of the vehicle was 10,120 kg (22,315 lb.). Geoff Capes, with superb pulling technique, was an easy winner, covering the 30-metre course in 42.6 sec. Wulfse was second and Okonkwo third.

There was a £1,000 bonus prize for the leader at this halfway stage of the competition, and this was won by Siem Wulfse, "Simon the Wolf." The muscular Canadian Tom Magee was second overall.

The overhead rock lift caused a few headaches—literally! The boulders weighed 84, 99.5, 103.5, 110, 115, 121 and 126 kg (185-278 lb.). Gamble succeeded with all of these. Sigmarsson failed the last only, but Wulfse had also done the 121 kg boulder so the two tied. (With current rules, where efforts are made to split ties, Sigmarsson would have won by fewer attempts). Magee and Capes, with the same number of attempts, tied at 115 kg, and Okonkwo and Kenady tied in sixth place.

Throwing the 56 lb. (25.4 kg) weight over a bar is a Scottish event as old as the hills, and the heights the strongmen achieved were much in line with those of experienced Highland Games competitors at that time. Standards have risen considerably since then, largely due to the interest taken by international strength athletes. Geoff Capes and Tom Magee both cleared 15' 6" and failed at 16 ft. Capes, having fewer failures, was given the verdict as outlined in the rules. Jon Pall and Siem were next, followed by Chris Okonkwo. Geoff had already been involved in Highland Games, but later all of those mentioned travelled to Scotland and competed with distinction.

A wool hoist with a 2½ cwt. (127 kg) wool bale was introduced in an effort to provide an ethnic event. The blonde Norseman, Sigmarsson, pulled it to 2 m 70.8 cm (8 ft. 10½ in.) to win. Geoff Capes achieved 2 m 7 cm (6 ft. 9½ in.), and this was New Zealander Allan Hallberg's best event, with a third at 1 m 15.6 cm (3 ft. 9½ in.).

There was now a change in the overall placing, with the Briton moving into first place over the previous leader Wulfse, who had dropped to fifth in the wool hoist. Sigmarsson was third, having hovered round there from the start. Tom Magee in fourth was still much in contention. Geoff Capes was now very confident but could not afford to relax, for although the more experienced Dutchman may have seemed to be the greatest threat, the highly motivated and supremely fit Icelander was still a big threat. What a finish it was!

The sacks of flour were a little light by current standards at 75 kg (165 lb.), compared with the 100 kg (220 lb.) often used nowadays. However, there were ten sacks, whereas it is now considered more appropriate to have as little as six loading objects for a test of strength. The wild Viking loaded all sacks in a splendid 1 min. 31.7 sec. to win the race. Geoff Capes heaved the sacks on the wagon in 1 min. 36.3 sec., pausing to take a swig of water from a well placed cup. It was not bravado in such a vital test, it was an indication of his careful attention to detail, which he always demonstrated throughout his career. The fine flour from the sacks covered the competitors and dried their mouths, and Geoff had anticipated this. Siem Wulfse faded somewhat during the lung-bursting trial, finishing more than 13 sec. behind Sigmarsson and 8 sec. behind Geoff.

In the final analysis, the title was won by Geoff Capes of England and Britain (it was only later that separate countries in the United Kingdom were given places). Sigmarsson was second, his performance and charisma already noted, and he was rewarded with a £1,000 "personality" bonus as the "Man of the Competition." Although he became a great and valued friend of mine, I did not agree with these bonuses for several reasons. I think they encouraged unduly extrovert behaviour, although in Jon Pall's case it was entirely natural and continued long after the bonus prizes disappeared. However the extra prizes also distorted the resulting rewards. Capes won a £3,000 first prize. Sigmarsson took home £3,500, (£2,500 second prize and £1,000 Man of the Competition) and Wulfse had £3,000 like the winner (£2,000 third prize and £1,000 for being leader at halfway).

The referee was Les Mills, a popular international athlete who became "mayor" of the Commonwealth Games Village at Auckland, 1990. He was ably assisted by my old weightlifting teammates and pals Precious Mackenzie and Georgie Newton. Precious was both a weightlifting and powerlifting champion and a fine acrobat as well. Georgie won many weightlifting titles and did the British team proud in international matches in the 1960s. Both had physiques which could have won bodybuilding titles if they had been so inclined.

It was Geoff Capes' first World's Strongest Man title, and he was quite emotional. Although he had long been at the top in athletic circles, this win meant a great deal to him, and he relished every second of his victory.

Mora, Sweden 1984

For the first time the contest was held in a cold, nay, *freezing* climate. Many TV viewers thought it made a nice change.

With DAF Trucks as the new multinational sponsor, it was not surprising that the first event should be a vehicle pull with a 10-ton DAF truck. Jon Pall Sigmarsson (Iceland) gave notice of the shape of things to come by winning in convincing style, with a time of 33 seconds over the 30-metre course. A new entrant in this competition was Ab Wolders, Netherlands' Strongest Man, a judoka turned powerlifter. He was truly a great strength athlete, strong enough to win European powerlifting gold medals, yet very supple and extremely fast. Ab was second in the truck pull, beating Geoff Capes in one of his favourite events (35.9 sec. to Geoff's 38.5 sec.).

Fourth was the African representative Pius Ochieng (Kenya), an outstanding result of 47.5 sec. as he was only 168 cm (5' 6") in height and 95 kg (15 st./210 lb.) bodyweight. Fifth was Rudi Küster of Germany (55.1 secs), who became a well-known figure in these competitions. Dave Waddington, who had competed in 1981 and 1982, represented America and placed sixth in the truck pull, ahead of Yngve Gustavsson (Sweden) and Daniel Poulin (Canada).

The timber toss involved tossing a log as far as possible from behind a line. It is based on a *stangstortning*, a traditional sport from the Swedish island of Gotland and is very similar to caber tossing in Highland Games. Three throws were allowed, with the best to count for scoring

Jon Pall Sigmarsson (Iceland) in the truck pull, WSM 1984.

purposes. The log was 5 metres long (approx 16½ feet), which is a good length for such an event, but it was light at 36 kg (79 lb.). Sigmarsson again won, throwing 56' 9" (17.30 m). Capes did 54' 11" (16.74 m), Waddington 49' 10" (15.19 m), Wolders 44' 3" (13.49 m), and Küster 34' 5" (10.49 m).

In the rock lift, the Icelander won his third consecutive event, lifting 125 kg (275½ lb.). Geoff Capes was again second, succeeding with 120 kg (264½ lb.). Wolders was third, and this order was reflected in the overall score. In general, the standard in this event was poor although the top men were up to par.

Ab Wolders came into his own in the horse hold, which was with a wooden horse weighing 25 kg (55 lb.). It was held in a forward hold with straight arms. This, like the crucifix hold, is a nightmare for officials as many competitors have poor arm locks, probably caused by previous injuries. On this occasion, Küster started with an invalid arm position and was stopped by the referee. Given a second attempt, Rudi finished third with 34.2 sec. Wolders did 46.9 sec. in first place, and Sigmarsson 40.1 for second. Waddington was down to 27.6 in fourth, Gustavsson 26.7; Capes, who hated all forward and sideways holds, did 22.6. Poulin clocked 19.2, and Ochieng a mere 11 sec.

At this halfway stage, Sigmarsson had a commanding lead at 31 points, to Wolders at 26 and Capes 23.

A race pushing a sledge came next, with a course of 100 m and the sledge and passengers weighing 250 kg (551 lb.). There were two heats of four, with the two winners and the two fastest losers going into the final. The others scored on their heat times. Wolders won heat one in 17.8 secs. Heat two was faster, with Capes doing 17.2, Sigmarsson 17.7, and Waddington 17.9 sec. The latter two went into the final as the fastest losers.

In the final, Capes and Sigmarsson were both faster but the order was the same. Indeed had heat times alone been used for scoring, the finishing order would have been identical: Capes 16.9, Sigmarsson 17.2, Wolders 17.4, Waddington 21.

In this year's loading race, eight ice blocks, each weighing 70 kg (154 lb.) had to be loaded on a truck set four metres from the starting point. All but Waddington succeeded with the eight blocks, and Wolders won again in 46.6 sec. Others were Sigmarsson 50.7 sec., Capes 53.5, Küster 56, Poulin 1 min. 6.9 sec., Gustavsson 2 min. 44.2 sec., and Ochieng 4 mins 45.8 sec. Waddington loaded only seven barrels. Poor Ochieng, accustomed to Kenya's scorching sun, suffered badly from the cold and long waiting periods.

A bench press, done with a series of logs, provided some interesting and unexpected results. There were no proper grips on the logs. Waddington of the United States won by lifting the eighth log—230 kg (507

Above: Jon Pall Sigmarsson (Iceland) in the bench press, WSM 1984.
Below: Ab Wolders (The Netherlands), left, and Yngve Gustavsson (Sweden), right, arm wrestling, WSM 1984.

lb.). Capes did 220 kg (485 lb.), which beat both Wolders and Sigmarsson, who tied at 210 kg (463 lb.).

Arm wrestling provided the final event, much against my wishes, but on this occasion I worried unnecessarily. Here are the results of the bouts:

1. *Sigmarsson beat Waddington*
2. *Wolders beat Gustavsson*
3. *Capes beat Ochieng*
4. *Poulin beat Küster*
5. *Waddington beat Ochieng*
6. *Küster beat Gustavsson*
7. *Sigmarsson beat Capes*
8. *Poulin beat Wolders*
9. *Ochieng beat Gustavsson*
10. *Waddington beat Küster*
11. *Capes conceded to Wolders; and Sigmarsson conceded to Poulin*

It was a good competition, well-handled by Maurice Woodman, brought in especially for arm wrestling only. Sigmarsson and Wolders were in unassailable positions by the time they reached their final bouts, hence the results.

Sigmarsson had fulfilled the promise shown in his debut the previous year and won the first of his world titles. Ab Wolders was second, and in third place Geoff Capes was not too downhearted, although he hated the Viking's victory roar, "The King has lost his crown!" In their version of the programme, Avro TV synchronised the music of this tune with Jon Pall's words. Capes had the same message for the Viking as Arnold Schwarzenegger made famous in *Terminator*—"I'll be back."

Cascais, Portugal 1985

I had long worked behind the scenes providing information for and advising TWI's producers Ken Hawkes and Margo Green. Margo brought me into a higher profile role by inviting me to referee Britain's Strongest Man in the early 1980s, and that dear old gentleman Ken Hawkes promoted me to referee for the World's Strongest Man in 1985. I worked closely with Ken until his final competition in 1992 when several changes took place. He and Simon Betts of the BBC created a good atmosphere for competition.

The start of a new era, the special, happy memories of Cascais have remained vividly in my mind. Camera crews from Britain, Netherlands, France and, of course, the host country filmed every muscle-searing movement and accompanying grimaces as powerlifters, throwers, pro-wrestlers, Highland Games athletes and Olympic lifters vied with each other. The brightly painted fishing boats bobbing in the bay made a colourful background to many events with a maritime theme.

With DAF Trucks as sponsor, the truck pull took pride of place and was won by Geoff Capes, pulling a 7½-tonne truck 30 m in 30.7 sec. Powerlifters George Hechter (USA) and Tom Magee (Canada) were second and third.

I had a sleepless night, having seen that the dead lift had to be done with a valuable old antique oxcart from an agricultural museum. It had been strengthened at my request, but not enough to ease my mind, knowing the kind of load it had to bear and the "dumping" it may have to suffer. With only three men left in the dead lift, it became very tactical. Sigmarsson and Hechter did 515 kg (1,135½ lb.). Cees De Vreugd, who proudly wore his gold medal won a week earlier at the powerlifting championships, took 525 kg (1,157½ lb.) and succeeded. At 535 and 545 kg (1,180 and 1,202 lb.), there were no takers. Sigmarsson and Hechter decided they could not risk more and tried 555 kg (1,223½ lb.) and both failed. Foxy Cees did not have to try any more, his 525 kg had been enough to win.

There had been a dramatic incident when Geoff Capes lowered the ox cart rather heavily, incurring the wrath of a highly placed TV executive. Geoff is not easily intimidated, "There is the referee," he retorted pointing to me. "He, not you, says whether it is a good or bad lift." It had been a good lift, and I passed it without any doubt, but I had qualms about the wooden ox cart. My worries however were unnecessary; the wooden wheeled antique withstood all the punishment it was given. Over the years I wish I could have said the same for the other objects provided for the competitions. Only since we have provided all the main items has this ceased to be a major problem.

Getting the Sack

No, I was not dismissed at this early stage—we got the sacks for the next event, a sack and barrow race. A 80 kg (176½

Geoff Capes in the oxcart dead lift, WSM 1985.

Jon Pall Sigmarsson lifting Grizzly Brown, WSM 1985.

lb.) sack had to be carried 50 metres, and the athlete had then to return 50 metres pushing a porter's barrow loaded to 350 kg (772 lb.). These were not specially made barrows, but ones "borrowed" from the airport on arrival! Geoff Capes was back in the picture, winning in 29.3 sec.—a fast time for 100 metres with such loads. His old rival Sigmarsson was hot on his heels, and the big Finn, Roger Ekstrom was third.

Boat Haul

A boat and its contents, total 233 kg (514 lb.) had to be hauled up a steep ramp. It was a good event, as any relaxation on the part of the athlete allowed the boat to slip back, thus losing time. Geoff Capes, now in great spirits, pulled the craft over the whole steep course in 19.9 sec. The first four places were exactly the same as the previous event: Capes, Sigmarsson, Ekstrom, De Vreugd.

"And the First Shall Come Last, and the Last Come First"

That was the result of the next test when two lovely brass bells, totalling 25 kg (55 lb.), were held for as long as possible with arms raised sideways. Grizzly Brown broke the world record by holding the bells 64.8 sec., and Geoff Capes came last with 22.2 sec., the event causing him great pain in the shoulder joints.

Grizzly is one of those amazing characters who have greatly enhanced the strength scene. While I was in California the previous year and covering a story about another amazing personality, the so-called "She-Beast," aka "Pillow," the latter told me about Grizzly, who had been causing tongues to wag with his strength records in incline pressing and in pro-wrestling with Ripper Ross. Of course the tongue that wagged the most was Grizzly's. He was a happy, voluble, massive strongman, 5' 11" in height and 5' 5" round the chest. His back was almost a yard wide, and his arms hung like hams from his shoulders. The media loved him. He always made controversial or amusing comments or had some funny antic to perform.

Second to the Grizz was De Vreugd, and the Viking was third. The overall score changed radically at this stage with Geoff and Cees first equal with 30 points, and Sigmarsson only one-half point behind. The rest were now virtually out of the running. This overall placing and differences remained exactly the same even after the next test, the port wine cask lift.

I classed this as a poor event because a change of barrel size at 120 kg (264½ lb.), a much larger cask than before, resulted in a multiple draw, although there were clearly great differences in respective abilities. Six men succeeded with 115 kg (253½ lb.). None of those did the 120 kg (264½ lb.) although Sigmarsson very nearly succeeded. Near misses don't count, so he got the same points as a person who retired without trying the weight!

The swingletree is an old Scottish test of strength, still widely practised in rural districts and is also popular with west of Scotland wrestlers. Opponents sit facing each other, feet to feet. They hold a bar, alternate grasp, ready to pull on the referee's signal. It is like a seated dead lift with the loser being lifted up by the strength of the victor's pull.

The two best won their places for entirely different reasons. Geoff Capes, the winner, had very fast reactions and pulled hard and fast on the signal, beating his opponents to the pull. Grizzly on the other hand, a superheavyweight with a very low centre of gravity, just sat them out. They could not lift him off his seat. Result: Capes, Brown, Sigmarsson, De Vreugd.

The final race was a tough speed and endurance race carrying ten 62.5 kg (138 lb.) lobster pots across the sand and up the steep boat ramp to load the pots on to a truck. This would be five laps, carrying two pots at a time. The position was very close at this final stage, with Sigmarsson and Capes known to be exceptionally good at loading. De Vreugd was still in contention but a likely third.

In the final analysis, the athletic Tom Magee was more than one-half minute ahead of the man from the Netherlands, and Sigmarsson was nearly a minute ahead of him to win the event. Geoff Capes came second with 1 min 57.9 sec., and this was enough to give him a victory overall. He had his revenge on the Iceman and savoured his victory. "The King has not lost his crown," was his closing remark.

Final placings: Geoff Capes (UK), J.P. Sigmarsson (Iceland), Cees De Vreugd (Netherlands), George Hechter (USA), Richard "Grizzly" Brown (USA), Tom Magee (Canada), Roger Ekstrom (Finland), Pierre Brulois (France). I thought the prize money was rather low for such an important and popular event: first £3,000, second £2,500 and third £2,000. Grizzly Brown got £500 as the "Personality of the Competition."

From left: Second place Jon Pall Sigmarsson (Iceland), first place Geoff Capes (Great Britain), and third place Cees de Vreugd (The Netherlands), WSM 1985.

Nice, France 1986

The Mediterranean sun glinted through the palms as with a Tarzan-like cry and abounding good humour, Jon Pall Sigmarsson regained the title World's Strongest Man against tough opposition from Geoff Capes and other titans of strength.

Sigmarsson glowed with warmth and friendliness towards spectators and fellow competitors, as he heaved, dragged, pulled and pushed his way back towards the title which he had first won in Sweden two years earlier. The eight massive contenders were a very colourful lot, and sharing superstar status with Sigmarsson was Britain's Geoff Capes, the defending champion. There was also Ab Wolders, a powerlifting champion and bouncer from Holland; Ilkka Nummisto, Finland's Strongest Man and veteran of four Olympic Games; Dusko Markovic, a Yugoslav-Canadian with a great personality; Klaus Wallas, the professional wrestling champion from Austria; Rick "Grizzly" Brown, the gigantic and popular Californian; and finally Jean-Pierre Brulois of France, the idol of the home crowd.

Highlights of the competition included the McGlashen Stones of Strength, transported all the way from Scotland to be used in this contest for the first time. The car turnover was another innovation which was wildly applauded. From an endurance point of view, dragging circa 227 kg (500 lb.) of sand and carrying 91 kg (200 lb.) barrels up a steep ramp tested the toughest.

The sixteen million TV viewers should remember that undertaking an unrehearsed battery of tests like these in televised conditions is very different from working up to maximum efforts on standard and well-practised feats; as so often happens there was a significant toll of injuries, including the arm injuries of Nummisto, who ripped his left biceps lifting the Stones of Strength. He decided to continue, and in the next event, the car turnover, he tore his right biceps. The muscles jumped to the top of his arms, and there was multicoloured bruising. In spite of this, heavily bandaged, he still tried the crucifix but after that, and while in third position, he had to retire from the competition.

Ab Wolders turned over three cars on a 40-metre course in the remarkable time of 18.1 sec., but as he dashed over the finishing line, he collapsed with a torn hamstring. He too continued and was in agony, during the dead lift in particular. Twenty-seven-stone Grizzly Brown took a tumble early in the car turnover and injured his back. The doctor came rushing with a needle and syringe, but the Grizz turned pale and point blank refused such treatment. Klaus Wallas's hands were very sore after the tug of war, and Jon Pall pulled a pectoral muscle. Geoff Capes suffered also but said little. The only one apparently unscathed was Dusko Markovic, personality prize winner of the event, "If I felt any better I wouldn't know what to do with myself." He always had a wisecrack and it won him £500 as the man of the meet.

The first event on the Promenade des Anglais was the truck haul, where a 7.2-ton truck had to be pulled over a 20-metre course, mainly using arm strength. Sitting on the ground with feet braced against a board, the trucks were pulled hand-over-hand at a remarkable speed. Most of the contestants considered this a good warmer. Geoff took the lead over Jon Pall and Ilkka Nummisto.

A Real Drag

The sense of confidence shown by competitors took a hammering in the next item where they had to run 50 metres carrying a 100 kg (220 lb.) sack and return the 50 metres dragging a 225 kg (496 lb.) sack. Let's face it, the big guys are not made for sprinting, although some of them can shift remarkably quickly when they have to. The sack carrying was easy but the return journey was more challenging. The first three finishers were Sigmarsson, Capes and Nummisto in that order.

The McGlashen Stones

Many considered this the best of the strength items ever staged in these competitions. It certainly was exciting: Five huge, smooth round boulders were laid in a semicircle which were then to be lifted, carried and placed on top of

Geoff Capes (Great Britain) on the McGlashen Stones, WSM 1986.

barrels. Many strongmen in the local community tried and failed to lift even the smallest an inch from the ground—then the competitors took over. It was absolutely fantastic the way they managed to do this.

Before the competition I would have been willing to place a bet that nobody would succeed in lifting the largest and heaviest stone within the competition. Previously Sigmarsson was the only man in the world to lift it, and that was outside competition. It was a feat which had earned him £250 for his effort. Only a handful had ever lifted the fourth stone, but there at Nice we were surprised at the way the stones were handled: Markovic managed three stones, Wallas and Wolders four stones, Nummisto five in 1 min. 23.6 sec., Capes five in 44.8 sec., and Sigmarsson five in 40.2 sec. It should be pointed out that in this competition standard wine barrels were used instead of huge whisky puncheons traditionally used in Scotland.

Stock Car Racing For Mastodons

Next came the dramatic car turnover with six cars in two 40-metre lanes, three cars to be overturned by each person. When one tries to calculate how long it would take these men to run a 40-metre course, having to stop and start three times en route, plus how long it might take to turn over not one, but *three* cars, their times overall are all the more sensational.

There was high drama throughout: There was the collapse of Ab Wolders and the fall of Grizzly Brown for starters. Grizzly opted to take the back of the car, instead of the front as others did, and as the weight of the engine was at the front, the car slewed round, causing Grizzly to slip and bang his head on the side of the car and collapse in a heap. First, as he fell, his hand went to his groin; later it appeared he had hurt his back. As referee I had a close-up of the action, and this one really worried me until the doctor came on the scene and Grizzly became his usual vociferous self. He is a great guy and can always be relied upon to keep everybody entertained.

Jon Pall also provided a shock for his supporters. He was one of the most athletic of strongmen and at the sound of the starting pistol he was off like a rocket. It looked as if he were going to go right through the first car, such was his acceleration, but suddenly he disappeared *under* the car. The world's strongest man had slipped on dog shit at speed—to think that such a mundane thing should happen to a Viking god! Quickly recovering he upended the car, and the others in like style, to finish in a time of 22.2 sec.—not enough to beat the old master Geoff Capes who finished with a remarkable time of 17.7 sec. Now that's really moving; to turn each car and run 10 metres in just over five seconds a time is no mean feat. Wolders did it in 18.1 sec. in spite of tearing his hamstring.

Under The Floodlights

The setting for the crucifix was one of the most pleasant sights of the series; by this time night had fallen and the fountains in the Espace Massena were now floodlit as was a picturesque church in the background.

In the centre of a little amphitheatre was a small stage and backboard. On two plinths were the largest bottles of champagne I have ever seen, the pair weighing just short of half a hundredweight, each Methuselah weighing 12.5 kg (27 lb.). As always, the idea was to hold them in the crucifix position, and Grizzly Brown was the favourite since he had broken the world record the previous year in Cascais, Portugal. He lived up to his reputation, winning with a new record 1 min. 12.1 sec., but there were other fine efforts, such as Sigmarsson's 1 min. 11.3 and Brulois' 1 min. 11.1 sec., which had the crowd shouting themselves hoarse. This was Geoff Capes' worst event, not only because he has long arms, but also due to injuries over the years; as I called out to him to lower the weights the pain on his face was very obvious to one and all.

Splashing Out And The Boat Lift

There was lots of fun in the man-to-man tug of war, where the loser finished up in a tank of water—that is, all except Jean-Pierre Brulois, who paid out the rope instead of going with it. He finished up in the water anyway, after a good-natured tussle with Jon Pall who threw him in to the delight of spectators. Again Geoff Capes was a worthy winner, Sigmarsson second, and Wallas third.

Next the rear end of a boat and trailer had to be dead lifted within 90 seconds, and as many attempts as required were allowed within that time. "On the signal 'down, good lift' he will lower the boat to the ground *without dropping it.*" I quote the procedure as there was a major problem during the event, and the real story has never been put in print until now.

Markovic did 340 kg (750 lb.); Wolders and Brulois, both competitive powerlifters of world championship standard, did 360 kg (794 lb.); Geoff Capes did a splendid 380 kg (838 lb.); and Sigmarsson did 420 kg (926 lb.) and had more in hand. The controversy was in Jon Pall Sigmarsson's first lift, a very easy 320 kg (705½ lb.). With a cry of, "I am the strongest man in the world," he lifted the boat with contemptuous ease. As referee I gave him the correct signal to lower, but instead of putting it down under control, he dropped it, and of course I could not pass that lift, telling him it was disqualified for dropping.

An official standing nearby had been complaining that Sigmarsson was not wearing the clothing provided, which was commercially important. At this stage, he and his associate told Jon Pall to get on his proper top with his name on it. Jon Pall was already temperamental about the

From left: Third place Ab Wolders (The Netherlands), first place Jon Pall Sigmarsson (Iceland), and second place Geoff Capes (Great Britain), WSM 1986.

disqualified lift and turned on those interrupting, telling them that he didn't need or want the top with his name on it: "Everybody knows Jon Pall, we don't need to show them my name." Jon Pall stomped off to the competitors' area. Most people did not know what was going on. TV staff were mystified; many thought the row was about the lift, as they were unaware of the dress problem.

The argument suddenly shifted when Geoff Capes and Mark Higgins pointed out JPS had not made a successful lift and the 1½ minute time limit had expired. There was general confusion regarding whether or not Sigmarsson had been disqualified. As far as I was concerned, only that lift had been ruled out for dropping. He and all other competitors were accustomed to having to repeat dead lifts or overhead lifts if they had not been completed properly. The only question was whether he had to be disqualified for not wearing the proper clothing. There was some hard talking between the two leading competitors and the two officials involved in the clothing issue. Since it was the same official who had fallen foul of Geoff Capes in the dead lift at Cascais, there was a considerable amount of heated discussion.

Finally Capes saved the day by accepting that Sigmarsson had been interrupted and should be allowed to continue—but wearing the correct clothing. There were many sighs of relief. It was clear to all that Sigmarsson did the lift easily and could do much more, but that lift had to be disqualified as he dropped it. However the official, no matter how important he was, should not have interrupted at this stage; he should have allowed Jon Pall to repeat the lift, which was well within his capabilities. Likewise Jon Pall should have made a second and good attempt before storming off.

The competition resumed and finished in great style, with a finish between Geoff and Jon Pall. Sigmarsson finally won, lifting 100 kg (220 lb.) more in the winning lift than he took in that offending first lift. Having regained his good humour, he took great delight in replacing the boat as gently as he would lay down a basket of eggs.

Roll Out The Barrel

The toll of injuries had grown, and Grizzly Brown, Ilkka Nummisto and Klaus Wallas, were out and now there were only five left to finish the competition. The last event, barrel loading, was in danger of being an anticlimax. The competitors had to manoeuvre a deep step, then go up a ramp to load six 90 kg (198½ lb.) barrels. The plastic barrels were difficult to carry, the deep step was a killer, and the ramp too steep for my liking. It was a very tough test.

Brulois of France went first and confirmed my worst fears. With great difficulty he made the first barrel only. Dan Markovic had proved a great favourite with the crowd in his first tilt at the title and was desperate to do well. He was matched with Ab Wolders, a strongman worthy of great respect. Wolders managed two barrels, leading Desperate Dan and stopped to encourage his opponent, who was struggling gamely. Dan finally heaved the second barrel on to the wagon, and Ab gave him a huge congratulatory hug and retired. Dan looked shattered, but told me he would not let me down.

"Bonjour!" he shouted to the crowd. They roared their replies and cheered him on. He rushed down to the next barrel and carried it like a man possessed. He had done enough to place fourth in the overall competition and gained an army of fans.

Capes and Sigmarsson lined up for the final heat and paced themselves well. Neck and neck they raced for the first two barrels. Sigmarsson went into a slight lead and looked comfortable. Geoff Capes finished the third with difficulty and signified that he had finished. Sigmarsson, although he now knew he had now regained the title, went on to delight the crowd with his sheer showmanship. His Viking declarations of triumph interspersing his exuberant posing left nobody in doubt that he truly was the World's Strongest Man of 1986. Once again the winners were the survivors in this most demanding of contests.

Final results:
1. J. P. Sigmarsson   59
2. G. Capes   55
3. A. Wolders   37.5
4. D. Markovic   34
5. J. P. Brulois   31.5
6. K. Wallas   22
7. I. Nummisto   19
8. R. Brown   14

(There was no contest in 1987)

Hungary 1988

The 1988 *World's Strongest Man* competition was probably the most hotly contested of all time. All the elements were there—a red-hot rivalry between the defending champion, Jon Pall Sigmarsson, and old war horse Bill Kazmaier, plus determined and impressive young newcomers such as Jamie Reeves, popular personalities like Ilkka Nummisto and Ab Wolders, and dark horses too—Laszlo Fekete and Joe Quigley.

The fans were not disappointed, for the clash between Kazmaier and Sigmarsson was all that was expected, with other athletes playing important roles. Sig had

The WSM 1988 lineup from left: Jean-Pierre Brulois (France), Laszlo Fekete (Hungary), Joe Quigley (Australia), Ilkka Nummisto (Finland), Jamie Reeves (Great Britain), Bill Kazmaier (USA), Jon Pall Sigmarsson (Iceland), and Ab Wolders (The Netherlands).

Bill Kazmaier (USA) in the dead lift event, WSM 1988.

beaten Kaz in eight out of ten events at Huntly Castle, and Kaz had won the World Muscle Power championships (by the same promoters, which seemed to indicate there was no favouritism). However, all seemed to believe that the World's Strongest Man in Hungary for the DAF Trucks Trophy and some £17,000 of prize money was the most important decider.

The first day's events took place on the ramparts of the beautiful Royal Castle, overlooking the Danube, and glorious sunshine favoured the competitors as they nervously got under way in physically demanding loading races. The strongmen had to lift, carry and run with six awkward, unwieldy objects, heaving them on to a truck before returning for the next one. With each object weighing 90 kilos, nearly 200 lb., this was a most searching test, as most had little or no handhold, and the time element made it really gruelling. The plastic keg was slippy, the loaded basket was flexible, the oil drum was bulky, and so on. There was also a sack of sand, a churn and a crate, each with its own inbuilt problems which could be overcome by strength.

There had been grave doubts about Sigmarsson's fitness to compete owing to recent injuries, but these were silenced when he turned in a scintillating 51.81 sec. He ran faster carrying 200 lb. than many people can without any load! Ab Wolders of Holland, supported by a vociferous, good-natured band of Dutchmen, took second place. Surprising many people, but not the connoisseurs, was veteran Ilkka Nummisto in third place, still demonstrating great strength and endurance.

Dead lifting followed, raising a traditional handcart on to which a huge cask of wine and many sandbags had been loaded. Although the overall weight was well over 454 kg (1,000 lb.), the first poundage was calibrated to equal 289 kg (637 lb.) on the handles. Bill Kazmaier, former world powerlifting champion, showed his superiority in his winning lift of 510 kg (1,124½ lb.), a new best in this competition. He ended with a little speech as he held the weight—a great feat. It seemed to some of the TV people that his words criticised the event, but Bill later said this was a misinterpretation. Jamie Reeves, successor to Geoff Capes in this competition and an excellent ambassador for Britain, came second equal with Nummisto, who was already a firm favourite with the crowd by laughing joyfully as he succeeded with each weight up to 480 kg (1,058 lb.).

Sigmarsson came next, now showing some evidence of pain, and blood had sprayed from his nostrils as he made his maximum attempts. Brulois of France, still a world champion powerlifter, was fifth equal with another powerlifting gold medallist Ab Wolders, and Joe Quigley of

Australia, who had done extremely well to equal such specialists at their own game.

At the end of the second event, Sig and Kaz were now neck and neck and Nummisto only a half point behind.

Moving back to our base at the enchanting Club Tihany on the shores of Lake Balaton, it was clear that the organisers had done well in getting such fine locations. The next test was pulling the massive DAF vehicles, Truck of the Year Award winners. These monsters, weighing 6½ tonnes and looking much more, had to be pulled over a 20-metre course *twice*. Normally there is only one pull but in an effort to minimise the differences in the course and the trucks, competitors switched lanes and vehicles for their second pull. There was a startling moment when Sigmarsson's rope gave way as he strained for the pull, and he crashed to the ground. I held my breath, expecting a tirade, but he good-naturedly made a joke of it: "Too much power," he cried. This Icelandic power proved good enough to win, and he finished a point ahead of Kazmaier, who in turn was a fraction of a second ahead of Jamie Reeves.

In log lifting these three re-shuffled to again fill the top three places. The setting at Tihany was like a lumber camp, and a superb set of logs had been specially made for the competition. This was a very exciting part of the contest, where great things had been expected of Fekete, the Hungarian competitor who specialised in lifting huge stones overhead, and also of Jean-Pierre Brulois, a former Olympic lifting champion of France, well accustomed to overhead lifting. Brulois looked good as he jerked 130 kg (286° lb.) using a split style, but it was not enough to give him an edge over the top men. Fekete was already feeling the effects of the hard work in earlier rounds and was unable to realise his true worth. Sigmarsson went to 150 kg (330½ lb.) and tried to conceal that his shoulder (amongst other things) was hurting badly.

Jamie Reeves lifted like a man possessed, roaring with pride as he exceeded Bill Kazmaier's old record of 161 kg (355 lb.) set in 1982; then the big Brit shed tears of emotion when the record was announced. Kaz responded with 170 kg (375 lb.) to regain the record. Jamie valiantly tried 175 kg (386 lb.), but the bulk and awkwardness of the tree trunk was too much on this occasion. We had witnessed another brilliant battle.

The forward hold was to be staged under floodlights, but as darkness fell, lightning flashed, thunder rolled and the heavens opened, sending us indoors to the Vitorlas Vigado, an attractive folklore restaurant. Huge rolls of ribbon decorated half a hundredweight of salami which had to be held forwards at arm's length for as long as possible with straight arms, the back remaining against a wall throughout.

The drama of the storm was heightened by the goings-on indoors—there was a missing vest, missing competitor, missing chalk and other complications, which rose to a climax in a heated scene which was not shown on TV. Jamie Reeves won this event fair and square, holding the 56 lb load for 57.7 sec. to beat the previous record set by John Gamble in 1982. Jamie had covered his head with a towel during the commotion, and his calmness paid off. Ab Wolders was a popular second with 48.93 sec., letting out a triumphant yell in his own language, which his supporters told other onlookers meant, "I've got the bastard!"

Jon Pall Sigmarsson came third, and as he was the last man to lift, he gave a little speech to the effect that they were there for good sport, and they wanted no more "bullshit."

At this stage Sigmarsson and Kazmaier were equal with 33 points each, and Jamie was still very much in contention with 31½ points. Ab Wolders was next and could not be discounted.

Sacked

In my view the sack race was the hardest event of the competition. In earlier days there was sometimes comment that timed events were out of place in strongman contests, but such views were uninformed and do not take into account the fact that enormous strength is needed to carry 100 kg (220 lb.) for 50 metres and drag 200 kg (440 lb.) for 50 metres, both within 90 seconds. Most of those who make such comments could not even significantly move 200 kg of wet sand. Even the strongest of legs trembled and collapsed under the strain of this event, and there is a special word of praise for competitors like Joe Quigley who, although inexperienced in such strength sapping contests, gave 100% effort in each and every discipline, where others packed in much earlier. Joe and Ab did the sack feats until they collapsed.

Only Bill Kazmaier managed to pull the 200 kg sack the full 50 metres within the time limit. He did this attaching the sack rope to his lifting belt while the others used their hands alone. His move was permissable, and it shows strongmen can be brainy as well as brawny. Sigmarsson was second, Nummisto, still hanging in there, was third, and Reeves fourth.

Lake Balaton was again bathed in sunlight as we crowded the jetty for the penultimate event, but there was tension as spectators realised that the titanic efforts of the last days were beginning to take their toll on the competitors. This was a crucial stage of the competition.

The first throws with the 56 lb weight over a bar were fairly uneventful and of the expected standard.

Then came a shock when Bill Kazmaier failed three times at 4 m 60 cm (15' 1"). He had been clearing this height throughout the summer, but although there were no adverse decisions or external influences, it was just too much on this occasion.

Reeves, Wolders, and Sigmarsson battled it out to a finish, and as things progressed, they seemed to enjoy it more and more. Ab's supporters out on the lake in a boat cheered themselves hoarse as Jamie and Ab tied at 4 m 90 cm, 16' 1", excellent performances. However Jamie had fewer attempts than Ab, so this split the draw and placed him second to JPS, who cleared 5 m 5 cm (16' 7") and didn't try any more. From being one point behind Bill, Jon Pall now had a formidable four point lead.

Jon Pall Sigmarsson (Iceland) winning the weight for height, WSM 1988.

The McGlashen Stones
It was confirmed that this is the most impressive feat of strength in these modern competitions. Five perfectly round and smooth boulders had to be lifted on to the tops of five upended barrels in the shortest possible time.

Only Sigmarsson and Kazmaier could lift all five: Kaz took over 2 min. and the Icelander did them in a staggering 27.47 sec. The merit of this can be seen not only in comparisons of times, but also by the fact that Brulois could lift only one stone, and Fekete, the famous stone lifter, took 26.80 sec. to lift just the three lightest ones. In third place again was mighty Nummisto, with four stones in 33.12 sec. Jon Pall's slalom-like lap of victory zig-zagging through the barrels was a fitting climax to a fantastic competition.

The final score saw competitors well separated, and it was a convincing win for the man they call "the Viking," a decision welcomed by spectators and met with the approval of most competitors. It is all the more meritorious as the Icelander was badly bruised and injured. When it was all over, I heard an interesting story.

Jock Reeves, Jamie's brother, told me that early in the contest it appeared that Sigmarsson might have to retire injured. He was desperate to carry on regardless of the pain, when Jamie kindly sacrificed some of his pain-killers to help his rival. This allowed Jon Pall to finish the event and afterwards gave the Yorkshireman great praise for this sporting gesture. "Jamie Reeves and his brother are real sports," he said, "it's what the world expects from British athletes."

To win when injured is admirable, but he had to pay a high price for victory. Sigmarsson had difficulty in walking, and his arms and shoulders were painful for a long time. In Iceland he received considerable medical attention but had to withdraw from lucrative bookings. Few people realise the toll taken by these contests.

San Sebastian, Spain 1989
With a scintillating display of strength athletics, Jamie Reeves of Sheffield took the coveted World's Strongest Man crown back to Britain.

The drama started before the contest had even begun: Tjalling van den Bosch, Netherlands' Strongest Man, was finally declared unfit despite the strenuous efforts of top physiotherapists and sports medicine specialists. Frantic phone calls were made by the TV companies, who faced a further dilemma, because in the Netherlands' Strongest Man there had been a tie for second place. Gigantic Ted van der Parre could provide a new face, but Ab Wolders was a tried and tested veteran who had competed with distinction over the years.

Ab made the selectors' job a little easier, saying he had been enjoying a season in Scotland with the Highland Games and was only in San Sebastian with his friends to watch the show, and he would be happy to see big Ted get a chance at the title. Avro TV officials accordingly invited van der Parre, but he had sustained an injury at the

European Muscle Power championships. So Ab it was, and such a relaxed approach had seldom been seen from any competitor. Wolders was injury free and going into the event at twenty-four hours' notice; therefore he had no previous pressure. He laughed and joked his way to victory in three of the eight events, enhancing his claim to being the world's *fastest* strongman, but all the while when the starting signal was given, he exploded with deadly serious, one hundred percent effort, finishing overall second to Jamie Reeves.

The Car Turnover

The competition itself was full of interest and excitement right from the start when the car turnover took place on the lovely Maria Cristina Bridge. Bill Kazmaier and "Dan" Markovic kicked off in heat one, and Dan received a stunning blow on the head and eye when at one stage the load fell back on him. He never quite recovered from this severe shaking, but he always managed to raise a laugh, speaking to the Basque in their own language. This made him very popular with the crowd.

The fastest heat was undoubtedly the third one where the current holder Sigmarsson was drawn against Ab Wolders. Here I would like to make a point about the draw. On previous occasions, Bill Kazmaier had rightly protested about the draw being done in advance. This had been done by the producers Trans World International to facilitate printing of starting lists, press handouts and suchlike, but Bill wanted a public draw, as he was felt that some of the pairings helped his leading opponents by giving them good competition while he was paced by "a pencil neck." While emphasising the fairness of previous draws, producer Ken Hawkes recognised that justice must be seen to be done, and a public draw was held in San Sebastian, the final stages of this being a blind draw which would seem to be the overall best approach.

Wolders and Sigmarsson were breathtaking in their power and speed, showing what modern strength athletics are all about. Ab covered the 40 metres (44 yards) in only 20.25 sec., stopping three times en route to turn over three cars! Sigmarsson was a fraction of a second behind with 20.47 sec. Interest was heightened by the way Jon Pall lifted the cars by the front wheels instead of grasping the sill in the usual fashion. Always interested in techniques, I later asked the Icelander about this new method. He held up a swollen finger, but he was not being rude. "During the warm up I pushed my finger through the rotten metal of the old car and so I could not use it to grip properly. I had to do something to get some points so I used my arms like a forklift on the tyre." It was later discovered that the finger had been broken.

Bill Kazmaier complained that a car or cars had moved during his attempt so both competitors in the first

The 1989 WSM lineup, from left: Jon Pall Sigmarsson (Iceland), Bill Kazmaier (USA), Hjalti Arnason (Iceland), Ilkka Nummisto (Finland), Adrian Smith (Great Britain), Ab Wolders (The Netherlands), Jamie Reeves (Great Britain), Rudi Kuster (Germany), Dan Markovic (Canada), and Lazlo Fekete (Hungary).

heat were offered a rerun, which Dan declined. Bill was a fraction of a second faster on the second run, but it did not make any difference to the overall placing: first Wolders, second Sigmarsson, and third Reeves with 21.08 sec.

Political Activity and the Log Lift

Moving on to our next location, we were astounded to find that Basque demonstrators had taken over the square and had numerous sheep roasting on spits over hot coals. They had set up a bar for drinks and a stage for music and were having a rare old time, so we moved to the equally charming Plaza de la Constitution for the log lift.

Rudi Küster, the West German title winner in both powerlifting and Olympic lifting, added spice to this test by neat split style clean and jerks, but like Nummisto and Markovic, the awkward size and texture of the logs resulted in failures at 130 kg (287 lb.). Sigmarsson, clearly doing minimal attempts, was last to start with Jamie Reeves. Sig failed at 160 kg (353 lb.), which left the way clear for a repeat of last year's finish between Kaz and Jamie. On this occasion, however, the lifts and the attempts were reversed, and Bill finished with 165 kg (364 lb.), while Jamie achieved 170 kg (375 lb.) fairly comfortably to take the top points. Reeves now led overall, Sigmarsson was second, and Wolders third.

The Churn Carry

Next came the churn carry, the event which we know as the farmer's walk or the Fergus walk, thus named after the place in Canada where it is an annual event. The competitors had to carry two 75 kg (165 lb.) churns around a course for the greatest possible distance. Difficulty was added by making them climb and then descend steps, two up, across, and two down. This gave Jamie his first win with Jon Pall second, and for the first time we saw the respect and rapport of these two great champions. As the churn handles were very thin, the competitors were allowed to wear gloves or tape their fingers. The big Viking was in heat two, and on completion advised Jamie not to wear gloves as they slipped. The Sheffield blacksmith took this advice and taped his fingers.

Just before the third heat, someone suggested to me as referee that Reeves had glue on his tapes, and as this was mentioned again afterwards, let me say for the record that on hearing the complaint, I immediately checked Reeves's hands and found that there was no glue or any illegal substance.

You could say it was a "walk over" for Jamie Reeves, as his distance of 97.06 metres was more than 20 metres further than Sigmarsson's, his nearest rival, and some of the others were very far behind.

The Basque Stones

Basque stone lifting was a fine new event, preceded by a great demonstration of different types of stone lifting by Goenatxo, a local champion. This fourth event in the World's Strongest Man was in two rounds. The first had the competitors lifting a smooth, round 100 kg (220½ lb.) stone to the shoulder as many times as possible within 90 seconds. Each time they lifted, they had to hold it there for a second to get the judge's approval, then drop it forward on to a pad before the next rep.

Four men lifted in each heat for the first round, then the best went on to lift a 125 kg (275 lb.) boulder. Fourth equal in the first round were Wolders and Fekete of Hungary, each doing nine reps, so both went through to the final. Reeves and Nummisto managed ten each, and Sigmarsson was best with eleven.

Jovial Ilkka Nummisto, Finland's hero of the Mexican Olympics, and Ab Wolders each lifted the 125 kg stone once—it was extremely difficult to do consecutive repetitions. Jamie Reeves and Laszlo Fekete, a specialist millstone lifter, each did four reps, and the incredible Sigmarsson, in a performance which was pure theatricals, did six reps—with action poses between each lift! He might have come unstuck and been left with "egg on face" if he had not been able to beat the count with at least five reps, but his confidence was justified, and he still had time in hand at the finish, having done more than enough to win.

There was now only a half point separating Jamie and Jon Pall, but it was Jamie who got the £750 for being leader at the half way stage.

The Cheese Hold

Half a hundredweight of *queso del pais*, Basque sheep's cheese, had to be held in the crucifix position, this time with a backboard and crosspiece which prevented the competitors from raising their arms above shoulder level, a worthwhile innovation, but it does not remove all the problems from this event.

The crucifix is probably the most dreaded test by competitors and officials alike. The TV companies love the emotion and facial expressions, which often reflect the agony of the contestant but, as already mentioned briefly, the problems of this hold centre round the fact that most of the regular contenders for strongman titles have permanently affected arm locks through badly injured arms and/or shoulders. This leaves the way open for discrepancies and malingering which makes it a nightmare to judge. For example, one European with a very poor lock in the crucifix was not at all bad in overhead lifting!

I can say without fear or favour that the winner Jamie Reeves had very good form when he held the two

Ilkka Nummisto (Finland) in the Basque cart carry, WSM 1989.

cheeses for 58.97 sec. Kazmaier had 43.71, and amazingly Markovic and Wolders had exactly the same time of 42.61 seconds.

The Basque Cart Carry
I am not at all sure that all the placings reflected the real abilities of the performers. What tended to happen was that because they had no targets or expectations, the earlier ones carried the cart much shorter distances that the later ones who successively topped each other. Sigmarsson went first, walking 45.30 metres round the circle. Jamie Reeves came next and beat this with 54.30 metres, which looked good at that stage. Next came Kaz who could not get as far as the big two, going to 41.30.
Things really hotted up when Nummisto went into the lead with 58.40; then the next man, Küster, beat this with 64.90 metres, only to be beaten by the next, Fekete, who did 68.40. Finally the last man, Wolders, won with 70.65 metres. The finishing result was *almost* a reverse order of the starting sequence, but Jamie Reeves managed to hold on to his overall first place, and Ab's 8 points pulled him up to second place, making Sig with 3 points drop to third overall.

Truck Pull
The fashionable Paseo Republica Argentina was the setting for this key event where massive, 6.5-ton DAF trucks were pulled over a 20-metre course. Two men pulled in each heat, and there were two rounds since they swopped trucks for the second round to make it perfectly fair, and the aggregate time was taken. Once again the winner was Jamie Reeves, doing Britain proud with an aggregate time of 46.25 sec., and breaking the WSM record set in 1981. Wolders' second place consolidated his position, and Sigmarsson was third, a calf injury sustained in Finland and bandaged since the start was now swelling to unsightly proportions.

The Loading Race
It was a weary, worn, but not sad group which assembled at San Sebastian's picturesque harbour for the final race. Six nautically associated objects had to be lifted and carried up an inclined jetty and loaded on to a flat bed truck. These objects included anchors, boxes of fish, barrels and oil drums, all weighing upwards of 90 kg (198½ lb.). The race was against the clock to see how fast they could be loaded. The weights had to be carried and not dragged.
Poor Rudi Küster came a cropper as he heaved the last of his load on to the truck; he dived and crashed against the flat bed, badly bruising his face and chest. Rudi is a remarkable man, for apart from his strength feats and championships, he is something of an electronics genius and makes fascinating holograms.
Wolders and Sigmarsson came first and second in this event, and both had great fun in their own way. Wolders' time of 40.88 sec. over the eight-metre course compared with Sigmarsson's record of 51.81 over a ten-metre course in 1988. On this occasion, Jon Pall took 43.98 and was still throwing poses and blowing kisses until the end. Jamie Reeves was third, and that was enough to win him the title World's Strongest Man.

Joensuu, Finland 1990
For the very first time we had a representative of the former Soviet Union, Aap Uspenski from Estonia. Representing America was O.D. Wilson at 6' 5" and 184 kg (29 st./406 lb.), winner of the world superheavyweight powerlifting title and world record holder. Adrian Smith of Corby represented Britain in place of Jamie Reeves. Another new face was Henning Thorsen, more akin to a Rottweiler than "the Great Dane" as he is known—a very tough but likeable individual. Tjalling (Charlie) van den Bosch of the Netherlands, Laszlo Fekete of Hungary, Ilkka Nummisto, the home favourite, and Jon Pall Sigmarsson completed the line-up.
Very much in evidence was the old spirit of camaraderie and mutual respect which makes it a joy for all concerned. This had slipped a little in Hungary and in Spain.

The Log Haul

As dawn broke on the first morning, we assembled on the banks of the River Pielisjoki for a fascinating first event, an arm over arm pull of huge logs bound into a raft weighing 22 tons! It looked a large load to pull mainly with arm strength, and when the biggest crane available tried to lift the lot out of the water the full, immense size of the raft could be seen, and the crane could not lift it on to the quay.

Three new competitors took the top places; British supporters were ecstatic when Adrian Smith won by pulling the 22 tons 20 metres in 50.32 sec., just 0.01 sec. faster than O.D. Wilson. Uspenski came next, and there was considerable comment at the low placing of Iceland's Sigmarsson. Seldom beaten in an arm-over-arm pull, here he was sixth. Was this a sign of his current form? Thorsen commented unofficially (he did not want to protest) that a passing vessel had given a strong backwash against the raft during the attempts of Sigmarsson and himself.

The Boat Lift

The sandy shores of beautiful Lake Pyhäselkä made a wonderful setting for the Karelian boat lift; the Karelian boat was a 40-foot traditional craft used on Sundays to take the good rural folks across the lake to church. It seemed that a few prayers were being said as the competitors prepared for the formidable feat of lifting one end of the vessel and cradle clear off the ground using the shoulders and upper back. Most of the contestants adopted a squat style rather than a back lift, although all used the hand rests provided for extra leverage and balance.

After each round, weight was added to the *front* of the boat so that it was right over the lifter, rather than give any mechanical advantage by locating the weights further back. Starting at 400 kg (882 lb.), the weight went up 50 kg (110 lb.) at a time until 650 kg (1,433 lb.) proved too much for Uspenski, Fekete and van den Bosch. There was drama when the Icelander badly strained his right shoulder girdle pressing down on the hand holds. The pectoral and anterior deltoid were clearly injured, and multi-coloured bruising soon appeared.

As usual there were several painful injuries, and one ministering angel to the competitors was lovely Taru Laukkanen, Finland's Strongest Woman. Her skilled help and pleasant personality made Taru a very welcome part of the team.

Jamie Reeves, "the Iron Man from Steel City," was helping the BBC with commentaries, and when earlier he was asked to forecast the winner, he had stuck out his neck: "Sigmarsson for sure," replied Jamie "If he doesn't win I will stand naked in Burton's shop window!" With the mighty Viking now in fourth place Jamie was being reminded of his declaration and told he would be held to it.

Mine Hosts and a Rock Concert

We then headed for the Outokumpu Copper Mine where a new form of the loading race was scheduled. I will pass quickly over the loading race as I was not at all keen on the

Hjalti Arnason (Iceland) in the boat lift, WSM 1990.

shovelling and carrying, feeling that it was more suited to a labourer's skill and judgment than for the world's strongest men. Some, like Adrian Smith, made a hash of it but not through any lack of strength.

After this, with some trepidation, we descended into the depths of the copper mine where in the gloom we could see moisture running down the rocky walls. Fortunately, any feelings of claustrophobia which may have been present were dispelled when the tunnel widened to a well-lit cavern, where huge rough boulders were laid out for the overhead rock lift. It was the most dramatic setting I had seen for any such event up until that time.

The lifting brought considerable changes in the result. From being last equal, the big Hungarian millstone thrower, Fekete, came into his own and beat all the other champions. It was a fascinating contest, with some going all out and excelling themselves and also, in my view, a few making tactical errors.

As it was, O.D. did 120 kg (264½ lb.) and missed 125 kg (275 lb.), letting it down rather heavily on his head, resulting in the need for a hospital checkup. Fekete alone had the good sense to try 125 kg; Thorsen and Sigmarsson, who both looked very strong, made valiant efforts with 130 kg (286 lb.), but the size and shape of the boulders made it an impossible task on this occasion.

Anvil Chorus

Jon Pall Sigmarsson's many fans saw the anvil lift as the turning point in their favourite's fortunes. He was supreme in the McGlashen Stones, which was very similar, and noted for his speed—he was, in their eyes, virtually unbeatable. Furthermore they felt that perhaps heavy lifting at speed would tax O.D. Wilson's capacity. How wrong they were.

Jon Pall, the blonde Hercules, lifted the five anvils, which ranged from 120 kg to 160 kg (264 to 352 lb. approx.), in an excellent time of 31.81 sec., making his supporters very happy, until massive O.D., showing an astonishing turn of speed and phenomenal strength, whipped all the anvils up in just 27.18 sec.!

It needs a little thought to appreciate the magnitude of this feat, for not only did he make five heavy lifts in this time, he also did five carries with the anvils and four runs without the anvils. Truly a magnificent effort, and now he had a substantial lead as they went into the last event. Before leaving the anvil lift, it should be said that Thorsen was a fine third and Nummisto fourth.

The Last Lap

The 200-metre track round the Linnunlahti Stadium looks a long way when you have 100 kg (220 lb.) of bricks on your shoulders, and every one of the strongmen completed the full lap in this gruelling race. Even to complete the course is a feat of great muscular and cardiovascular endurance, and to do it after three days of the toughest competition imaginable deserves the heartiest congratulations. Often competitors have to drop out before the last event, but this time they all finished in good style, although weary and worn.

At the start of the event, O.D. Wilson of the USA had 46 points to Sigmarsson's (Iceland) 40.5 and Nummisto's (Finland) 33. The latter was the favourite for this event, one for which he had trained hard.

The issue was kept in doubt until the very last race, in which the two leaders were matched. As they lined up for the starter's signal, it was known that USSR's Uspenski was fastest so far with 52.92 sec., and Nummisto next with 55.62, while Fekete was relatively slow at 64.22 and van den Bosch at 79.17. It looked good for O.D. To win, Sigmarsson would have to beat every other athlete including two very good times, and even if he did this, then O.D. would still win if he beat the times of the injured Dutchman and Fekete.

On the signal, the two strongmen were away fast, the huge hods of bricks piled on their shoulders and back. The fair Scandinavian contrasted with O.D.'s rippling black skin, and as both were great sportsmen, popular with colleagues and supporters, the cheers were for both these finalists.

As they came to the first bend, Sigmarsson went into the lead, running faster than many men could without any load. O.D. was trailing, yet clearly speedier than some of the others, but as the distance increased his speed slackened. Sigmarsson finished in the fastest time of 50.92 seconds, and O.D. with 72.80 was seventh, failing to beat Fekete. In the very last lap, Sigmarsson had once again won the title of World's Strongest Man. O.D. Wilson was second and Nummisto third.

I should perhaps finish at that point, but I am going to express my strongly-held personal opinion. Both men were great friends of mine, and I knew Jon Pall over a longer period, so this has nothing to do with personalities. I felt that O.D. was the strongest man that year and deserved the title. The tests favoured the muscular endurance aspects of strength rather than raw power. Regardless of whether or not it makes good TV, I hope that the correct balance will always be achieved in future.

Tenerife 1991

The sheer scale and savage beauty of the scene penetrated the senses and stamped itself indelibly in the minds of the beholders. The eight stern-visaged, muscular phenomenons vying for the title of World's Strongest Man waited quietly before the weird shapes and forms of the Rocks of Garcia in the crater of an extinct volcano. Nature had sculpted this lunar-like petrified world into a grandiose landscape, and in a different way, the principal figures in the unfolding drama had fashioned their bodies into equally diverse shapes in striving for this world title, which was the prime objective of their lives.

Under the blazing sun there on Mount Teide, the normally silent scene was soon shattered by hoarse yells and dull thuds as dead lifts were performed or dropped. The competition was nearing the midway mark and hopes and fears were crystallising. This is my most lasting memory of the 1991 competition.

Tenerife, belonging to Spain, is the largest of the Canary Islands and lies in the Atlantic off the northwest coast of Africa. The first day's events in the golden shell of Las Teresitas Beach had seen Magnus Ver Magnusson (Iceland) storm into a convincing lead, loading six 100 kg (220 lb.) objects in less than a minute. This was the heaviest loading race to date, and the nine-metre carry was up a slight gradient from the sea. The seven-foot Dutchman Ted van der Parre looked in good form taking second place, with Henning Thorsen, the great Dane, placing third.

It was a disastrous start for Britain's Gary Taylor; he loaded five of the six objects in excellent time then hit the dreaded "wall" where the oxygen debt demands payment and weird things happen. In Gary's case, he dropped the keg and tried time and again before he finally succeeded in lifting it on to the platform.

Magnus Ver's performance was brilliant. In total he shuttle-ran 108 metres, and for 54 of these metres carried 100 kg (220 lb.); he did 12 lifts (six lifts from the platform and six heaves to load) *all in 58.02 seconds!* It was an amazing feat.

Barrels of Fun?

Wine barrels and beer kegs were filled with sand, water and barbell discs and had to be lifted to an overhead position

The 1991 WSM lineup, from left: Henning Thorsen (Denmark), Gregg Ernst (Canada), Gary Taylor (Great Britain), Ted van der Parre (The Netherlands), Ilkka Nummisto (Finland), Manfred Hoeberl (Austria), Markku Suonenvirta (Finland), O.D. Wilson (USA), and Magnus ver Magnusson (Iceland).

and held there momentarily; a full lockout was not considered essential owing to the shape and method of lifting the loads. The old Spanish kegs were not capable of withstanding the punishment handed out by the competitors, but fortunately we had two beer kegs and a specially made British barrel which took all the pounding it was given with the heaviest loads.

Competitors were allowed up to six choices of weights and could make as many attempts as they wished within the 90 sec. allocated per increment. If they failed, they could not proceed to another weight.

All who elected 90 and 100 kg (198 and 220 lb.) succeeded. All but Markku Suonenvirta (Finland) managed with 110 kg (242 lb.). The 120 kg was a brute of a weight, with moving sand and water beating all but Magnus and the fabulous "Nightmare," O.D. Wilson (USA). The popular American went on to 125kg (275½ lb.) while the Icelander Magnusson did an easy 130 kg (286½ lb.) and still had an attempt in hand.

Keep On Truckin'

The DAF truck pull was held in the Plaza de Espana, Santa Cruz; the busy street was closed for the occasion or those pachyderms would certainly have caused a traffic jam. Here we had a new winner with the very determined and dedicated Henning Thorsen showing why so many people considered him a strong contender for the title.

There were two rounds, and the competitors changed lanes and trucks for their second pull. Each pull was 20 metres (total 40 metres). Henning averaged 25.56 sec. per pull, just over a second faster than O.D. Wilson in second place. Van Der Parre was third, and Magnusson's fourth was enough to keep him in first place overall. Wilson was now second equal with Thorsen in the cumulative score. British supporters were devastated by Gary Taylor being last at this stage, but Gary was not too downhearted. "Tomorrow is another day," he said philosophically, and he was right.

On the Rocks

We zigzagged up the mountain road as the rising sun broke over the volcano Teide, the highest mountain in Spain. The setting was the most striking for any strength event I have seen in the fifty years I have followed the exploits of the most powerful men on earth. It was the pivotal point of the contest.

The first day had been fraught with difficulties of locally provided equipment and had been as frustrating as a forgotten punchline, whereas now we would use tried and tested gear which I knew would meet all demands.

Two super-strong, and thus, very heavy "cages" were used in the dead lift, and several husky Spaniards who

Gary Taylor (Great Britain) in the loading race, WSM 1991.

tried to lift them *empty* could not budge them a fraction from the platform. Into these receptacles rocks were loaded, to start at 280 kg (617 lb.). Some spectators thought the starting weight on the high side, but we knew that the competitors would find this suitable and had estimated that the best would be well up on 400 kg (882 lb.), even with this strange apparatus to which they were unaccustomed.

It was a great competition, with colour and character emerging to give superb entertainment. Gregg Ernst, a bearded hillbilly-looking farmer from Nova Scotia, had come into the international circuit this year, a quiet and yet demanding contender. He had settled down more comfortably and was welcomed into the strength fraternity where camaraderie and mutual support are the order of the day. Having negotiated 280, 300 and 320 kg, Greg was struggling with 340 kg (750 lb.) when Markku, the unpredictable Finn, rushed forward and tugged on Greg's long whiskers. "Just do it," shouted Suonenvirta. A bewildered Ernst, the adrenalin now flowing freely, made an all-out effort and slowly hauled the weight up to tumultuous applause.

It's typical that the man who stood to lose most was the person who deliberately helped Greg succeed. Later Gary Taylor put it succinctly, "It's not like any other sport. We all know the pain and the superhuman effort needed when you are stretching yourself to the absolute limit. We know how much the support of friends means, so we give that support willingly knowing we in turn will get the same. It's a case of mutual respect."

Manfred Hoeberl of Austria was a truly sensational newcomer to the competition. His swashbuckling appearance on the scene, in denims ripped as if by a cougar, and wearing a bright bandanna, made a terrific impact. At 6' 5" (196 cm), the 24" arms revealed by the torn-off sleeves were the largest muscular arms in the world. There and then I predicted that he was destined for stardom.

Manfred found the heavy back work tough on his slim waist, and between every event, physios and doctors worked frantically to ease the pain and prepare him for his next effort. The Austrian showed tremendous determination and made a great, gutsy attempt at 360 kg (794 lb.) before making his exit, grimacing in pain.

O.D. Wilson, one of the world's top dead lifters, was also "hurtin' bad" to use his own expression, as he battled it out with the doughty Dane Thorsen, former champion powerlifter. Eventually they both did 380 kg (838 lb.) to share third place points.

A rejuvenated Gary Taylor finally showed his true potential with six good lifts, going to 410 kg (904 lb.). Crafty Magnus, playing a fine tactical game, won with 420 kg (926 lb.) and still had one attempt in hand. Although not in the heaviest bodyweight category, Magnus had the highest total and was the top performer in that year's European Powerlifting Championships, and his prowess put him in an almost invincible position in this contest.

Getting the Sack (and Barrow)

A few hours later, having travelled many miles to Puerto de la Cruz, a 100 kg (220 lb.) sack had to be carried 35 m, and 560 kg (1,235 lb.) had to be taken back the same distance on a hand barrow. The event gave me problems as hand barrows are not made to carry 1,235 lb.! Not without difficulty, we got two barrows strong enough to each carry over half a ton of anchor chains and couplings. In the second World's Strongest Man competition back in 1978, the competitors used barrows with a mere 340 kg, 220 kg less, and they didn't have any sack carry. How things change.

Magnusson took an early lead, covering the double run (70 m total) in 23.65 sec. In the next heat, Thorsen almost caught up with a 25.44 sec. effort, and in the final run Gary Taylor, now better acclimatised and settling down, tore up the course to record a fine 22.20 sec. to take first place. His many supporters were ecstatic; from being last after a bad start, he had now pulled up to fourth place behind Magnusson, Thorsen and Wilson.

The Crucifix

It was a balmy night on the Lago Martianez with a gigantic floodlit fountain shooting into the air to form the backdrop for the crucifix. The backboard and crosspieces introduced here eliminated some of the most blatant faults and provided competitors with tangible guidelines. Times were down on some previous occasions for two main reasons: Firstly, the weight of the bananas and handles were slightly heavier than usual, being 13.25 kg each side (total 58.4 lb.); and secondly, there were three experienced, strict, but fair judges invigilating. The extra weight (triple checked) may not seem much, but even a little means a lot in a long lever lift like the crucifix.

Here the winning result was surprising to the uninitiated, as the overall last man, Markku Suonenvirta,

Manfred Hoeberl (Austria) in the barrel lift, WSM 1991.

had a convincing win. Those who follow the sport however, knew that the Finn is one of the world's best in this event, and his technique is superb. He clocked an excellent 40.17 sec. to top Magnusson's 36.77, which was also very commendable. Gary Taylor's third place raised him to that position in the overall table. His tail was up; he was now amongst the leaders and pushing Thorsen with two events to go.

The Stones of Strength

The famous McGlashen Stones were transported over land and sea from Scotland to be centrepiece of the animated scene at the Playa de las Americas, the island's cosmopolitan resort. Five smooth round boulders, graduated to 140 kg (308½ lb.) had to be lifted on to large wine barrels in a timed event. All but Manfred Hoeberl were well acquainted with the manhood stones, and secretly part dreaded and part relished the challenge. The opportunity to join the elite band to lift all five was welcomed, but all the competitors knew that in the process, real blood would be shed. Sure enough, skin was torn from arms and muscles from the bone.

Thorsen maintained his reputation as one of the best stone lifters ever seen and lifted all five in 30.87 sec. Gregg Ernst, with a heart-warming performance, also lifted the set of five to place second. With the lapping of the waves murmuring uncomfortably close, Magnusson, Taylor, Van Der Parre and Wilson lifted four stones and placed in that order according to timing. Markku lifted three and poor Manfred, his back excruciatingly painful by this time, had to be content with one stone only. (Years later, on becoming the World Muscle Power champion, he lifted all five).

There was another casualty. The fifth stone and the cumulative stress of the tough competition finally proved too much for big O.D.'s back. There had been a whisper on the muscle grapevine that he was having some back trouble, but the courageous giant had blocked out all negative thoughts, mindful of his promise the previous year that he would be back to win. Numerous helping hands tenderly carried him on a stretcher to the waiting ambulance, and as it sped away with wailing siren to a nearby hospital, one of his opponents sighed sorrowfully, "There goes a great guy."

The Last Lap

Magnus Magnusson was in an invincible position, but he is a proud Viking and intended to go all out right to the end. Another Norseman, Thorsen the Dane was in second place and as they lined up he gave an evil grin. "I'll make the bastards work," he promised—and he did. Gary Taylor, in turn, was after Thorsen's blood, and with O.D. retired from the competition, Ted van der Parre was still in strong contention.

A 450 kg (992 lb.) speedboat and trailer had to be pulled hand-over-hand from the water's edge up a very steep ramp, as far and as fast as possible to a maximum of 10 metres. Done in reverse order of the overall position, Gary Taylor beat all previous efforts by pulling the load the full distance in just 29.68 sec. The next pull by Thorsen is one I will long remember. As referee I had to keep in line with the front of the trailer, so I could ascertain how far the boat was pulled in event of it not being hauled the full course. The tremendous surge of power as Henning Thorsen made his first pull was mind-boggling. The boat zoomed forward as though engine powered, and the second pull took the vessel beyond some of the best efforts of other competitors. It took him only 21.86 sec. for the full course, more than 36 feet, while some others had done less than 4 metres in the allocated 2½ min.

Magnus Ver, last to pull, made a bold bid to beat the Danish champion but was over 7 sec. slower. However, he just beat Gary Taylor into third place by a fraction of a second.

The final tally was probably a true reflection of the situation: Magnusson, Thorsen, Taylor, Van Der Parre, Wilson (who should have placed higher had he not been injured), Ernst, Suonenvirta and Hoeberl.

Magnusson took the £6,000 cheque and the DAF trophy, Thorsen got £4,000, and Gregg Ernst won £1,500 as the "Best Personality of the Competition." I can think of much easier ways to earn a living, but this isn't all about money. It's about rightfully earning the title of World's Strongest Man.

Reykjavik, Iceland 1992

The land of ice and fire provided an absolutely unique setting for this World's Strongest Man competition. In a beautiful, remote valley with massive cliffs towering over a russet tinted landscape, a deep flowing river reflected Viking graves and the remains of the oldest Parliament in the world. In this lovely setting, the competition was reaching its climax. The final test was with the legendary Husafell Stone, said to have been carried round a sheepfold in the 1700s by a Lutheran priest, who was a warlock and poet as well as being the strongest man since the saga of Grettir the Strong.

The stone weighed 186 kg (410 lb.), and as we pick up the story a man with all the attributes of the Biblical Samson, determined to succeed where others had failed, strode down the path to where the stone lay. Not everyone could lift the boulder, but this reincarnation of the Hebrew strongman, his uncut hair tightly braided round his head, hoisted the huge rock and set off unsteadily down a long, stony trail. The efforts of previous competitors had been pegged, their names clearly shown on the bright red markers.

One by one he passed the marks, his face becoming a purple hue as the massive relic pressed on his burly chest, cutting off his breathing. The encouragement of the crowd changed to cheers as he passed the furthest mark and then rose to a crescendo as he went on and on, right to the end of the 200 ft. long path! It was one of the greatest feats of strength and endurance I have witnessed in the half century since I first became obsessed with physical power. You'll find out more about the feat and its performer as you read on and follow the competition through the various stages to reach this point.

It's a Drag

The first demanding test was two pulls with 13½-ton trucks, the heaviest ever used in World's Strongest Man competitions. The contestants went in heats of two, and having pulled one truck, switched over to pull the other vehicle. The aim was to pull as fast as possible for 20 metres, but where the load was too much, marks were given for distance. Ted van der Parre (Netherlands), James Perry (USA) and Jamie Reeves (UK) pulled both yellow-coloured monsters over the full double course to win the top three places in that order.

Moving rapidly into the town square, a huge crowd gathered for the cart lift. A milk cart had been specially strengthened to cope with an enormous load and modified to incorporate a bar at shin height for dead lifting. The actual weight on the bar was calculated to give the true load, as opposed to simply stating the weight on the cart. For example, although a 100 lb. (45.4 kg) churn may be added as an increment, the true weight would only be 50 lb. (22.7kg), owing to the leverage advantage given by placing it in the cart and not on the bar. Fans gained true appreciation of the tremendous efforts of the competitors.

Jovial Gerrit Badenhorst, the first South African to compete in this event, was a popular winner with 465 kg (1,025 lb.), and his ready smile and rapport with the knowledgable fans gained him many supporters. He had a ding-dong battle with Magnus Ver Magnusson (Iceland), who did 452.5 kg (998 lb.), but Gerrit always looked confident and capable of more. Jamie Reeves, James Perry, Ilkka Nummisto (Finland) and Gregg Ernst (Canada) were all in the running.

Monsters of the Blue Lagoon

A real culture shock came next at the picturesque and romantic sounding Blue Lagoon. Iceland is full of natural wonders; it's as if Mother Nature experimented there and was showing off. Here we had a loading race different from all others in the past. Six 90 kg (198½ lb.) drums had to be carried from the mineral-rich lake and loaded on to a platform. The drums felt light in the water, and the full weight not experienced until the objects were lifted clear of the water. At that stage, the liquid *inside* the barrels swilled around to make a very volatile load, which the men found most disconcerting. On top of that although the lagoon was hot, causing clouds of steam to rise, we were nudging the Arctic Circle, and the bitterly cold wind chill created an amazing contrast between immersed legs and exposed torsos. It was a weird experience hitting all the senses. On one side a harsh, silent, tortured "moonscape" of crusted lava, on the other a steamy blue lagoon with noisy,

The Blue Lagoon, WSM 1992.

unclothed bathers enjoying the spectacle as officials froze on the shore.

As occasional gusts of wind cleared the steam, one might have imagined palm trees would come into sight but instead there was a huge, dominating, geothermal heating plant, creating a background more in keeping with *Terminator 3*—and the sulphurous smell was straight from Hell. It was a good time for the Danes to remind us of their view that the Devil, piqued by God's creation, tried his own hand—and created Iceland!

There were some surprises in the results, with Ted van der Parre and Henning Thorsen (Denmark) pacing themselves beautifully to show the way to go, while others who went all out from the start hit the "wall," where the oxygen debt just had to be paid. Big Ted finished third, the Great Dane second, and local hero Magnusson stormed to a convincing victory.

Day one ended with the Icelander in first place, Badenhorst second and Reeves and van der Parre third equal. British hopes were still very high.

All Craters Great and Small

Next day, long before the crack of dawn, we drove some two hours to set up at Gullfoss, which means Golden Fall, taking its name from the arching rainbows so often framing the scene. A series of tumultuous waterfalls, nurtured by melted snow and gushing into the frothing river, was a fitting end to a drive, where we saw such a diversity of geological phenomena—majestic volcanoes, with live as well as extinct craters, barren horizons, hot gushing geysers, plumes of steam and frozen glaciers.

Our excellent field crew of Icelandic strongmen, supplemented by Ossian from Ireland and our own Jim Pollock and Andy Anderson, set up the lifting rocks in record time and went on to assist Trans World International, the organisers, and Tonka the sponsors. Having done their work, the lads had their own competition with the rocks and some very fine lifts were recorded. In a country where only the strong has survived, nature's selective breeding has given us a race with the world's highest strength ratio per head of population, and the Norsemen appreciated the efforts of the World's Strongest Men at Gullfoss where the strength athletes competed not only with each other, but also against the elements, for the weather conditions were not conducive to good performances. Yet good performances there were in abundance, with Ernst, Badenhorst, Reeves and Magnusson most prominent.

Gerrit Badenhorst showed determination as he held on to the 120 kg (264° lb.) rock and staggered around until he finally had it overhead and under control for referee Olafur Sigurgeirsson's signal. Magnus Ver broke the world record with 130 kg (286½ lb.); and in turn, an attempt at 135 kg (297½ lb.) was made by Jamie Reeves, a great overhead lifter with barbells, logs, kegs and stones. He had very tough luck with this and got it to arm's length, although it tilted in the final stages and, by a whisker, failed to get approval. I have no doubt that he would have got the 130 kg had he tried it, and this would have had a decided effect on the final result.

Magnus tried the awkward 140 kg (308½ lb.) and nearly got it overhead, but he had already done enough to beat his three nearest rivals. More accustomed to the cold than anyone else, he showed the greatest respect for the elements by wrapping up with a warm ski suit over his track suit. I am sure this sort of attention to detail played an important role in his performance in these hostile conditions.

I congratulate the TV crews, under BBC's Dave Pickthall, for their wonderful filming of these events, this one being a classic example, for they managed to frame the lifters and the waterfalls in the same shot, as though the competitors were lifting on the very edge of the craggy escarpment.

Big Geezers

A few miles down the road, Thor's Hammer was thrown against a spectacular background of hot, erupting geysers. The place itself is called Geysir, the original 700-year-old waterspout giving its name to every other similar geothermal commotion. The symbol of Thor, the Viking God of Thunder, is his heavy hammer, and we had just such an implement specially made to test the explosive power of the strongmen. In these contests there has to be a blend of static strength, dynamic strength, muscular endurance, etc., so that the battery of tests truly covers every aspect of human might.

The hammer had to be thrown for height, and chucking a 27 kg (60 lb.) implement like this over a high bar is only for the strongest. Three attempts were allowed at each height, and those who succeeded went on to greater heights as the bar was raised. There could be a dozen or more tough throws by each man in the course of such an event.

Outstanding throwers included Gerrit Badenhorst fourth, Gary Taylor third, and Jamie Reeves second. The big surprise, however,, was Ted van der Parre, not normally known as a superlative weight thrower; but here he was taking full advantage of his height (7') and progressed to 4.90 m (16' 1") without a single failure—a notable achievement, which had everybody viewing him with great respect. Experts were now seriously considering him as a potential high placer.

As Ted went on to win at 5 m (over 16' 5") with only one failure, attendants rushed to put more ground protection under the bar, for there was molten rock and boiling water not too far beneath our feet. As throws were being made, the steamy potholes simmered away like perking coffee pots, and every five to seven minutes, a geyser would erupt and scalding water would shoot about 40 ft into the air in a show of nature's power. Jon Pall Sigmarsson, who was badly injured at a Finnish competition three days earlier, said that he often visited such places to enjoy and benefit from the generation of power. "I can feel it inside me," he declared.

At the end of the second day, the overall placing was Magnusson 42 points, Badenhorst 38.5, Reeves 38.

Axe Me Another

Ancient and modern history converged next morning at the Summit House, where world leaders had met to put an end to the Cold War. On the steps, a platform and backboards were erected so that competing strength athletes could face each other in pairs, holding huge double-

Gregg Ernst (Canada) in the Husafell Stone, WSM 1992.

headed Viking axes for as long as possible. The forward hold has never been quite so tough as the axe had to be held *horizontally,* creating difficult body leverage problems. I had to be inside the house, marshalling competitors, so only saw one effort, that by Jamie Reeves holding for 56.56 sec. to place third, and it was done very strictly. Gary Taylor of Wales, suffering from flu, had not been producing his best, but he managed to place second to Ted van der Parre, who again took top place to go into the overall lead.

Plane Sailing With The Big Fokker

Over the years the big guys have repeatedly brought traffic to a standstill in order to do truck pulls in city centres, but this time they closed down a whole airport, because team buses, sundry vehicles and the TV van signals interfered with radar beams on a foggy morning.

The test was to pull an Icelandair 50-seater Fokker 50S weighing 13.666 tons by an arm-over-arm pull for a distance of 20 metres. This proved well within the capacity of every competitor, although they were tired after three hard days of competition. There are ways of making such a pull easier, but none of these were employed. Indeed such was the calibre of the competitors that air was taken from the plane tyres, giving much more "drag." Marks were made on the runway so front and back wheels of the plane went to the same place every time, but in spite of all precautions, there was a "hiccup" for Jamie Reeves. As two daring camera men raced under the plane to get an unusual shot, a camera cable wrapped round a plane wheel so Jamie was awarded another pull at the end of the round.

Magnus Ver Magnusson gained another first to draw even overall with van der Parre, who was second in the plane pull. Gary was third, and Jamie's fourth put him only three points behind the two leaders in overall ranking.

As we reached the final event, the competition was still wide open and there was tremendous tension. Magnus seemed confident of winning, why else would he have a supply of champagne and glasses on hand? Jamie, stern-faced and saying little, was fighting hard, but some couldn't help feel that his many recent competitions and two major arm injuries had taken a bit of a toll—but he was certainly still very capable of winning.

Stoned

A fifty minute drive from Reykjavik took us to our final destination, the beautiful valley of Thingvellir, a very special, historic place for Icelanders since Viking days. It was here that the world's first parliament was formed, and the wonderful vistas had producer Dave Pickthall quite thrilled. A ridge of austere crags skirted the valley, where the lowering rays of the sun made the flora and ground cover glow in lovely shades of green, brown and red. On each side of a river, paths stretched from ancient graves to a hostelry appropriately named Valhalla, the special paradise to which the souls of Vikings slain in battle were transported. The heart-shaped Husafell stone had to be carried along one of these paths.

Imagine, if you can, lifting and carrying an awkward boulder much heavier than the heaviest McGlashen stone; it was too tough for some men who had given maximum effort for three days, competing each time until exhaustion. On the other hand there were some tremendous carries, most notably Gregg Ernst, the Pentecostal farmer from Nova Scotia, who now wore leather apron and faded jeans. He hoisted the stone without ceremony, and it was he who had the spectators cheering themselves hoarse as he traversed the full course to create a world record of 68.60 metres. Gregg was jubilant: "This made it all worthwhile," he gasped, his breath rasping hoarsely after his Herculean effort. It was even more demanding than back lifting a team of oxen, the feat which hitherto had made him famous.

But the title was still very much in doubt. Any one of the last four men could win. Gerrit Badenhorst carried the rock 52.90 m, which eventually gave him third place in the carry. Jamie Reeves beat him with 53.82 m, but was it enough to win? Next went Magnus Ver Magnusson, and he managed only 45.10 m, fifth in the event and equalling Jamie overall. Excitement was reaching fever point, and there was considerable speculation. Would it end in a draw? Could big Ted conceivably beat the previous winners, much better known and more experienced? Many considered this unlikely, but Ted had other ideas.

The initial lift was convincing although he seemed to be carrying the stone too low. Most competitors lifted it high to clear the legs, even though this seemed to hinder breathing. Van der Parre's stature grew with every step as he surpassed opponent after opponent. He knew what he had to do to win and as soon as he passed Magnus Magnusson's mark, he dropped his prodigious load and lifted his long arms in a victory salute, acknowledging the wild shouts of the crowd. What a finish!

Soon afterwards in the last rays of the setting sun, Ted raised his arms once again, this time with the gleaming Tonka trophy firmly in his grasp. It had been a classic strength competition, and one of the best TV programmes to find The World's Strongest Man.

Orange, France 1993

The World's Strongest Man 1993 was a live event, held under imaginative lighting in a 2,000 year-old Roman arena in the department of Vaucluse in southeast France. This year the concept was totally changed, using a more dramatic approach and setting, with the events held in two late evening shows, all at the same location; the accent was on

WSM setting, Orange, France 1993.

producing an entertaining, spectacular display rather than a sporting event.

This was obvious from the opening ceremony, when these modern gladiators made their individual entrances through a smoke-filled arch, going downstairs into the arena, where "vestal virgins" danced a greeting and led them to their places on stage, the maidens turning their backs to show flags indicating the nationality of the competitors.

This latter ploy was quite unnecessary in the case of Iron Bear Collins, the American powerlifting champion, who is also a genuine full-blooded Native American Indian brave of the Lumbee tribe. Iron Bear, decked in his beautiful feathered headdress and all the tribal accoutrements, did a war dance, fiercely waving his spear, challenging his stalwart opponents. One or two of the others responded in like style, with Magnus Ver Magnusson of Iceland, carrying a mighty battle-axe and wearing a Viking helmet he had won as a prize in the national competition. Jovial Gerrit Badenhorst of South Africa doffed a fine safari hat to the crowd, and so it went on until through the smoke—the mists of time—marched a bagpiper followed by massive referee, my friend and

From left: Magnus ver Magnusson (Iceland) second, Ted van der Parre (The Netherlands) first, and Jamie Reeves (Great Britain) third, WSM 1992.

The 1993 WSM lineup, from left: Iron Bear Collins (USA), Gary Taylor (Great Britain), Hjalti Arnason (Iceland), Riku Kiri (Finland), Gerrit Badenhorst (South Africa), Henrik Ravn (Denmark), Magnus ver Magnusson (Iceland), Berend Veneberg (The Netherlands), and Forbes Cowan (Scotland), all cheering Manfred Hoeberl (Austria) pulling the rope.

colleague, Douglas Edmunds, kilted and resplendent in full Highland evening wear.

In addition to the competitors already mentioned were Manfred Hoeberl of Austria and current World Muscle Power champion, Riku Kiri of Finland, Berend Veneberg of the Netherlands, Henrik Ravn of Denmark, and Welshman Gary Taylor representing Great Britain. During the show there were many special effects and pyrotechnics, with cannons firing as finishing lines were crossed, creating a dramatic atmosphere to end each heat.

Inclined To Win

There were a number of new events. In the first of these Iron Bear showed his worth in winning the leviathan lift, which translates as repetition incline presses with a log instead of a barbell. The heats took place in pairs, to give one-to-one competition, and the Indian brave managed a superb 20 reps with the awkward 105 kg (231½ lb.) tree trunk, which he did well within the 90 sec. time limit. Hoeberl of Austria was second, equal with the much-fancied Riku Kiri of Finland.

Samson's Barrow

Samson's barrow was an entertaining event where a specially-made wheelbarrow, weighing close to half a ton, was filled with eight beautiful dancers. The load had to be pushed the full length of the arena as quickly as possible. Rockets were automatically triggered off as the barrows crossed the finish line, which proved to be another crowd-pleasing device.

The experienced men came into their own, with Gary Taylor and Magnus Magnusson first and second, covering approximately 25 metres in 12.56 and 13.40 sec. respectively.

The Clash of the Titans

Better known as the pole push, this is a sumo training practice adapted for competition. Contestants commenced facing each other, each with two rope handholds on a heavy pole. On the referee's signal they had to try to manoeuvre the opposition out of the square, marked by a thick rope. No part of the body other than the feet was allowed to touch the ground, and if anybody fell, they lost the point. The best of three rounds determined the winner of the bout.

In the many times we have held this event over the years, we had never witnessed such ferocity as on this occasion. Gary Taylor was like a man possessed and powered young Dutchman Veneberg out of the "ring" in double quick time. The Welshman's class showed when he beat Magnus Magnusson, who had disposed of Iron Bear.

Meantime Manfred Hoeberl was looking good but very excited as he beat Henrik Ravn of Denmark and lined up with Riku Kiri. The pair were evenly matched and fought like tigers, both appearing greatly psyched up for the bout. Just when honours were even, Manfred went down and appeared in difficulty. The expert medical team from London's Vision Group Sports Clinic, Harley Street, rushed in and took over, but they could not revive Hoeberl in time for the final round and Kiri was given the bout.

The resulting final between Kiri and Taylor will remain long in our memories, and I believe the excitement of this bout alone secures a place for the pole push in many future competitions. Regardless of desires for high-tech, media-attractive duels, I believe there is always a place for "primitive," man-to-man events.

The Car Carry

It sounds almost impossible, but a French car, in working condition, would be lifted and carried as far as possible by the competitors! The car was reversed to the starting line, the seat removed, a chained harness fastened and the first competitor called forward. Riku Kiri was the insiders' favourite, and his supporters claimed the arena course was not long enough. He actually finished third behind Magnusson and Taylor, who, last to compete, carried the car just enough to win and looked good for more. There was an element of fun in the Fred Flintstone-like appearance of men walking inside a car, but there is no doubt that it is a genuine gut-busting feat.

The Atlas Stones

The McGlashen Stones have provided the classic strength test of many TV programmes and it seems very hard to improve on this. Many felt that the innovation of 1993 with ten stones, two matched sets of five, was even more exciting as it featured two men in each heat, giving a series of great races.

In this finale, the two closely matched leaders, Taylor and Kiri, met in the last heat. At first they lifted and carried stone for stone, then suddenly there was high drama as Kiri, in sheer excitement, rocked the barrel, fumbled a stone, dropped it, and had to lift it again, slowing him down considerably. Gary Taylor lifted in precision style, and knowing he had a fast time (indeed the fastest), punched the air in triumph. The World's Strongest Man title had returned to Britain again. The Welsh Dragon had repeated the triumphs of Jamie Reeves and Geoff Capes.

The ancient and beautiful arena was suddenly lit up by a spectacular display of fireworks as Gary walked down the steps between the vestal virgins to receive the coveted Tonka trophy. High above this animated scene, the statue of Caesar looked down impassively, the only unemotional face in sight.

Sun City, South Africa 1994

The previous exotic location in a 2,000 year-old Roman arena was hard to beat, but the 1994 location was even more amazing. There in Sun City, some 150 km north of Johannesburg, is southern Africa's most luxurious resort, synonymous with good living and excitement, the centrepiece of which is the Lost City.

It is an awesome place. According to tradition, long before intrepid explorers pierced their way into darkest Africa, even before western civilisation, nomadic tribes found this land of peace and plenty in a secluded valley, shaped by a volcanic crater. The nomads settled and mined the area, creating a small city and a marvellous palace for their benevolent king.

One terrible day, folklore maintains, an earthquake destroyed their homes, fields and mines, leaving only the foundations of the palace. Vegetation gradually concealed the ruins until all that remained was the legend of a Lost City. You may have seen variations of such folklore in stories or seen it in films of the Tarzan genre. In more recent times, the area was "rediscovered and recreated," and the Lost City is now a fantasy world of splendour, barred by massive wooden gates, a Bridge of Time, with rows of rock-sculpted elephants down each side, the whole scene overlooked by a huge sphinx-like leopard crouching on a ledge as though guarding the Temple of Creation, in which an eternal flame burns day and night.

These and many other such fascinating features formed the backgrounds for the world's strongest men, locked in combat under the scorching sun. The format for 1994 was a complete change from the past. Sixteen contenders split into four qualifying heats, two in each heat going through to a final. In addition there were two excellent testers, Andreas Gudmundsson of Iceland and Claude Parnell of South Africa. These men had an even more demanding time than some of the competitors, as they had to do numerous camera runs as well as testing the equipment.

The enlarged field of entrants was a welcome improvement, giving the opportunity for much more TV coverage. The original idea was to have the eliminating heats at a Scottish Castle long before the finals, thus giving ample time for recovery and the healing of injuries, which are common in this demanding contest. However, schedules being what they are, the heats and finals had all to take place within seven days. This, in blistering heat and at high altitude, made it extremely difficult for competitors.

Group 4 consisted of Steve Pulcinella of USA, Heinz Ollesch of Germany, Gerrit Badenhorst of South

Africa, and Riku Kiri of Finland. Their first event was the car roll where the competitors raced, in two-man heats, to turn over a car on to its side, then on to the roof, over on to the next side and finally back on its wheels again!

Cars were complete with engines, so it sounds an impossible feat, but all succeeded in excellent times. Steve took 46.78 sec., which would be great in any other company; Heinz clocked 18.94 sec., Riku Kiri 13.78 sec., and Gerrit, the local hero, pipping him with 13.50 sec. Give these times a bit of thought, and you will understand the calibre of these men—to roll these cars right over, from wheels over to wheels in under 14 sec. is just fantastic.

Next the group moved to the Monkey Plaza for incline presses with a heavy log. Monkeys abound in this area and have a special place in the affections of the natives, as these animals are said to have helped them find water in their direst hour of need. Now a fountain, with water flowing from the palms of the monkeys, has been erected to honour the memory of those bygone saviours. In the shadow of the fountain, the 105 kg (231½ lb.) log was incline pressed 9 times by the American, and 14 times by South Africa's representative; Ollesch the Bavarian did 17, and the Scandinavian Kiri created a new world record with 21 reps to beat the previous best by Iron Bear Collins the American Indian, a popular figure at world powerlifting championships.

A most gruelling tug-of-war contest came next, with the men harnessed together and pulling on a fixed rope to prevent slippage. It was a body-taxing event, as are all such man-to-man confrontation events with such proud and determined individuals as we have in the World's Strongest Man contests. They ask no quarter and give none. Some real blood was spilled, and in the final analysis, the result was Kiri, Badenhorst, Ollesch, Pulcinella, in that order.

The final event remained, with the competitors carrying one of the Atlas Stones over marked a course. Three out of the four unexpectedly carried it the full distance, all in under one minute, with Gerrit Badenhorst sprinting, yes *sprinting*, the 25 m in 22.50 sec. with the huge boulder in his arms.

Riku took 29.59 sec. but won the qualifying heat with 14 points to Gerrit's 13, and both went through to the final.

One of the most popular groups featured Magnus Magnusson, the insiders' choice. Twenty-one-year-old Anton Boucher from Namibia had won many friends that season with his gutsy performances, and it was a toss-up between him and Wayne Price, South Africa's "Perfect Gentleman," to go into the finals with Magnus. Henrik Ravn of Denmark was obviously much bigger and stronger than last year, but he had really tough opposition.

Car turning took the place of car rolling, and here three cars were spaced at intervals over the course. All these autos had to be turned on to their sides as quickly as possible. Once again all cars were complete with engines. The power and speed of these huge men is something to behold. Anton Boucher took only 25.86 sec. to cover the course and turn all three cars—and he was the slowest! Henrik Ravn took 23.95 sec. Wayne Price looked great with 20.15 sec., but even this was beaten with a tremendous new world record by Magnus Ver Magnusson, who ran some 5 m, turned car one, another 5 m and turned car two, (the heave was so explosive), ran another 5 m to turn number three, and ran to the finishing line in about as

Wayne Price (South Africa) in the axe-hold, WSM 1994.

much time as it took to type this. A world record 15.08 sec.—one of the greatest feats I have ever witnessed in a lifetime of strength sports.

By marked contrast, the next event was a static strength event, the Viking axe hold, in which all expected the Icelander to do well. Instead Magnus made a big mistake, concentrating on his left, the weaker arm; his right arm strayed from the crucifix position, and he recorded a mere 24.79 sec. The crucifix also proved to be the downfall of Ravn the Dane. After 17.21 sec., he winced in pain and an exclamation showed clearly that he was injured. After examination, our doctor, surgeon Rick Reyes informed us that Henrik could not continue with the competition.

The Africans were jubilant after this event for Wayne Price managed 36.06 sec., and jolly Anton Boucher won with 67.80 sec.

It was now a three-horse race with little separating the contestants as they moved to the old favourite, the loading race. In these scorching conditions, it may still have been the crowd's favourite but not the contestants'. They dreaded the effects of altitude and their fears were well-founded. Five 90 kg (198½ lb.) oil drums were set in a picturesque lagoon in the Valley of the Waves. Each competitor had to wade through knee-deep water carrying the barrels, one by one, to the shoreline, where the drums had to be loaded on to wagons.

Wayne Price showed most clearly the effects of oxygen debt when he hit the dreaded "wall," after having loaded five barrels. Although under normal circumstances he could do a great many repetition lifts with such a weight, now when he was gasping with the physical exertion and water resistance, plus the climatic conditions; the spirit was willing, but the flesh would not respond. He tried time and again to lift the last barrel on to the truck but couldn't quite make it. Magnus won, taking 66.54 sec. to Anton's 84.97 sec.

They went into the last event with Magnusson in the lead, and he wisely didn't overexert himself in carrying the Husafell Stone, thus saving a little more energy for the final. The 186 kg (410 lb.) stone had to be carried as far as possible. Wayne lifted it far too high on his chest and overbalanced, thus ruining his chance of being in the final. It was hard luck for such a worthy contender.

Magnus dropped the stone after 15.70 m, knowing he had a safe lead, but Anton Boucher had something to prove, and he carried it 41.2 m to join the former powerlifting champion in qualifying for the final.

In another round we had two physically amazing characters, the 1992 World's Strongest Man, Ted van der Parre, a Dutch giant over 7' in height, and Manfred Hoeberl, possessor of the world's biggest muscular biceps now at 25½". Laszlo Fekete, Hungary's Strongest Man, and French Canadian Ron Trottier were the other two in this heat.

The first test was to pull two fully loaded safari trucks over a 25 m course, which proved easy enough for these well-matched strongmen. The results were first van der Parre 22.90 sec., Fekete 25.44, Hoeberl 26.84 and Trottier 27.56. The expected winner had placed third, but there were those who believed he was conserving his energy.

Hoeberl won the throw for height quite comfortably, with a height of 6 m. A "gold" block was thrown over a wall which was gradually raised as the contest progressed, the set being well laid out with two massive stone-carved animals at each side of the wall. The big Dutchman came second, making 5.75 m; Trottier did 5 m,

The weight for height, WSM 1994.

and Fekete cleared 4.50 m, having difficulty in mastering the necessary technique.

On then to the McGlashen Stones; as previously mentioned, now there were two sets of stones, five on each side so that two competitors could race at the same time, placing the stones on oil drums as quickly as possible. The races were really exciting. The boulders weighed 95 kg, 105, 115, 125 and 135 kg (209-297 lb.). The weights are deceptive; lifting is made more difficult by having to bend right down to the ground to get the hands under the stones: These being perfectly round and smooth with are no handholds, this makes it impossible for most people to lift them.

Fekete is a champion stone lifter in his own country, where millstone lifting is traditional, so some favoured him to win. However, the long-armed Hoeberl is no stranger to the McGlashens and clocked 23.35 sec. to Laszlo's 30.23. Van der Parre beat Trottier, doing 35.83 to Ron's 37.53.

The last event in the round was the farmer's walk, with two 85 kg oxygen cylinders with very thick handles. The men carried the 170 kg (375 lb.) for 75 m as quickly as possible. Manfred again won with a snappy 23.93

sec. Fekete was next with 30.84, and big Ted did 31.28 sec. He could do much more, I am sure, if he gave up smoking.

Manfred Hoeberl was a clear heat winner with 14 points, but it was a close thing between Ted (11 points) and Laszlo (10 points), and the Austrian and Dutch champions went through to the final.

Group one had Britain's two great hopes: Gary Taylor of Wales then the current World's Strongest Man, and Forbes Cowan of Scotland, who had been peaking for this great event, a long-standing ambition. Also in contention was Koala Bill Lyndon of Australia and a colourful Western Samoan, Joe Onasai, who looked tremendous. Little was known about Joe's abilities in such competitions although he had a formidable record in more formal strength sports.

Cowan got off to a great start, winning the arm-over-arm pull with safari car and passengers. He pulled the load over the course in a fast 33.02 sec. Lyndon was second with 34.48 sec. Gary was a disappointed third with 39.02 sec., as his recently torn biceps had let him down in this event. Joe needed just over a minute to complete the feat.

The log lift was completely different. All took 120 kg (264 lb.) and succeeded. Joe and Forbes took every lift offered, Bill took only one more lift. Forbes Cowan and Bill Lyndon went out after doing 140 kg (308 lb.) with the awkward log. Joe and Gary went on to succeed with 150 kg (330 lb.), then jumped to 160 kg (352 lb.) where Joe failed.

Gary made it look very easy, he was well within his ability in winning this part of the contest as probably the best overhead lifter in the world—in 1994 he heaved 270 kg (595 lb.) overhead!

Sumo wrestling then created a stir. I personally feared the consequences of this type of combat event with these mighty men. They get very excited and could do untold and unintentional damage to each other. I was glad that they had changed from back-hold to sumo as it eliminated *some* of the danger of falling on each other, but the risks were still high.

Gary Taylor beat the big Aussie with ferocious attacks. He seemed very psyched up from the starting gong to his final expletive, on gaining the winning fall. Joe Onasai beat Forbes Cowan, who told me later that every move he made was skilfully countered, and his own strength was no match for Joe's skill. In the semi-final Koala Bill took the first fall against Forbes, but the determined Scot, although several stones lighter, never gave up and took two straight falls to win third place in wrestling. Joe Onasai was definitely the star of this event. Looking very controlled, he beat Gary in an excellent bout to gain four points to Gary's three.

There was little to chose between the leaders. Four points went for a win, three for second, two for third and one for fourth place. In the event of a tie, the most first places would gain premier position.

In the farmer's walk for distance, Gary badly needed points to ensure qualification, but Forbes Cowan won again, doing 83.50 m carrying the two cylinders, a total weight of 170 kg (375 lb.). Joe was second (67.30 m), Gary third (66.10), and Bill did 59.80 m.

It had been a very close battle, it could not have been closer with three men all scoring 11 points. On countback Forbes had won two events so he went into first place. Gary had one first and one second. Joe had one first and two seconds so took second place overall, thus knocking Gary out of the final! It was a shock for the British supporters.

Gary was disappointed but, as always, philosophical. He knew he had been let down by his biceps injury, which had particularly hindered him in the arm-over-arm pull, and he also revealed to me that he had a bad groin injury which later required surgery. He acted like a true champion and stayed on, not just to present the trophy to the eventual winner, but also to help Forbes Cowan, the man who had won the heat. Forbes was extremely appreciative and could not praise Gary highly enough. It is actions like this that make strength athletics a very special sport. The toughness of the competition brings the competitors really close together.

Joe Onasai (Samoa) takes down Gary Taylor (Great Britain) in sumo, WSM 1994.

Manfred Hoeberl (Austria) in the farmer's walk, WSM 1994.

A new titleholder was now assured, but who would it be? The finalists were Forbes Cowan, Joe Onasai, Manfred Hoeberl, Ted van der Parre, Anton Boucher, Magnus Magnusson, Riku Kiri and Gerrit Badenhorst.

The 1994 Finals
After the totally exhausting heats, the finalists had a couple of days in which to rest and partially recuperate. They were far from idle, having rehearsals and filming of an elaborate and colourful opening sequence with African drummers and beautiful, exotically dressed girls.

As the jungle drums throbbed their hypnotic rhythm, the competitors entered the Lost City, singly, over the Bridge of Time, carrying their national flags. Each was accompanied by one of the torch-bearing maidens, and the pairs emerged from a curtain of mist, between rows of elephants carved in stone. It was a spectacular and inspiring opening.

The final events took place over two days, the first in the vicinity of the lovely Royal Baths, also known as the Roman Pool, and the programme started with a harness and rope pull with three safari trucks, heavily laden with passengers. There were no starting blocks, simply a rope on which to pull. The intention was that competitors could use upper body strength as well as bodyweight and legs to move the heavy load. The course was 25 metres long, and the standard was high.

Manfred Hoeberl (Austria) certainly used a lot of arm work, employing his enormous biceps to good effect. He was the only one to cover the distance in under 30 sec., with a time of 29.65. Magnus Magnusson (Iceland) was second with 33.66 sec. Then three men were *very* close, Gerrit Badenhorst (South Africa) 34.05, Ted van der Parre (Netherlands) 34.07, and Forbes Cowan (Scotland and U.K,) 34.51. Sixth was Riku Kiri of Finland with 36.68 sec., a bad time for him—he expected better.

A Pick-Up For The Boys
Samson's barrow gave a whole new meaning to the term "pick-up truck": Handles had been attached to the rear end of a couple of pick-up trucks. The athletes, in two-man heats, had to lift the back of the trucks so that the wheels were completely off the ground, and then push the trucks on their front wheels like wheelbarrows!

During testing it was found that it was too easy for men of this calibre, so water-filled barrows were loaded on each truck to give added weight. Great care was taken to get the weights exactly alike—there was the same amount of petrol in each tank, and drivers Billy and Jim were weighed and equalised by the use of small weights.

Not all competitors could cover the full course. Joe Onasai (Western Samoa and Hawaii) lifted and pushed the truck 5.60 m while Ted van der Parre travelled 12.90 m. The remainder were timed over the full course: The fastest was Riku Kiri in a remarkable 14.25 sec. Manfred and Magnus were again close with 16.10 and 16.21 sec. respectively, and plucky Forbes Cowan was hanging in there as usual, with 17.43 sec., to beat some of the favoured strongmen.

Getting Boulder
Moving to a lawn in front of the picturesque, cascading Hidden Cave Waterfall, a row of rough rocks were lined up for lifting. Nothing could be further from the well-balanced, revolving barbells to which such top men are accustomed, but they know what to expect in these contests, and they were unperturbed as they began with 100 kg (220 lb.).

Tactics were much in evidence, and several attempts came unstuck because of the awkward shapes of these ill-hewn boulders, much rougher than those used in New Zealand and Iceland. In the final analysis, Gerrit Badenhorst got first with 135 kg (297 lb.), which is tremendous, considering the grip change necessary at the shoulders and the precarious balance as the weight is put carefully overhead. After all, who wants a huge stone like this dropping on his head? Gerrit *pressed* the stone and then stood on one leg to show how easy a world record was for him.

Anton Boucher, the astounding twenty-one-year-old Namibian, did 130 kg (286 lb.) in just two attempts. Magnus Ver Magnusson was third, and Manfred and Forbes Cowan lifted the same, 120 kg (264 lb.). All competitors had expected to do better, and more than one promised to exceed the world record by a considerable margin. Unfortunately, apart from the awkwardness factor, they had not taken into account the physical demands of preliminary rounds, the intense heat and effects of altitude.

It was a bloodied but unbowed group who went on to end of the first day finals in the dreaded car carrying race.

Carry On

Two identical cars were driven into the arena, the drivers stepped out removing the seats to reveal that the floor as well as the roof had been taken out so that the competitor could stand inside the car in order to lift and carry it. This was done with the aid of straps, placed over his shoulders. This year two cars were used for the first time, so that there were four heats of two competitors racing each time. On the starting signal, the car had to be lifted clear of the floor and, while wheel touching was permissable, dragging the car was not allowed. Wheels were locked to prevent any advantage from occasional touches on the ground, but this was almost irrelevant because the men were unbelievably impressive in this event.

They all picked up the 380 kg (836 lb.) load with ease, and some literally *ran* down the 25 m track carrying the car without it touching the ground. Forbes Cowan beat 20 sec. for a new personal best of 19.34 sec.; this was only good enough place him fourth! Riku Kiri did 14.78 sec., and Manfred Hoeberl 13.60 sec. Tremendous, but the performance of Magnus Ver Magnusson still has experts slack-jawed for his astounding time was 11.75 sec.! It was a sight I will never forget.

At the end of the first day of the finals it was an incredibly close result. Magnusson scored 27 points, and Hoeberl was only one-half point behind. Badenhorst with 22 was just two points ahead of Kiri. The bulldog Brit Forbes Cowan, with 18½ points, had now shown the world why he is so highly respected in Europe. Lurking right behind Forbes and giving notice of great things to come, was young Anton Boucher, who had just received the good news that through a legacy, he was now a millionaire! Joe Onasai, unaccustomed to the heavy toll that such strength athletics puts on the system, was struggling gamely and impressing all with this first appearance. The old-timers know how important experience is in these strongman contests, and those who have toured on the circuit learn to adapt to the mental as well as the physical demands.

Poor Ted van der Parre was plastered. His leg, which had let him down in the past, had finally given out, his limb now covered in plaster of Paris from toes to thigh. He was hobbling about on crutches, proof of the musclemen's adage, "In these events there are no winners—only survivors."

"The Gods Are Angry!"

The last four events were to be held under floodlights in the gladiatorial-like Royal Arena of ancient design, but the air was heavy and humid as darkness approached, and a strange, tense atmosphere pervaded the scene. Everybody seemed edgy, last night nerves, they said, but it was more than that.

Suddenly everything went still and the heavens opened, thunder rumbled and lightning lit up the arena. It was absolutely awesome, and one school of thought was that this would make a spectacular finale. That idea was quickly dispelled, with the thought of competitors standing in a metal frame holding metal handles, or slipping on a water-covered platform. The evening performance had to be cancelled, which was regrettable as it would have been a beautiful sight, and a big crowd had been guaranteed.

The show went on next morning in the same location, and although the atmosphere was very different with daylight in an almost empty arena, the competition was everything one could wish for in a final. Proceedings started with the Hercules hold, with the handles supporting 130 kg, total 260 kg (572 lb.). The sustained effort showed very clearly on competitors' faces.

Joe Onasai, whose picturesque traditional tattoos had been a major topic of conversation, went first holding the contraption for 38.30 sec. The equipment looked like a pair of scales loaded with huge gold ingots and gold coins, appropriate to the location, and the heaviness of gold being well-known to most people. I think the event is more impressive with two huge barrels. Gerrit Badenhorst was disappointed with 30.34 sec., which hindered him in his battle with Riku Kiri, who won the event with a fine hold of 53.54 sec. In second place, was Forbes Cowan with 52.63 sec., then Magnus Magnusson with 43.16.

Next came the dead lift, done with two glass-fronted, gold coin-laden money safes, very similar to the apparatus used by Paul Anderson for the squat in his professional strength act. Gerrit Badenhorst, last in the previous event, placed first in the dead lift, which was not very surprising since he was once powerlifting world record holder in this feat. He went to 420 kg (924 lb.)—great lifting!

Right on his heels was Magnus Ver Magnusson, another gold medal winner in powerlifting succeeding, with 430 kg (946 lb.); Riku Kiri was third with 420 kg. Then came Manfred Hoeberl, Anton Boucher, Joe Onasai and Forbes Cowan in that order. Forbes has always been a competitive strongman, never a weightlifter, and he sometimes feels a little out of his depth in lifting events, but he is never a quitter, as we saw in the next test.

Pole Positions

The pole push is a head-on contest based on a sumo training activity. Rope handholds on a wooden log are grasped by the two competitors, who then try to push each other out of a marked area. It is a vigorous combat sport without personal physical contact.

The TV directors felt this was one of the most exciting parts of the programme, and I am not inclined to disagree. However, as a personal friend of most of the athletes, I felt extremely sympathetic towards them as even under perfect conditions this is a gruelling event. Therefore at the end of the toughest of all competitions, it was almost heart-rending to see their maximal efforts and total exhaustion. The medical room was like a battle zone as Rick, Stef and their medical team strived to get competitors fit to continue. Surgeon/sportsman Rick Reyes would like to see this event dropped from the programme because of potential injuries.

Having said that, it is a tremendous, man-to-man confrontational situation, yet eliminating the close physical contact which could render some combat sports lethal with these levels of strength and aggression. Riku Kiri won the event and once again challenged the overall leaders.

Two bouts are worthy of special mention as these were all-time classics. Manfred Hoeberl came second to Riku by winning a closely matched bout with Joe Onasai. Time and again it looked as if Joe would win, but Manfred had learned well from a similar bout last year and kept remarkably calm (I nearly said "remarkably cool," but with the thermometer showing over 100 degrees, not even the spectators could keep cool). The crucial point was being contested and apparently neither could gain the edge, when suddenly Manfred seemed to relax. Joe, who was pushing with every ounce of strength, stumbled forward and went down while Manfred nimbly retained his balance to win the bout.

In another classic battle, Forbes Cowan and Magnus Ver Magnusson were extremely well-matched. They asked no quarter and gave none. Magnus was very much on the offensive in the first round and eventually took the first point, the contest being decided on the best of three points to win the bout. Forbes Cowan, his chest heaving with exertion, went into the next bout like an enraged bull; in Scotland he is nicknamed "Red Bull," and folks here could now see the reason for this. After a Herculean struggle, first one gaining the advantage and then the other, Forbes pushed Magnus out of the ring, equalising the score.

Many of the other competitors were now taking a great interest in the proceedings, most of them cheering on Cowan, as a win by him would reduce Magnus's lead and leave him very vulnerable. It was now one point each, and the third and final round would determine the winner of the bout. After a frantic battle, with raw courage and dogged effort shown in great abundance by both contestants, the Scot beat the Viking. It was a magic moment for the big fellow in his first bid for the World's Strongest Man title. He took third place in the event, but there was a big price to pay. Cowan's ribs were badly damaged, and he was physically shattered, but somewhere deep down he found the will to carry on to the very last event.

The Stones At Las'

The Atlas Stones, brothers of the McGlashens, are two sets of stones of increasing weights which had to be lifted and carried different distances to be placed on a stepped plinth. In this exciting finale, contestants were paired to race according to the cumulative scores at this final stage of the competition. In a way it was a bit of an anti-climax after the pole push, where excitement had bordered on hysteria. Now the competitors were subdued through exhaustion; Joe Onasai joined Ted van der Parre on the sidelines, leaving only six out of the original sixteen competitors.

Forbes Cowan was thankful of the great support he got from Gary Taylor, but his face contorted with pain in every lift, and he could not lift the final stone. The issue was in doubt right until the very end. Magnus and Manfred went into the last round on even terms. They had to beat Riku Kiri, who had done all five stones in 35.61 sec.; Anton Boucher had 38.41 and Gerrit Badenhorst 38.88 sec. Neck and neck they raced, stone for stone right until the end. Little separated them, only .86 of a second; Magnus achieved 29.01 to Manfred's 29.87 sec. Magnus was overjoyed to gain the single point he needed for victory; Manfred was very disappointed, but both were very professional and handled their positions extremely well.

In a cave by the Royal Arena, these two relaxed alone before the prize-giving ceremony. As I went to call them to take their places I witnessed a touching scene where Magnus sincerely consoled Manfred, who was being a good sport although feeling low at that time. Magnus said that the competition could have gone either way, and that it had been a great battle—it was a simple but accurate summary.

Out in the blinding, scorching sun Magnus, the man from the frozen north, regained the crown he had first won in Tenerife, Canary Islands in 1991.

Paradise Island, Bahamas 1995

According to legend, a magnificent island paradise was lost at the bottom of the sea. In recent years Atlantis has been recreated on Paradise Island in the Bahamas. This was the setting for TWI's World's Strongest Man of 1995, the biggest and best ever strength contest.

Atlantis, the very name evokes wonder and mystery. Just as its beauty and splendour was said to have changed the course of history, the twenty strongmen gathered there created their own history and demonstrated real feats of which legends are sometimes made.

They came from seventeen different countries, big impressive men, champions in their own right. There were a number of new faces in the competition, including Nathan Jones a 6' 10" (208 cm) Australian powerlifter, appropriately known as "Megaman." There were several others of and around 6' 6": Torvi Olafsson (Iceland); Magnus Samuelsson, a Swedish Adonis; and Mark Varalahti (Finland), who looked more like a basketball player until he started to compete and then displayed outstanding strength. Of course, there were old favourites too, like Magnus Magnusson (Iceland), Gerrit Badenhorst (S. Africa), and Gary Taylor (Wales). Other popular Brits were Forbes Cowan of Scotland and Bill Pittuck of England. America was represented by the magnificently-built Curtis Leffler (Hawaii) and Phil (Stonehenge) Martin, who at 6' 5" (196 cm) was the smallest in his group!

It was the biggest TV strength competition ever held; with a line-up of twenty top-liners and twenty-nine tests, it is impossible to cover all in depth. The groups were as follows:-

    1. Anton Boucher (Namibia), Berend Veneberg (Netherlands), Joe Onasai (Western Samoa), and reigning champion Magnus Ver Magnusson (Iceland)

    2. Stasys Mecius (Lithuania), Wayne Price (South Africa), Gary Taylor (Wales), and local hero Spinks Rolle (Bahamas)

    3. Colin Cox (New Zealand), Bill Pittuck (England), Heinz Ollesch (Germany), and Gerrit Badenhorst (South Africa)

    4. Curtis Leffler (Hawaii), Flemming Rasmussen (Denmark), Markku Varalahti (Finland), and Forbes Cowan (Scotland)

    5. Phil Martin (USA), Torvi Olafsson (Iceland), Magnus Samuelsson (Sweden), and Nathan Jones (Australia)

The competition got off to a great start when contenders carried a car over a course nearly 100 feet in length. Powerlifters Joe Onasai and Magnus Magnusson did this in under 21 sec., with the car weighing over 363 kg (800 lb.).

Curtis Leffler (USA) in the car train, WSM 1995.

Placings were the same in repetition incline press with an awkward 100 kg (220 lb.) log. Joe and Magnus did 23 and 22 reps respectively. The organisers try to minimise skill factors by using implements like logs and boulders instead of revolving barbells. In the dead lift hold, a standard car with passengers was driven on to a frame weighing half a ton, and the end of the car was lifted and held for as long as possible. Veneberg of Holland held this very heavy load for 1 min. 4.54 sec.

Eight McGlashen Stones were lifted on to 52" barrels in 46.98 sec. by Magnusson to win the next event, with the smooth round boulders weighing up to 136 kg (300 lb.). It was a new world record.

The following heats included anchor pulling with 218 kg (480 lb.) and 100 kg (220 lb.) anchors; holding 280 kg (616 lb.) barrels by grip strength; boat loading; carrying two truck engines (more than 317 kg/700 lb. over 65 ft. in 16.27 sec.); Bavarian rock lifting; pulling six cars simultaneously for around 100 ft. in 30.84 sec., and many other interesting tests.

The traditional Bavarian rock lift left the competitors bruised and injured. Bill Pittuck's multi-coloured, multiple bruises were one of the most seen and most colourful sights in the Bahamas. Gerrit's abdomen went from purple to black with the passing days, owing to a severe rupture which would have crippled a lesser human. It was a miracle that these men could continue.

The fourth round was most closely contested. Cowan won Samson's wheelbarrow, with its load of human passengers; Rasmussen won the confrontational murder ball. This is a man-sized rubber globe filled with water which the strongmen aim to push out of their opponent's area. Varalahti won the Atlas stones and went through to the final. The Scot and the Dane had tied on overall points and had to do an extra event to see which would join the Finn. The tie-breaker was a race between the two men in which each carried an Atlas stone. On the starting signal Forbes hoisted the stone on to one shoulder while Flemming carried his in his arms. Half way down the sandy course on this pristine tropical beach, Cowan stumbled in a hole and dropped the stone. The jubilant Dane was on his way to the final.

I would rather forget the fifth round, which included arm wrestling. Here Megaman Jones beat Phil Martin by two straight falls and went on to face European arm wrestling champion Magnus Samuelsson. The first bout was truly dramatic, a battle which raised the crowd to a frenzy. Jones was like a man possessed, but the experienced Swede kept cool and held on until he sensed the right moment, then with a mighty effort he pinned Megaman. Nathan seemed dazed and could not comprehend that he had been beaten.

They squared up for the next bout, and again they seemed very well matched, although the Swede gained a slight advantage by turning his opponent's wrist backwards. Nathan Jones gave a roar and put everything into a bid for recovery, when suddenly there was a nauseating crack and a pained blood-curdling scream the like of which I had never heard before. Megaman's mighty arm was broken. Our surgeon Rick Reyes and his team were immediately and calmly in action, dealing very professionally with the grisly situation. It turned out to be a bad spiral fracture of the humerus. Sad, as the likeable Aussie had been one of the favourites to win.

The final started with the best vehicle pull ever seen in these TWI TV contests. A beautiful old 35-ton fire engine had to be pulled for 25 m (over 81 ft.). Ex-world powerlifting champion Badenhorst of South Africa did this in 33.24 sec. and also won the next spectacular event, car rolling. The cars were turned completely over, to side, roof, other side and back to wheels in as little as 13.91 sec.

A Fred Flintstone-like barbell with discs of rough, solid stone were lifted from *behind the neck* on a non-revolving bar. Gary Taylor, who was superb at the Los Angeles Olympics, easily lifted 210 kg (462 lb.) overhead in this manner. He has already done 270 kg (595 lb.) without a split on an Olympic bar and intends to be the first to do 600 lb. Onasai astonished the crowd by heaving up 205 kg by brute strength, not a vestige of technique. Magnusson, who makes no claim to being an Olympic lifter, put 200 kg (401 lb.) of stones overhead in very easy fashion.

The farmer's walk developed into a startling race, with two heats of five men *running* downhill and uphill carrying 115 kg (253 lb.) oxygen cylinders full of water in each hand. The winner Varalahti (Finland), 6' 9" in height, carried the awkward 506 lb. weight 217 ft. in 33.65 sec.! Magnus was second and Gerrit third, both completing the full course.

Tossing the caber for height had the men throwing a 16 ft. tree trunk over a bar into the sea. Their task was made more difficult by having to throw from shallow water against the incoming tide. In spite of this difficulty, Rasmussen, the winner, threw the log 17' 10" high. Varalahti and Taylor followed.

A platform with school children was used for squats. Bearing in mind the fixed path of movement and other restrictions of such a contraption, Magnusson's 437 kg (962 lb.) was meritorious. Gary Taylor and Gerrit Badenhorst were next in line.

The final event was a loading race using sacks of wet sand, treasure chests, and anchors—all around 91 kg (200 lb.), plus barrels and a massive chain estimated at close on 900 lb. These had to be loaded on plinths of various sizes. The big Finn, Varalahti won again, but it was not enough to pass the leads already established by Badenhorst, who came second overall, and the proud winner of the title for 1995, Magnus Ver Magnusson, joining the elite by taking the crown for the third time.

Joe Onasai (Samoa) on the Flintstone barbell, WSM 1995.

Mauritius 1996

Venues for the World's Strongest Man competition have become very exotic in this era. There was the ice and fire of Iceland; an ancient Roman arena in Orange, France; simulated earthquakes in Sun City, South Africa; and in the Bahamas, Atlantis beneath the sea; then for 1996, remote Mauritius, in the Indian Ocean some 500 miles east of Madagascar.

Descriptions of this idyllic island frequently use the word *paradise*: "paradise caressed by the sun," "a little known paradise," "a perfumed paradise." We found all these to be very apt. Competitors were particularly pleased with the warm welcome and friendliness of local people. Many of these fine islanders have living conditions which are light-years away from the enveloping cocoon of first world luxury we were enjoying at Coco Beach, yet there was absolutely no scrounging for tips or favours.

Trans World International's annual event with their incredible TV coverage has made this the main strongman competition each year. Having attended more of these contests than anyone else, it is my considered opinion that 1996 was the very best in nearly every way. There was a record lineup of twenty-four great strength athletes from all over the world. It was good to see the Iron Curtain gone for good and several entries from the old Socialist States. Included were great Olympians and many record holders.

There were twenty-four interesting and entertaining tests, the settings were superb, the competitions fascinating, production, organisation, back-up and all the essential ingredients were of a high standard. These competitions go from strength to strength (pun intended).

The Heats—Group 1

The first of the four heats proved there are always surprises in sport. Magnus Ver Magnusson, the defending champion, was the favourite although he had not had a great season, placing third behind Kiri and Ollesch in Finland and Lithuania. Nathan (Megaman) Jones, on the other hand, had been out of competition for a year because of the broken arm in the Bahamas. Jorma Ojanaho had shown well in Finland, a country noted for its tough competitions. Vladimir Tourtchinski the good-humoured Russian TV Gladiator, Dynamite, was strong and very fit, but his opponents were all much bigger and heavier. Pavel (Paul) Lepik, had dual nationality—Estonia and Canada, and like Stasys Mecius of Lithuania, has a superb track record in lifting weights.

Megaman had a good start. Sitting with feet braced against a stop board, he pulled, arm-over-arm style, six cars over a 30-metre course in 44.6 sec. for a new record. Ojanaho of Finland was second in 47.01 sec., and Magnusson third, 56.88 sec. The surprises had started.

Keg loading in the water proved to be a tough event for these strongmen. The kegs weighed 104 kg (229 lb.), and the combination of sea and sand, along with the heavy weight, made sprinting difficult. This time Jorma Ojanaho was first and Megaman second. Magnus came third again, so the first two tied overall at 11 points, with Magnus at 8 points. Dynamite and Mecius were equal at 5 points each.

Paul Lepik came into his own in a tremendous squatting competition. The magnificent efforts and thoughtful tactics were appreciated by strength connoisseurs. A platform was increasingly piled with concrete blocks, and a contraption like a Smith machine ensured that the squat was done with a fixed path of movement to a

Megaman Jones (Australia) on the platform lift, WSM 1996.

specified depth. Although much harder than an ordinary squat, good weights were achieved. Magnus showed all the qualities of a champion in working up to 410 kg in five single lifts. Paul lifted the same, 904 lb. in *six* increments. With tactics much in evidence, both passed on the intervening weights on offer, each opting for 425 kg (937 lb.), but it was not to be. Ojanaho was third and Jones fourth, so there was a big change in overall positions.

Going into the last event of the heat, the big Finn was in the lead, Megaman and Magnus now second equal, only one point behind. Paul Lepik and Dynamite

Jorma Ojanaho (Finland) in the log lift for reps, WSM 1996.

were also equal, so all were trying hard to maintain or improve their placings.

A log lift provided the final for the first group, going in pairs and making as many reps as possible within 75 seconds. Megaman was confident he would do well in this and do enough to get into the final. The logs had been 110 kg (242½ lb.) but had dried out and had to be adjusted; both were exactly 105 kg (231½ lb.) of awkward timber. Again results were close. Magnus did an amazing 14 reps, many of them snatches, the last ones taken from the belt. There was a little controversy about him tucking a towel in his belt, but this was approved by the chief ref Dr. Douglas Edmunds, a very experienced judge. He pointed out that this was sometimes done to prevent injuries, such as nipping the skin between weight and belt.

Jorma Ojanaho was determined to beat Magnus but finished just one rep behind at 13 reps. This was enough to put the hotly-tipped Nathan Jones out of the final; Jorma and Magnus went through with twenty points each. It was a triumph for the new boy from Finland.

Group 2

These men were all very well-known to strength enthusiasts. There was Gerrit Badenhorst, the South African champion who had been a top finalist in these events; Forbes Cowan, Scotland's "Braveheart"; Hjalti Arnason, Iceland tester in many world championships; Bill Lyndon of Australia; and a new entry—the great Evgeny Popov, Bulgaria, Olympic lifter and powerlifting record holder.

Samson's barrow was the first test. The athletes had to pick up the back of a *pick-up truck* and push it as fast and far as possible over a 30-metre course within 90 sec. Forbes Cowan was an easy winner, pushing the truck all the way in one single push without any rests. It took him only 20.99 sec., a phenomenal performance. Those eagerly awaiting the debut of Popov were not disappointed. He came second with 54.39 sec., and Badenhorst was third, less than 2 sec. behind the Bulgarian.

A tremendous loading race came next, with a range of heavy objects to be lifted, carried and loaded onto platforms of increasing heights. There was a 250 kg (551 lb.) anchor chain, a 100 kg (220½ lb.) anchor, a 110 kg section of a mast, a 60 kg keg (132 lb.), and a heavy sack of sand, which had given Gary Taylor such a problem the year before. Again Forbes Cowan was a good winner, taking only 54.09 sec. Gerrit Badenhorst was second (and second overall), taking 59.05 sec. Third place went to Bill Lyndon, 69.49 sec.

In the third event, the back of a car filled with passengers had to be lifted and held for as long as possible. It was well suited to powerlifters, and Badenhorst is one of the best dead lifters in the world. He held the load for 99.18 sec., an easy winner. A surprised second was Forbes

Bill Lyndon (Australia) in the car dead lift, WSM 1996.

Cowan, who is neither a weightlifter nor powerlifter, simply a competition strength athlete. It was with the greatest difficulty that he lifted the car until he stood upright, but once there, he held on grimly for 74.17 seconds. He told me afterwards, "I was right on my limit for the dead lift part. I nearly didn't make it. If any of the passengers had more coins in their pockets, I would have failed!" A gutsy performance, and he was still first overall, but he had a price to pay, his back was badly injured.

The leg press was with ten girls seated in two rows of seats on an incline machine. It was at least 550 kg (1,231 lb.), and some believed that with the apparatus it was more than the stated weight. The maximum number of reps had to be done within a 60-second time limit. Bill

Lyndon, greatly improved from his previous appearances, took first place with 22 reps and put up a fine performance. Hjalti Arnason, his normally jovial face turning many shades of red and purple as the set progressed, was second. Gerrit Badenhorst beat Evgeny Popov by just one rep to take third place. Forbes Cowan did only one rep because of his back injury. His two previous firsts were enough to keep him in second place overall. He and Gerrit Badenhorst went through to the final. Evgeny Popov was third overall, an excellent place for a first appearance in the World's Strongest Man competition. America's Phil Martin, a massive and former finalist, had a difficult year and was disappointed at not being in top form on this occasion.

Group 3

Group 3 began with the super yoke, where two truck engines were carried on a metal bar supported across the back of the shoulders. The engines weighed 325 kg (716 lb.) and had to be carried over a 25-metre course as quickly as possible.

Raimonds Bergmanis of Latvia, who had competed with distinction at the Olympic lifting events in Atlanta, started well by winning in 22.52 sec. Heinz Ollesch (Germany), ranking number two in the World Strength Grand Prix 1996, was second with 22.67 sec., and there was a sensation when Regin Vagadal (Faroe Islands) took third place with 24.50 sec. He made a dash for the line, stumbled, and fell on the ground; the yoke grazed his head and took with it a chunk of hair and skin. He may have been shaken, but continued as though nothing had happened. Fourth place went to Colin Cox, New Zealand's Strongest Man.

The wheel flip is a great strongman event when 400 kg (882 lb.) tyres like these are used. They have to be lifted and turned over, not rolled, until a 20-metre course has been covered. There was a time limit of 90 seconds. Colin Cox was one of the favourites here, but it was the heavy-muscled Dutchman, Berend Veneberg, who was first over the line in 48.69 sec., and Regin Vagadal second in 67.8 sec. Heinz Ollesch was third in the wheel flip and joint overall leader with Vagadal.

A huge platform with bleacher seating on three sides was especially built over the rocks on the water's edge at Coco Beach, and this made a tremendous setting for several events. The axe hold, in crucifix style, had the Olympic lifter Bergmanis back in first place. This bright new star, with more experience, is a potential champion. He held the two axes, total over 22 kg (50 lb.) for 65.57 sec. Great effort is needed to keep the axes firmly pressed to the overhead contacts as bells ring when contact is broken, ending the attempt. Second place went to the arm wrestler, Magnus Samuelsson of Sweden, who did well, considering his long arms, which are a decided disadvantage in this test.

We had to get up at 5:00 A.M. to travel across the island to the capital, St. Louis. It was a lovely run, past the spectacular Moka Range of mountains with their sharp peaks and peculiar knolls. Everywhere there are sugar cane fields, each with a huge pile of black volcanic rubble reminding us that eruptions created this island some ten million years ago. We drove into the heart of the port to the town square, which was thronged with people to watch a spectacular race, the weight carry.

All six men in the heat had to run at the same time, carrying a large solid 200 kg (441 lb.) in weight! Many locals tried to lift the blocks off the ground, but not one of them succeeded. The competitors, however, had to lift and then carry the weights over a 50-metre course. It must have been a shattering experience after hard previous events, and torrential rain made underfoot conditions difficult.

Regin Vagadal was a splendid sight, coasting home in 28.2 sec. Raimonds Bergmanis took second in 32.62 sec., and Veneberg third in 39.3 sec. This also reflected the finishing order for the group. The big surprise here was the elimination of previous finalists, Heinz Ollesch and Magnus Samuelsson.

Group 4

The favourite was undoubtedly Riku Kiri of Finland, and many believed that he could beat Magnus Magnusson in the final, as he had bettered the Icelander earlier in the season. Riku went off to a great start winning the carry and drag,

Heinz Ollesch (Germany) in the super yoke, WSM 1996.

where a 100 kg (220½ lb.) anchor had to be carried for 30 metres, and a 250 kg (551 lb.) anchor chain dragged back over the same course. It took the Finn only 53 sec. to do the double 100 metre journey with these loads. Derek Boyer, "the Island Warrior" from Fiji, took second place in 89.24 sec., while Flemming Rasmussen of Denmark was third.

Kiri won the Atlas Stones, carrying and loading the five varying boulders in 35.88 sec. Rasmussen took 42.36 sec., and newcomer Svend Karlsen, a Norwegian gym owner with great potential, was third with 45.52 sec.

The Flintstone lift provided some of the greatest highlights of the round. A very primitive barbell with stone discs had to be lifted overhead either from in front or behind the neck. Five attempts were given to reach maximum, and it was clear that some could have lifted more

Derek Boyer (Fiji Islands) performing his *haka* after the car walk, WSM 1996.

with extra attempts. Svend Karlsen was a jubilant, crowd-pleasing winner with 200 kg (441 lb.). He has no pretensions about being a weightlifter, so his efforts were quite amazing using such primitive apparatus. Rasmussen was second; Bill Pittuck (England) lifted the same 190 kg (419 lb.) but took more attempts.

A special word of praise in this event goes to Brian Bell (Scotland), who had travelled to Mauritius as a tester but had then been brought in to lift at the last minute, owing to the withdrawal of Tarenenko, the Olympic weightlifter. Brian pushed the Flintstone winner, Karlsen, all the way and indeed gambled on first place with a 205 kg (452 lb.) final attempt. He got a great reception from a large crowd for his splendid efforts.

The last event for this group was the car walk, one of the most popular events, as everybody understands the enormity of the test. Karlsen was still hoping to overtake one of the overall joint leaders, Kiri and Rasmussen.

The competitors went in paired heats, the cars each weighing 380 kg (838 lb.). Greatly improved, Derek Boyer won the event, covering the 25-metre course in 20.37 sec. He jumped onto the top of the car and did his *haka*—a war dance particular to his own island in the sun. The crowd loved it, and when he was asked to lift two young lads for photographs, he first held them in crucifix style then spun them around. Second was Bill Pittuck with 21.59 sec., but it was not enough to get him into the final. Riku Kiri was third but had injured his ankle and foot and was clearly in considerable pain. He had won the heat, but there were serious doubts about his ability to compete in the final. Flemming Rasmussen was the other finalist, just one point ahead of Karlsen and Boyer, who were making their first appearances in this important TV competition.

The Final

The harness and rope pull, first event in the final, always gives a good indication of all-round bodypower, so it would be a good indicator of Kiri's chances of continuing. This was a particularly tough pull and would not have been a good event had it been any heavier. Tractors are notoriously difficult to pull, and here there was a big tractor plus an enormous trailer full of sugar cane, weighing approximately 20 tons overall! Jorma Ojanaho (Finland) and Gerrit Badenhorst (South Africa) finished closely, covering the 20-metre course in 34.24 and 34.53 sec. respectively. Magnus Magnusson was also close with 34.67 sec.—what a tight finish!

Car rolling races are usually done only in the biggest and best shows and so are always a treat. The test here was over a 20-metre course during which each competitor had to run to his car, turn it over on its side, over again to its roof, keep it moving if possible onto its other side, then back on its wheels! The competitors then immediately sprint for the line because the time is taken only when they have covered the complete course.

Gerrit Badenhorst set a new record with the 720 kg (1,588 lb.) car, doing the turns and two sprints in an incredible 11.51 sec. for a new world record. Riku Kiri's second place in 12.43 sec. silenced all those who thought he would not finish the competition. Third position went to Flemming Rasmussen who finished in 14.14 sec. Forbes Cowan, trying the event for the first time, got a nasty blow on the face when the car came back on him, but bleeding profusely, he finished in 21.24 sec., which was a good time for a first-ever attempt.

Throwing the weight for height was next. Riku Kiri was outstanding, his injuries not being greatly affected in this test. Throw after throw cleared the massive wall with space to spare. After all others had dropped out, he still had power left at the finish with 6.60 metres. Magnus came second with 6.30 metres, and again, the hitherto little-known Regin Vagadal of the Faroe Islands was highly placed as third.

A new style of Hercules hold was seen for the first time in the World's Strongest Man. Two cars faced each other on sloping ramps and between them stood the athlete holding handles with chains attached to the cars. On a signal car brakes were released, and the athlete had to hold the cars by grip strength alone. Competitors had to stand erect at all times, and the strain on their faces was very obvious.

There were no surprises here: The favourites were Riku Kiri and Forbes Cowan. Ojanaho split these two top grip men, but with a fast-growing respect for the young Finn, high placings were now expected of him. Kiri clocked 49.19 sec., Ojanaho 47.81 sec., Cowan 46.62 sec., and Magnusson 35 sec. Riku Kiri had increased his overall lead to 27 points. Magnusson was next with 23, and Badenhorst had 20 in third place. Now many thought this would be the finishing order.

Cask strength, another innovation for TV, featured next. Two huge wooden casks were suspended on a horizontal metal pole, which pivoted and rotated on a capstan-like support at one end. Competitors held the free end of the pole in the crook of their arms and carried the load as far as possible without dropping the rotating apparatus, ensuring a circular path of movement. Markers were placed for each competitor's maximum distance and points awarded accordingly.

There was some controversy when Rasmussen left a large loop on his belt, hoping to gain advantage from such support. After this, referee Dr. Edmunds would not permit this again. Magnus Magnusson objected strongly as he wanted to do the same. There was some debate, but finally the proud Icelander used the incident to motivate himself, and his 946 degrees was above reproach. Latvian Bergmanis was a superb second and had a growing army of fans. Once again, the remarkable Regin Vagadal finished in the top three.

The overall placing after cask carrying was Kiri and Magnusson first equal and Scotland's Forbes Cowan in third place with only three events to go. He had been one of the favourites in the cask carry but stumbled. He had hoped that a win in this and the farmer's walk would build up points before his poorest event, which was yet to come.

In the farmer's walk, the total load to be carried in the hands was the heaviest yet, 238 kg (523½ lb.). It is difficult to imagine the strength, muscular endurance and cardiovascular efficiency required for a race over 60 metres carrying such an enormous weight. Four men ran in each heat, and was an amazing, inspiring sight. The fastest time was by Magnus Ver Magnusson, who covered the 60 metres in 28.19 sec. This is phenomenal when one considers that after 30 metres, they have to make a complete about turn for the return journey over the same course! Rasmussen was second and Kiri third.

The contest was still wide open with Magnusson two points ahead of Kiri in the overall results. Cowan and Rasmussen followed, each with 28 points.

Forbes Cowan (Scotland) in the cask carry, WSM 1996.

The penultimate event was a dead lift with Flintstone weights; I thought the natural stone much more primitive and impressive than the bright colours used here. The whole idea of using a rusty, plain steel bar, loaded with rough stones, was to move away from high tech and razzmatazz, but we soon ignored appearance when powerlifting began. Handstraps were allowed in this splendid competition, but it was clear that some of the competitors had no idea how best to use them. It was also most interesting to see different styles, such as Bergmanis lifting huge weights in the pulling positions he used in Olympic lifting at Atlanta. A closely guarded secret now became public knowledge.

Forbes Cowan had two slipped discs early in the 1996 season, but his back had stood up well until the car hold, when the injury re-occurred. He made a token dead lift with 230 kg (507 lb.) and finished with only one point, which ended his hopes of placing in the overall top three. It is quite amazing that Kiri and Cowan could compete at all with their severe injuries, but these are very determined and brave men.

Kiri was going well and did 370 kg (816 lb.), but in doing so hurt his back, thus multiplying his injuries. Such cumulative strains often occur in extended, fatiguing competitions. His effort placed him third ahead of the amazing Bergmanis, who did 350 kg (772 lb.), although he has never before done powerlifting.

Magnusson and Badenhorst, two superb powerlifting champions, gave us a great contest with all the cunning and tactics to be expected from such past masters. In the end, Gerrit had a well-deserved and popular victory; his good humour and friendliness throughout the whole contest, in success and failure, had won him many admirers. His winning lift was with 410 kg (902 lb.) without any failures; it was clear that he could have pulled more had Magnus not conceded. This win had pulled the South African from fifth to third position.

Another new event, the power stairs, provided an exciting finale. Competing in pairs, one on each side of six-tiered structure, the competitors tried to lift three 200 kg block weights up a series of six steps. It was a very tall order at the end of tough heats and a tougher final. To get all three weights up six stairs meant eighteen successful lifts, and of course, time taken was an important element. Gerrit Badenhorst finished strongly and lifted all three to the top in 48.45 sec. Jorma Ojanaho took 53.66, Magnus ver Magnusson 57.89 and Cowan 61.14 sec. Riku Kiri, with an injured foot, ankle and back, lined up for the final heat. However, he had calculated and knew that he had already scored enough to place second, so when the signal was given he made no attempt to lift.

Finishing points for the top six were Magnusson 52, Kiri 43, Badenhorst 41, Rasmussen 35.5, Cowan 34 and Ojanaho 32.5. Mauritius' Honourable Minister Jose Arunasalon and other dignitaries presented super awards while traditional dancers whooped it up to make a fitting end to a fabulous competition—and a fourth WSM title for Magnus Ver Magnusson, equalling the record of Jon Pall Sigmarsson.

CHAPTER 6

Beef Encounters

The Crunch Bunch

On one much discussed occasion some of the world's biggest, strongest and most well-built men teamed together as "the Crunch Bunch" and made a sensational debut in a unique game in Glasgow in 1988, which heralded a landmark in the history of American football. The heavy athletes of the Highland Games and the new-style strength games are famous and extremely well-liked in Scotland, but they hit a new high in the popularity stakes when they accepted a challenge from the famous Glasgow Diamonds, premier champions in American football in this country at the time.

Although the Diamonds knew they would be dwarfed in size and considerably outweighed by the strongmen, they reckoned their speed and mobility would save them from annihilation. Well, they deserve full marks for cheek! The Crunch Bunch's roster was like a Hall of Fame: Bill Kazmaier (USA); Jon Pall Sigmarsson and Hjalti Arnason (Iceland); Ab Wolders (Netherlands); Tjalling van den Bosch (Friesland, The Netherlands); Basil Francis, Jamie Reeves, Mark Higgins, Peter Tregloan, and Tom Hawk (all of England); and Iain Murray (Scotland).

Although most of the overseas strongmen were brought in especially for the occasion, many people thought that this would just be a bit of fun and nothing more. They were wrong. Sure it was lots of fun and great entertainment, but the two teams were deadly earnest and the musclemen were a revelation. They were nimble and tricky, showing flashes of brilliance and ingenuity, even if they did bend the rules as easily as they bend metal bars.

First to impress was Mr. Universe, Basil Francis, displaying a turn of speed that burned up the grass and the opposition. I bet this guy could put out the light at night and be in bed before the room is dark. This 20-stone streak of lightning scattered Diamonds left, right and centre as he made a 50-yard dash to touchdown and celebrated with a little victory dance. Although it is on record that Iain Murray, Scotland's Strongest Man, converted, I believe that it was Hjalti Arnason, Iceland's toughest bouncer and powerlifting champion, that was behind the mask and under the enormous padding.

Mark Higgins's great height (6' 9") allowed him to intercept many passes meant for the opposition, and Ab Wolders had an effective way of stopping the opposition. As one of the larger Glasgow Diamonds ran at great speed towards the Crunch Bunch line, Wolders emerged from nowhere and stood right in his path and didn't budge an inch under the mighty impact; it was the attacker who bounced off. Is this what they meant when they said Ab was a bouncer?

The bravest player on the field, however, was a slip of a lad who must be mentioned in despatches for the uninhibited way he tackled Bill Kazmaier, only to be body slammed for his pains; the intrepid player tried again with the same result, and as he went barging in for a third time, Kaz growled, "Just stay down," and en masse the Diamonds blocked their own doughty tackler to save him from grievous bodily harm. Tom Hawk, a new boy to strength games, pulled a hamstring and limped disconsolately off the field.

The Crunch Bunch's moves were masterminded by Bill Kazmaier, who had previously played with the University of Wisconsin's famed lineup and more recently for Green Bay Packers and Jacksonville. Throughout the game he went through the opposition like a dose of salts.

In this galaxy of stars it was Strongest Man in Britain, Jamie Reeves, who was nominated by the Glasgow Herald as "the Star of the Show," for in the final play,

The Crunch Bunch (back, l. to r.): Peter Tregloan, Jamie Reeves, Mark Higgins, Tjalling van den Bosch, Jon Pall Sigmarsson, Ab Wolders; and (front, l. to r.) Iain Murray, Bill Kazmaier, Hjalti Arnason, Basil Francis, Tom Hawk.

Gordon Brown of the Diamonds gained possession, only to find himself grabbed by the massive Jamie (6' 4" and 23½ stone), who then ran down most of the field at full speed carrying Brown and the ball, only to be brought down some five yards from the line.

It was a great game, quite different from the usual fare on the gridiron, and the game Glasgow lads probably still have the bruises to prove it, but they had the consolation of coming out on top, sneaking the winning move late in the match.

It's Tough at the Top

As previously mentioned, the annual World Muscle Power championships is generally held in Scotland. However, the seventh World Muscle Power championships were held in North America for the first time in 1991.

The good folks of Fergus, Ontario, presented their three-day festival with enthusiasm and panache, and there was a galaxy of real strength stars all out to gain this major title, the most important live competition of the year. Space does not permit me to describe this or the others in the series, but I use it to highlight one of the darker aspects of strength events. There is no denying that strength athletics at the highest level is extremely demanding and hazardous, with even supremely fit athletes suffering severe injuries.

In the run up to the World Muscle Power event that year, Markku Suonenvirta of Finland had to withdraw through injury, and Aussie Joe Quigley, last seen as a strongman in TWI's spectacular from Hungary, hurt his back and retired on medical advice. I was present at the examination so know that it was totally genuine. Magnus Magnusson was put in as a replacement to make up ten first class entries; the Norseman had earned his place by winning the European powerlifting title at 125 kg with a total which exceeded everybody else in the competition regardless of weight. He had also a recent strongman victory over the fabulous O.D. Wilson, USA's world powerlifting champion. Although he was a late selection he was in tremendous form.

In the finals of the World Muscle Power, there was sensation in the car turn over when the Soviet entrant Arvydas Svegzda collapsed with apparently broken ribs. In a Finnish competition about that time one of the favourites, Arto Lukkenen, fell under the car he was turning and suffered crushing and multiple injuries, including two broken legs. In the Canadian competition, we used spotters who rolled oil drums under the cars as they were lifted, but only touching the cars in cases of emergency as in the case mentioned.

Concern and anxiety was further expressed when Arvydas, the gallant injured Lithuanian, bravely decided to carry on. He had previously badly bruised his thighs in the loading race where competitors had to lift and carry six unwieldy objects, each weighing around 100 kg (220 lb.), hoisting them on to a wagon as quickly as possible. One of these items was a massive tractor tyre, which was probably the most awkward object ever to be included in such an event. Fortunately the initial diagnosis was incorrect, and Arvydas was absolutely O.K. the next day except for bad bruising.

The world title was won for the fifth time by Jon Pall Sigmarsson (Iceland), with Jamie Reeves taking second place for England. Magnus Magnusson was third; the muscular Welsh dragon Gary Taylor, fourth; and O.D. Wilson, fifth.

The competition over and a good time had by all, it was a happy group that flew back to Europe, but that was changed a few days later when first of all Jamie Reeves dead lifted 383.6 kg (845 lb.) and in doing so, snapped his biceps. After consulting his local hospital, he was rushed at speed to Glasgow where he had another operation similar to the one undergone the previous year when his biceps were torn from their insertion in turning a car in the Scottish Power Challenge in George Square, Glasgow. This time it was the other arm.

Hot on the heels of this came a phone call to inform me that Ilkka Nummisto (Finland) had broken two fingers and would be unable to compete in Henning Thorsen's Hercules of Denmark International. Could things get any worse? Indeed they could. In the competition's car turning event in Denmark, Jon Pall Sigmarsson suffered an identical injury to that sustained by Jamie—the Viking's biceps finally gave out. They had been bothering him for some time, but he had been careful and not tempted providence: For example in Canada, although he had the fastest time for turning one car, he didn't try to turn the second once he felt the strain on his biceps. His major injury prevented him from defending his World's Strongest Man title in Tenerife.

As had been said so often, in this sport there are no winners only survivors. It is probably the most demanding of all activities and we must constantly remind young strongmen eager to get into the big time that there are many hazards and how tough it is at the top.

The Ultimate Challenge

Bill Kazmaier's T-shirt said it all: "There can be only one" it proclaimed, indicating that the titles World's Strongest Man and The Strongest Man That Ever Lived are very exclusive, and only one individual can merit the title concerned. Whenever strength followers meet, they compare the greats of past and present—Arthur Saxon, Louis Cyr and Apollon are compared with the heroic figures of today and there is general agreement that in terms of overall strength, power and versatility (as opposed to specialities), strength champions of today win hands down.

The arguments then become fierce. At the conceptual stage of the competition about to be described, we wondered how Bill Kazmaier, of Alabama, USA, three times winner of the World's Strongest Man title would compare with Geoff Capes and Jon Pall Sigmarsson, who took over the title from the unbeaten Kaz, and had each twice won the coveted title. Jon Pall went on to win two more WSM titles.

Victor Ludorum (Sports Promotions) consisting of Dr. Edmunds, Colin Finnie and me, decided to organise a competition in 1987 to clarify the situation. This was to be the ultimate challenge—to decide who was the strongest man that ever lived, and the big three, each of them a legend in his own lifetime, met almost in secrecy in an ancient ruined Scottish castle to settle the matter.

Early morning mist swirled around the floor in the upper reaches of Huntly Castle as the three mighty men stood motionless, each holding a huge claymore horizontally in one hand, the other hand of each man clutching a studded shield to their brawny chests. A few inches under the swords all three had a glass goblet on a silver tray, and the purpose of these would soon become clear. The height of these was precise, as each man had been measured at the request of one contestant, allowing no advantage or disadvantage to any individual.

Gradually Geoff Capes began to quiver and Jon Pall Sigmarsson turned his head slowly to look first at one opponent and then the other, perhaps trying to psych them out. With 44.28 sec. on the stopwatch, Geoff dropped his arm, and the sword smashed the goblet and sent the tray spinning. After what seemed an eternity, Kaz began to show signs of the strain and his arm shook as he held on valiantly. At a seemingly endless 1½ min. (0.94 sec. to be precise), his mighty thews gave out, and the sound of splintering glass again echoed round the old stone walls.

With a bellow, "There can be only one!" Sigmarsson "the Iceman" deliberately brought down his claymore to shatter the third goblet and end the first stirring event. How far he was from exhaustion will never be known, and it heralded the shape of things to come.

In the Courtyard

Outside amongst the castle's broken walls, lay three of the famous McGlashen Stones of Strength, weighing respectively 100 kg (220 lb.), 110 kg (242 lb.) and 120 kg (264 lb.). These stones are round, smooth and without handholds; therefore the warriors had to bend right down to the ground to even begin to budge them, and Bill Kazmaier let out an oath as he tried the stones for the first time.

With the great accumulation of experience in scores of competitions over the last four years, the Europeans were at a slight advantage in knowing the stones, but they were totally unprepared for this new event. Here at Huntly instead of simply lifting the stones, the contestants had to *carry* the boulders a distance of some 35 metres and load them on to an ancient cart. Nor was the course a straight one, they had to negotiate bends round the remains of the old castle walls.

All three employed the technique introduced by Holland's Siem Wulfse at the World Muscle Power championship; there Simon the Wolf lifted the rocks upon his shoulder before depositing them. Sigmarsson again placed first, but Geoff Capes beat Bill Kazmaier to even their scores, and this must have shaken Kaz's confidence a little at this stage.

Cannons and Cabers

Going round to the castle moat, the next event involved a formidable solid iron cannon, weighing around three-quarters of a ton, and the rusted wheels had seldom turned since the days it had first been hauled into position at Culzean Castle to defend the Clyde Coast from an anticipated invasion by Napoleon. The strongmen had to pull the cannon *up a slope* using a hand-over-hand pull on a thick rope. The cannon had been brought from Culzean Castle just days before the event and had been in a blacksmith's shop to have the wheels freed, so none of the contenders had any opportunity to try it out, and in any case the gradient was an integral part of the severity of the test.

It was a gut-busting, back-breaking, muscle-burning event, demanding abnormal strength and a high degree of muscular endurance. Great determination was also needed as the pull neared completion, and all three

Bill Kazmaier (USA), left, and Jon Pall Sigmarsson (Iceland), right.

displayed an abundance of the required physical and mental qualities.

Jon Pall was still unbeatable and was now amassing a formidable lead; he completed the pull in 23.11 sec. Geoff did it in 25.39 sec., and Bill 45.86 sec. The cannon was pulled up a trackway of conveyer belting, so it had to be a fairly straight pull. In Geoff's effort, one wheel went off the belting quite a bit before the end of the pull, which slowed him down. Jon Pall got the cannon a little further before going off, and Bill's pull was best in this respect, but he was visibly slowing down at the end of the pull after making a good start. He would have liked knots in the rope, and the TV producer decided to put in a different event which would have a knotted rope as suggested by Kaz at a later stage of the competition

Jon Pall now had 17 points, Geoff 10 and Bill 9. Nobody except Hjalti Arnason, the tester, had predicted or expected such a result at this stage.

Tossing the Caber for Distance
Experts will tell you that an ability to toss the caber Scots style is a decided disadvantage when it comes to tossing the caber for distance, and so it proved in this event. At Highland Games the clock face method of judging ascertains how *straight* the caber is tossed; distance does not matter. The result is that throwers use a technique to gain height and turn. Although Geoff Capes is undoubtedly the best of this trio in normal caber tossing, he came third after a ding-dong competition in which all three had the lead at one time or another. The final result showed the Icelander with 39' 3", Bill Kazmaier with 38' 8½", and Geoff 38' 7", a very close result indeed, and nobody could tell the result until all the throws had been measured.

Throwing the Weight for Height
All three are world-class at this event, and we were hopeful of a record. On the day of the competition the confirmed world record was 17' 2", but the task was made much harder by the inclusion of a castle banner draped over the bar to add a touch of pageantry and tradition to the proceedings. To put in perspective the heights achieved, let me remind readers that many amateur competitions were being won at around 14' 6", and many professionals had taken first prizes with 15' or thereabouts. On the international circuit, Capes, McGoldrick, Grant Anderson and Sigmarsson often fought it out around 16', sometimes going to 16' 6" if the weather was good and competition was strong.

At Huntly Geoff Capes went out at 16' 3" with but one failure, and complained that the breeze blew on the banner, unsighting the cross bar. Sigmarsson went to 17' 3", thus exceeding the confirmed record, but Bill was in devastating form, doing 17' 6" and looking good for more. It was in this event that he broke his first world record in Highland Games when I took him to Braemar in 1979. At that time, the record was held by Grant Anderson at 16' 1". Now he was beating that by 17"!

Kazmaier had shown that the Icelander could be beaten—would the tide now turn? That was the question on everybody's lips.

When Darkness Fell
Originally a new type of harness event had been scheduled, but a hoist pull with a knotted rope was substituted to suit TV requirements. This was the only item not tried and tested by Victor Ludorum, the organisers, and many adjustments had to be made with scaffolding, which must have cost a fortune. After a lengthy wait, in a dramatic evening setting with bonfires and torches casting eerie shadows amongst the trees, huge cannonballs in a net, were pulled upwards by a rope and pulley.

Again Geoff Capes and Jon Pall renewed the rivalry so well-known to followers of strength contests, and the intensity produced a really close encounter with little more than one-half second separating them in the pull. The Icelandic athlete finished in 11.05 to Britain's best with 11.6. It was somewhat ironic to note that towards the end of the pull, the knots seemed to get in Kaz's way and broke his pulling rhythm, so he finished with 14.89 sec.

Up Above the World So High
There was drama galore in the log lift. Firstly, Capes pulled out of the competition at 127 kg (280 lb.). I had been with him the previous weekend and knew he was suffering badly from strained trapeziums. Indeed, he had to go to a hospital at Inverness for urgent treatment in order to fulfil commitments, and he went on to compete at Aviemore with numerous acupuncture needles in his body! True grit.

Sigmarsson warmed up with 113.5, 127 and 136 kg (250, 280 and 300 lb.) to get the feel of the log, whereas Kaz took 127 and 145 kg (280 and 320 lb). Six attempts were allowed and both skipped the 150 kg (330 lb.) increment, sizing up each other and beginning a tactical battle of wits. The blonde Viking then took 154 kg (340 lb.), and Kaz replied with 159 kg (350 lb.) to go into the lead. Taking a 9 kg (20 lb.) jump from his previous attempt, JPS did 163 kg (360 lb.), but it could have been near his limit. Kaz took 165.7 kg (365 lb.) and failed; all hell then let loose.

They were lifting on a fairly narrow platform, placed on the roof of a castle arch. It must have been very disconcerting for the lifters, heaving weights overhead in limited space, without a barrier to the front or to the rear. Kaz staggered forward and let the bar down rather than risk going off the platform. He used up his remaining attempts at this weight, but let everybody know his feelings about the unusual lifting conditions: "You should string us up in the trees like monkeys," he shouted, or words to that effect, and stomped off to create havoc behind the scenes.

Jon Pall had collected another three points and showed no sign of wear and tear.

The Cannonball Barrow
In the cobbled courtyard stood a very heavy metal wheelbarrow designed to carry the heaviest of cannonballs, and in this was placed McGlashen stones and sundry rocks to make it unshiftable by the average man. The competitors had to trundle this barrow round a varied course, weaving

between ruins and through a narrow gap in a low wall, back to the starting position. Even that experienced and powerful tester Hjalti Arnason could not complete the course, regardless of time, but the two stars remaining in the competition struggled through remarkably quickly. They were both extremely impressive, and bearing in mind the very different types of strength called for in these varied tests, we were left in no doubt that we were watching the world's strongest men, the strongest of all time.

Sigmarsson completed the zigzag course in 1 min 27.28 sec., and Kazmaier took 1 min 41.61 sec., which would surely have been enough to win in any other company.

A Strange Dead Lift

Imagine if you can, a barbell having a 3" x ½" hand grip with four edges. Rough, eh? An old cart axle of this description was used in the competition instead of the standard 1" round and knurled bar, and the cartwheels plus balancing weights made up the basic starting poundage of 236 kg (520 lb.).

The two contestants scorned straps for the first few lifts, making their attempts as soon as the weights were loaded. There was no procrastination at any time, simply mutual agreement on the increases, and they got on with the job in a very efficient workmanlike fashion. First was 236 kg (520 lb.), Sigmarsson entertaining us with one of his philosophical homilies: "There is no reason to be alive if you can't do the dead lift," he roared. The weight increased to 277, 322, 370, 420, 443 and 456 kg (610, 710, 815, 925, 975, 1,005 lb.). We could hardly believe our eyes or our ears, but it was all there, filling us with wonder.

At 475 kg (1,047 lb.), a Glasgow powerlifter commented to me after Bill Kazmaier's lift, "You wouldn't pass one of mine like that, Dave Webster." Personally I had every confidence in referee Bill Anderson OBE, a man whose integrity is well-known and respected in Scottish sporting circles. It should also be explained that the rules allowed the weight to be hauled up in any style, but the small criticism mentioned to me was about Bill not *completing* the lift, and sure enough at 489 kg (1,077 lb.), the referee ruled Bill out for just this fault. Kaz was not amused, but some of his keenest supporters endorsed the referee's decision.

Jon Pall remained impassive and having won with 489 kg (1,077 lb.), asked for more. On to the wheels went 523.5 kg (1,153 lb.), a weight never before lifted in any style of dead lift, and up it went. On the completion of the lift this extraordinary man even indulged in one of his berserking bellows, but his voice broke to the amusement of his colleagues.

The Finale

Since I first discovered the legend of the Dinnie Stones, the most famous Clach Nearts (Stones of Strength), I have done everything in my power to publicise them, and over the years thousands of strength worshippers from all over the world have visited Potarch Hotel, near Banchory in Aberdeenshire, to see the Stones of Dee, which were first used by travellers as tethering points for horses.

I have arranged for many of the world's greatest strength athletes to try these stones, and the legend of Donald Dinnie shines as bright now as it did back in the early fifties when I first brought this to public notice. Now we were to see what Sig and Kaz could do with them, but instead of being asked to carry the stones the *width* of Potarch bridge, they were required to carry them the *length* of the Huntly Castle bridge, which was some 25 metres. Naturally they elected to take them one at a time instead of both at once, as Dinnie is said to have done.

Kaz went first and he astonished everybody by carrying the first stone in just 40 sec. and both in a total of 1 min. 16 sec.—that was including the return journey for the second stone! Instead of carrying the first stone by the ring, Jon Pall lifted it bodily and carried it in his arms halfway across the bridge, and by the ring thereafter. This slowed him down, and his time was 10 sec. slower than Bill's. One of his supporters scolded him for his initial method, but the Iceman shrugged his shoulders, "I gave them a show, didn't I?"

It was the end of a fantastic and colourful strength event; Jon Pall Sigmarsson had 28 points, Bill Kazmaier 19 points and the injured Geoff Capes 10 points, having missed three events.

To compete in such an event is an honour in itself, to survive these most demanding tests is something of a miracle, and for Jon Pall Sigmarsson to beat so convincingly such tremendous athletes as these two most worthy opponents is a memory which will always live with those who were fortunate enough to see it in person for themselves.

We had witnessed the on-going saga of Capes v. Sigmarsson and had seen how over the years they have both improved beyond recognition. However, when I saw Bill Kazmaier again after an absence of some years, I was astounded at his wonderful muscular condition and thought that if there was anyone in the world to beat these two, then this was the man.

I have a feeling he was surprised at the improvement in the standard, and on our last evening together at Stranraer, ten days after the competition, he told me, "I will be back, and next time things will be different."

Jon Pall Sigmarsson received the Budweiser Pure Strength Trophy from the sponsors of the Grampian TV programme with a modesty which is at variance with his programme with a modesty which is at variance with his competition demeanour. This man was an enigma, for although on stage he was a tremendous extrovert, exuding confidence, at most other times he was quiet and thoughtful. Regardless of which was the real Jon Pall, he was a very worthy champion whose exploits earned him a press description "the Legend," which was, incidently the working title for the TV show at Huntly Castle.

I See a Strongman Die

I was one of a cheerful group of international strongmen and officials gathered for the 1996 World Grand Prix in Lithuania, a country long noted for great strongmen, such as Pyotr Krylof (1871-1933), Alexander Zass (1888-1962), Valentinas Dikulis (1938-), and Jonas Ramanauskas (19 April 1912 - 8 July 1996).

Like their forefathers, modern Lithuanians give great support to their strength athletes, so there were three rounds of this major event organised by the dynamic Bronius Vysniauskas, a former weightlifter, now coach and organiser. After preliminary rounds in the capital Vilnius and Panevezys, the finals took place in Klaipeda, where the waters of the Curonian Bay met the Baltic Sea. We were accompanied throughout the tour by Bronius' attractive wife, Delia, who was our splendid interpreter, and little Jonas Ramanauskas, a veteran circus and stage strongman, who although retired, still took a keen interest in his modern competitive counterparts. At every stage of the tour, adoration was lavishly bestowed on this modest gentleman, who has been the honoured guest at each Lithuanian strength contest and given the best seats amongst the honoured guests.

Never seeking the limelight, he revelled in awe at the superhuman strength of Hercules' heirs of today. I was overjoyed at the opportunity to meet and have a little time with Jonas, and I was most grateful to Bronius and Delia for the arrangements they made on my behalf. Meeting him was a revelation. He was a very dapper, impeccably dressed chap, and seldom have I met such a charming, unassuming and enthusiastic old-timer. I will never forget his pleasure in thumbing through *Sons of Samson, Volume 1*, and his jubilation at seeing featured in it his former colleagues and friends. It made all the burning of midnight oil during my research and writing of the book worthwhile.

"We taught each other many tricks," he said pointing to Vladimir Hertz, "I know him well. Here's Heinrich Schmidt. I have his weights in my museum." So it went on. He particularly admired Zass, "the Amazing Samson," and wanted information on his life and death in Britain. "I want to go there and see where he is buried, say a prayer for him and return something of him to Lithuania his homeland." Naturally we had some language problems, but I understood Mr. Ramanauskas to mean to return with a little soil from Zass's grave. His reference to prayer later took increased relevance. He may or may not have been a religious man, I don't know, as he made no reference to any religion. What I do know is that he had terrific faith in the power of prayer.

A huge crowd was required for the finals in order to cover the enormous costs of the Grand Prix, but the morning of this event was very dark and gloomy, and on meeting Jonas I pointed to the sky and screwed up my face in distaste. He waved away my disappointment, telling me convincingly that it would be okay. He had a few words with Delia, who then explained smilingly that Jonas has prayed for the athletes and for good weather. She said he *knew* it was going to be a nice evening in spite of weather reports, and indeed it did turn out fine—except that it became cold later.

We spent some time talking of our respective collections, our little museums, and of his wife. He had married her when she was only fifteen years old, and they

Jonas Ramanauskas.

were still very close although he was now eighty-five years of age. He looked and moved as though he were twenty years younger.

When we went to the finals he introduced me to Vytas Nemius, the Minister of Sport, and asked if I would be photographed with them. We had a pleasant interlude before I went back to my colleague Dr. D. Edmunds, as I had to open the proceedings, and Doug briefed me on what had happened in the past. Many hours later, towards the end of the competition, Phil Martin (USA) was injured, and I was called to help. I requested an ambulance to take Phil to the hospital for a checkup. "Another ambulance?" queried the medic, "We have already had one for Mr. Ramanauskas." Worried about this remark, I made enquiries and discovered that the strongman had become cold and was excited during the event, and perhaps as a combination of circumstances, had suffered a heart attack.

It was past midnight before we returned to our hotel and too late to disturb him, so ever-energetic Bronius arranged for us to visit Jonas in the hospital the next day. Bronius drives like a rally driver (which he had been in his younger days), and his manoeuvres on our drive to see Jonas nearly gave *me* a heart attack, and after this James Bond style car trip, unlike Bond's vodka martini, I was shaken *and* stirred!

Jonas was lying on his bed looking sad, but got up nimbly when we entered, hugged us, and thanked us profusely for coming to see him. He informed us he would be going home later that day. Bronius went to see if he could get some information from the medical staff, and Jonas sat down to autograph his picture in my Grand Prix programme. He had written some lines when Bronius and a doctor returned. The doctor, shouting, told Jonas he must stay for three or four days. I disliked the shouting, Jonas' hearing aid worked very well.

The old strongman was very distraught at this news and held his head, protesting because his wife needed his attention and support. He told me that she had a severe knee problem which somewhat immobilised her. Jonas was agitated. The doctor ordered him to bed. Bronius decided to telephone Jonas's wife and tell her that her husband would be in the hospital for several days, and he left with the doctor. A nurse came in and gave Jonas an injection in the stomach and left.

Almost immediately Jonas became more perturbed and looked around at the top of his bedside cabinet. I offered him his spectacles and a glass of water, the only things on the cabinet, but he shook his head, clearly disturbed. He pointed a little higher and I saw a red panic button. I pressed it hard, but it did not seem to work, it seemed stuck. I ran out into the corridor and summoned medical aid. Two nurses hurried to assist, the doctor came too. The strongman was now moaning continually, and a trolley was brought . . . .

Further details are superfluous. Bronius returned, and we tried to console each other. The big, kind heart of our dear little friend finally gave out. It was a devastating experience. The contrasts of the happy affectionate greeting and his unfinished message to me, ending abruptly, were his last written words.

Jonas had a super strongman act which brought joy to many people. The respect in which he was held by ordinary folks to the highest in the land brought status and honour to our activities. Most of all he was one of us, a valued member of the strength fraternity, travelling in the competitor's bus, cheering on the athletes, and visibly praising their endeavours by his body language which surmounted all linguistic barriers.

His personality and demeanour brought together the traditional circus strongman and modern competitive strength athletes—the subjects of this work—and the timing and nature of Jonas's demise cannot be forgotten. To keep his memory alive in Scotland, we now have a Jonas Ramanauskas Memorial Sash, which is worn by the champions at our main strongman events.

Do me a favour, if you can find the will, please say a little prayer for the soul of Jonas, a very worthy Son of Samson. He would appreciate that.

Most of this book was concluded soon after the World's Strongest Man competition in the Bahamas. My heart went out to the strongmen who day after day performed magnificent feats in soft stamina-sapping sand under a blazing sun. Like true professionals, they took these hardships in their stride; it's all part of being among the world's strongest men.

Looking over the empty scene at the conclusion of the last event, I thought to myself that their strength and courage had made even deeper impressions than their footprints. I recalled the words of the American poet Henry Longfellow (1807-1882):

> Lives of great men all remind us
> We can make our lives sublime,
> And, departing, leave behind us
> Footprints on the sands of time.

It is hoped that readers will have enjoyed my efforts to perpetuate facts and figures pertaining to modern strength athletes, who will surely leave their very deeply impressed footprints in the sands of time.